A SIMPLE SOUL

Vadim Babenko

Ergo Sum Publishing
www.ergosumpublishing.com

Published by Ergo Sum Publishing, 2013

Translated from Russian by Christopher Lovelace and Vadim Babenko
Russian text copyright © Vadim Babenko 2009, 2013
English text copyright © Vadim Babenko 2013

E-book ISBN 978-99957-42-05-8
Paperback ISBN 978-99957-42-06-5
Hardback ISBN 978-99957-42-07-2

This novel is a work of fiction. Names and characters are the product of the author's imagination and any resemblance to actual persons, living or dead, is entirely coincidental.

Cover design: damonza.com
Editor: Robin Smith

www.ergosumpublishing.com
www.simplesoulbook.com

CHAPTER 1

One July morning during a hot, leap-year summer, Elizaveta Andreyevna Bestuzheva walked out of an apartment building on Solyanka Street, the home of her latest lover. She lingered for a moment, squinting in the sun, then straightened her shoulders, raised her head proudly, and hurried along the sidewalk. It was almost ten, but morning traffic was still going strong – Moscow was settling into a long day. Elizaveta Andreyevna walked fast, looking straight ahead and trying not to meet anyone's gaze. Still, at the corner of Solyansky Proyezd, an unrelenting stare invaded her space, but turned out to be a store's window dressing in the form of a huge, green eye. Taken aback, she peered into it but saw only that it was hopelessly dead.

She turned left, and the gloomy building disappeared from view. Brushing off the memories of last night and the need to make a decision, Elizaveta felt the relief of knowing she was alone. She was sick of her lover – maybe that was the reason their meetings were becoming increasingly lustful. In the mornings, she wanted to look away and make a quick retreat, not even kissing him good-bye. But he was persistent, his parting ritual enveloping her like a heavy fog. Afterward, she always ran down the stairs, distrusting the elevator, and scurried away from the dreary edifice as if it were a mousetrap that had miraculously fallen open.

Elizaveta glanced at her watch, shook her head, and picked up speed. The sidewalk was narrow, yet she stepped lightly, oblivious of the obstacles: oncoming passersby, bumps and potholes, puddles left by last night's rain. She wasn't bothered by the city's deplorable state, but a new sense of unease uncoiled deep inside her and slithered up her spine with a cold tickle. The giant eye still seemed to stare at her from under its heavy lid. She had a sense of another presence, a most delicate thread that connected her to someone else. Involuntarily, she jerked her shoulders, trying to shake off the feeling, and, after admonishing herself, returned to her contemplation.

Old Square gradually came into view, revealing the church that once stood over public executions, and the commercial section next to it crowded with merchant stalls and cars parked willy-nilly. Elizaveta navigated like a seasoned pilot, her shoes squelching in mud seemingly left over from centuries past. Finally, she reached the flimsy fence that, by some strange design, had no gate. She shook her head, stepped gracefully over a massive chain, and found herself in a park with the cool shade she longed for, even though it was still early in the day.

Then began the long journey up the hill. Elizaveta winked at Saints Cyril and Methodius, who stared bleakly at a plaque reading "From a Grateful Nation" – a bitter joke about a nation that never learned how to be grateful. She skirted a bench with a sleeping bum who exuded an unbearable stench, and, after a brief hesitation, took the left alley, which was slightly more shaded than the right.

The promise of another blistering day loomed over Moscow. The park was full of people – victims of morning hangovers, refugees from the nearby office buildings, clutching their beer cans. The adjacent bar was also far from empty. The waitress wandered lazily between the tables, fully aware of the power she wielded. Elizaveta surveyed the unfriendly territory. She noted the casualties dispassionately, without registering their faces, which looked blank in their identically aloof, self-absorbed expressions. She walked with virtually no effort, pretending to float above the sidewalk, the meager greenery, and the bushes filled with trash. Only once did she stumble – and it brought back the sense of that persistent, hidden gaze. She was probably only imagining it, but her heart remained heavy and her thoughts disintegrated into a confused jumble.

As she reached the top of the hill, the sun sliced into her eyes, and the smell of asphalt and burned gasoline filled her nostrils. Elizaveta crossed the road and arrived at the Polytechnic Museum, which cast a much better shadow than the despondent trees. Many years ago, this spot housed a zoo. The museum had fallen on hard times – possibly the hardest since the zoo's Indian elephant broke under the persistent attention of gawkers and went on a rampage. The fate of the museum, much like the fate of the elephant, was regrettable, but Elizaveta had her own concerns. She continued to feel uneasy and even glanced over her shoulder. There was nothing there. She hesitated at a theater poster framed behind glass, watching the wavy reflections, but they looked harmless enough. Then she snorted, frustrated with herself, and read the advertisement inviting passersby to learn about varieties of packaging at a Packers' Club that had found a home in the impoverished building. For a moment, she felt amused, and her unease took on a mystical, ghostly quality. Past the museum, Elizaveta gave the menacing Lubyanka building a cursory look and descended into the underground walkway, which led to her office building on Maly Cherkassky. With a glance at her watch, she hastened up the stairs – but the exit beckoned her with its bookstalls, and she gave in and began to examine the covers.

One of the books caught her attention. She opened up an imposing black tome, but somebody jostled her elbow and the book tumbled out of her hands, wreaking colorful havoc on the neatly arranged stand. In the resulting commotion, the woman next to Elizaveta yelped with surprise, a man's deep voice muttered an apology, and the proprietor of the kiosk rushed to straighten out his wares, worried he might get robbed. Elizaveta tossed an absentminded "It's okay" in the direction of the voice, whose owner's face she never saw, and stepped aside to leaf through another book with a picturesque dust jacket. Its contents, however, proved to be too serious, and the second page was branded with a triangle that nearly covered the entire sheet. She immediately remembered something she once read:

The triangle is a grand figure; it controls souls. It was an ill-timed sign, a dumb hint verging on mockery. Embarrassed, Elizaveta cast a furtive glance around, set the book down, and hurried away from the racks toward the old, five-story building that housed small companies and underfunded government offices.

Elizaveta's colleague, a staunch feminist, Masha Rozhdestvenskaya, who called herself Margot, greeted Elizaveta amiably, seeming not to notice her lateness. The reason was simple: Masha was dying of curiosity. Not long before Elizaveta's arrival, a messenger had knocked on the door and handed the dumbstruck Masha a large bouquet of roses wrapped in golden tinfoil. "For Ms. Bestuzheva," he said and disappeared, dissolving into the Moscow smog. The card clipped to the edge of the tinfoil said nothing but *From a suitor* written in ornate cursive with fancy flourishes.

Masha had never seen a card like that, and she was surprised beyond measure. The moment Elizaveta stepped into the office, she was barraged with questions, which, unfortunately, found no answers. The occurrence had no explanation; all they knew for sure was that Bestuzheva had a secret admirer, a fact so strange that it irritated rather than thrilled or entertained. Elizaveta's life held no mysteries, and having little faith in lucky accidents, she preferred to choose her admirers herself.

"You know," she said to Masha pensively, "I stopped by a kiosk, they had a book... Can you imagine, I opened it, and there was a triangle on page two. I have no idea what it means."

"It's for fevers," Margot explained, her eyes narrowing, matching the sarcasm in her tone. "A triangle spell is the best cure for it. They draw it on a piece of paper, or on wolf skin like they did in the old days. It clears the illness right up."

"Come on," Elizaveta said, offended. "I'm serious. Triangles control the soul. It said so right there: *Thy soul is not thy body.* Then something else I couldn't figure out, and at the end, *Thy soul is love...*"

"*Thy soul is love,*" her coworker repeated thoughtfully. "Wow.

Your life is never boring, eh, girlfriend? Liz the little vixen."

Elizaveta felt awkward. She responded with an absent smile and went in search of a water jar for the flowers while Masha continued to cast sidelong glances at the strange bouquet, as if still trying to find the key to this mystery that was eluding both of them.

A fervent enemy of mysteries – especially those concerning the opposite sex – Masha Rozhdestvenskaya had no faith in signs and solitary bouquets. She'd had strained relationships with men since her youth, each more like a protracted war than a romantic dream. Many thought she was weak-willed, so they used her without compunction in exchange for compliments, presents, and small favors. Once they got what they wanted, they would disappear without a trace, leaving the inconsolable Masha to lick her love wounds. Over time, her heart grew hard and men continued to treat her like a toy in their hands. Her illusions wilted, and it hurt more than the loneliness to which she was beginning to grow accustomed.

Eventually, Masha went on a counteroffensive. It proved to be successful: she managed to turn the tables, convincing first herself, then others it was she who used her lovers indiscriminately, walking away with pleasure, money, and more gifts and favors. And if they happened to disappear too soon, it wasn't a problem. There were plenty of fish in the sea; she just had to cast the net.

People began to respect and sometimes even fear her. The victim had turned into a lioness, albeit with a somewhat cornered look she had learned to hide. But the metamorphosis drained her of vitality, and she was now building it back up brick by brick, ruthlessly dismissing, as frivolous whim, all that defied rational cynicism. According to the latest fashion, she interpreted the eccentricities of love and the ensuing thrills as a chemical defect in the brain, like the warring energies of different colors that can't find a balance. Feelings were transient; colors tended to merge into a dull gray. In her current state, Masha didn't think they were even worth talking about. Instead of looking for implausible meanings, it was much more fun to discuss haircuts, Tarot cards, and dogs. She loved dogs: her pug slept right in her bed, and she thought of her greyhound, who had recently died of old age, as the incarnation of some kindred spirit.

Though not particularly friendly, she and Elizaveta weren't openly hostile, either. Their work was boring; the travel agency was nothing more than a front for the machinations of some big shot whose name was never said out loud. As such, the company had to provide perfect form with no pretense of substance. Business was slow; the agency was mostly in the red, but a certain young man never failed to deliver their salaries, which were rather high by Moscow standards.

All in all, everyone was happy. Masha and Elizaveta covered the walls with posters, littered their desks and the windowsill with brochures, and filled the office with Tibetan music and Chinese figurines. African masks hung on the wall to the right of the entrance, across from the glossy map of the two hemispheres crisscrossed with flight paths, as if to validate the company's readiness to send a client to the ends of the earth if necessary. If Mr. Big Shot ever decided to drop by in his free time, he would like what he saw. To the disappointment of both women, however, his time was never free. Would-be travelers were also a rare occurrence. The women spent their days in the virtual world of the Internet and the pages of books while their presence livened up the somewhat drab office, like butterflies decorating a dusty bush.

Of the two, Masha was the more alluring. Her dark hair was nothing short of splendid; her eyes were big, her mouth sinfully sensual. Her cheekbones were a bit on the wide side, but some would consider that another asset, as it suggested a similarity to the women of the Transvolga known for their insatiable appetite for love. Her overall appearance constantly reaffirmed the tumultuous nature of life. But she knew reality could be duller than appearances, so she was no stranger to somewhat shocking urges, especially in the company of people of privilege. Still, she never sank to the level of full-blown indecency.

Next to Masha, Elizaveta looked like a Cinderella relegated to the background. Plus, she was four years younger than her coworker; she'd turned twenty eight the month before. They couldn't have been more different in their demeanor and, while the eye first rested on the *femme fatale* Margot, the two quickly balanced each other out and it was impossible to say which one stood a better chance in sustained battle.

Either way, a helmet of dark blonde hair perfectly framed Elizaveta's narrow face, with its graceful nose and green-speckled, catlike eyes. She did resemble a large cat from the front, but in profile she looked more like an exotic bird. All this was augmented by very delicate skin and narrow wrists and ankles – a legacy of her aristocratic lineage, lost in the quagmire of intermarriage but still evident in her last name and proud bearing. All she knew for sure was that one of her grandmothers was of the Polish gentry. It seemed that grandmother's genes had skipped a generation to define her refinement and grace, and maybe to predispose her to pragmatic romanticism, which the rules of metropolitan life forced her to hide. Not that romanticism was lacking in the Russian three-quarters of her wild family tree, but she knew next to nothing about them. She didn't give much thought to the past, being content with the present, with all its bustle – and with herself, exactly as she was.

Elizaveta Bestuzheva knew her own world quite well. It was mainly an internal rather than external matter, an easy subject for analysis, though she did her best not to indulge too much in self-contemplation. Things were occasionally confused in her mind, but the important stuff was undeniably clear: she knew she held an entire universe inside her, replete with heavenly bodies. Some of her planets were inhabited, and she could hear the voices of all the countless creatures who lived there. Sometimes, the voices tortured her; sometimes, they made her irrationally happy. They resonated in her heart with joy and anxiety, and in her body with its unique physiology, as well. To Elizaveta, hers was the best of all possible worlds.

She noticed others who carried their own inner universes, which doubtless seemed just as perfect to their owners. Of course, this complicated life considerably: that's why, she told herself, signals from one individual to another often got scrambled and were bound to be misinterpreted. They encountered so much interference, how could a message reach its target without distortion? Not to mention that everyone thought in a different language... People were utterly wretched when it came to communicating meanings. She could hardly believe they understood each other at all. It took tremendous effort to concentrate on an external stimulus, to capture Morse code or some other cipher, let alone translate it into words.

She was considerate of others' weaknesses, aware they could be hiding the complexities of their own private spaces. People valued her compassion – though she was callous with those whose worlds were empty, not bothering to hide her boredom. This wasn't malice on her part. She didn't think she was better than anyone else – it just happened that way. The Morse code got lost in the vacuum with no hope of a reply. Unfortunately, most men she knew were carriers of this vacuous, non-resonating space.

It must be said that unlike the implacable Margot, Elizaveta harbored no ill will toward the stronger sex. She believed love was the most important thing in life – in the traditional, old-fashioned sense. It was a conscious challenge, a notion of extreme romanticism she inherited from her Polish grandma or from some nameless Russian ancestor with a passionate heart and a sentimental nature.

There was a contradiction here: between the external and the internal, between a declaration of self-sufficiency and the expectation of a fateful encounter. Sometimes, Elizaveta asked herself resentfully, is her precious inner world really alive? Full as it was of life-giving juices and warm plasma, was it all just a lie, since she still pinned all her hopes on simple happiness?

She recognized her emerging impulses, unchecked and capable of surprising anyone, but she needed help to awaken them and set them free. When flirting with men, she tested their courage in hopes that their shameless gaze would help her find something deep within herself. At times, she was ready to sacrifice almost anything, even the scattering of her internal galaxies encased in perfect form, for a moment of insight. What if she could eventually just toss the fragile structure up into the air and then fail to catch it? Let it crash, let it splinter into shards of glass?

This thought scared her. It was distressing to think that somewhere inside this warm plasma the gears of negation and decay were ticking away. Maybe one day she would meet someone – a man who would determine how far they could both tumble into madness... This, of course, left ample room for fantasies. Elizaveta was a big fan of fantasies. Still, she had no doubt that, when reality caught up with her, she would meet it with dignity and not miss her chance.

She had learned all she knew about love from the books that filled her parents' home, crammed onto shelves that stretched from floor to ceiling. Elizaveta spent her childhood buried in their pages. Nobody bothered her; her older brother lived his own adult life and her parents had their own problems: the Bestuzhev family was not a happy one. Her father worked at Intertrade, and though he had been considered quite a catch back in the Soviet era, he had married a modest waitress, to the surprise of his friends and relatives. He had his own motive: complete, unquestioned authority, and that was what he got – along with the opportunity to demean his wife over the course of many years. But the children knew full well that, in actuality, their mother was secretly in charge. And then the father died, still young, from a rare bug he caught on a business trip to Africa.

On her diet of books, Elizaveta grew into a young lady resembling Turgenev's heroines. She loved Kuprin, cried over bad poems she spent hours reading in the local park, and shunned all displays of rudeness. Soon, however, the wild nineties shook up the values in her pretty head. Her older brother began to work for a living, curse profusely, and smoke pot. Her friends landed men with secondhand German cars, and she fell in with the leader of a local gang. As a result, she finally lost her virginity at nineteen, blushing at such outrageous conservatism.

Then the century came to an end. Elizaveta mourned her gangbanger as he found himself in a cemetery, befitting the career he had chosen. She did her time at university, got her completely pointless degree, and moved out on her own, despite her disapproving mother and brother. They had no genuine connection after that. She grew more distant, refusing their advice and money. Finally, her brother left for another continent. Her mother sold the flat and joined him. And Elizaveta felt truly free.

Her first marriage soon followed. It came on a fleeting, feverish whim and left no trace when it ended. The man she had chosen proved to be a nobody: a mediocrity, a total waste. She quickly grew tired of him and breathed a sigh of relief when she found an excuse to kick him out.

After a bout of severe self-pity, she befriended a certain Sara, with a hazy past and a streak of bright red hair. Sara was inclined to extremes, and something in her entranced Elizaveta, especially the glinting edge of the narrow switchblade with which she was never parted. They invented game after game, and Elizaveta forgot her troubles. She would often daydream about the blade that tasted so many secret parts of her body – along with Sara's playful tongue and her own sweet shame. No one had ever been so maniacally jealous about her – and this only fueled the fascination. Then Sara disappeared, leaving suddenly for the Altai Mountains, and Elizaveta knew the worst was behind her. She was ready to get on with her life.

A few well-mannered, mature lovers helped her fully reclaim her confidence. The desire for fire and passion quickly returned, but they proved elusive despite her cheerful disposition and energetic search. As a result, Elizaveta's personal life was reduced to compromise and a quest to satisfy her lust. This held its own brand of passion: risky and shameless, with a sharp, musky aftertaste. Her outward detachment would give way to a surge of stormy intensity; she seemed to break free of her cage, growing unrestrained and insatiable. It had little to do with crude sensuality; the nature of these whirlwinds that tossed her about was much deeper and subtler. Elizaveta had no name for it, but with a bit of work, she could convince herself it was the energy of love.

Time passed, and nothing changed. One by one, her girlfriends started families of their own. Elizaveta held no grudge: she knew a different fate awaited her, and it should not be rushed.

Men fell for her, flocking like corpulent moths to her wicked glow and silent call. Eventually, however, she grew up and became stingier with her charms. She was tired of variety; the ranks of her admirers thinned out, and only a lucky few were granted permanent status. And yet she couldn't develop respect even for them. The hollow vacuum they personified didn't resonate on any frequency, made no echo on any wavelength, yielded no light or word. At first, she resented them, but eventually they became merely amusing. She accepted it as fact that in her country, the stronger sex was much worse than the weaker. This knowledge helped her reconcile with reality, providing a common ground for isolated episodes. Having an answer made life easier: she watched with a smile, even a sort of maternal concern, as her lovers moved about the room, gestured, squared their shoulders, and threw furtive glances at the mirror; as they tried to put on airs and take up more space; as they ate, drank and smoked, simulated thoughtfulness, and studiously knitted their brows, only to dive with relief back into familiar patterns, from house chores to sex to driving. She knew the real value of their lies and insinuations, their vague promises and frequent whining. She knew how easy it was to confuse them, to knock them right off their feet, to flatter them into giving her what she wanted, to get them to talk or to fall silent with doubt. She held power over them, yet she didn't much like this power. Control over events offered convenience, but when things didn't work out, she took it lightly, refusing to get sucked into an argument and feeling no regret.

Her latest lover was going on six months. Bestuzheva valued his devotion – a quality that had gradually worked its way to the top of her updated priorities. He was easy to deal with, so he would probably be a convenient life partner, but she knew that was something they would never get to test out. This chapter, too, was coming to an end. In the mornings that followed their stormy nights, she could barely contain her hostility, looking at the bustling "Sasha," as he'd taken to calling himself to please her. His obedient stare caused her nothing but irritation and disgust. She even began to hate this diminutive nickname, and after a few insulting outbursts, "Sasha" turned into a gloomy "Alexander," all tangled up in consonants. After that, she tried to avoid the name altogether. At least she didn't have to say *that* out loud.

Alexander was well liked by her friends, including Masha and a few old classmates. This used to flatter her; now, it was another source of irritation. Yet, generally, Elizaveta didn't care what anyone thought. She'd long realized that every opinion was one-sided in its own way – and besides, you could never expect to hear the truth. Everyone chased their own private goals, and she knew herself what a goal could mean – a clear, well-defined one, something doable within given deadlines. She had a whole list of them that she loved to inspect while drifting off to sleep – taking inventory and outlining new horizons. At those times, many things would fall neatly into place – many, but not all. Some matters stood apart, defying every kind of list; they beguiled her with their elusiveness and remained a permanent dream.

CHAPTER 2

Noticing Masha's disappointment, Elizaveta sorted the office mail and switched on her computer. The inbox was almost empty, but one e-mail caught her attention. "Fortunate!" the subject line blared. This was quite strange. Elizaveta glanced at the bouquet, feeling out of sorts, clicked on the message, and began searching for meaning in the tiny symbols that comprised the image on the screen.

"Masha, check this out..." She was about to wave her co-worker over, but the screen suddenly sprang to life. The symbols swirled, danced, and settled into the shape of a large heart. It turned crimson.

"What?" Masha said, looking up, but Bestuzheva waved hastily at her, "Nothing, nothing," feeling a blush creep across her cheeks.

The words "Click this!" appeared on the screen. She poked it obediently with the mouse pointer, and the heart was replaced with a list of short commands.

It was a formula for calculating her "Soul Number" – at least that's what the bold-face heading said. Intrigued, Elizaveta followed the instructions twice to make sure she made no mistakes in the calculations, and typed the result into the box at the bottom, above the *Decode* button. She didn't have to wait long: "Your number is SIX," the screen blinked. "Your sign is VENUS. Your stone is DIAMOND. Your nature is LOVE, MOTHERHOOD, DOMESTIC BLISS."

The words disappeared and the heart returned, only to

disintegrate into shards and dissolve into nothing. Elizaveta tried to bring the image back, but to no avail. The e-mail refused to come to life again, giving her nothing but a scrambled row of symbols.

Bestuzheva felt unreasonably sad. She glanced at the bouquet again, as if it could give her a hint. When that didn't come, she shook her head and leaned back in her chair, thinking about her morning, her Soul Number, and her entire life.

She languished like this for the rest of the day and left work with a headache, irritated at everything. The bookstalls had disappeared and fruit dealers, southerns with oily eyes, had taken their place. Elizaveta got a fleeting sense of the transience of her surroundings, with the office and her apartment providing the only tenuous stability. She walked downstairs, crossed the square, and headed slowly down Bolshaya Lubyanka, shaded by the famous edifice that still oozed menace and struck inexplicable fear into some people's hearts.

Elizaveta wasn't affected by the granite building or any other specters of the Soviet epoch she barely caught and had no reason to take seriously. Moscow boasted brand-new values, and Bestuzheva was quite content with them – especially since she didn't have a choice. She turned toward Kuznetsky Bridge, which sparkled with boutique shop windows, and headed toward Tverskaya Street. The high-end stores neither she nor most of her fellow citizens could afford had long ago lost their allure. Her eyes glided absently across expensive clothes, bedding, and accessories illuminated by brilliant lights, safe behind thick glass. Next was a row of jewelry stores. Elizaveta slowed her pace, thinking back to the diamond from the morning e-mail, but felt suddenly ashamed and sped up again with a slightly arrogant expression on her face.

The workday was coming to an end, and Kuznetsky Bridge was packed with pedestrians. Elizaveta noted with annoyance that they all looked alike, like drops of wax or some other liquid that easily shifted form. It was some kind of trick, she felt, an offensive injustice, though she couldn't tell how or why it should be different. The setting sun, along with reflections of other people's lives, diluted and distorted the figures around her, making them seem unremarkable, nearly incorporeal. They glided back and forth like shadows or characters from hastily written novels, their movements guided by the simplest of instincts and needs. Their desires, ambitions, and problems were all too predictable. The city had given them a respite and they submitted to it, just as they had succumbed to the burdens of their workday: the rudeness of their bosses, the headaches and accusations, bad food at the nearest coffee shop. They lacked something crucial, and Bestuzheva didn't want to put a word to that something; naming it would only make things more depressing. She felt like a foreigner to all of them, an alien from another planet, though she quickly reminded herself that this sentiment was fleeting and she would eventually have to grow up.

"Eventually, but not now," she mumbled. "You lucked out, gorgeous!" With secret satisfaction, she thought there could be no other way. And that "gorgeous" no doubt defined her very well.

Beyond the Rozhdestvenskaya Street intersection, the Kuznetsky went downhill, literally and figuratively. Boutiques gave way to regular stores and cafés. Elizaveta entered one of them, named after a Hindu god, and ordered a citrus smoothie.

She sat and watched the bustle outside. The structure across the street housed the embassy of some newly minted country, irrelevant and largely unessential. The store next to it offered foreign trinkets. Farther down the street, the once-famous Writers' Bookstore now sold postcards and souvenirs, its only window blocked by a billboard advertising cranberry lipstick. The advertising slogan, like the taste of a lingering kiss, reminded Elizaveta of last night, which left nothing but fatigue and frustration.

Suddenly, her back prickled with cold goose bumps again. She felt she was being watched from somewhere nearby. Elizaveta craned her neck – abruptly, angrily – to catch the interloper, then leaned back in her chair and closed her eyes. "My nerves are completely fried," she complained in a whisper. "I'm just imagining crap."

She was mistaken: her suspicion was not unfounded. From a reasonable distance, a nondescript man was watching her every move.

Earlier that morning, he could be glimpsed outside the gray house on Solyanka – and everywhere else Elizaveta went. He followed her like a relentless shadow.

The nondescript man was a private investigator. His first assignment was to give the subject a hint of his presence, but not so much that she could spot her pursuer or even be sure she was being tailed. So far, he had lived up to his reputation and carried out the task brilliantly. He didn't know the client; all he had been told was that the man was from out of town. That was enough to fill him with sympathy for Elizaveta, caught by misfortune in the web of some provincial fat cat.

But the fat cat was far from provincial: born on Ordynka, he'd spent his first twenty-seven years in Moscow. Had the PI known this, his remorse for Elizaveta's plight might have morphed into solidarity with a fellow Muscovite. On this account, though, he would have also been wrong. Contrary to stereotypes, the client had an enduring hatred for Moscow.

His name was Timofey Timofeyevich Tsarkov. Once upon a time, he had been one of Bestuzheva's classmates: a poor student who got his education somewhat late in life, after a youth wasted on black-market dealings, amateur rock, and a stint in the army. Through it all, he never lost his optimism and easygoing nature. One day, their eyes met over flasks and Bunsen burners – they got to talking, then to urgent groping between the sheets, and then to infatuation and fervent passion. Elizaveta fell for him like a teenager, with a wide-open heart, and he loved her youth and vigor. Yet their romance was short-lived. The city dealt Timofey a mortal offense, and his life changed forever.

It was the slippery road that did it. Timofey's car skidded and crashed into an expensive Jeep. The two vehicles drifted across the highway, hitting a few others along the way. Miraculously, there were no injuries in the ensuing pile-up except the totaled cars. As Tsarkov, slight and skinny, climbed out of his demolished ride, the owner of the Jeep stomped over, tossed Elizaveta aside, ignoring her terrified squeal, and smashed his fist into Timofey's face, hard enough to give him a serious concussion.

In the hospital, he realized he could no longer live like this. He lost interest in college, friends, and Elizaveta Bestuzheva. His life narrowed to a single point: the desire to take vengeance on the world. He wanted to do it with the same weapons the world had used against him: brutal force, money and power, and a right to be cruel. His uncompromising nature set a high bar for his future endeavor. But he was a reasonable man and knew he couldn't reach his goal in the capital – he had neither the cash, nor, more importantly, the connections. And so Timofey Tsarkov's heart hardened with a bone-deep loathing of Moscow.

During the first two days of his hospitalization, Elizaveta barely left his side. But he was sullen, distant, burdened by her presence. She got upset, and her visits grew infrequent. Then, right before he was discharged, Timofey had a quickie with one of the nurses, which he admitted to Bestuzheva with secret relish. He couldn't forgive her for witnessing his disgrace; he wanted to punish her, and he succeeded: they ended on a very bad note. Soon after, he dropped out of school and fell completely off the radar.

Having disposed of his past and made his present a blank slate, Timofey moved to Ekaterinburg, closer to his uncle, a jeweler. He found no overnight success and the uncle proved to be a real scoundrel. Eventually, however, fate smiled upon him. As is often the case, fortune came in an unexpected package.

One day, he did something he had never done before: he approached an unconscious man lying helplessly just outside a bus stop. To his surprise, there was no smell of alcohol. Timofey flagged down a cab, took the guy to the hospital, and, as it turned out, saved him from almost certain death.

The man happened to be an out-of-town hot shot with business interests all up and down the Volga. He had come to the Urals incognito on highly personal business, and it had nearly cost him his life: on his morning walk, he had an epileptic seizure and lost consciousness. The physicians said this was caused by a nervous disorder, combined with a congenital vascular defect. Without immediate treatment, the seizure might have killed him.

Within two days, the patient was patched up and discharged. He carefully recorded the obscure diagnosis in his notebook, said a few choice words about his hometown doctors, who were obviously in for a severe punishment, and headed to the nearest church to donate all his cash. When he returned to his native Sivoldaisk, he took Timofey along as his personal aide.

That was seven years ago. Working side by side, Timofey Tsarkov and his *patrón* didn't waste any time. The *patrón* moved into local government, where he was even more at liberty to do as he pleased. Timofey, in the meantime, discovered in himself an aptitude for financial scheming and built his own little "outfit," as he liked to call it. His assets were quickly approaching the levels he'd once conceived of in his hospital bed.

Disaster, like good fortune, came out of nowhere, in the form of the *patrón's* daughter, who had suddenly grown up. Her zealous father wanted nothing but the best for his child and had long been exploring various matrimonial prospects. But then, his "little girl" – who, at twenty-something, became a burly Russian matron, dressed to the nines and accustomed to denying herself nothing – took matters into her own hands. All of a sudden, she fell head over heels for Tsarkov, whom she'd known since she was a giggly kid with freckles and a ponytail.

Now that she was an adult, she scared him. She embodied a thousand devils, a handful of hardened bitches, and Albert Einstein adapted to the Russian plains. She was stronger, smarter, and more ruthless than anyone he knew. Her temper terrified everyone around her. Timofey imagined she could probably bite her lover's head clean off like a female praying mantis. Plus, he didn't like chubby women. In other words, catastrophe loomed on his horizon, and all his senses screamed to get away.

After the first failed attempt to lure her would-be husband into bed, the daughter, Maya, marched into her father's office and demanded a wedding. "Love will come later," she explained. "That's how everyone does it these days." And, really, who could resist a treasure like her?

Nobody, her father agreed, slightly dazed by her onslaught. Placated for the moment, Maya took off for Cleveland on a cultural exchange program, tasking her parents with making all the arrangements. She was scheduled to return in three months or so. The first month was nearly over, and Timofey realized this delay – a generous gift from the gods – was his only chance of escape.

His *patrón* called him in for a man-to-man talk. Both chose their words carefully. In a shrewdly perceptive move, Timofey brought a modicum of ambiguity into the situation. He was suitably incomprehensible and mysterious, alluding to some vague events from his past he couldn't talk about just yet. His speech was peppered with "honor" and "duty," words that resonated in the heart of his *patrón*, a member of the old guard, shaped by obsolete rules. The conversation resolved nothing. It only proved that both parties had serious intentions and the hapless bridegroom was in for hard times.

If Timofey was going to defy the dangerous clan, he needed a damn good reason. His *patrón's* bruised pride – not to mention the fury of the rejected Maya – could crush him like a bug. He could tell them he was into men, but that wouldn't work in Russia's backwoods; no one would ever shake his hand, let alone do business with him again. He was left with just one option: he quickly had to arrange an alternative marriage – a retroactive and sufficiently credible one. He put everything else on hold and dove headfirst into this project.

Finding a fake spouse proved to be a hard task. Timofey needed someone he could trust completely, and, mulling over the candidates' credentials, he felt increasingly hopeless. He knew plenty of women – now he saw them from a new perspective and even thought he had treated many of them unfairly, with little regard. But still, they were local, living in plain view, with pedestrian biographies, transparent right down to their birth. There was no way he could change that. He needed an outsider, but all his old contacts were gone. What was he supposed to do – invite a stranger, the first one who came along, to join this delicate and cunning game?

Timofey was close to despair, but then a brilliant thought occurred to him. He congratulated himself and breathed a sigh of relief. His salvation might not be a slam dunk, but he certainly had a chance.

He had to marry Elizaveta Bestuzheva, who fit nearly all the parts of the profile. She knew how to hold on to secrets, knew how to keep her word – he just had to press her into making a promise. Unlike almost everyone else, she was honest and incapable of deceit. Timofey had a soft spot for sincere people: he never failed to be surprised they hadn't gone extinct.

Yet she was stubborn, and that could be a serious problem. He saw that clearly, thinking back to the turmoil of their breakup seven years ago. Still, he had no other avenue of retreat. He had to bank on Elizaveta's big heart and romantic nature – and his own charm and skill – to get his way.

It took him a single night to come up with a detailed plan. It might seem too intricate to idle eyes, but Timofey disdained easy solutions. He always relied on complicated schemes, and they miraculously paid off, to the surprise of his hardheaded partners. His customary tactics relied on piling up a heap of accidents until they grew into a clear inevitability – or at least into the likeness of one. Inevitability was something you couldn't argue with – this was the secret of success. And so, armed with an understanding of causation, Tsarkov made bold decisions and knew no doubts.

He approached his pre-existing marriage plan in the same way. Unseen patterns began to swirl around Elizaveta, building a chain of disparate events that moved along the same vector, aimed at the spot soon to be occupied by Timofey himself.

The private eye, who stood motionless behind the door of an office building catty-corner to Elizaveta's café, was unaware of the plan's complexities – he was merely the man on the ground. He felt compassion for the young woman who was obviously headed into trouble, but it didn't stop him from doing his job as best he could. He didn't mind bringing emotions into his thankless business; he even cultivated them. At times, he felt pity for his assignments; at other times, he hated or disdained them. This helped him bear the inconveniences of his work and provided comfort in the dark days of blunders and failures. Not that those were common. He was highly respected in certain circles and had no shortage of clients.

The PI glanced at his watch, pushed a button on his cell phone, and said a few words to the person on the other end. A minute later, a girl in leggings and a pink top ran out of the neighboring building and trotted up Kuznetsky, holding a large rose wrapped in tinfoil. Her provocative appearance drew everyone's attention. Passersby turned to stare; patrons of the open-air café gaped at her in shock.

She made a sharp turn to stop directly in front of Elizaveta and handed her the rose with an old-fashioned curtsey. The flower was the same color as the morning bouquet, but bigger and more vibrant.

"For you," the girl said, peering into the irises of Elizaveta's eyes. "Just one, but it looks like a ruby. The diamond – that's for later." Her face diffused into a cunning grin, and Elizaveta realized she wasn't as young as she seemed.

"What is this?" Elizaveta asked, bewildered. The girl simply smiled again, giving Elizaveta's palm a quick caress with her cold hand, and ran off at full speed, melting into the crowd.

Elizaveta sighed, shrugged, and set the rose on the table. Completely baffled, she was oblivious to the fact that all eyes were on her. A plump waitress brought the bill and stared with undisguised curiosity. Elizaveta suddenly felt sad. Tears stung her eyelids. She paid the bill; grabbed the rose, pricking her finger on a sharp thorn, left the café and headed quickly toward Tverskaya.

Half an hour later, she sat on the couch in her small apartment on Gnezdnikovsky Lane, staring at the flower that now jutted from the narrow neck of a vase. "I am Venus, my stone is diamond," she whispered as if trying to cast a spell against some alien force that had invaded her life.

CHAPTER 3

That very morning, Nikolai Kramskoy, a forty-year-old Muscovite, walked out of his apartment block onto a quiet Gilyarovsky Street and hiked off to the Garden Ring Road. The large, two-tone edifice where he had lived since birth was well-known throughout the neighborhood. Three of its arches directly linked narrow lanes to bustling Mir Avenue and were frequently used by all manner of vagrants, so the inhabitants were accustomed to disturbances and police raids. A black band ran right through the middle of the building, dividing it in two. The upper half, painted blue, was considered to be a refuge for aristocrats, and suicides of both sexes had jumped from its roof on more than one occasion. Among them was the Austrian ambassador's lover, not to mention several lesser personages.

Nikolai had slept poorly that night. He was unshaven, fatigued, and glum. On he went, maneuvering between cars parked right on the sidewalk, descending along a sleepy street that resignedly sheltered the prosperous classes of various years who had all rolled into one and lost their distinctiveness. He had a dismal aspect, and an old scar on his cheek, resembling the outline of a tiny hand, showed up more than usual and gave him a rather ominous look. The heat was picking up. A sort of steam seemed to be rising from the pavement, and even in the early morning the surrounding environs imparted no joy.

Upon reaching the Garden Ring, noisy as a race track, Nikolai habitually looked in the direction of Sukharevka and waited until the tower saluted him with its silent sheen. He winked in reply and turned toward the underground crosswalk leading into the twilight of the old streets. There, he knew, coolness and tranquility awaited him, rare as they were for summer in the city.

Today, he decided to go through Trubnaya, which was narrow and echoing, like a bent pipe. Nearly all the houses once belonging to the merchant nobility had been preserved in the stormy years of transition. They were now the property of banks that had expelled the institutions of the Soviet era and gradually pushed out the ordinary tenants. Nikolai walked without haste, examining the multicolored buildings as if recalling acquaintances in whose faces you expect to see premonitions of bitter days. They were beautiful, standing out as spots against the grey, but beautiful to no effect, as there was no one to admire it. The grey advanced, occasionally covering itself with insipid mottling; inept government carelessly held sway. The evolutionary tree was shedding its unneeded leaves to be trodden underfoot. Like many Muscovites, Kramskoy had learned to take this lightly: society deserved its leaders, and those left in the minority should just chalk it up to bad luck.

Reaching the square where there had once been a pet market, he shook his head and chastised himself for taking the wrong route. The space was now taken up by a sprawling construction site, which was dug up length and breadthwise, cut by ditches, inundated with scaffolding and lumber. There was no way back though, and Nikolai, like the other unlucky pedestrians, set off across the wobbly walkway laid out with boards and sheets of metal – picking his way, it seemed, through the craters left after a bombing. Threading his way somehow to Rozhdestvenka, he took a breath, wiped the sweat from his brow, and began to clamber up a hill of uneven asphalt that now seemed the pinnacle of perfection. He wanted to imagine how luxurious coaches had once trundled through here as they sped from outlying estates to the radiant Kuznetsky Bridge, but for some reason, his heart harbored only frustration and bile.

"Hadn't someone written," he recalled gloomily, "that 'to make a Russian do something decent, you must first smash his face in?' That was an astonishingly accurate observation. People in general have a true penchant for self-destruction. And, along the way, they manage to get torn down all around."

The sun was now shining right in his face, making him squint and blink in irritation. "How hard it is to overcome Moscow's distances; it's as if you're wandering in the desert or a boundless impasse," he thought, getting short of breath as he climbed amid the ruts and puddles left from the previous night. "At times, you don't even know whether you'll make it to where you need to go. Then once you finally get there, you feel that your strength is all dried up. Survival in this city demands constant little victories. It is surprising how they consume every resource. For serious efforts, no strength remains – isn't that a mockery of Moscow's arrogance?"

Of course, Nikolai was exaggerating, deliberately laying it on thick. The reason for this was a strange sadness he had felt ever since morning. It concealed a threat that had no explanation; Kramskoy could not fight it off, which was why he was irritated with both his surroundings and himself.

Something similar had happened to him before; the world occasionally showed its cruel face – but not often, and usually for a good reason. Despite an inclination toward meticulous contemplation, Nikolai was no misanthrope. He accepted reality as it was, blaming no one for his troubles or his state of mind. That was not easy, and of course he wanted to lay the blame on many. But he knew to restrain himself, being afraid of turning into a complainer, which would signify the onset of aging and the loss of his fresh perspective. He had once developed the habit of thinking out loud – this helped him maintain his composure. And besides, his mental balance was guarded by the personal worldview he had worked out during sleepless hours and would never share with anyone.

It was nearly indescribable; the necessary words were desperately lacking. At its heart, like an inscrutable beast, resided a ruling organism that lived its own life, where each particle, molecule, and tiniest element was assigned a specific role. Nikolai Kramskoy was such a particle, and he did not yet know whether that was something of great importance or small. His thoughts and inner impulses, his desires, aspirations, and plans – all of this was the product not of a chance, but rather of metabolic reactions whose complexity could not be depicted within the confines of human judgment.

This was an entire universe; maybe that was where God lived, to put it in familiar terms, which Nikolai did not want to do. The consequences sufficed without it: for instance, there was no point in deluding oneself about personal rights and freedoms. The ruling organism was not generous with them, and perhaps did not offer them at all. Kramskoy could never quite figure that out for certain, yet he knew that the rest, who frequently felt too much of their own importance, were not as independent as they would like to believe. They themselves were no more than particles and, moreover, it was not yet clear whether their roles were even slightly distinct from each other. The majority of them were ballast, energetic material suitable only for the simplest chemical reactions. Still, this didn't make anyone better or worse. After all, there's no way to manage without them, and, besides, a signal worth decoding may arise within any ordinary point. There was just no need to get upset when you realized that signals seldom get through, and the universe distorted and jammed them according to the rules of the game known only to it.

Thus, there was no sense in complaining. Today, as always, his mood was determined by higher planes – an intricate design from beyond, which was not possible to comprehend. Nikolai obediently bore this, transporting it as if it were a fragile burden, over the hill and back down to the city center, past pawnbrokers and fake antique shops, the Architectural Institute and the Sandunovsky bathhouses, to Kuznetsky Bridge, seething with life. There he should have turned to the right to go straight on to the place he needed, but at the last instant, it was as if someone's hand pushed him in a different direction. He decided to walk around, even pop in to his favorite bar at Lubyanka, on the top floor of one of the new buildings. He had already reached the entrance when he noticed bookstands close at hand. After taking a fleeting glance at them, he was about to turn and leave but bumped someone's elbow and caused a small stir. A voice cried out, and a tome in black binding fell from the arms of a girl standing next to him. The young bookseller, keen to maintain order, started breathing down his neck. Nikolai made a soothing gesture, muttered an apology, and lifted the fallen book, which had opened in the middle. "...*he rolled a four – two deuces on the jagged dice – an odious symbol of the head of Rakhu, hewn, as it were, of hessonite, the contour of destiny, in which there was neither joy nor warmth, but only ennui and arduous toil...*" he read with displeasure, quickly looking away as if ashamed. Then he stepped back to the glass doors without buying anything, frowning all the more.

Things went better for him upstairs. Ultimately, the prophecy was probably intended for another; he had simply stumbled into someone else's business, which had happened to him more than once. Really, people here were too fond of prophets, oracles, soothsayers, and magicians of all kinds. He himself didn't mind peering into things to come, but there was no point in becoming like those who believed in obvious rubbish. Of course, if the mind had no other sustenance, then even rolling deuces or the dragon's head could be taken seriously, but he wasn't foolish enough to be afraid of who-knows-what!

They brought Nikolai a fruit cocktail; he sipped it in small gulps and looked at the square below and the pandemonium of cars and the headquarters of the former KGB. The view wasn't bad, but was not much of a joy to behold. He would have preferred to be transported back in time, a hundred years or so into the past. He wanted to see the coachmen's tavern, funeral carriages at the corner, and soft-spring broughams; to hear not the cacophony of horns and tires, but rather the clop of hooves across the causeway, the jingle of chains and buckets, the din and shouts of people. The nineteenth century, and even the twentieth including the tumultuous events of the last years, attracted Kramskoy much more than the faded world of the moment, which made him want to pucker his face as though from the bitter aftertaste of a hangover.

The city of today awakened no warm feelings within him. Moscow, hospitable and proud, full of secrets and indomitable spirit, was promptly losing its former charm, similar to the magic tablecloth, soiled with greedy fingers, shrinking into a small rag like Balzac's Magic Skin. It was changing into the capital of a miserly world, a consumer society yearning for toys in bright wrappers. And it succeeded in this by denying its former qualities while desiring to neither create nor discover anything new, and certainly not to use its greatness to feed those who could not stand the pervasive primitivism. The variety of forms it bore no longer – inclining toward standards set by alien prescriptions, intentionally simplifying itself, losing its voice and hearing. Nikolai's head sometimes spun in confusion, as if he were asking where he was, what was happening to him, and what had become of all the people who had surrounded him a decade ago.

He, however, did not wish to be embittered over a temporary difference of opinion with the city where he was born and had spent his whole life. Excessive bitterness smacked of weakness, which he despised utterly. Of course, the immensity of the creature into which he had been so cleverly implanted predisposed him to expand his scales of measurement. The vicissitudes of one destiny, even his own, did not seem such a serious matter. But even individual destinies were imbued with meaning – otherwise, why were there so many complications with human bodies and spirit, unquiet reason and instincts? No, everything's not so simple; and he himself, though no giant, was also no dumb speck of dust. Nikolai firmly knew this; however, he hesitated to extol its importance too much. In such a grandiose picture, there was no place for complaints, just as there was no room for boasting or excesses of conceit. The universe acted according to plan, and life flowed by the laws of "predestination" – getting to know this predestination was the most important objective. Having accepted this, it was easy to tolerate annoying trivialities – for example, the sneers directed at anyone claiming the rightness of his own view, or, at least, of its plausibility.

However, the inconveniences were not so great – the "personal metaphysics," as Nikolai called it, did not prevent him from making a decent life for himself. He had received, free of charge, a broad range of very useful knowledge – at the expense of the USSR, which was already on the verge of collapse. Then he spent seven years working in the Academy of Sciences, which fell into decay as soon as the USSR was no more; and now he was nostalgic for both – the empire as well as the Academy – soberly admitting such a sinecure could not last forever. When the crash occurred and a legion of scientists rushed to save themselves on their own, Nikolai successfully hooked up with a group of computer gurus with beards and PhDs who had not yet found a road to the West. Into a common pot, he threw everything he had done for the former government that it was suddenly unseemly to mention, and his life became quite comfortable by the standards of those tough times. Over the next two years, they collected a whole assortment of dead theories from the Soviet research institutes, bolted them together with garish interface functions and, writing *Technology T* on top of it, started looking for a big buyer. The scheme was too adventurous and doomed to fail, yet they succeeded, in accordance with the strange laws of Russian absurdity. This was aided by the stupefaction of the world as a whole and, in part, by the shortsightedness of Europe, which had decided to believe the myths of Perestroika. One of them turned out to be spot on, and, intoxicated by it, the emissaries of a large Dutch corporation bought the Big T – not even haggling much and paying real money at the realest of prices.

The case was unique, and it taught someone a lot – at least one of the notorious myths probably expired because of this – but the fortunate heroes didn't give a damn. However, almost all of them quickly lost what they had earned as they rushed headlong into the murky world of New Russian commerce. Only Nikolai Kramskoy, who had no interest in commerce whatsoever, lived on his share a little at a time, trying one thing, then another, in search of the main solution to the riddle: what did the colossus of the universe really want from him? Over ten years passed in this fashion. There was still enough money left for about forty more years, which was enough, he was certain, to figure out the answer or, at least, to make significant progress toward it.

Having funds and free time, Kramskoy used them to the fullest. The initial shock from his sudden prosperity subsided quickly, and he was smart enough not to consider himself rich. He understood, however, that he was provided for; he accepted this new freedom and managed to handle it in quite a sensible way. Living in a city of gregarious habits, he avoided the temptation to conform to the rules that had ruined so many, to force himself to be the model of "success" imposed upon him by others. He didn't even buy a car, as he was squeamish about the chaos of the Moscow streets. Likewise, he didn't bother to change his living quarters or acquire luxury goods. Instead, he hid from everyone for a week in a dull guesthouse not far from Moscow that was hardly a third full in the cold December weather. And there, wandering through the winter woods and warming himself with homemade punch, he outlined a rough plan of long-term actions, which turned out to be reasonable enough.

The main point of it was extensive travel, to which Nikolai dedicated himself with full fervor. At first, he was flustered and stuck to tour groups but understood that too much gets left unexplored, so he made the effort and learned English, achieving independence from the guides after about six months. This didn't come easily, but he was persistent, studying many hours each day, contrary to the notion of Russian slothfulness. Once he started talking and shed his shyness, he realized his eyes had been opened and the world was accessible to him in all its variety – something he could only dream about before.

Kramskoy lodged in the best hotels, enamored instantly with five-star luxury, but then he would mostly wander in rather poor places, far from the trails blazed by tourists. He sought the ordinary; and once he found it, he drank it in, not shrinking back from dirty roadways or sidelong glances. He inquired of housewives and oldsters, pretending to look for a forgotten address, bought all sorts of trifles in local shops, walked into smoky dives and struck up discussions with random people. The language barrier no longer existed for him, even if only a few spoke English in the country where he chanced to be. Remembering his efforts and proud of them, he – like the thoughtless Yankees – convinced himself it wasn't his problem, and he learned to maintain such poise that his interlocutors believed the same. Later, he grew so bold he began to meet women, sometimes expressing himself only by gestures, having found, to his surprise, that the number of intelligible words played no decisive role. He even experienced a few fleeting successes; one in particular caused him to long maintain warm romantic memories.

Within a few years, Kramskoy had visited all the continents except Africa, which for some reason did not entice him in the least. Finally, the variety of the world revealed several dominant forms and took on a nearly pyramidal structure. This was a sign of saturation: things started to repeat themselves, regardless of the geographic coordinates. Nikolai then spent some time reading books, buying himself an entire library little by little, but finally became fed up with idleness and acknowledged that his search for predestination was progressing way too passively, spreading in breadth to the detriment of in-depth penetration.

It even felt as if he were slipping or running in place, and that was unacceptable. So Nikolai resolved to transition from nonchalant observation to active creation. He began to concoct small business projects, devoting rather careful preparation to each. The precondition was the return of his invested capital – preferably within the very first year – so he would not be in the position of a loser. This always worked out – probably because the sums were not large – and afterward, he would usually shut down the project for good and start ruminating on something new. He did it with ease, as though ridding himself of a heavy burden; his ambitions extended far beyond paltry businesses. Still, this seemed more satisfying than his recent inaction, to which he would now never wish to return, and he even found some interest in these schemes of his, especially in the theoretical part which he was sometimes able to see from a philosophical angle and abstract out the accounting and other boring stuff.

The Astro-Occult Parlor, with which he had started, concerned itself with plumbing the depths of ancient sciences somewhat related to his own ideas. Of course, the positions of the stars seemed like a simplification bordering on ignorance, and the essence was left in the subtext, concealing the mechanisms and offering short-cuts; but, on the whole, it was a pleasure for him to spend time studying tables and charts that gracefully juxtaposed the positions of cold stars. Then disappointment came in because of the unacceptable remoteness from reality, so the next project was utterly realistic. He opened a practical sexology center, buying himself an authentic-looking diploma and offering patients advice in the spirit of Hindu-Chinese routines. Their unique techniques he fearlessly united into one, albeit only in theory not committed to written treatises, and developed his own method for reconciling the Daoshis with the Krishnas in matters regarding the mysteries of love. His reputation soon spread and the enterprise turned profitable, so Nikolai exercised his whim and stopped accepting men as clients. Rather, he limited himself to the fairer sex, who was much easier to work with. During his sessions and conversations, he frequently got inviting looks, but he had firmly decided he would not take advantage of any of his patients' trust – for ethical reasons, as well as fear of exposure – and he never deviated from that rule, despite a multitude of temptations.

Later came other schemes, also connected with the Orient, according to the Moscow fashion of those years. But eventually, Eastern topics were taken in hand by serious people, and Kramskoy knew he was being pushed out of an enticing niche. At about that time, he came up with his current plot, slyly called Heraldic Inquiry or Heraldic Inq. for short, which – contrary to his rules – had already existed for two years, confidently keeping afloat and even bringing in profit.

One way or another, he had not yet come upon his true mission – this he recognized honestly, telling himself it was all still ahead. There were other reasons to hold tightly to his businesses; they were like a thin umbilical cord connecting him to real life, which he admitted with some reluctance. The financial independence freed him from humanity, gave him the ability to wriggle out of the system, to escape from the humiliating contest with his peers, all fighting over crumbs. Yet, being on the outside, he noted that everything was not so easy, and the very freedom he now could not do without – just as he could not live without food and air – concealed danger he had not detected before. He had become a different man over these ten years: unlike his former self, which was nothing special, but also distinct from the rest, which was rather vital. The system was monolithic, but he stood on his own. He stood and hesitated, not daring to move far.

The sensation of being separate from the others came to him gradually, often accompanied by alarm and anxiety. Kramskoy was not stupid, and he knew how to foresee losses from the first sign of changes in the wind. He understood that the divergence of views, as innocent at first as private theater, could soon develop into a chasm impossible to overcome. Imagining this was depressing, especially since his fantasies could take him quite far. He saw, as if firsthand, how the distance grew between himself and the normal world, the lights of inhabited places concealed from sight, and his surroundings were becoming more and more hostile every day. He knew any caution misleads you occasionally; any compromise becomes obsolete. Sooner or later, only one possibility remains: cry out in protest while you still have the strength; make it heard, if you have the means; throw all on the altar of that illusive temple and incinerate yourself with no hope of revival. Of course, the flames may be bright, and there is a chance the crowd will notice, turning their heads away from their daily trivialities – but so what, and what's the point of it? No, this is only suitable for those who wish to change the world, which is funny in its own right, but which is, unfortunately, totally unfeasible because one has to negotiate with the chief authority, the ruling organism that decides destinies. And it, obviously, will not even heed the impudent. All that remains is to vibrate in solitude, sending negligible impulses into the void and stirring up only an extremely small locality.

All this disturbed him considerably. At first, before isolation had become a habit and the animosity of the world seemed to increase each day, Kramskoy tried to challenge the course of things by inventing methods of combating the inevitable. From the outside, this appeared to be useless zigzags, but he saw a coherent protest in his actions. This protest, however, was brief and ended in nothing, yielding only, as was often the case, an opportunity for Nikolai to laugh at himself.

Having renewed old acquaintances, he promptly rejected them again: in inexplicable unity, traces of the past brought him to the exact same place, an arising class of managers with whom there was nothing to talk about. Their posturing seemed absurd to him; the corporate games, which they took seriously, caused him to irrepressibly yawn. He started to think he now knew what genuinely unfortunate people looked like, but then he doubted this knowledge because of the overabundance of these unfortunates who, in addition, exuded complacency to the utmost. Whatever the case, he realized he had to search somewhere else, so he set about studying the alternatives, mainly in places where the needy population was concentrated – like cheap taverns and public baths.

They were enchanting in their own way, especially a handful of surviving vodka bars where the interior was dominated by the seventies with a hint of antiquity. It smelled there of bleach and sour beer; dim lamps flickered beneath the ceiling; waitresses nimbly scampered about with sagging breasts and the faces of overexhausted mothers. The patrons did not like bright light. They hid in the corners and covered their faces with their hands, but Nikolai would deliberately sit in the very center as if he wanted to draw everyone's gaze. He punctiliously noticed details and tried to follow etiquette – drinking low-grade alcohol, cursing the same as the rest, and echoing the laments over times long gone. At first, he was usually able to blend into the crowd, but he would soon spoil the whole picture with one or two careless words. His companions recognized in Kramskoy a stranger and rejected him with contempt, or else they shut down, falling into inexplicable grief, even though he would try to revive the conversation with witty jokes.

"You don't even want to get drunk with me," he would tease those sitting around him. "You don't want to know my secrets, coax them out of the depths of my soul. Fat chance of you meeting anyone else with so much in his soul. You suspect as much, but don't want to believe it. The boring rules of the megalopolis are more important to you than a whisper of eternity. Have it your way; I'll get drunk alone!"

People glared at him and laughed derisively, but they didn't go for rapprochement – something about him was false, not striking the right tone. There were even displays of drunken aggression, and he was dragged into conflicts a few times. Once, it led to a real fight. Nikolai got a cracked lip, but he held his own, answering his opponent Yasha with a weighty hook to the jaw. They quickly reconciled, however, and settled up together with the cop who responded to the disturbance. Having become fast friends, they bought more vodka and canned fish and went to Nikolai's house, contrary to his strict rule not to let strangers into his place.

Yasha won him over with his open mind and erudition, rare even for the fallen intellectual. *"They smote me, but I felt no pain; they buffeted me about, and I felt it not; when I awake, I will seek the same again,"* he quoted from Ecclesiastes, and inquired in a sober voice, "What's that about, Kramskoy?" Then he clarified, "It's all about the same thing: boozing," and added with a grin, "On the whole, I agree with the prophet. But I need to know: what was King Solomon's schedule for getting soused? In particular, I'm interested in the frequency and time of day – because, in my opinion, I'm doing it wrong."

Nikolai was surprised – it seemed to him he had found someone who spoke his language. Later, he chastised himself for his unexpected foolishness and noted with irony he really had blended in with the majority that day, quickly drinking and falling into a stupor like a blue-collar worker, passing out right at the kitchen table. Upon waking, he found his friend Yasha had disappeared like an Englishman – without saying goodbye – and he had lifted – quite like a Russian – the spare cash from the sideboard and a brand new

Japanese camera. Kramskoy was not so sorry for the money and the camera; he thanked fate that at least he hadn't been poisoned by the canned fish – taking one look at them in the morning was enough to horrify him. Nevertheless, this episode brought a close to his attempts to master mimicry with the objective of merging with the surrounding environment.

"It is senseless to again aspire to what, of its own accord, had long ago ceased to make sense," he told himself, accepting as a postulate that free flight was unavoidable. He needed only to carefully calculate a trajectory – to move not in a straight line further and further and further, but rather in a more intricate way: moving away and returning, waltzing and spinning, gliding on one skate and tracing out figure-eights. He would have to be clever and maneuver among the human masses without being carried away like a comet but allowing for only those interactions which he needed himself.

This was genuine art – quite difficult to learn, but it had to be learned if one wanted to achieve comfort. Kramskoy assimilated it gradually, sometimes taking notice of kindred spirits, cautious shades dressed in carefully adjusted masks. They could be recognized by their walk, the manner in which they laughed, sometimes just by a glance. They were called "observers" or else "outsiders." They were alone in a world used to monotony, and they accepted loneliness with heads held high, conscious of its implacable nature. For Nikolai, at times, it became worrisome when he thought of this and asked himself: was he already one of them? The question went out into space on unseen wires, but the response was lost somewhere without reaching its recipient. Perhaps he was unable to distinguish it from the whispers and noises. And besides, he was cunning enough not to strain his hearing.

CHAPTER 4

By noon, Nikolai Kramskoy had finished the cocktail, eaten an orange, and felt more cheerful. He still didn't want to go to his office, but the day could possibly unfold better than it had seemed an hour before. He was about to get up but suddenly detected the aroma of perfume, exciting and spicy, teasing his imagination and reminding him of something that had not yet come true. The source of the smell was behind him, where he heard the rustle of pages and a bit of commotion, so Nikolai sat there for another quarter of an hour, fantasizing and already nearly falling in love with a stranger he had never seen.

"How easy it is to get excited if you discard all the nonessentials," he thought later as he went down in the elevator. "Really, there are just a few things that rule the world. Sometimes it's perfumery – ask the Parisians, they'll tell you, though they'll probably mislead you as usual. All the same, they're right in a way: just go into a luxury store and take a whiff of how it smells all around. They clearly know how to manipulate sensations!"

Kramskoy wandered along Nikolskaya and meditated upon the unpredictability of the olfactory senses. For some reason, he recalled a crippled girl who looked like a small mouse whom he had met in a library a few years ago. Her scent was naïve and touching; she explored his body with her greedy mouth and in the morning looked at him with cheerful astonishment. The recollection was pleasant, but it quickly dimmed and was replaced by the unsteady image of a wife he never married. Half a year they spent engaged; she even lived in his apartment, but then ran away in a huff, slamming the door and accusing him of all sorts of sins. She was fond of Laotian aromatic sticks, and their bitter smell was ingrained in his memory, being firmly linked with arguments over nothing, frequent, shy sex, and a sense of disaster.

After the first week, Kramskoy knew he wasn't cut out for cohabitation. He tried to turn it all into a joke, but his would-be bride did not accept jokes. She made herself at home and spread out her possessions, not willing to give up the territory she had won. Nikolai started to panic; his hands shook and sleep eluded him. Soon, his whole physical being rose up in revolt: he got a skin rash, started to have convulsions, night spasms, and stomach cramps. He thought he would die, so, in order to save himself, he pretended to be an insufferable killjoy, exhausting his flatmate with grumbling and nagging. She, however, bore these things with resigned patience. Then, as a last resort, he decided to become a cheapskate, counting pennies and limiting expenditures, and this finally had an effect. His girlfriend took serious stock and, one fine day, disappeared with all her belongings after instigating an ugly parting scene.

Nikolai then understood a lot about Russian women, their flightiness and tough temper, and later he considered himself an expert, deducing the rules he never used. Friends, of whom he had many at that time, laughed at him when he would interpret the features of the female nature. They didn't have a moment to look into it themselves – after getting into quick marriages, they dropped out of Nikolai's existence, departing for places where it's customary to demand, tolerate, and subsist within the prescribed boundaries. And there they had remained ever since, getting divorced, dividing up children, apartments, and money, hooking up again and building a "home," having neither time nor the habit of reflection. Observing their spouses, Kramskoy noticed the majority of women did not picture life as it truly was, but instead expected too much of it for no reason. Granted, they were prepared to give a great deal in return, thinking they were capable of it and misleading those around them. Nikolai's friends took the bait and were later surprised at their own blindness, but they would repeat it all over again, often more than once. He soon ceased to share their astonishment, deciding it was no wonder they screwed up: when a girl believes in her own substance, it's no less inspiring than the substance itself. It causes her face to light up and her eyes to shine – and it's impossible to figure out what a bright spring bud will blossom into. Then nearly everything turns out phony, only the demands remain high; but it can't be helped, and you have to make do with what you yourself have chosen. And, besides, the choices are not so great if one judges soberly – all Nikolai's acquaintances had gone through the same process, to his considerable disappointment.

But now he had nearly no friends, and those whom he considered as such, he saw no more often than once a month. Their interests had diverged too far, which didn't bother him much. He had matured and had little need of anyone after he accepted the fact the world was terribly short-sighted, with no desire to recover its broader vision. He was uninterested in their lives, and they, perhaps with secret envy, explicitly or implicitly rejected the excessive freedom he asserted by his lifestyle and bachelor mores. Of course, he was often slandered and even experienced open sneers – especially from his friends' wives. He was an eyesore for them, like a gaudy necklace, with his pretense of exclusivity and his animosity toward normal life; that understandably exposed him to confrontation bordering on direct calumny. A rumor had even circulated once about his "inclinations," and the news was gleefully snatched up and twisted every which way. Then, suddenly, a certain childhood friend turned up out of the blue and volunteered brave fantasies that had just come up to be put to the test. Indeed, being gay was fashionable at the time, and people liked to talk about it. But all of it was built on shaky soil – nobody saw anything, nor did they know anything for certain. Besides, Nikolai had, in fact, always been extremely hetero, offering not even a single piece of evidence to support the gossip.

Finally, they left him in peace, but he continued to feel bitter for a long time and even harbored something akin to hatred for the insidious sex, the source of the universal lie, it would seem. Naturally, he was being unfair and laughed later as he recognized this, recalling how he had once been filled with contempt – first for the wives of his friends, and later for Moscow girls as a whole. They began to irritate him in almost every way. Behind their languid grace, he sensed the clumsiness of their whims and the coarseness of their movements. He looked at them through an unkind scowl, registering their impudence and insolent impulses, which would instantly come to naught at the first sign of resistance. And he also saw their true nature: an endless readiness to be humiliated, which was written on their faces in the invisible ink of lachrymose masks. They believed humiliation was inevitable and obediently took it for granted, taking revenge on those few who cowered before them or idolized them – but even this they did with caution, with concealed timidity that could not be eliminated. "Where is the dignity?" he asked silently. "Where is the quiet confidence and proud bearing? Why do almost all of them appear to be such beggars in their soul? And they are also so fond of pity – toward the downtrodden, the worthless, the weak. Yes, Russians have a tradition of pitying the wretched; that's nothing new."

Until he was about thirty-three, Kramskoy tortured himself and suffered, feeling he had been deceived and didn't get what was promised in the past. Then the acuteness of his bad experiences faded; he grew stronger and stopped blaming others for being the way they were. Also, he admitted Muscovite women could be attractive and spontaneous like nymphs, and as desirable as tasty candies. The main thing was not to expect too much – as soon as he realized that, the obstacle he had built for himself instantly broke down. Consequently, the opposite sex became more comely to him, and he himself, without noticeable effort, began to incite interest from them. This he made use of liberally, according to his mood and available free time.

The heat grew ever more intense; sunbeams beat down and melted the asphalt. Kramskoy walked to Teatralny Proyezd and began the descent toward the corner of Petrovka. Upon reaching the TSUM Department Store, which cast a heavy shadow, he breathed a sigh of relief; but then a melodious trill rang from the pocket of the shirt plastered to his body. Nikolai glanced at the screen of his cell phone, frowned with displeasure, and answered with a gloomy "Yes?"

From the ringtone itself, he understood right away he shouldn't expect anything good. The harmonics of the caller's mood probably infiltrated the radio signal, and the old Korean phone resonated in a minor key. It even managed to occur to Kramskoy that his morning melancholy was a premonition of the conversation that had long needed to take place. Furthermore, the one to blame for this situation was none other than himself.

A client was calling who had commissioned Kramskoy's services three weeks before. He was disgruntled and abrupt – and unsurprisingly: Nikolai, after receiving his deposit, became lethargic, lax, and unable to force himself to deal with the order. Even more bizarrely, this order was the only one for the whole summer, so it had nothing to do with a lack of time.

Now the client demanded a report. Nikolai believed him to be a patient man, not disposed to getting upset over minor issues, and, in the main, that was true. But today it just so happened that problems were closing in from all sides, and he wanted to take it out on someone. Kramskoy fit the bill perfectly: the stipulated term was coming to a close and the total lack of results was a good reason for discontent. The client escalated to discontent quickly, exercising notable restraint to keep himself within the bounds of decency.

Nikolai, for his part, tried not to be rude in his responses. Every time there were setbacks in one of his business deals, he had the urge to walk off and say to hell with it all – explaining to his clients he really had no need of them or their money. This impulse, he knew, had to be vigorously quelled, and he fought it: counting mentally to ten, pinching his arm, and trying to take slow, deliberate breaths.

To refuse the client and return his money would mean to incur a substantial operating loss. Though that was not dangerous in light of his general prosperity, it was still unpleasant, like an alarm or the shadow of misfortune – and not just in his own opinion. There was one more interested party that Kramskoy took into account, and he could not allow himself to show weakness by giving in to the whim of a moment. The situation had to be saved; he had to fight for the client and, indeed, to comport himself as befitted a small businessman who was not firmly standing on his own two feet.

However, there was no answer to give, so Nikolai, maintaining the proper tone, dispensed the usual line, assuring the client the order was being handled around the clock, and that those efforts were just about to pay off. They needed only to wait a bit, and the result would not disappoint, he insisted, wishing he could believe that himself. The client prattled on some more, making Kramskoy repeat the same thing over and over, and they ended the call coolly, agreeing to be in touch again in three days. In that time, Nikolai knew, real progress had to be made – otherwise, the order and the deposit would be lost. The inactivity had to stop, regardless of his mood and temper.

There was no sense going to the office now; the material he needed was to be found elsewhere. Nikolai stood in thought for a minute, then made up his mind, marched back to Kuznetsky and entered a majestic building covered in pustules of plaster molding. There, he knew, hid an Internet café, cool and cozy, serving nondescript food.

Hours later, after six pm, Kramskoy left the establishment, exhausted and with his eyes tearing up. Recoiling from the bright light, he ponderously ascended toward the subway station. The search had produced no results: rummaging through a host of articles, Nikolai had not encountered a single idea, and now he was just as angry at the client as the man had been at him a few hours before.

At least the day was coming to a close, he thought gloomily, muttered a curse under his breath, and then was overtaken, nearly bumped into, by a girl in leggings with a large rose in her hand.

Kramskoy's eyes trailed her, but someone close by called his name. Forgetting the girl, he gazed down in amazement at the drunken-faced beggar who was addressing not him, but the neighboring bum on the pavement.

The beggar spoke loudly, like a town crier; people were staring at her, some even slowing to look. Nikolai was at a standstill, not even sure why himself; after halting there for a few moments, he began to hunt for change in his trouser pockets. Several gawkers stopped around him. The beggar studied them with surprise, yet not skipping a beat in her inspired speech. Then someone suddenly guffawed; an insult rang out, then another, and she began to curse in response, then to sob and complain bitterly. Her neighbor spit over her shoulder, right on the sidewalk, and murmured with a sigh, "Now, here she goes wailing, the crazy bitch..." – and Nikolai, feeling somewhat uneasy, hastened on toward the open terrace of his favorite snack bar.

He wanted a cold beer, but there was no alcohol on the menu, so he asked for a citrus smoothie, looking the pimply waitress full in the face as she took the order with an indifferently imperious gaze. "Fish!" he thought glumly. His mood did not improve, and his overworked eyes still ached. Nikolai sought an ashtray, found it on the next table, and rose clumsily, nearly overturning his chair; then he thought better of it, waved his hand, and resumed his seat. "Well, no, that won't do," he declared in a low voice. "They're trying to lure me into a net again. Somebody wants to use my anger to his advantage."

The waitress, who had arrived with the glass and a napkin, looked at him in consternation, clearly thinking he was a weirdo. Kramskoy winked at her, but she sniffed and hurried away.

"A fish, really," he thought again. "Or a chicken. I wonder if anybody's sleeping with her? Probably not; that's why she has zits. Look how she glowers. Isn't she afraid of me?"

The acne-face maiden was discussing something with her compatriots in a distant corner of the terrace, glancing occasionally in his direction. Nikolai relocated to the next chair so he could sit with his back to her, lit a cigarette, and looked at the street filled with the evening sunlight, willing himself not to give any more thought to the client or the wasted day.

"The rabble is homogeneous indeed," he contemplated idly. "The types are all the same; variety is harder to find than a needle in a haystack. There are more faces than heads, and there are even less souls, as Karamzin used to say. It's hard to disagree with that. I'd only add that men's faces sit atop uninteresting bodies, and women have the opposite: interesting bodies are supplemented with faces. And, of course, women get flashes of thought more often. Today's men have a tough time venturing a thought. Stress smothers them and their emotions are shallow; even the feelings that do occur become face masks – and the faces accept this because they're tired of arguing. Consequently, they're twisted and beaten down; those are the signs of submission after a short struggle. And many more seem to shout, 'How can someone love me if I have no money?' Meanwhile, a woman thinks about the permanent. To her, by and large, there's no one with whom to engage in dispute: the universe has determined everything for her. I wonder if they sense the tingling vibration of the universe. Or are they just arguing over trinkets?"

Nikolai extracted a new cigarette from the pack and squirmed with disappointment: thoughts of money drew him into remembering about the client. "They're all the same, all in a hurry," he thought angrily, "as if every average nobody has somewhere to be. Well, I'm not an average nobody, and I, for example, have no place to hurry to. But I have to do it anyway because of someone else's rush that makes no sense. Nothing but veneer and foolishness – run, run... The majority have it written in neon on their foreheads: 'I'm part of the rat race,' and you can't erase the label no matter how you try. It's not shameful, it just sounds pitiful. They're not so bad, these races – they keep you from being bored. Life goes by quickly, and the anxieties are the same for all. There's something to be proud of – if you hustle faster than your neighbors. And there's something to reach for: being even quicker and more tenacious. Here they scrape their claws along the asphalt – demonstratively, looking down upon the rest. But so be it: this is their time, and everybody else is on the sidelines. The arrangement changed, maybe forever."

He took a gulp from the narrow tumbler, squeezed up one eye, and peered into it with the other, as though it were a kaleidoscope or spyglass. The contents of the tumbler were cheerfully multihued, like the Sunday morning comics. "An entertaining pattern," mused Nikolai. "What am I angry about, anyway? Such is city life, and it could be worse. I should probably enjoy it. Economics is to blame – oil is skyrocketing and thieves don't get their hands slapped, so they grow fat and happy. The city will wake up only when the winds change. Then everybody will stop, think a bit, become more open, kinder. All that's needed is a financial crash, though I wish no one ill..."

"From its gluttony, the vulture fell, unable to rise, ripe pickings to be bludgeoned," he recalled from who-knows-where. "Keep running, keep running, all is ahead – you will have your fair share. And why doesn't fate tire of treating all alike?"

Nikolai set down the empty glass, sighed deeply, and stretched his body. It responded with the pleasant lassitude of muscles that had worked out at the gym. "Tomorrow I'll do the weight machines," he determined, businesslike. "But something has to be done with the evening. It's no good giving up and slacking off."

He realized the day's heat had abated. The smells of the night already wafted on the air. The decision took form right away, as if of its own accord, though it was obvious from the very beginning.

Kramskoy waved into the distance behind his back and they brought him a bill worthy of a trendy Manhattan bar. "Keep the change," he grumbled to the waitress as she hovered over his shoulder like a reproachful shade. She left without thanking him. Nikolai took out his cell, made one short call, and, feeling young and energetic, hurried toward Petrovka to catch an obliging taxi.

CHAPTER 5

On the very same July morning, Frank White, Jr., a thirty-year-old American, turned out of his driveway onto River Road, the main street in Potomac, MD, his tires squealing as he sped toward I-495. It was early; the sun had barely risen and the traffic lights still blinked yellow. His brand-new Dodge flew like a bird; there was not another soul on the road. Lush green grew in thickets right up to the roadside, arousing a sensation of sylvan freshness. This perception was facilitated in no small measure by the car's air-conditioning: the damp heat on the other side of the glass was already intensifying, but this did not spoil the amenity of the perfect morning in the least. A wild deer revealed itself, standing right up against the edge of the roadbed, sensitively flaring its nostrils. The highway exit soon appeared; the Dodge valiantly pulled into the empty left lane and headed toward Dulles International Airport. Frank White, Jr. was utterly filled with joy.

He was flying to Russia, of which he had once been enamored. This love had begun in his distant childhood, and it continued to stir his soul. Many years ago, Frank's father had been offered the opportunity to head up the Moscow office of an influential Washington newspaper, and he accepted, to the surprise of his whole family. Afterward, no one regretted this except for White's colleagues in the main bureau, who liked their coworker's dry humor and the firm principles he inherited from his Puritan forebears.

This was a time when the Soviet system flourished, passing gradually into decline. Cloak-and-dagger zeal was tightened into a hard knot, and the pressure on officials was significant, forcing them to be vigilant to the point of absurdity and to select their acquaintances and words with care. The White family braced itself for living in tough conditions, to anxieties and privations, to being on the front lines, but life there turned out to be much easier than expected. It was even quite fun – much more fun than everyday American life.

Quick to adapt, the Whites acclimated to the Western circle, which in Soviet Moscow pertained to the *beau monde* of the highest order. Consequently, the Westerners were overwhelmed by Russian hospitality – altered by the realities of Socialism but retaining many national features, including generosity and indefatigability. Europeans and Yankees, brought up on precise accounting and the tedium of tight control, easily adjusted to the opulent excesses of the pyramidal system and found themselves on the inside of a warehouse of pleasures operating around the clock. Receptions, performances, and feasts for no reason followed one after another in dense succession. The variety of acquaintances they made surpassed their wildest expectations, and boredom was totally out of the question. Besides, Frank's father was terribly busy at work, and his mom, along with the wife of some Frenchman, supported the hungering underground in the best of missionary traditions under the attentive, though invisible, eye of the KGB.

At her insistence, Junior attended the public school rather than its ambassadorial counterpart – though that would have been more befitting of their status. Her formal reason was the Russian language, and the aspiration to study it to such a lofty degree it could not be provided by any university. Unlike her husband – who considered Russians to be amusing but completely uncivilized, and thought their country was doomed to a slow death – Mrs. White, enchanted by the Bolshoi Theater and the ingenious paintings of the drunkard Zverev, suspected Russian power could exist for a long time and that linguistic freedom would help Frank to achieve a great deal in his future career. There was something else, not quite expressible in words, that didn't fit the stiff atmosphere of the embassy classes – but, whatever the case, White Sr. merely shrugged, fully trusting his wife in matters of education and upbringing. As a result, little Frank began to attend a special – albeit fully Soviet – institution with in-depth instruction in mathematics, for which he showed no aptitude whatsoever.

His school years awakened much in him, and he recalled them as the brightest time in his life. His peers accepted him, and he was no different from the rest until his senior year, when Mrs. White realized he required private tutoring for Harvard. On this she insisted, yet even then he spent a few hours almost every day in the company of his classmates, as close as possible to dark-haired Natasha, who had taken hold of his teenage heart. It was with her, at the age of sixteen, he had his first experience of passionate necking, and with her he had fallen in love with Moscow forever, feeling much more at ease there than in his native country, where the Whites only spent brief holidays.

The end of his father's assignment struck him like a thunderbolt out of a blue sky, though rumors had been circulating in his family for a while about some opportunists waiting for the right moment to take their place. That moment came suddenly, soon after the death of an elderly Soviet leader, who was replaced by a man still hated by Frank and despised by the entire White clan. He, of course, had done nothing amiss to them personally, and it is unlikely he knew about their existence at all. Frank White, Sr. even admitted with a laugh that for a couple of years he had sincerely believed in Gorbachev's Perestroika, failing to notice – like many others – the petty-mindedness of the main players. Whatever the case, that "breath of fresh air" changed the life of the American newspaper. Some were even forced to retire, pushed out by new rhetoric and new people, and, to tell the truth, the director of the Moscow office had already occupied that spot longer than he was supposed to. The Whites were recalled, and they returned to Washington. Frank's heart was shattered into many pieces, like the country that had accidentally fallen into the hands of hopeless numbskulls.

Nevertheless, he adjusted to his homeland quickly, and his timely experience at Harvard imparted the necessary luster to him. Once, he visited Moscow with a group of Slavic literature majors and came back disappointed: Natasha had married and was expecting a child; his former classmates had run off to who-knows-where; the city was delirious with cheap trade and easy money. People were thrilled with the "changes" and suddenly transformed into simpletons and morons. The hated young Party leader shone his bald pate on TV, and there was little to remind Frank of the school days of his youth. Upon returning to the States, he firmly resolved to forget Russia forever.

The Delta Airlines Boeing 747 taxied slowly out to the runway. Frank White, Jr. sat by the window next to a doughy blond man who huffed and puffed over his disobedient seatbelt. The cabin was dominated by French cologne and Russian speech. Only the stewardesses chirped away in English, smelling of nothing at all. Frank caught himself thinking he perceived both languages as one, just inflated with nonessential slang. His neighbor, having finally buckled up, mopped the sweat from his forehead, looked at Frank, and joyfully asked in Russian, "One of us?"

"Who?" asked Frank, jumping in surprise.

"You," his neighbor explained, pointing a finger at his chest for clarity.

"Uh, not quite," Frank White cautiously replied, flashing his wide American smile.

The neighbor muttered, "Okay," and turned away with a frown – and Frank almost burst out laughing, feeling in full measure that his adventure was truly about to begin.

The blond's mistake astonished him slightly – Frank White didn't look Russian at all. The descendant of ruined barons from Sheffield, he had a physical appearance that, making some allowances, could be considered flawless. He was tall of stature and broad-shouldered, possessing classic facial features and a straight, aristocratic nose; only his eyes seemed too lively for the heir of such ancient genes. Over ten years had passed since he had been to Russia, and he had a poor reckoning of what country might have arisen to replace the one he knew. Since then, too many things had changed – and had done so more than once. The growth of Frank's career left much to be desired: contrary to the hopes of Mrs. White, the bilingualism he had acquired in his youth was not put to further use, and the nature of his endeavors was far from the journalistic spheres of the family. At Harvard, he had earned a degree in the history of Ancient Rome, to the amazement of both parents, who did not venture a direct prohibition, since they reasoned, quite sensibly, that everyone in their country should have at least a small taste of freedom. The secrets of the Roman Empire, including the refined practices of Machiavelli, did not impress his employers much. On top of that, once he had received his coveted degree, Frank felt his interest in science had vanished, and weighty history tomes induced boredom in him.

He knocked about from firm to firm, always playing a secondary role, until fate wound the next coil and the Russian theme resounded anew in his life. At a party being thrown by the acquaintance of a former roommate, Frank heard a random word spoken in Russian as he shuffled about the rooms; thus, he met Axel Timurov and disrupted the unsteady equilibrium of his rather wretched existence.

At first Frank took him for a Western European – Axel knew how to put up a smokescreen and hide the obvious for his immediate benefit. On top of that, unlike the majority of *homo sovieticus*, he had a pretty good command of English and left a powerful impression that some kind of success awaited him right around the corner. Nearly everyone speaking with him took this bait, and even the phantom of the American Dream came to life in his foreign presence – as if in reproach to the local keepers of the flame who had lost their former passion. Very soon, however, a vague concern arose, the suspicion that something was not quite right; and then, after a few minutes, the indisputable fact became clear: Axel Timurov was hopelessly dense.

His dull-wittedness was all-embracing and absolute; it clouded his eyes and stopped up his ears. However, that did not contradict the notion of the "dream" – his new acquaintances soon understood where the problem was concealed, and were not surprised any more by his wildest comments or inability to retain even the simplest thought. Moreover, that even created the illusion of comfort: it seemed the key to Axel was easily obtained, so quite often the very lack of intelligence served him as a ticket into fairly serious circles where foreigners, and especially Russians, were not generally welcome. But Timurov, sporting a badge of good luck as if it were pinned to his lapel, was admitted as a completely harmless exception that was also able to benefit the affair. They tolerated him like an aborigine who, fortuitously, had assumed the face of *homo modernus* – though, of course, no one missed the chance to laugh behind his back, making him the hero of the most absurd fables.

As far as absurdity was concerned, he himself was an endless source of it, providing plenty of material to his detractors. The most comical was the legend of his origin and enviable pedigree, which he made up soon after arriving in the States, and of which he was particularly fond. It had been started at a reception for the Belgian consul, where Timurov had been admitted for reasons known to him alone, and where, after getting thoroughly drunk on champagne, he confessed to one of the embassy secretaries that he was a distant descendant of the last Russian emperor. The Belgian, showing professional restraint, didn't bat an eye and told him, in reply, of his love for Tchaikovsky and Faberge eggs. Nonetheless, since then, Axel never missed an opportunity to corner his next victim and ask him with grave seriousness, "Did you happen to hear I'm a member of the Tsar's family?" This minor weakness of his quickly became known as yet another myth about "mysterious Russians" who couldn't live without fairy tales. Some scoffers even spoke to him directly about the problems of royal dynasties that had weathered bad times. And Axel noticed nothing; he merely took on an enigmatic air and proudly cast his gaze about.

Within half an hour of meeting Frank White, he was already

hinting about his relationship to the Tsar. Frank was taken aback at first but quickly learned to deal patiently with Axel, enjoying the occasion of speaking Russian again and suddenly missing Moscow. They began an inconspicuous friendship, and then Timurov had a fling with a cousin of Frank's who had a thirst for the exotic. As a result, he met the whole White family and made a good impression on them. Perhaps nostalgia for the happy past played a role here, especially for Mrs. White, who took a serious interest in Axel and introduced him to her relatives and friends, among whom were well-to-do, rather influential people.

One must admit that, for all his oddities, Axel had an irrefutable talent. He always managed to get people to like him the first time they met, seeking out with his sixth sense an occasion for subtle flattery as the phantom of success soared about like a nimbus, generously compensating for those follies he poured out as though from a horn of plenty. Where that success – or, more precisely, its imperceptible shadow – came from, Frank could never quite figure out. Before meeting the Whites, Axel's affairs were not too good; his own business, which he raved about, wasn't bringing in a cent, and to make a living, he had to work at the National Institute of Health, where the German boss, who didn't like Slavs, treated him like a lazy child. Nevertheless, nearly everyone was ready to believe in his shining future, and Axel regarded that as the only real chance to find and apply his long-awaited luck.

He easily convinced Frank of the prospects of a joint venture. They became partners and started looking for money; instead of counting on banks from which you couldn't get a dime, they turned to the same group of Whites, who were favorably disposed toward the undertaking. By this time, Axel had already learned by heart the advantageous parts of his long-suffering business plan, and Frank's diploma with its impressive Harvard stamp also came in handy. In just a month, they collected a lot, which allowed the enterprise not to die right after being born – and connected the two of them, like it or not, for the long haul.

Since then, five and a half years had passed. They tried many things, including Russian wolfhound puppies, merchandise made of birch bark, and even rare earth metals – which caused some unpleasantness with the FBI. Ultimately, the most profitable import item turned out to be Russian programmers, which the entrepreneurs settled on after entering a fashionable niche of protection from the hackers who had inundated the world.

The programmers were reticent and timid. They had to be taught the simplest things, like using deodorant and driving. When the bosses showed up, they would huddle in a bunch and hide their eyes with a twisted smirk, but, on the whole, they were good-natured and quite efficient. Business was on the rise; Axel Timurov grew fat and disagreeably arrogant, but with Frank he remained the same as before – because Frank White, like nobody else, learned how to manage the programming team, and that made him irreplaceable. For his part, Frank had already come to seriously dislike Axel, having discovered in himself an intolerance for idiots, which was rare for an American. He even considered leaving the company for good, but every time he sensed a regret originating from his school days, and for some reason he didn't feel like fighting it. Besides, he was attached to the programmers in his own way: they were strange creatures who possessed a gloomy, timid trust in him; that was to be valued. So, Frank came to view Timurov as a symbol of another Russia unknown to him, where so much was alien but, alas, incontrovertible, unless one wanted to try arguing with the laws of time and space. He even spoke of him as a New Russian, having seen the popular term somewhere and wishing to highlight, with the naiveté of a bystander, that Russians were different before. Then they happened to encounter the real New Russians, and Frank realized he was wrong. There was yet another shift in his consciousness; Axel Timurov became for him a timeless variation of the omnigenous Slavic type. White worried only that others, looking at his partner, who became even more obtuse and resembled a peacock, could reach the wrong conclusion about a country that was worthy of a more thoughtful appraisal.

There was one more thing that served as a source of anxiety

for Frank: for quite some time now, he had been sensing a lack of firm soil beneath his feet. It seemed to him that he again wanted to go *there*, and for this there was no one to blame but those very same programmers. Two continents were beckoning, and at times it seemed he was right between the two, suspended over an indifferent ocean, powerless to swing to either side definitively. Some connection existed for him with Russia, like an invisible umbilical cord, though when he spoke with Russians in his own country, Frank White, Jr. felt all-American down to his bones. Amid his compatriots, however, he had been experiencing uncertainty from time to time, looking upon his environs like an outsider with foreign eyes, as if through a thin but strong pane of glass. This bifurcation was tortuous at times. The sense of indistinct longing did not occur often, but it came regularly and did not leave Frank so easily anymore. He was even seen by a doctor who found nothing amiss; then, being truly troubled by it, he turned to an expensive psychotherapist. However, right in the second session, the shrink started to ask questions with an unpleasant subtext about his childhood, and Frank decided he was throwing his money away.

The pressure built inside; he was waiting for a sign or impetus. Then, exactly one month ago, something outstanding took place. Frank came across a man named Nilva – his surname was as strange as his clothing and appearance, and he would tell no one his first name out of some unclear superstition. They got acquainted at Axel's house, where Nilva was introduced to White, Jr. as a neighbor from the block in St. Petersburg, a childhood friend who had turned up out of nowhere. Indeed, he had appeared in the States only recently, coming to a Jewish community outside San Francisco. Family affairs, he claimed, brought him to the other coast, though his family was still waiting in line for departure papers in that gloomy, windswept Russian city.

Nilva attacked Frank White like carefully stalked quarry. In an hour or so, he admitted he was burdened by a secret, the details of which he disclosed forthwith. Surprisingly, Frank believed it immediately, as if recognizing that fate had long been pushing him toward it. For this exact reason, he had been taught to speak Russian, hooked up first with Axel and then with his childhood friend, and been constantly enticed by that distant land, as if being held in reserve for some unique mission. As it turns out, Nilva the Jew, with his sad, all-knowing eyes, suggested to him that very thing. Wrinkling his brow and frowning, he informed White, Jr. that he had in his hands an original map to a very rich trove – maybe not as rich as the famed burial site of Genghis Khan, but still enough to comfortably set up for life the happy soul who found it. This hoard was nothing less than a part of the plunder stolen by the brigand Pugachev, and the priceless document had fallen into Nilva's hands by a series of coincidences, or by the will of the stars being properly aligned.

He then began speaking in a rapid-fire staccato, spitting when he talked and sometimes transitioning to a whisper. There were no bright colors in his story, but its ordinariness neither spoiled the impression nor generated doubts. All began with an altruistic impulse, an act of assistance to the backward boondocks: in the Hermitage Museum, where Nilva had worked since his youth, a container arrived with old manuscripts taken from the archives of provincial towns. Each of the employees got a few boxes that no one had looked into for many decades. The manuscripts were strewn about without order, and the condition of some was terrible. Specialists from St. Petersburg could only sigh as they beheld this disgrace. Nilva himself, to be honest, was not thrilled about the thankless task, but later, as often happens, he took a liking to it and got buried up to his throat in old documents. Here an unlikely surprise awaited him.

"The boxes were given to us, for one," muttered Nilva, doubling a crooked counting finger into his palm. "Then two: one of mine came from Sivoldaisk – a city that, between us, is noteworthy for almost nothing. But that's if you judge it out of context, and this box was *in* context. That is, the context itself, partially stricken with mold, was in the box, filling it completely. For almost all we got from Sivoldaisk," he said, bending a third finger, "was from the famous time of Pugachev – that's three. Now, I knew enough about Pugachev to have my interest piqued then and there because it was right outside Sivoldaisk that the outlaw suffered a shattering defeat. That was the place where he was utterly routed and went on the lam. He retreated in shame with just a handful of people, including those who were to betray him, and quite soon, as it turned out."

"So, now we have four, five, and six," Nilva said, crooking his fingers. "At the fortress of Sivoldaisk, Yemelyan Pugachev could sense his impending demise. The ice cold touched him there, and he began to lose his faith in mankind – becoming morose and withdrawn, and frightfully dark of countenance. And there, in one of his fits of despair, he commanded two of his most loyal men to bury half the treasure in a secluded corner and to keep their mouths shut about it to avoid theft and betrayal. What he wanted to spend that half on is known only to God and his sorry brigand heart, but the rumor of this deed took on a life of its own, though the ones who did it were silent as the grave, and they soon wound up in a grave when the emperor's bullets took them. The treasure itself was far from modest: it included gold and jewels collected from ransacked houses, and since the houses robbed were without number, even half would suffice to make anyone's eyes pop. Attempts were made, as one would expect, to find the hoard, but it was all for naught, because how can you look for something if you don't really know where. But now, 'where' is known. I know *where!*" Nilva yelled out, and quickly covered his mouth in fright with the palm of his hand.

Later, once he had rested and attended to the drinks on the counter, he finished relating the story. The ending turned out to be rather sad. The paper with the map – a faded, ordinary-looking leaflet – came into his hands during the process of recording documents of the era, which were tossed in a disheveled heap in the aforementioned box. Its authenticity was, obviously, the weakest point of the whole account, but Nilva began with such passion to put forth arguments, citing chemical tests as well as graphology and corroborating dates, that Frank, soon lost in the confusion, agreed without listening to the end.

"After all, you're a specialist yourself," the new acquaintance summarized in a slightly injured fashion. "You should understand

I'm not conning you here." At this, Frank White, Jr. hastily nodded, and Nilva kept on talking, now with a rather doleful face.

Really, he deserved sympathy. Convinced of the significance of the fortune that had befallen him, he almost undertook to plan concrete steps, but here fate played a cruel joke. All of a sudden, he turned from a respectable citizen – albeit vegetating ignominiously along the roadside – to being a member of the criminal element, with the prospect of spending the next few years behind bars. Russia is full of such metamorphoses. It cherishes and knows them beyond count – and, with him, all happened quite foolishly and was not his fault at all. Old friends convinced him to enter into a partnership – concerning another matter not connected to Pugachev's treasure. After considering it hundreds of times over, he consented and affixed his ill-fated signature, soon after which men from a very serious organization materialized and started to ask questions. Some money issues surfaced that he knew nothing about, along with angry creditors and debts… He had been set up, that is the essence of what happened. He was forced to flee Russia, taking only what he could carry, a little bit of hard currency and the document that opened a path to riches and luxury. Luckily, his passport still bore a multi-entry American visa – Nilva had visited his relatives in New York and returned quite recently – otherwise, it would be good-bye to his freedom, and maybe even his life. So, the only steps left were to transfer his patient family to America and find an adequately reliable person to extract from the earth those Pugachev's treasures awaiting the opportune hour.

Therefore, he continued, grabbing Frank by the sleeve and looking him affectionately in the eye, therefore he was so happy with their pleasant encounter: White, Jr. – who already knew the language and was acquainted with Russia firsthand – was practically the only person whom Nilva, an extraordinarily cautious man, could genuinely trust.

"Russians," he motioned with his head toward Axel's guests on the porch, "Russians are guaranteed to cheat you, and then they'll be proud of it. People are jealous, jealous and spiteful, and ready to gouge their neighbor's eyes out. It didn't used to be like that..." and he launched into memories not connected in any way with their joint enterprise.

They saw each other two more times, discussing basically the same thing, and then they shook hands. The agreement they arrived at was to divide the money in half. Frank suspected this was unjust, but his partner became unexpectedly tough when the talk turned to percentages and shares. A minor hitch also arose over the question of guarantees: Nilva did not doubt Frank's honesty, but knowing the fickleness of human intentions, he wanted proof of his partner's commitment. A sum of several thousand dollars, Nilva said, would fully convince him that Frank would not change his mind and get involved in something else while Nilva sat around and wasted time. Then, seeing White, Jr.'s hesitation, he decreased the amount from several thousand to just one, but he wouldn't go down any further. To this Frank finally agreed, assuring himself that everyone should have insurance for the contingency of lost opportunities. As a result, a solemn exchange was made of a photocopy of the ancient document for a short stack of hundred-dollar bills. Then each went about his business: Nilva, to get moving on his family's emigration; and Frank White on arranging a quick vacation and packing his things, which, it turned out, were few.

The priceless photocopy was in the inside pocket of Frank's jacket as he flew over the dreary Atlantic, rather pleased with himself. Despite the fantastical nature of the project, he firmly believed that success lay ahead. Considering Nilva's offer, he studied tables of star signs; everything pointed to Pegasus, an admirable creature who soars above reservations, knowing its luck, its own special fate. The plan of the heavens was complicated and stretched on for years – and why shouldn't it be that way? In the spheres where the decisions were made for Frank White, there was neither commotion, nor haste, nor the fear of being misunderstood by others.

The last thing in the world he wanted was to scare off this fortunate chance. Chances arose for him too seldom – even less often than he thought of them, as he recalled his classmates who had really soared high. Frank experienced no envy, but he also didn't consider himself deserving of a worse fate. Consequently, quite in keeping with the spirit of his country, he carefully nurtured his optimism every time there was an occasion for it. And now, gazing out the window of a Boeing at the veil of cirrus clouds, he didn't fuss over re-examining his motives. Rather, he reflected directly on the consequences – for example, what he would do with the riches he obtained – painting pictures full of speculation and cliché. In his head, in odd succession, spun houses, cars, and yachts, expensive women and their whims, palm trees against an azure seaside, his own cook and bodyguard. He realized this was naïve and very childish; however, he supposed a few fantasies could hardly do any harm.

Then his musings took a more rational turn. Frank began to assess the implementation of a dream he had long held, one upon which he would not be sorry to spend a portion of his future money. The dream smacked of a certain madness, but it possessed ambition on a grand scale, which made him secretly proud of himself. The turbines hummed steadily, and his thoughts flowed as smoothly as lines on paper. Meanwhile, the clouds below combined in intricate patterns that traced out silhouettes, or letters, or the outlines of strange buildings. At times, even numbers seemed to appear: threes linked in a chain, or fives, the embodiments of unpredictable Mercury, promising so much in multifaceted Moscow.

CHAPTER 6

Rattling along in a shabby, black Chevy, Nikolai Kramskoy's taxi was making its way through narrow alleys as it tried to bypass Kutuzovsky Avenue, frozen in a traffic jam. Kramskoy suffered from the heat and dust but looked upbeat and twitched impatiently. His mood had changed, as if by magic, and not a trace of his recent melancholy remained. Jumping the curb, the car turned onto a side street, weaved to miss an open manhole, and picked up speed. Nikolai reclined in his seat and whistled a cheerful tune.

"Going to see a girl, isn't he?" the elderly driver thought. "Must like chicks, this guy."

The driver was right: the upsets of early youth were long forgotten, and women had occupied a significant place in Nikolai's life. He was drawn to them by an acute curiosity that had not run dry in all his forty years, and that had nothing to do with an overabundance of hormones. He was still willing to see a mystery in them – the kind that could captivate and disarm, if only for a brief instant. He was excited by the impulse and the response, and often thought he was born in the most ideal of places: regarding ephemeral mysteries, Russia stood out, and trips to other countries only convinced him of the obvious.

The women of his motherland did not cease to amaze – by a combination of sensuality and innocent posturing, by a blend

of modesty, albeit feigned, and a boldly expressed sexual facet –
in their breasts and hips, covered with clothes, in their voice and
walk, which could not be concealed. Some of his girlfriends were
difficult to arouse, though their bodies often responded before their
consciousness, on guard unexpectedly before an invisible force field.
But then, once the step was taken and emotions got the green light,
all the chains fell off and the consciousness soared ahead, pulling all
in its wake. The elation of what was imagined, often without outside
effort, caused reactions unachievable by any art of love. All that
remained was to submerge in the female essences, taking a gulp of
air now and then, not hoping to return to *terra firma*. And, afterward,
to long remember the elements and the depths, the madness of
storms and the calmest breezes, each of which had its own meaning.

When the bodies settled down, everything became duller.
There came pretentious habits, and the suddenness of discovery
gave way to the old, well-known game. The depth then and there
became a shoal; Nikolai just smoked and thought of his own affairs,
distractedly nodding to the affected whisper. Some remained always
sincere, but such were contemptuously few. With all the others,
it was apparent the heat of amorous passion had a quite variable
magnitude. It depended entirely on the moods of his partner, which
changed too frequently. At first, he was angry and even offended
at times, but he soon learned to take this for granted too, finding
interest in endless unpredictability and elevating it to the rank of
those national virtues that have been carried unchanged through the
ages and societal customs.

As he matured, Nikolai grew much more tolerant in general.
After an abortive marriage he, in the main, avoided permanent
relationships and the commitments of cohabitation. Only when the
separation from the others really alarmed him did he again, albeit
briefly, initiate a search for a partner for his remaining years, a link
between him and those "others," between the position of outsider
and everyday life. However, as soon as he was ready to buy into
constancy, all the seductresses, apparently available and willing,
suddenly became attached, and Kramskoy was left with no one to

choose.

Ultimately, he met a tall and slightly slouching translator from the Ministry of Foreign Affairs; yearning for sex, she threw herself on him like a tigress. Her drive was so strong, he interpreted it as a testament to true feelings, but after a month his new girlfriend began to regard him with doubt and was in no rush to profess any intentions for the long term. Then Nikolai decided the problem was in the inertia of the female mind, so he set out to prove the improvable, showing his chosen one with all his might that he fit the role of a "real man." Another month passed that way, during which he exhibited methodical persistence in repairing domestic appliances, zealously discussed guns and cars, and expressed sympathy toward the notions that women, by their fragile nature, need understanding and protection. As a result, the translator broke things off, telling him he was too much of a bore – so Kramskoy ended up in the same place where he started, regretting only that he had behaved foolishly, not noticing in his potential bride a tinge of unusualness seldom encountered.

Right after this incident, without even time to catch his breath, Nikolai was inflamed with desire for a saleswoman at a men's clothing store, who had amazed him with the perverse curve of her lips and the sharp collarbone of a schoolgirl. There was nothing else schoolgirlish about her – she was a year and a half his senior – but something got deep into his soul. He suffered and tormented himself for real, conquering this woman like it was the most important thing in the world. Once he experienced her and spent a few days in passion, he concluded this was genuine closeness, which he had never known with anyone, and that the fair-haired Ludochka was the most delightful, inspiring being. Soon it became clear, however, that her compliance was too pragmatic; and then he learned Ludochka had an ex-husband she continued seeing, for she could not resist his charms. The protests of Kramskoy, who was dumbfounded by this last revelation, were incomprehensible to her. They quarreled rather unpleasantly and his feelings dried up in an instant – so that every recalling of them caused nothing but shame.

For a change, Nikolai escaped for two weeks to Prague, which was full of available, enterprising Czech girls. He returned from there considerably refreshed and resolved that romanticism was henceforth permissible only in measured doses. He became stingy with flowery words – many of his girlfriends found this amusing, as usual confusing the consequence with the cause. And, when some of them got upset, Nikolai explained everything quite sincerely, not wishing to play games with no purpose, and justifying himself with the labors and thoughts that consumed the ardor of his heart. "Behind them stands eternity," he humbly admitted. "Therefore, they are worthy of great effort!" And he just joked in response to every accusation, thus all understood that nothing could be done to change him, and they entertained no illusions, considerably simplifying his life.

At about thirty-five, Kramskoy began to consider the shallow nature of his romances to be normal, and he learned to regulate their duration and frequency. And then an event occurred that suggested something more: a different perspective and a new trajectory. He met Sweet Yana, a twenty-year-old gymnast, affectionate and limber, shameless and always cheerful. She changed lovers often and gave each of them only a small part of herself, but from that part, she created the coziest little world, a most comfortable space you never wanted to leave. Her men adored her and put her on a pedestal, fawning, head over heels. And she would just purr and stretch out full length, always knowing precisely what she wanted and why.

With her, Nikolai acutely sensed the difference in years and the gulf between worldviews. This was welcome; it harbored novelty and delicious pain. He understood that youth was an astringent poison of unbearable strength and you could do nothing with your own tenderness, which you just wanted to spend nonstop. There was no future in it, nor was there any double game – making it all the more intense to feel the present. And this permitted everything, including the aforementioned romanticism, which was now harmless, for it could deceive no one.

They didn't see each other for long, but the experience taught him a lot. He felt he shouldn't open himself up to her quickly, breaking barriers and letting down his defenses. Knowledge should be accumulated piece by piece – and he dispensed it a piece at a time, hiding what was most important, laughing it off and slipping away, carefully selecting ambiguous words. Sweet Yana accepted the game with relish; the phantom of secrecy, like a mystic glow, excited her imagination and her sensual ardor, uncovering common ground with her own feminine mystery, which had no end. Thus, Nikolai discovered a lucky formula for himself: he now found his flings among young girls who preferred older men to their brawny contemporaries with the manners of the street. Many of them had had sharp shark teeth, but they possessed open minds and had not even begun to tire of life or fear things that were not scary. The age difference seemed huge to them, big enough to contain anything, and he threw out hints so they made up their own fables, becoming more excited by him and arousing him all the more with themselves.

Kramskoy, moreover, attracted them with his appearance: they saw in him a hero, in the dark Mephistophelean sense. He was tall and lean; his dark hair hadn't perceptibly thinned, but silver strands could already be detected – and this also incited noticeable interest. His grey eyes, too, and his gaze itself also served as good bait – his thin lips and a barely perceptible scar made it demanding and daring, which sometimes, especially in the twilight, worked rather flawlessly.

These affairs, as a rule, lasted briefly, but this was taken for granted. Besides, Nikolai found to his surprise that there were more young beauties wishing to have a passionate interlude with him than he could have imagined. They weren't looking for a life together, a faithful bulwark, or a strong manly shoulder. They wanted to enjoy themselves, without thinking about marriage or the complexities of existence. This suited Kramskoy fine. He even started looking younger and livelier in spirit. The burdensome thoughts of aging and loss of sex appeal ceased to occur to him at all. He briskly scanned the Moscow masses and considered his private life to be in tip-top form.

The one he was now rushing toward, fidgeting on the backseat of the battered car, was altogether a different case, though she, too, was barely twenty-three. They had already known each other for several years and the time had long passed when their passionate interlude should have evaporated. Nevertheless, cheerful voices resounded in his heart and his fingers drummed on the dusty plastic of the armrest.

He had met Zhanna – who carried the humorous last name of Chizhik – three summers ago, not far from the Kremlin. The night before, he had had a strange dream: it featured a young woman wandering the city, walking a tiger on a leash. The vision stuck in his mind in the morning, and Kramskoy took it seriously: he canceled business and went meandering about the streets, on the lookout for a girl with a tiger, which was her only telling feature. In one of the alleys, he startled a black cat, then got trapped in a maze of Zamoskvorechie backyards and had a hard time making his way back to a familiar area. By noon, he had utterly despaired and, having ended up at Red Square, struck up a conversation with the first female stranger he met, a girl who looked utterly provincial and simple.

The dream and the tiger on a leash were already far removed; the black cat had probably forgotten him long since; everything was ordinary and boring. "Would you happen to know where they sell champagne around here?" he asked Zhanna Chizhik as she enthusiastically consumed an Eskimo bar. At this question, she merely rolled her eyes and shook her head. "Well, I do," Kramskoy informed her. "Want to come with me?"

They drank champagne in a hotel bar where people cast glances at Zhanna with a snicker. Then he took her for a ride on the water bus, followed by an inexpensive meal, and later they went to his place and made love without mincing words. She figured she should pay him back, and Nikolai, for his part, was gallant and fascinating to her. Of course, at home she wouldn't have allowed such liberties as he took with her in his Moscow apartment, but in the big city they seemed quite natural, and some of them were strangely pleasant. By the following day, Zhanna had decided she was captivated for good and grew so impassioned that Kramskoy became bewildered and even scared.

A dilemma, well-known to many, thus arose. He wished to avoid complications but he had no desire to lose Zhanna so soon: she attracted him, striking a deep chord. Nikolai's heart remained calm, but his mind opposed separation, especially since Zhanna Chizhik had no intention of returning to her tiny burg on the Volga. She had decided to begin a new life in Moscow, with Nikolai or without him.

He was perfectly aware of the chasms and precipices waiting behind his door, ready to swallow her up along with thousands like her, to crush, maim, remake her into third-rate detritus and spit her into the rough, vulgar crowd. She had courage, sincerity, freshness. These virtues were uncommon there, and he wanted to possess them in her or at least have access to them, but not to the detriment of his freedom and habits. Therefore, frowning at his own trickery, he began to wriggle and squirm; then, once he devised a successful plan, he used all the persuasive powers he could conjure. And Zhanna showed sobriety of mind, probably realizing all her dreams at once were too much to achieve. Consequently, they found a compromise acceptable to both, though she cried a little as she felt sorry for herself and her romantic sentiments. But the tears rapidly dried, thanks to an abundance of amusements and her easy-going nature.

Nikolai rented Zhanna an apartment and got her enrolled in a second-rate university. He also paid her a secretary's salary, fearlessly involving her in his business, which she took to in earnest. The money was small, but Zhanna did not demand much. Her requirements were quite modest – at least until the arrival of some future which Nikolai sometimes talked about. Its details were not disclosed and never discussed at length. Zhanna didn't even try to speculate about them, feeling she still harbored unspent fervor that would one day erupt on the surface. For the time being, she liked her life and wanted no other.

For Nikolai, everything turned out to be more complicated, though not by much. They became friends, called each other every day, and sometimes slept together without attaching great significance to it. Kramskoy didn't know whether she was involved with other men; he assumed she was but didn't think much about it. He was tormented by other things: for example, by the true meaning of the entire affair that he couldn't properly formulate. Having expended so much energy in capturing Zhanna Chizhik, he could not be satisfied now with something small – a "mistress" or "kept woman" would offend his inner hearing with its excessively primitive sound. The proper word would just not come to mind, and this frustrated him like something left unsaid. And later, after a year or so, another matter arose that left a thorn in his side: he continually caught himself thinking that having Zhanna in his possession meant he was given too much, and for that he could be severely taken to task in the future. Kramskoy could not shake the apprehension that someday she would vanish from his world and find another where there was no place for him.

This fear was invigorated by another vivid dream, or more precisely, a series of nocturnal visions linked by a common thread one stifling night when the sheets stuck to his body and the open window admitted sounds but no freshness. The dream was long; it featured Zhanna, a seaside city, and a bright amethyst stone: she left him for good and took the stone with her. He woke after having slept until nearly midday, his face moist from tears. For a long while, he could not comprehend why the image came upon him with such force. The amethyst had looked real and the rest remained a riddle he didn't wish to reflect upon yet. He sensed only that Zhanna Chizhik had some power over him, which was an alarming revelation and could destroy the stability of their union.

Nikolai then lost his calm, overwhelmed by a new rash of emotions; and he quickly convinced himself he didn't want – and was probably unable – to fall in love with Zhanna or anybody else. But the aftertaste remained and he understood he might suffer a terrible loss without experiencing love first. The ill-fated dream was indelibly etched in his memory, and he began at times to feel fear facing the impending casualty. Then he learned to stuff it deep inside where it was almost silent, and the sensation of stability was restored – though he began to watch over it with great care. He even treated his businesses differently since Zhanna occupied her modest niche in them: now he couldn't afford to fail and look like a loser, even in the short term. And he was afraid to leave her idle, giving her space to be filled with something else.

He accustomed her to good music and fine arts; he also brought her books but never forced her to read. Gradually, she developed taste. Sometimes her questions stumped him, which could not help but please him and bring satisfaction. He began to fantasize that Zhanna Chizhik was a secret weapon waiting for the right time, that when she was finally "ready" he would realize how to use her talents and abilities. However, the details of the upcoming battles where they fought side by side had not occurred to him yet, which angered him considerably. Then Nikolai reminded himself about the will of the higher power that had obviously planned something for him again. Thus, it was wiser to concentrate on the present, which was giving him tangible pleasures, than to try to peer into the future. In any case, he noticed with a proprietor's satisfaction that the former provincial was still transparently honest and not overly sure of herself – and so she was not yet able to deal with the realities of Moscow life on her own.

Zhanna was not shy, but sometimes she showed bashfulness about the most unexpected things. Above all, she despised the railway – all her childhood had been spent at a remote freight yard in the family of a switch operator and a machinist. Shortly before she started school, her parents divorced and her father married a train inspector who worked in the same depot. This elevated their social status, but relations with her step-mother never quite jelled, and Zhanna was sent to a military boarding school she loved with all her heart. Even now, she kept the skirt from her uniform and the cadet epaulets, symbolizing virtue and honor, no less. Removing the epaulets, or even one of them, for some unbecoming act was the most shameful of sanctions for a cadet, and it embodied the worst possible disgrace. This was imprinted upon Zhanna Chizhik's consciousness forever.

She generally liked herself, though she noticed that much in her was far from ideal. It seemed to her, for instance, that she too often resorted to cunning, though her wiles were utterly naïve. As a child, her mother would hide the chocolate candies from her since she had a consummate sweet tooth, but she would find them and eat the exact number that would not arouse suspicion. Later, when she had grown up a little, her older brother forbade her from using his video game deck, which attracted her like a magnet. She wasn't so innocent anymore and became more inventive and crafty, tracking it down like a true detective and learning to cover her tracks. Since then, having seen in herself the propensity for such things, Zhanna had considered herself a bit rotten, though in fact she was ingenuous and open – due to either her cadet training or simply to her personal integrity, which she would not yet trade for anything.

Her appearance, though, seemed to indicate differently. She was a natural redhead, with gray eyes and a few freckles. It was easier to envision her wandering rooftops or flying on an obedient broom through the night than to imagine her diligently poring over the fundamentals of psychology and PR in her university studies. Her smile at times recalled a fox's grin; she knew this, and in her next life she wanted to become a sky fox. She would have been able to deceive nonstop – with the naturalness of a whisper or a sigh – to confound and bewilder, to prevaricate and get what she wanted. But deceit was alien to her and, despite her cunning profile, such a bright feeling emanated from her that soon everyone knew she could do no harm. Probably a single meeting was enough to make her hard to forget – Nikolai even supposed there were whole throngs wandering Moscow who had caught a fleeting glance of her and had been enthralled ever since.

After settling up with the driver and running effortlessly to the third floor, he paused for a moment before the call button, as if indecisive or collecting his thoughts. This was silly, and Kramskoy cursed at himself in a quick whisper. Then he responded with a rather cool grin to the hot kiss and was deliberately all business as his redheaded agent, her eyes sparkling, gestured with her hands when she informed him of all that had happened lately.

As usual, she had plenty to relate though it was only half a week since they had seen each other. Nikolai always noted with envy how many events fit into her days and how she found some new meaning in every one of them. He took it easy around her, losing track of hours and minutes – Zhanna's time flowed without hurry, despite the brisk pulse of the city outside the window. Here in her apartment, she lived according to her own rhythm, which took more of a hold on Nikolai than he would have liked to admit.

The main subject of today's story was a call from a distant relative – from the same town where she had spent her childhood and youth. Generally, she spoke seldom of where she was from, fed up with the wretched squalor that began right after the Moscow beltway. She remembered only drunken faces, poverty, and ennui, which she wanted to flee without looking back. On top of that, this relative was a regular boozer and lived in destitution punctuated by occasional small earnings. And yet, having spent the money on the long-distance call, he requested books, not cash. This was beyond strange, and she took it as an absurd whim, looking at Nikolai a bit plaintively, as though asking for support. Kramskoy savored the notion that Zhanna still belonged to him and needed him as a counselor and mentor. Then he thought lazily that he would never agree to help anyone with money, but to refuse such a touching request as this was, frankly, not easy.

"You know, why don't we send him a package?" he suggested, suddenly remembering a certain friend he hadn't seen for many years. That guy also lived along the banks of the Volga now, and in his last letter – God only knew when that was – he had requested the same thing of Nikolai: books, in his typically jocular fashion.

"Oh, and send books, Nikolya," the friend wrote, and there was something else funny in the letter. But he had forgotten, of course, as he was caught up in business. That was a shame, and Kramskoy shook his head, slipping into thought and ceasing to hear Zhanna Chizhik. Regaining his senses, he realized she had stopped talking and was looking at him with conspicuous bedroom eyes. All was familiar and well-known, and the time was passing intimately, just as both of them wished. The arrogant megalopolis remained outside, weighing down on the others, who meant nothing to them. Nikolai only managed to think that any equilibrium is capricious and demands constant supervision. Then he rose, walked over to Zhanna, and she extended her hands without averting her eyes, which became completely shameless, but still hid in the depths of their pupils a barely perceptible flicker of deviousness.

Still, that flicker could appear by happenstance, he mused later as he went out into the warm night. And if it wasn't there, all the better: that may be why he wasn't troubled by manly jealousy. His heart was light; life seemed quite tolerable; he now felt on top of the world – somehow even in spite of the all-powerful universal organism – and he nurtured this power within him, just as that morning he fostered thoughts seemingly imposed from outside.

"Well, this may be what distinguishes the times of the day," he muttered and even walked a few blocks on foot, though the outskirts at this hour were unsafe for pedestrians. Then something rushed across out of the gateway and disappeared behind a Dumpster. Nikolai stumbled and, not wishing to tempt fate further, went to the motorway and hailed a ride.

Once in the car, a squeaky, dirty-white Ford, he recalled his friend from the Volga again. They had once sold Technology T together to the Dutch, but then parted ways. This friend quickly lost some of his money and returned to his native Sivoldaisk, resolving to engage in literary work. Nikolai suddenly thought it might be nice to visit him. This idea went round and round in his head and even took a practical turn, facilitated by the evening he spent with Zhanna Chizhik and her come-hither look. It was unfortunate, of course, that she came from another city, but Sivoldaisk also seemed to have a connection to her. There, Kramskoy imagined, hordes of provincial girls probably roamed the streets. They were like her, and at the same time slightly different. No, not slightly – definitely, definitely different. Distinct, enigmatic, unknown – but with the same direct, shameless look.

CHAPTER 7

Strange things had been happening to Elizaveta Bestuzheva all week. Somebody yelled at her in a crowd, coming up really close and calling out her name, but when she glanced over her shoulder – startled, annoyed – she saw the voice could not belong to anyone nearby, and it was impossible to pinpoint the stranger. This made her feel even more detached from the city, and her modest travel agency came to seem like a saving grace, a shelter from the anonymous assaults. Yet even there it was impossible to find peace: in the morning, the computer generated batches of e-mails from odd addresses, different ones every day. The messages mostly contained photos – dazzling, sumptuous flowers that all but gave off a scent. Margo spitefully called them "the genitals of plants," probably because she was slightly jealous of her associate. As for Elizaveta, she soon got used to the flowers and even became fond of them. Still, she admitted that, beautiful as they might be, they were completely incomprehensible. And then, to top it all off, her answering machine began to act up from time to time: somebody was calling her at home, during the day, at weird times when she couldn't possibly pick up the phone. There were no words on the recording, just coughing and sighing, quite indecent. She noticed, however, they held a trace of sadness and mild longing rather than vulgar carnality.

But more than anything else, it was the stalking that bothered

Elizaveta. At times, it seemed the eye from the store window on Solyanka was hovering around her in the summer haze, soaring over the rooftops and tacking between the buildings – here tearing up from the exhaust, there squinting in the bright sunshine. And this, by the way, was a harmless fantasy in comparison with what was actually going on: she was now being shadowed quite openly, had long since identified her observer, and had begun to recognize his face. Her skin had become too sensitive; she would shudder, suddenly feeling the stranger's pupils fixed on her – as if from tickling or light breathing. He followed her everywhere, like on an invisible leash, insistent and indefatigable, a predator pursuing its prey. Elizaveta even felt puzzled: she was defenseless and couldn't rebuff him, so why didn't he dig in with his teeth and nails? Sometimes it was impossible for her to resist; she would whirl around and walk toward him, pushing people out of the way, intending to put some harsh questions to him, getting excited at the very thought of how uncomfortable he would be. Yet each time he easily slipped away, dissolving into the crowd, proving as elusive as a predator should be; and, moreover, Elizaveta possessed no knack for making scenes, assiduously avoiding them her whole life.

In his own way, her tail got used to her too, learning her schedule and routes in detail and considering the two of them old friends after a few days. As he plodded along the Moscow streets in her footsteps, he relished their temporary, clandestine union in pleasant melancholy. In his mind, he was an errant knight who did not dare draw too near, the preserver of her peace who was always ready to come to her aid, even if that wasn't included in his list of duties. He took to Elizaveta more and more but he didn't forget the job was his top priority, knowing no sympathy could interfere with his fulfillment of the instructions down to the letter. Fortunately, they were innocuous enough and let him undertake the assignment without any unnecessary distress.

His associates knew him simply as Dimon. That's how everyone addressed him, not even contemplating whether it was a pseudonym or the name he had been given before becoming an ethereal shadow.

He had grown up in the Moscow working-class district of Lianozovo, in the stinking, steaming air of derelict five-story buildings, in the humidity and dirt of courtyards – or rather rat traps – which were engulfed time and again by clouds of smoke from the enormous pipes of the neighboring factories. This was a strange world with its own color spectrum: poisonous greenery and puddles producing reddish-yellow lichen and rosy moss oozing into the cracks of the Khrushchev projects. It seemed only naughty birds and packs of nomadic dogs, as dangerous as hyenas, could make a life in this place. But human life thrived there all the same, with its fetishes and passions, knife fights and love stories, cruel morality and drunken habits – and it was in this world Dimon felt at home, only embarrassed by his Ryazan roots, which always served as targets for jokes. His sister, a few aunts, and grandfathers still lived in the town, and he loved to travel there on holidays, dragging bulky bags filled with food.

In Moscow, however, he was ashamed of his round face and gently apparent provincialisms, which could not be avoided no matter what he did. When he wasn't working, he tried to uphold some style, nurtured his liking of flashy shirts and dried his hair with a blow dryer before combing it back with a dash of hairspray. Yet something evaded him despite these efforts and he felt he was playing out a weird game and striving for the impossible. It was only when he went out on another assignment that he calmed down, disguised and blending in if that was required, or lurking constantly in the background, as he did with Elizaveta, exhibiting the most average of all physiognomies, wherein lay the promise of success.

It's difficult to believe, but back then, in the company of Lianozovo thugs, he was quite conspicuous, having an intransigent personality and getting into lots of arguments for any reason and for no reason at all, defending his habits and convictions down to the very last. Nothing could change him, neither the laws of the street nor his first girlfriends, dominating and prevailing over him in every sphere of life. He had a strong core that remained intact from his very boyhood, an integrity he had inherited from his parents, calm

Russian folks who always respected their neighbors and were ready to share anything with them, even when it was a disadvantage to themselves. Perhaps that's why he appeared always on the outskirts of prosperity, inhabiting uncomfortable places and unable to push through or – worse still – to lie to anyone's face. For some time, he had tried to fit in, hanging out with former friends, giving his all to become their equal, flexing his muscles and thrusting out his chest. But all he received in return was the leftovers, frequently with scarcely concealed ridicule.

Once, in despair after his latest failure, he got drunk in a third-rate dive and woke up in a stranger's car the next morning without his phone and jacket, remembering almost nothing. He got out, slammed the door, and strode blindly through unfamiliar courtyards, giving no thought to where he was or where he was going. The sun had just risen, and the city was quiet and thoughtful; it looked mystically new, as if all links to the past had broken and the secret of life had opened a crack. But this lasted only an instant; a quarter of an hour later he saw the sign for the old familiar bar and the sleepy bodyguard at the door. After chewing him out for his forgetfulness, they handed Dimon his rumpled jacket, his phone still in the inside pocket. Everything was the same as yesterday, except his hangover and throbbing head. At that moment he realized how pointless it was to fight for elusive luck if your legs carry you in circles and your soul gives birth to nothing that has not been tried before. He acknowledged this and chose humility, which was not far from the very obscurity that helped him to find a reliable niche, turning habit into professional experience.

On Thursday, after he had followed Elizaveta to her office on Maly Cherkassky, already aware he was doing this for the last time, Dimon wandered down Teatralny Proyezd at a leisurely pace toward the Metropol Hotel and thought about how every occupation involves too many compromises. His assignment had been carried out almost to the end. This day would come to a close; gloomy Monday would arrive soon, with the burden of the aftermath following the short weekend; and he would force himself to forget about this woman forever, no longer remembering any of her addresses, not even the fact of her existence. That was the unwritten rule: no contact afterward, even if surveillance was completely secretive and the risk of being discovered was close to zero. That's how it had been with the other contracts; to some of them he had become even more attached, and he had long since gotten used to the bitterness of that parting, as one does to anything inevitable.

Upon reaching the Bolshoi, the PI went through the passageway under the street to the famous square, a symbol of homosexual love. There, he sat on a bench by the fountain and made two short calls. The first was to a well-known older actor to confirm their earlier agreement; the second to a madam, a friend of sorts, who always had a whole army of expensive girls on hand. She remembered him, which was nice, and he dragged out the conversation with relish, tossing his head back and marveling at the cloudless blue for a second before adopting a strict tone and instructing her to send him a brunette with big tits, talkative, cheerful, and not fat.

"You going to take a break?" asked the madam respectfully.

"Yes, I want to rest a bit," the PI confirmed and hung up. "Rest," he repeated once more, feeling very tired indeed for no apparent reason.

At that same time Elizaveta Bestuzheva was sitting at her desk, absentmindedly glancing over the flyers that came with the day's mail, ashamed to admit she was expecting more from the post. She had spent the last few days in vague anticipation that something crucial was about to happen in her life. She didn't feel any threat but languished in uncertainty, slept poorly, and woke up irritated and testy over nothing. Meanwhile, her thoughts lingered far afield, returning with difficulty to her everyday routine.

More than anything else, Elizaveta mulled over loneliness these days. Something made her want to feel sorry for herself, driving her almost to the brink of tears. There was no tragedy in her fate, though; things in general happened in a sensible manner – not counting, of course, the oddities of the last week. Loneliness as a way of life did not weigh on her; on the contrary, she found it comforting at the moment. When she snuggled into her cozy sofa with a book, or laid out her belongings and spread her aura over her small apartment, it became clear there was no space for anyone else.

Her first marriage had taught Elizaveta not to believe in the clichés of happiness, and it might have lasted longer if she and her husband had slept in different bedrooms and knocked before entering. Certainly, the great passion that was supposed to overcome her at some time would be capable of changing everything. But in its absence she didn't understand why one should tolerate inconveniences and exchange established comfort for the supposed joy of living together, which her men had cautiously alluded to sometimes. Now that the flow of life had suddenly been interrupted, however, she was consumed by doubts. She wanted somebody's presence near her at night – and during the day, evening, and at all times in general – and her inner world shriveled up into a hard lump, buried and not showing any signs of life. The empty apartment became uncomfortable; the creaks and rustlings were frighteningly unusual; and even the furniture, which was very sparse, started to evince its character and reveal its sharp corners.

Her present lover she had forgotten completely. He was baffled and called daily, feeling hurt and mumbling something or other, but Elizaveta was always extremely cold to men in whom she had lost interest. They stopped existing for her, as if they had been put behind a transparent wall that repelled each and every word. She didn't waste her energy on explanations of any kind and refused to reply to protests – not because she was heartless, but because conversations like these were intolerable torture. This subdued the men entirely; they became pitiful and even whiny at times, excelling at importunate entreaties, which naturally led nowhere. Elizaveta couldn't help them, and her only real hope was that they would find comfort in someone else.

Now she was the one who needed some comfort, though it was pretty obvious no man could provide it. After thinking a bit, she went to see her Aunt Helga, who for some reason had changed her name to make it harmonize in German, something that many people considered an act of unacceptable eccentricity, even saying that Olga-Helga had gone slightly batty. She lived in Yasenevo, right at the edge of Moscow, and it was only infrequently that guests came to pay her a visit. Elizaveta, however, was a completely welcome guest, a favorite from childhood, so Helga was glad to see her, kissed her on the cheek, and they drank tea with wild honey. The tea made a flush rise to Aunt's cheeks and even lent her face a certain warmth, though, sadly, Elizaveta noticed the signs of age in Olenka, as she called her, the traces of not having a man around – even if her smile, which reflected her soul, was becoming ever younger.

The entire situation elicited her aunt's greatest interest. She cross-examined Elizaveta, pumping her for information on this and that, especially the flowers and melancholic sighing. Then she got her cards and laid them out on the table, but they were silent, not revealing anything and unable to provide any help.

"An evil spirit is circling around," said Helga, chewing on her lips. "An evil incubus. Asmodeus is his name, or even Defiort, but yours is certainly Asmodeus: he whispers in your ear but doesn't show his face. I'll say a magic spell..." And she hugged Elizaveta, jabbered something over her shoulder, and then gave her a little dark liquid in a small vial.

"Keep this *voshchanka* in the headboard, and don't be afraid. This is thistle; it won't do you any harm. Otherwise, I don't know what to do," she added upon parting. "When winter comes – winter and the first snow – wash your face with snow water from a silver dish. The dish I have – it's real, very old. Nothing else will help; be strong, Lizochka. God be with you. Hopefully, it'll pass."

"If he's really an incubus, then by winter he'll have seduced me a hundred times," Elizaveta laughed and said good-bye to Olenka warmly, feeling as if her worries had been assuaged a bit. She even waved to the stalker who followed determinedly in her wake, thinking with a hint of mischief, "Maybe he's the one – Asmodeus the devil?" But later she became uneasy again and had bad dreams that night, despite the *voshchanka*, murky in the vial, which she had obediently placed at the edge of the bed.

Besides her aunt, Elizaveta decided to confide in her only friend who had any pretense of being really close. This friend, in contrast to Helga, was not prone to mysticism and interpreted reality on the basis of objective facts like the philosophers of the dullest schools. They drank sweet maté in a coffee shop on the Garden Ring to the accompaniment of a summer downpour, catching men's gazes with sidelong glances. The cafe, which had opened not long ago, had still not had time to come into its own, revealing the eclecticism of its design, as if tuned to trivial harmony against its will. Everything here looked like a game – the Japanese paintings, the hookahs on pedestals, the streamer of a Spanish soccer club above the pillar at the bar – Elizaveta would not even have been surprised if she had seen a jester's hat on her tireless voyeur. But he was not in the mood for jokes and streaked by the glass with his usual inconspicuous aspect, darting somewhere to the side, escaping the big drops, so a second later there remained in the window only the dirty, gray silhouettes of the high-rise buildings on New Arbat, which resembled open books with faded pages and covers, permanently defaced by the glitter of expensive casinos.

Her friend had a proletarian name, Zoya, which harmonized well with her last name, Klimova, bringing to mind everything from having a dad in the military to the Young Communist League and the Russian hinterlands. And that's how it had all been, more or less. Their family had arrived in Moscow from completely unremarkable Tambov, thanks to an enormous effort her father made just before retirement. Young Communist romanticism just barely touched Zoya, not helping her to recover from preteen shyness and complexes. But once she got married, she became comfortable with herself and learned to deal with the opposite sex. Now Zoya Klimova was aware of her worth, and it wasn't easy to throw her for a loop, although traces of insecurity were left concealed within, reminding her of their existence by erupting in baseless exaltation or, even worse, by leaving her bewildered and at a loss for words. That often happened, to her embarrassment, when she was interrupted at the wrong time, so she tried to talk a lot and, if possible, without pausing.

Having listened to her friend, Zoya became sad and furrowed her brow. "Forget it," she said. "Someone's just fooling around with you. No good will come of it; you'd be better off going to the police. Perhaps you'll get lucky, seduce the boss, and everything will be just hunky-dory."

Soon, it became clear Elizaveta wouldn't be able to get a word in edgewise – in addition to the disparity in their opinions, Zoya was also having problems with her husband and couldn't think about anything else. "He doesn't like my cat," she said, slumping and drooping her shoulders. "He gets angry, screams, threatens to chase him out of the apartment – I have no idea what to do. The cat is so domesticated – he has a diet, haircut, filed claws… On the street they'd be speechless when they saw him; he can't go there, he won't survive. He's gotten used to sleeping in bed with me, and has become effeminate and slothful. Men don't understand these things. They think everything should bend to their will. And the cat, of course, despises my husband in return."

Elizaveta listened for an hour, then another, and when it had all nearly bored her senseless, Zoya Klimova grabbed her hand and burst out in hysterical sobbing in front of everyone, making it necessary to calm her until evening, no longer ordering maté, but tequila and gin. They spent several more hours together, and still Zoya was not satisfied and said something nasty when they parted.

That was yesterday. Now Elizaveta had a headache and was thinking gloomily about how friends in general are useless. Carefree Margo looked at her cautiously but decided not to pry, knowing very well that her companion's temper had temporarily worsened. The clock had just chimed noon, lunchtime was approaching, and it was at that moment the event finally happened, the one that would mark the end of uncertainty and expectation. Elizaveta Bestuzheva received The Letter.

At first there were steps: somebody was walking from the elevator to their open door. That alone was not surprising – there were a number of offices farther down the corridor – yet both women sat stock-still and pricked up their ears. There was something in those steps revealing a rigidity of intention; Fate herself could have that kind of footfall if she were ever to stroll down that floor. The next moment, a visitor appeared in the doorway and Margo let out an involuntary, "Ah hah!"

It was not that the man entering had come clad in a dark raincoat thoroughly out of place in the July heat or that he was wearing a wig with ringlets, black like coal, which framed his thin face. It was that before them, between the doors, stood a well-known actor, beloved at one time by the whole nation. And to meet him here, in a small travel agency, seemed so unbelievable that Masha Rozhdestvenskaya wanted to pinch herself in a soft spot or poke her arm with a pin. Elizaveta was also stricken dumb at first but remained calmer than her coworker, already knowing the stranger had come for her and could not have done otherwise – only somehow he had waited too long.

In the meantime, the man in the raincoat scanned the office with no apparent haste, politely bowing like a gentleman to each of the girls and addressing Elizaveta directly. "I have been given the honor of bringing a message to Miss Bestuzheva," he said quietly, though filling the room with his words. "That is you, no doubt. Having beheld you with my own eyes, I know I cannot possibly be mistaken. So please accept this letter and be so kind as to excuse my sudden intrusion in the middle of your workday."

He pulled a snow-white envelope out of his raincoat and extended it to Elizaveta. She stood up, gracefully approached him, and took the letter, smiling and briefly lowering her eyelashes in thanks. For a second or two, they looked at each other. Elizaveta's head was spinning; his movements, his words, and his husky, entrancing voice were all filled with such latent authority that she couldn't counter her infatuation. In the room, another reality had come into being, created by him in the flash of an eye without any visible effort, and she couldn't let herself hit a wrong note now by saying an incorrect word or making an improper gesture.

"You are very kind," she said after a pause, trying to keep her voice from shaking. "But who is he, this secret admirer? You must admit..." and here she got confused.

The stranger smiled vaguely, bowed, and kissed her hand. He knew all the power of his charm and the power of talent in general, and was able to appreciate a proper response. He liked Elizaveta, mused in passing that she was sensible enough and capable of something real, but quickly squelched these thoughts; this was not his business. And, apart from that, there were countless others – gorgeous, intelligent girls with inbred distinction – though recognizing them was really becoming harder and harder now.

"I wouldn't be anxious if I were you," he said with a slightly crafty grin. "There's good reason to believe that the writer's intentions are perfectly innocent. I am honored."

He bowed again to both of them and left without turning around. Elizaveta stood and followed him intently with her eyes. Soon, they heard the sound of the elevator, the clang of doors, and everything became quiet. Only then did she gaze upon the letter and shrug indecisively.

"Of all things," said Margo loudly. "My goodness, that's incredible! Well, why are you standing there frozen like a pillar of salt? Read it!"

"Wait a minute." Elizaveta brushed her off, turning the envelope over in her hands and pacing up and down the room. "Give me some scissors, okay?"

A palpable silence hung in the office air – and the secret letter deserved this tribute. From the outset, the author named himself, and color rose rapidly to Elizaveta's cheeks although she had hardly thought about Timofey over the last few years. But now, when her senses had become ultraresponsive and her soul craved answers, anything definite seemed desirable, like a sign promising the revelation of all other secrets. Her heart throbbed, akin to a frightened rabbit, although she was not the timid sort, not known for being shy. The tension in the air condensed as though a thunderstorm were approaching. Electricity tickled her eyelids, and unsolicited moisture clouded her vision.

Right from the start, Timofey admitted his guilt, mercilessly castigating himself before eliciting some hope for the future and just one more chance. He eschewed poetic phrases, stridently avoiding trite metaphors, yet somewhere within the austere simplicity and restraint there erupted serious passion, clearly living inside him all these years since they had broken up. Then and there, not sparing any ink, he illustrated his progress and success, which had brought him – what was there to hide? – enviable prosperity. But his heart... – and he broke off. But his soul... – and again he stumbled, as if uncertain how to proceed. Then, having finally decided, he scrawled out all those precious words and fell silent, devastated, even slightly astonished at his own eloquence and ardor, yet firmly insisting on what was his and from which – doubts be gone! – there was no turning back now.

The letter made an impression, perhaps because it had been written by a professional who possessed considerable talent and was paid generously. Timofey Tsarkov believed that path would be better in terms of the final result. And the result really was perfect – he almost cried himself before sealing the envelope – and Elizaveta now sat in a strange daze, held entirely captive by the magic words. Then she reread the letter one more time, carefully studied the attached train ticket, put it all in her bag, and sighed deeply.

She wasn't surprised – for what was so surprising if she were honest with herself? Nothing worth mentioning had happened since those days of her youth – nothing that in any way resembled the cherished past hovering in the murky distance. And a quiet thought had been creeping into her head: perhaps they, in teenage ignorance, had missed the most important thing back then. At least he was brave enough to admit it first, assuming he wasn't lying. But why should he lie? Nobody had put a pen in his hand, and he had nothing to gain from her – nothing except herself, that is.

She said his name out loud in her mind and listened cautiously. No unpleasantness ensued; quite the opposite: she wanted to smile, and all her past malice was gone. The thought of finding herself at his side did not seem that foolish any longer – no, actually, it even stirred something inside her. And although it was not clear how the town of Sivoldaisk fit in, and what Timofey could possibly have been doing in such a dump, Elizaveta didn't let these matters distract her from the main point, the only one of significance. She hid her face in her hands, feeling the corners of her lips stretch into a smile while the flush on her cheeks became still more evident.

"Well, my friend?" Margo was unable to bear it any longer as she fidgeted at her desk. "Come on, tell me what's going on. Why all this torment?"

"There's nothing to say. Someone has invited me to visit him," replied Elizaveta tranquilly. "He's an old friend; you don't know him. I guess I'm taking a vacation, starting tomorrow."

And she didn't say another word, utterly disappointing her coworker.

CHAPTER 8

Nikolai Kramskoy's office was located at the corner of Kamergersky and Tverskaya, in a two-room apartment in a five-story building. He got the flat to rent from a client who had long ago gotten rich and become tired of opulence, so he decided to concern himself with the search for eternal truth. Recently, he travelled to China, and there he finally fell under the sway of something "eternal" – in his last letter, the former client wrote that he did not intend to return for several years. This was great luck: Nikolai paid very little for such an enviable spot, especially now that Moscow was bloated with free-flowing cash.

The office windows looked right out onto the box office of the Moscow Art Theater. From the decorative balcony, one could flick a cigarette butt right on the monument to Chekhov as the provincial doctor and moralist glowered tiredly at people devouring cheap pizza, crowding around the tables right at the base of the statue. Further, beyond the ticket windows, rose masterpieces of sculpted architecture, tastelessly emblazoned with the red and yellow logos of the local proprietors of mobile networks. Eclecticism here had reached the peak of absurdity, a disturbing hint of universal anarchy, but the edifice stood firm and the iron door at the entryway, a defense against anxiety, did not admit outsiders. After restorations and major repairs, there were plans to put the building into the hands of the ubiquitous mayor's officials, but they were left with nothing. Among the apartment owners were some rather serious men, and the furious attack by the powers-that-be was met with resistance no less fierce. Rumor had it someone had really suffered a debacle over this, and then everybody admitted the reallotment of property here had already taken place – at least until the next powerful, muddy wave.

Kramskoy's clientele was never simple – probably because all his businesses tended toward the exotic, not quite familiar to the masses. The present endeavor, related to genealogy and heraldry, attracted, as a rule, people of substance who wished to confirm in a demonstrative manner the nuances of origin that were at times unclear. "Getting to their roots" or "reaching the sources," as Nikolai would call it when they met, or else just "obtaining proof," as he later came to denote it when the discussion turned to concrete business. These affairs were fairly sensitive, but he wouldn't undertake simpler projects: routine lineage searches were the domain of competitors working under the patronage of the government. People came to him who were disappointed with the findings – the ones who had paid considerable money and, after waiting for a year or two, received not what they wanted: whether it was not all they sought, or not what, or not as much.

There could be a multitude of reasons for that – gaps in the archives, lack of diligence, or occasionally the obstinacy of historical facts that didn't draw the projected picture. In any of these cases, Nikolai offered help, promising to do everything quickly, conclusively, and for a reasonable fee. He was aware, of course, that many of the proofs demanded simply did not exist; and he never concealed from the client that he was going to re-invent history rather than ruin his eyes by uselessly scrutinizing the smudged tracks of the past. But here he added that any truth was full of falsifications anyway, and made-up stories, as everyone knows, are no worse than genuine ones.

"And sometimes they're even better," the client would agree with relief, convinced Kramskoy knew how to peer into the very nature of the issue, which could almost never be reduced to a heap of open lies. More likely, it required some scrupulous cleaning, polishing, and smoothing out of curves – or sometimes just adding a few touches to transform the mosaic into a single whole. It was hard to call this a fake in the coarse, vulgar sense: here was a game of shades and half-tints. Each step beyond the invisible boundary was masked by a reference to fully truthful details extracted by diligent archive rats. Even to the discerning eye, it wasn't easy to sort out the certainties and distinguish which of them were beyond the subjective line. Besides, the present state of technology allowed much to be achieved and opened up space for maneuvering, since almost no one asked for the originals.

Perhaps this reflected the *zeitgeist* of modernity, a gravitation toward surrogates, or else it just insinuated that humankind was used to getting by on a little. But, in any case, it substantially simplified life. Copies, as everyone knows, are just that, allowing tampering capable of improving them – because, to tell the truth, there are almost never exact duplicates. Sophisticated software made it possible to do amazing things that far surpassed the requirements of applied genealogy. Nikolai didn't even have to resort to the services of calligraphers; and, in any event, this was a simple part of the work, albeit sometimes time-consuming. The main thing was to construct a strategy of surgical intervention capable of maximum credibility to provide the needed result.

The demands on that result differed considerably from order to order, just as the clients were distinct, one from another. For some, the point of the affair was to satisfy their vanity. Others had a practical interest, at times even admitting the key to their present success lay in the impenetrable darkness of the past. The latter paid more generously, but they were mistrustful and capricious. Nikolai agonized with them as he groped for choices that wouldn't cause doubts. He had occasion to assist a manufacturer who was pushing out his competitor, and a hereditary magician slandered by a group of old believers. Petty politicians who wanted to get ahead would come to him as well, but the most fastidious was a stockbroker who had taken up with an impudent Scotswoman, a continuator of an ancient clan long since due to be married.

This story was worthy of placement in the annals as a practical case of the triumph of imagination. Estimating the pros and cons with professional precision, the stockbroker fed Mary a line about a concealed family secret. The secret placed him among the ranks of the descendants of Russian nobility, but he faced the bullish obstinacy of her father and brothers who did not buy a word of it and demanded certifiable evidence. Their reaction was understandable: his house in Rublyovka, luxurious by Moscow standards, could not compete with their patrimonial Edinburgh castle, and the stockbroker had nothing else to present besides his Russian passport and a bank vault full of cash. Unaccustomed to backing down, he hired the best forces, but the result was extremely modest: it lacked the patina of centuries and the marks of noble degeneracy. Time passed, nothing happened, and the Scottish family grew nervous and did not return calls. The noticeably distraught stockbroker was all ready to abandon his dream of a noble union. But then he turned to Nikolai, grasping at straws with no hope at all; and Kramskoy thought up the ingenious solution of sketching a family crest in special ink over a seventeenth-century manuscript that had almost completely faded anyway. The sketch bore a remote similarity to the logo of a firm the client owned, and this was presented as the observance of a family tradition. It was enough to compensate for the deficiency of the other data in the eyes of the Scots, who valued tradition above all else. The image of the contemptible *nouveau riche* was overlaid with shades of bearded Russian princes – especially since Mary was really quite mature not to be betrothed. So things went rather smoothly for the stockbroker after that, but how it turned out precisely, Nikolai never found out: they parted in mutual displeasure after a disagreement over the final bill.

His current client was not marked by avarice: he himself offered a deposit worthy, if not of a stockbroker, then at least of a successful merchant. He found Nikolai through the newspaper, made a personal appearance, but then vanished, as he said, "to make inquiries" because Moscow, as everyone knows, is full of swindlers and con artists. The inquires took about a month, and the client was apparently satisfied: he got right down to business without ambiguity or mincing words.

The crux of the problem, as always, was in the identity of a distant ancestor, but here all was simpler at first glance because the client knew this ancestor perfectly well. He was certain he descended from the Russian rebel Pugachev. His last name, Pugin, attested to this since it was only slightly distorted by time or some frightened clergyman. It was also supported by additional facts that, though not very convincing separately, gave a rather accurate image when taken as a whole.

Interest in the past arose for Pugin as a byproduct of reading the novels his young wife foisted on him. He started reluctantly but later grew fond of the books and suddenly noticed his own life, which was full of victories and defeats, had quite a bit in common with the fortunes of characters whose bodies had long ago turned to ash. This was another reason to be proud of himself, which had never occurred before to him or his friends who loved to show off, and Pugin used it to the full, sensing prospects far surpassing the standard pretensions of the New Russians. He consumed book after book, skimming over the boring parts and tirelessly applying epochs and lands to himself as if in search of a suitable reference point on the illusory map of space-time or amid his brethren of earlier ages, near in spirit, if not by blood.

He was particularly fascinated with the crusader knights. Their hard fates and faithfulness to the quest, courage and unrelenting struggle with the confusion of an ungrateful world seemed for Pugin to resonate with the uneasy realities of his own craft. The Crusades recalled Russian gang wars in the years when the first monies were accumulated. The majority of the knights perished before reaching maturity, but those who came back alive became wealthy, reckless lords who recognized no authority but their own – which bore a strong resemblance to what had happened to him and his business colleagues over the last two decades. They served as somewhat of an example for him as the cosmonauts or the first Russian millionaires once were; and Pugin, who always tended to be a man of action rather than thought, began by doing what every crusader must: he seized land on a lake just outside Moscow and set to building the family castle. The construction progressed slowly but surely. The local administration was compliant; and as for the blockheads from the capital who didn't recognize the upstart, he was in lengthy legal proceedings with them but not really worried about it.

The next step was a coat of arms – which every knight is obliged to have in addition to a castle – and thus began Pugin's acquaintance with the science of heraldry, which initially angered him considerably by its inflexibility. He eventually adjusted to it, however, perceiving in the canons a guarantee of authenticity, and agreed to what was offered by the experts. As a result, for example, the victorious eagle in the center of the composition was replaced by a more traditional bear, and the shield in the whole retained nearly nothing of the crusaders, but this did not bother him much. They provided an idea, which in itself was a lot, and Pugin wanted further development to proceed within the confines of his native symbols and concepts.

He was an inveterate Russophile – at least he didn't hesitate to declare it publicly. He wanted to be proud of his Russian roots and expressed this pride explicitly, selecting as a starting point a name that was not last in the history of man. Yemelyan Pugachev – that was an honor, and it was the right choice. Pugin didn't wish to claim what wasn't his: for example, descending from refined aristocrats, which would match neither his appearance nor the surrounding beastliness. Pugachev, that suggested malice and fury, and Pugin loved his own whims of malicious rage, whether they happened under the influence of alcohol or on their own for no reason at all. And, finally, Pugachev was a protest, and Pugin wanted a protest: in his heart, he considered himself a mutineer, even if he didn't yet have a clear, mutinous goal.

He was born in Muscovite Mytishchi, and there his parents spent their lives. But his grandmother, a severe woman who he took after in spirit, spoke time and again of her freewheeling childhood in the boundless steppes beyond the Volga. This alone prompted the right thought, though it couldn't be taken as proof – as they quite transparently hinted at in an archival agency catering to the Moscow elite. Very unpleasant people gathered there; it was difficult to deal with them. They expressed themselves with half-words and wanted money all the time, not even concealing that the desideratum would likely be unobtainable. Pugin wasted a whole year on them, after which the investigation reached a deadlock, leading not to the Volga, but to somewhere in Archangelsk, which was of interest to no one.

He was incensed and prepared to respond harshly, unaccustomed to retreating from what he intended; but then, fortunately, rumors reached him of Kramskoy's small firm. Nikolai warned him at once he didn't fabricate open forgeries – that was the business of dishonest men with no sense of history. However, getting a document from the period into appropriate shape so one wouldn't be ashamed to show it to others – this he would gladly undertake, knowing firsthand how merciless time was to ink and paper. Sometimes, the writing becomes completely undecipherable and many documents are lost forever, so the only ones available are mostly those of a minor grade, subject to ambiguous interpretation. Therein lay the problem, but it also implied the solution: why not take a secondary detail and augment the essence of the fact it masked, especially when the client had no doubts regarding the very contents of this fact. And the contents might then lead them further, and the form might be reconstructed accordingly. So, everyone could get what he wanted – but as a result of reconstruction only, not of roughly hewing a fake from scratch. Here Nikolai was firm and made no exceptions.

They quickly understood one another and got on well. Pugin counted off a handful of bills and departed, quite content that the matter was moving forward from the impasse. Real progress didn't happen soon, however – at first, Kramskoy simply had no ideas, and then he experienced an attack of inexplicable laziness. He took on the Pugin project in earnest only after the notorious phone call, when there was nowhere to retreat.

Now, five days later, he finally felt all was under control. The Pugin-Pugachev business, the old friend requesting books, and, in the long term, the Zhanna Chizhik's shameless look were gradually converging into a single point.

During this time, Nikolai, showing remarkable activity as if to reprove himself for the lost weeks, groped for a solution capable of linking the roving villain and his annoying descendant. He was helped in this by material placed on the Web by an unknown author who had collected a bunch of data about Pugachev and his final days. No self-interest was evident on the part of the author, but he took the work seriously, dug deep, and was fastidious regarding material evidence, which included papers and letters found among the villain's personal effects. There, among the rest, something revealed itself that led to the right clue.

It was a note informing Yemelyan of the death of his bastard son. It had been written by the chief of the Chumovo settlement, which was located not far from the fortress of Sivoldaisk. The note itself, along with the other manuscripts, was stored in the Sivoldaisk city museum. Nikolai's unjustly forgotten friend also resided there, which was, of course, a sign and not just a coincidence. And Kramskoy's heart fluttered: it became clear he hit the right spot and everything was on the point of uniting, of linking up by the edges and slots like a child's puzzle.

The rest was simple; it was only necessary to strain the imagination ever so slightly. Of course, someone's death in his first year could not by itself certify continuation of the family line, but it pointed to something obvious: seduction, an affair, probably even passion that had once arisen in the village of Chumovo between the legendary outlaw and a country girl who lost her head at once, surrendering like an outpost without firing a shot, under only the pressure of those mad, black eyes. In terms of times and dates, it was clear outlaw love visited the settlement as Pugachev traveled up the Volga when he was still at his height and taking one town after another. Before a fair-eyed maiden with firm buttocks and a thick plait stood not a weary animal, but rather a ravenous wolf in a coat of sables and a blue Oirat cap. Such girls crossed his path without number, but for some reason, this one enthralled his heart. So he stopped in Chumovo for about two days, or even three, to grant himself a respite. The walls of her hut shielded him from the fate that ruthlessly propelled him forward, to a false crown and immense power...

Nikolai gazed through the window that looked out on Kamergersky and drummed his fingers on the table as he thought up the details. It was clear this demon of free rage left the pretty girl with a child – in addition to jewelry from burned farmsteads, a brocade shawl, and hot kisses. This was an established fact, and starting from that, one might cautiously move forward step by step. Yemelyan, without doubt, couldn't forget his beloved and made provision for her future – and his offspring as well – by sending gifts and money. This was why the mayor wrote, and the man would know better than to bother Pugachev over nothing. He had probably been ordered to look after and take care of them, which he did as best he could. And here, look: the child has died, but the chief informs him of this fearlessly, with customary bureaucratic courtesy. Why is that? Why did he not cower and repent in sackcloth and ashes, saying that he's guilty, asking for forgiveness?

"Because..." Nikolai gave a whistle of significance, "because the child may not have been the only one. Weren't twins ever born in Rus? Of course they were, lots of them. One died, no great loss, the second was left, and all hope was placed on him. Let's accept that as fact: there were two boys, and only one of the brothers was left alive. Well, that may solve the riddle for us!"

It was a good version, and completely feasible. Hastily, he estimated what could be done with the chief's letter and concluded the task was not difficult at all. Just appending a few words, copying letters and matching style – a day or two of meticulous work. The winning cards were in his hand. Kramskoy felt their weight and thought, biting his pencil, of how to present the information to the client. He had to dispense with all questions at once and convince him the solution was in the bag – or more precisely, in the remote museum at Sivoldaisk, probably moldering in poverty and oblivion.

Finally, he dialed the number and, with phone in hand, paced the room. Pugin answered after the third ring. "Hi there!" Nikolai began cheerfully, sensing right away he had rung at a bad time. "To hell with it," he thought, and changing to a dry, official tone, concisely outlined the heart of the matter.

Pugin acted disgruntled, pretending he was still not pleased with Heraldic Inq., but Kramskoy knew right away he had the client hooked, and this one wasn't giving up the bait. "A very interesting document has come to light," he said as dispassionately as possible, and to Pugin's impatient, "Well?" he added, "It's a museum piece being stored in a dump. But it solves the problem one hundred percent. Does the name Chumovo mean anything to you?"

"And what's it supposed to mean to me?" Pugin responded irritably. "You tell me. I'm the one paying you, after all."

His voice seemed to rustle with hundred-ruble notes and clink with the metal of kopecks. "Asshole!" thought Nikolai to himself, and out loud he continued, "Absolutely right. Let me tell you then: Chumovo turns out to be the very place where the person of interest to you once sired a son out of wedlock – apparently, your direct ancestor. They named him Yemelyan, after his father, and gave him your last name – so it was related, but not quite the same. What do you think of that story?"

There was a click and a sigh on the other end of the phone, a frightened woman indistinctly said, "I'm sorry," and stillness hung in the air once more.

"The story?" Pugin asked, after a pause. "The story's good. I can come up with such a story on my own. Now, do you have a document to back it up?"

"Exactly," Nikolai affirmed. "There is a document. That's what I've been telling you about. We found it – with difficulty and expenses, of course, but we did. There's a letter from the mayor where your great-great-great-grandfather is mentioned at a tender age on account of the demise of his twin brother. The quality, of course, is good for nothing; the paper is quite scored and scratched. But if we polish it up, it'll be like new, no worries. You'll need a copy anyway. The original is quite dilapidated."

"No worries..." Pugin repeated thoughtfully. "All right then. Fine, if that's how it is. So how are you going to do it, this copy? Or are you going to ask someone?"

"Why ask? It's just a matter of going there, making arrangements, and doing it," Nikolai said in a dull voice. "Let me take a look." He rustled some papers on the desk. "Here, I'm free at the beginning of the week. I could leave in about three days, if we're basically in agreement."

"Basically..." Pugin repeated again and let out a deep breath. "All right, we have an agreement. Basically... But you snag the original from them too, so nobody else gets any fancy ideas."

This guy's a piece of work, Nikolai thought and then inquired as if he didn't understand, "What do mean *snag*?"

"You grease somebody's palm. With moolah, man," Pugin explained in irritation. "Otherwise, what's to keep other interlopers from coming along and sniffing around? No, it shouldn't be left there. I'll put up the cash," he added, interpreting Kramskoy's silence as a question of funds. This gave the latter no choice but to affirm he would do everything that was possible.

"And everything that's necessary!" the client boomed forcefully and concluded with surprising cheerfulness, "Let's keep in touch." At that, the conversation ended, leaving Nikolai with a sense of mild disgust. Giving it some thought, however, he decided he had gotten his own way and even broke out whistling a tune that floundered after the first well-known notes.

Afterward, in the evening, the tune was still stuck in his head on his way home in the crowd that filled Tverskaya Street. On route to the boulevard, he phoned Zhanna Chizhik and informed her in a serious voice of his impending business trip, during which time she would have to "take care of business herself" while he "closed out the project." They were not expecting any business, but Zhanna received the news with the appropriate decorum, which was pleasant in itself. At Pushkin Square, he veered right, considering over and over how well everything was linked in a single chain: the friend he had not seen for many years, the outlaw Pugachev and his unfortunate bastard, the evening with Zhanna that teased his fantasies, and Pugin, who was not going anywhere now. One could even think the events had lined up in a row on their own, pushing him toward this quite ordinary trip.

"So then, Sivoldaisk. Maybe one more sign," he said thoughtfully to himself as he grinned, engrossed in his own meditation, almost bumping into a man with a frozen look who stood by the newsstand and peered into the showcase window.

CHAPTER 9

Meanwhile, the man at the newsstand, though he turned when Kramskoy apologized, looked around and through him, not noticing Nikolai at all. Other people did not interest him now; he was consumed by his own burning thought. His name was Alexander Alexandrovich Frolov; he lived on Solyanka Street. It was his apartment that Elizaveta Bestuzheva had left that July morning nearly a week before.

Since then, Alexander had known no peace. He mulled every moment of their last meeting over and over in his head, desperately trying to understand the reason for the misfortune that had befallen him, but he couldn't identify a single disquieting detail, nothing noteworthy or out of the ordinary. Yet the misfortune was obvious; his living space was rapidly decreasing in size, and it seemed the whole world was crumbling around him.

They hadn't seen each other again, which was not odd in itself. Their meetings occurred infrequently; that was typical in a city that allowed no one to breathe freely. Now, however, he heard the threat in every sound, saw its footprints, sensed its smell – and was beside himself with panic. Between him and Elizaveta the link disappeared, some frayed thread was severed – that was irreversible and permanent. Frolov slept little, ate nearly nothing, and couldn't think of anything else. Among his acquaintances a rumor spread about his sudden mental illness, which was not far from the truth. Inadvertently, he threw fuel on the fire by speaking mostly in interjections, breaking off conversation and hanging up abruptly – though just moments before he had rushed to the ringing phone across the room at full speed. Even at work his bosses started to regard him dubiously: he had become inefficient, which the administration could not help but notice. He thought distractedly that a conflict could arise soon with the company, followed by dismissal, the collapse of his career, and the loss of his source of income. This didn't bother him in the least.

No matter where he was or what he did, he was tormented by thoughts of Elizaveta Bestuzheva and the fear of losing her forever. Their romance had drawn out for more than half a year, and he was convinced this woman, like no other, gave meaning to his monotonous life. Now that meaning was slipping away, sinking into sand, leaving an emptiness in its wake, and the sight of this emptiness was so frightening that Alexander's mind refused to believe it. Only an extreme exertion of will prevented him from cornering Elizaveta at the door of her residence or calling her more than once a day. At times, the despair receded for a brief instant and Alexander surveyed the world with a more or less sober view, even planning actions that could put an end to the humiliation to which he had subjected himself. But it didn't last long; very soon his sullen nerves took the upper hand again. He rushed about the apartment like a sick animal or ran outside and roamed the streets until weariness dulled the pain inside. That was one of those moments, when Nikolai Kramskoy saw him and walked past without distinguishing him from the others.

Alexander no longer remembered Liza had once seemed simple to him, not very experienced in matters of the heart. At that time he was full of himself, sincerely thinking he played first fiddle, acting a bit arrogant and a little careless. She wouldn't allow his gaze to penetrate deeply, but this didn't trouble him much; he concocted what he couldn't see, playing with illusions pleasant to look upon. Quite soon, however, he fell for her seriously. Perceiving in Elizaveta an age-old modesty through the deceitful lens of his imagination, he decided that deep inside she held some genuine feelings toward him – and he set a goal, as if from curiosity, to awaken in himself something that matched them. The illusions turned more malignant; his curiosity was deprived of its sight and left to wander in darkness. Soon, he realized he needed her more than the other way around, but it was already too late. The demons had awakened and had free reign. A poisonous fog infected his consciousness, overcoming and subordinating it. Over time, the situation only worsened: he banished his imagination for its betrayal, and many of the exposed particulars were not that pleasant to look at. He only consoled himself with the assumption that Liza was too reserved, but their mutual passion was intense enough to link them forever. He had long since lost the courage to contradict her, and he tried to comply in everything, unable to endure her coldness and sarcasm. In a word, he succumbed to dependency, which he accepted with resignation, not finding the strength to be ashamed of it or to change anything.

At the same time, in normal life, no one would think him able to dance to another's tune. Frolov knew how to make money and establish himself in his circles; and now, when the caste structure had been deposed, these circles expanded considerably. They admitted anyone who knew how to survive the Moscow jungle, grabbing a piece for himself – and Alexander fit right in. Besides, he could be fun, always having some cool joke in reserve for just the right occasion. This was even taken for intelligence, especially by the women who considered him interesting, and, in actuality, it was based on a system that no one around him knew about just yet.

The system was simple, but it was related to issues of a higher order, including the meaning of life in general. Like many unlucky others, Frolov, very early in his life, experienced the fear of physical death, the inevitability of the end, and since then he had tried – again, like the rest – to find, if not a way around it, then at least a shadow of one, to which he could direct his thoughts when an icy wave of terror overtook him. The recipes for immortality offered to the broad masses were unreasonably naive; religions that reduced the question to a set of populist dogmas annoyed him with their inept lies. Quite soon, it became clear he must combat the fear with his own mind and strength. To Alexander's credit, this revelation didn't break him or make him give up. It just added a little bitterness to his attitude toward the world, for which he had never before harbored any ill will.

The struggle lasted for years and ended, one might say, in a draw: neither side achieved a clear advantage. After being promptly disappointed with the techniques of physical rejuvenation, Frolov addressed the spirit as the only possible area in which to search for salvation. This concept promised much, but was weakened by an absence of clear forms. Soon enough, he understood the noncorporeal could not be depended upon. The only answer was to find something material in the ephemeral and identify it as a firm core from which to take further steps.

This task was hard – even the creators of major religions didn't always succeed at it – but any effort is eventually rewarded if one demonstrates persistence and accepts reasonable compromise. So Alexander finally chose for himself a tangible symbol of the spirit – or, more precisely, a product of it – that was suitable to be transformed into a material model, at least to start with. He resolved to consider as such a product any original thought arising inexplicably in the chaotic morass of neurons, which either vanished into nothing and was thus useless for his purposes, or else was subject to being recognized and captured as a new atom in his patiently created environment.

Of course, the idea was not without fault, and it raised questions that, under close scrutiny, could extinguish any enthusiasm. Too much was left unsaid, including the next step to be taken when the "environment" reached maturity. Even the present phase left much unclear, but there was no use in hesitation. Nobody knew how many bricks had to be laid in the foundation to form the critical mass, and Frolov, hoping for the best, decided the time had come to act, not to think. He started to peruse encyclopedias and directories, to listen and look around, picking out other people's thoughts that were worthy of consideration wherever he could. He read them, overheard them, and nearly stole them, learning them by heart, etching them in his memory until he reached home, where he deposited them, using his favorite fountain pen, into a special ledger already comprised of two dozen notebooks.

This in itself calmed and encouraged him. He liked very much the look of the ink lines on white paper. The fat notebooks, heaped in piles, gave the sensation of visibly growing volume and, peering at them, he was convinced he was not idling or standing still. How good the result would be is always hard to determine in advance; many thoughts seemed strange to him or overly willful. Others duplicated or even contradicted each other, but Alexander faced this with tolerance and recorded them without amendment, believing careless intervention could only do harm. He cared for the notebooks with all diligence – protecting them against dust with a special cover and punctiliously bookmarking the months and years. For each thought apprehended, he also specified its source – with pedantic thoroughness worthy of an accountant or a pure-blooded German.

This thoroughness, however, had no Teutonic roots. Alexander's grandfather, Frol Frolov, the son, in turn, of another Frol, came from a prosperous family of Kulaks from the Urals. He didn't get along with the Soviet authorities and was dispossessed several times, but he rose yet again and acquired a homestead, to the envy of the revolution-minded poor. The last time, at the very beginning of the thirties, they took everything and sent him to build the Uralmash factory, along with his wife, who was pregnant with Alexander's father. There was icy cold, there was hunger and back-breaking labor, but they survived and she bore a child. A year later, Frol fled back to his village, where he again built a house and began to get rich. Through some sort of oversight, they didn't touch him again, though he didn't hide or conceal his success. Each autumn, he would travel to vacation by the sea in Sochi, and in the winter, he relaxed and liked to read Dostoyevsky during the long, boring evenings.

So the grandfather carried on the Frolov name worthily, but nature decided to stop with him and even take a few steps back. The issue, perhaps, was with poorly chosen monikers, but Frol's children turned out much worse off than he, and the best of them was Alexander's father, also called Alexander at the heated insistence of his mama. He grew up thoughtful and quiet. When he reached adulthood, he moved from the country to Sverdlovsk, married a high school French teacher, and preferred Chekhov to Dostoyevsky, reading the same short stories time after time. Alexander Alexandrovich himself, apart from his accuracy with bookmarks, inherited quite little from his grandfather but still resembled him: stately and broad-shouldered, though not very tall of stature. Upon his shoulders sat the hollow cheeks and pointed chin of a Russian intellectual; his expressive eyes seemed to sit too close together, and in his youth, he had poor health and was generally inclined toward reflection, which was unprecedented for the Frolovs.

This was facilitated by the fact that the family of the elder Alexander Frolov had happened to relocate to Moscow and lived on Baumanskaya, in a very dismal place. The windows of the nondescript building looked out on ancient workmen's quarters, sullied and half-burnt, probably because the specter of revolution that still dwelt among them could not grow beyond an abstract idea. There were neither trees nor grass there, just echoing paving stones and asphalt distended by the tramway tracks. Men and women with sagging shoulders wandered around, drinking beer straight from the bottle and desiring nothing. The area smelled of bad heredity, sickness, and early death. In such a landscape, depression bloomed in magnificent color, and Alexander Frolov the younger got his strength up only as he approached thirty, already in his own studio on Solyanka. The decision to create a ledger, which expanded his horizons, played no small role in this, as did the grandeur of his grey apartment building, the festively colored church next door, and the whole Kitai-Gorod area, boisterous and noisy, as if even today it retained its spicy spirit of opium smoke.

Of course, collecting the thoughts of others was not done randomly; it included periods of certain themes. Alexander would be taken for a time with a particular phenomenon or simply a word that seemed to harmonize with the records of the current notebook. His last interest before meeting Bestuzheva involved the peculiarities of great wars, which one way or another excite the soul of every man. He often muttered aloud quotes that impressed him, for example, "In war, all is simple; but the most simple thing is extremely difficult," or, as Napoleon once observed, "War consists of unforeseen events." But then fate took a turn and served up an unforeseen event caused not by war at all: Elizaveta intruded upon his reality, pushing everything else from his mind. And now, though he still scribbled in his notebooks sometimes, he did it mostly from habit rather than from his former drive.

This drive notably cooled when Alexander tried to tell Bestuzheva about it, to sort of prove himself, because at that very point, their relations started to lack parity. Unfortunately, he chose a bad moment: Elizaveta was not in the mood and suspected Frolov was being arrogant and putting on airs, hinting at her own lack of education, which she thought about whenever she heard unfamiliar words. She wanted to take revenge and told him in response of her first love, Timofey Tsarkov, exaggerating a little at the part concerning their carnal pleasures and hinting for some reason at certain anatomical details. This grieved Alexander extremely and unsettled him for a long time, though Elizaveta wasn't at all serious. Besides, anatomy didn't mean much to her, and as for Tsarkov and their best moments of affection, she had received the greatest pleasure when he brought her to the heights of arousal by skillfully caressing the vertebrae in the small of her back.

This, clearly, she couldn't share with Alexander since it was a detail of too intimate a nature, and he never recovered from the blow caused by her thoughtless remark. Soon, he noticed his feelings were getting out of control, surpassing in their heat the total of her emotions, of which little were intended, alas, for him. Little by little, he lost interest in everything else; his days and weeks were broken up into periods of anticipation – of the next meeting, the next call, the next favorable omen. He forced himself to believe their bond was becoming stronger and that Bestuzheva was getting more and more attached to him. That very soon she wouldn't be able to manage without him, and then she would finally dare to fall in love. More than once, he was about to take the decisive step, a desperate attempt to win complete control of her, but Elizaveta's freedom-loving spirit cooled his courage. Frolov understood the first shot had the greatest chance of success; therefore, he waited, showing patience worthy of an ancient stoic, though his blood boiled and it became unendurable for his heart at each parting after the short night.

Now, as all sped toward the precipice, Alexander's strength was sufficient merely to keep himself from committing irreversible folly. More than anything else, he wanted to force Elizaveta into an open discussion, but this, he knew perfectly well, would likely lead to a definitive split. Any impulsive act threatened to be fatal, so he stayed away from her usual routes, which he had long known by heart. He roamed like a phantom along the dusty streets, grabbing his cell and then immediately stashing it back in his pocket, forbidding himself to even think of making another call, fearing to worsen the situation, although – he sensed in anguish – it was already intolerably bad.

Now, in fact, his route was deliberate and had a particular purpose. Alexander was going to meet Masha Rozhdestvenskaya, as agreed upon the day before. The time had come for extreme measures; neither his dislike toward Margo nor his fear of making himself look ridiculous had any further meaning. Of course, on the phone he had tried not to reveal his desperation, but Masha instantly understood Frolov was grasping at straws. She suggested they meet that very evening and not put it off. Another time, she would probably have let Elizaveta know about this – out of her congenital bitchiness and a desire to witness the drama from different angles – but now, angered at her colleague for her scandalous surreptitiousness, she decided to entertain her own mystery. It was now her turn to keep secrets from Bestuzheva, who was clearly stuck up. Besides, Alexander was not a bad-looking guy, and Masha, though she despised men as a whole, couldn't deny they existed and were quite necessary sometimes. Certainly, he wasn't good for much now: he remained Elizaveta's property, which she determined unmistakably from his falsely buoyant tone. But circumstances have a tendency to change, and here it was obvious big changes were approaching.

They met at the Belarussky train station in a café styled after a Pullman car. "This really reminds me of something," said Masha, feigning absentmindedness. "Now, what was it? Oh, yeah!" and she told him about the train ticket on Liza's desk.

"Well, then," thought Frolov with a downcast face, "that explains everything, no further questions needed." He diligently kept up the conversation though, as he stared into his cup of green tea. The glass was an old pattern in a massive metal holder, also constructed according to the railway theme.

Alexander had practically no doubts left: she was leaving forever. The thought of Tsarkov appeared as an uninvited answer to the riddle that chilled his heart. "Sure, even anatomy is on his side," he thought dejectedly. "They say women can't forget that. So there's no chance, no fighting it."

"Many catastrophes occur right on schedule," he blurted out, cutting Masha off in midsentence. "Sorry, Margo, I was lost in thought, not paying attention."

"Did you come up with that on your own?" Masha asked in surprise. Then she put her hand on his, making him look into her eyes, and asked in a soft voice, "What? Is it all that serious?"

"Yes," he said simply, shrugging his shoulders. She made no effort to console him, seeing nothing could help, but suggested finding out more and informing him without delay because not knowing is the worst of all tortures.

"You must understand," she said, taking his hand again, "women can be totally heartless."

"Yes," Frolov replied with the same, solitary word, pursing his lips into the grin of a loser, and Masha, slightly puzzled, pledged to do all she could. It was clear a great intrigue was developing around her coworker – and it was intolerable for her to remain in the dark.

CHAPTER 10

Frank White, Jr. held high hopes for his trip to Russia. Of course, the search for Pugachev's hoard remained his main goal, but there were others that inflamed his heart and stirred his blood. Not all were suited for discussion with Axel or Nilva, so Frank was rather evasive, avoiding the inquiries and counsel pressed upon him. Meanwhile, he engaged in planning the journey with the appropriate seriousness.

The first week he decided to spend in the capital, yielding to recollections, even if they had faded over the years. Nostalgia, however, was merely a screen. What he really wanted was to forget all goals and be totally carefree, rushing headlong into the whirlpool of emotions which Russia would, as before, offer in abundance. Frank wanted to cut loose and get drunk, to exult, suffer, pine, and pity himself – building up a reserve of passion and heartfelt dramas for the years ahead, which were so lacking in his measured, American life. Now, on the sixth day of his Moscow vacation, he observed with morose satisfaction that he was performing the task well. Plenty of experience had been gathered – it even felt like there was no place left for a single thing more.

Frank White was tormented by a hangover, and, to some degree, regret. He felt like a pig, and this feeling was neither a burden nor a shame. On the contrary: it seemed in conformity with the surroundings – Frank sensed with every inch of his skin how attractive disgracefulness really was, and he chuckled knowingly, running his palm across his unshaven cheek in anticipation of the first Bloody Mary of the day. He had even become accustomed to hangovers, since he suffered one every morning. As happens with nearly everyone, he recognized in himself – after a short battle – that Russian habits lived in him always, merely waiting for their chance, covered with an American veneer. In the evenings, he drank to get drunk, relishing the thought he was wretched and slipping into a chasm. Taking in the world with a clouded-over glance, listening attentively to the cacophony of life, looking at his own reflection in numerous nocturnal mirrors, he was surprised but did not reproach himself. The part of his mind that always remained sober noticed the whole experience was nothing more than an amusement park ride, a carousel that would stop spinning at the appointed time. And it would be possible to step off – even if on wobbly, failing feet.

The main point of the Moscow program, however, was by no means alcohol. Having received a photocopy of the secret map from Nilva, folding it into fourths, and tucking it into his jacket pocket, Frank felt his heart skip a beat from thoughts unrelated to treasure hunting. In the final days before his flight out, he completely stopped dodging the fact that the approaching adventure, every now and then, turned into dreams of beautiful Russian women waiting for him beyond the sea. This was also facilitated by the memory of his high-school girlfriend with whom he had been forced to part so suddenly, and by the revelations of Axel Timurov, who loved to brag of his former conquests, the number of which approached the infinite, even adjusting the account for error by approximation. Books also played their role: though Frank was not in the habit of reading much, he still had time to consume his share of Russian literature, which couldn't help but affect his notions of Slavic girls, as well as the female sex as a whole.

Perhaps for this reason, in a simplified American life, on the artificial soil that did not nourish sensitive natures, he endured one misfortune after another with his compatriots. Thus it was at university, and thus it continued afterward, at times becoming ridiculous and eliciting serious doubts. Frank could recall only two more or less successful long-term forays, but even in those cases, his girlfriends eventually left him on their own after a year or so. One of them ended up preferring the college roommate she couldn't forget over vulgar masculine love; the other just moved to another state after finding a job there for a higher salary. Since then, his personal life was so poor, he didn't want to think about it. It even reached the point of wet dreams at night. He was terribly ashamed of them, like a teenager still popping pimples, and he sometimes wondered with bitter irony whether he should buy himself a lovely rubber doll he might manage to get along with.

Obviously, against this backdrop, thoughts of Russia caused a powerful surge of hormones. He dreamt of large women with fair hair, grey-eyed divas of proud Slavic bearing, graceful brunettes and their fragile shoulders like his dear Natasha once had, or blonde, green-eyed kittens with claws so playful, they scratched without pain. He imagined them at all hours, saw them in his sleep, and sighed helplessly as he awoke. On the plane, incapable of coping with his impatience, he looked around furtively, as if trying to guess the whole film from its opening shots. Even the stewardesses, pure-blooded Americans, seemed to be representatives of another breed, not the one left behind the demarcation line where the Puritan spirit hovered. One of them was clearly from the Midwest, where the mores were more relaxed than on the coasts. In her fleshy face, Frank perceived something from his shameful dreams and, taking courage, he struck up a conversation with her, trying to look relaxed – though it didn't work well. The girl, however, smiled readily, gave her name – Shirley – and probably even waited for more, sparkling at him with her mascaraed eyes, but he wanted nothing from her and had already spent his reserve of boldness.

In the airport as he waited for his luggage, he looked over the female passengers and their gloomy companions. In the hotel, forgetting himself, he stared intently at the cute, feisty receptionist. Hardly unpacking his things, he put on his sunglasses and went out, confidently heading for the city center. Moscow greeted him with heat and the stench of exhaust fumes. The sidewalks flowed with a motley throng; Frank walked along at its heart, trying to merge with the environs. He strode without hurry, soaking in the details, voraciously comparing reality to the pile of recent fantasies that now seemed entirely useless.

All was just so, and not so: the street smelled different, not as it had in his schooldays, and women turned out not as he imagined, though they were remarkable in their way. No stunning beauties walked among them; moreover, some of the girls he noticed were frankly plain. Frank White was astonished at their tastelessness and artifice, their inept makeup and poor clothing, which was quite apparent, even to him, although he was not used to judging such matters. But then he stopped focusing on the inconsequential and accepted it as fact that they were gorgeous all the same – for he had no intention of thinking otherwise. They decorated the space like bright spots against the dirty gray: aspiring, as it were, to dispel the despondence of the grubby hues. He wanted to straighten his shoulders and help them with this – or at least encourage them, let them know with a cryptic gesture that he saw and valued all. In their faces he endeavored to discern the defenselessness of innocent victims – which might explain and reconcile a lot of things. He imagined he was brave and strong and capable of more than anyone would have thought – especially in his own country, where no one considered himself a victim or sought empathy in others. Frank even grew taller – at least, that's how it seemed to him – and it was immaterial what was really going on with these girls, or what disappointment awaited a stranger if he succumbed to temptation and got to know them better.

"Russian women have a good appetite, and they get pregnant way too easy," one of his acquaintances observed ironically upon returning from Russia and added with a knowing look at the desperately blushing White, "yes, this is where their strength is. This is the quality of their genotype and the potential power of the nation!"

Frank didn't like him, but his words about potential power

sank into his soul. An unknown world seemed hidden in them and he sought the means to unlock it. That said, he didn't intend to surrender to mere dreams, understanding well that his free time was limited, and he shouldn't procrastinate with steps of a practical nature. He wanted to meet a thoroughly simple girl – a shop assistant or waitress, a secretary or factory worker. During the two hours he spent in the central streets, he encountered the most delightful of specimens worthy of admiration, infatuation, perhaps even of love. Frank White liked tall women, large bodies and heavy hips, veiled eyes, and the scent of cheap perfume. In this, he saw the precipice of unspent passion; it was hard to even believe that so much could be given to one man: flesh, soft skin, smells, sighs. He flinched and recoiled, then mustered his determination anew; but he didn't make himself talk to anyone and finally ran away in cowardice, taking cover in a tacky old-fashioned restaurant to pause and catch his breath.

The break was helpful enough. After a filling lunch where Frank drank two shots of vodka to deceive his jetlag, he finally made a move – and suffered a complete fiasco. In the hot summer day he caught a whiff of the cold of the snowy steppe and the indifference of vast spaces. He was too foreign and clumsy, his tongue sputtered from being unaccustomed to spirits, people dashed aside from him and looked on in his wake. Very soon it was clear Russian girls could be timid and cold-blooded like no other and knew how to reject men even better than American ones. Brutal strength and coarseness of heart suddenly peeked out from beneath their features, and he noticed the hands of some were unkempt and rough, similar to the hands of fish wives, as he imagined them to be. Something wasn't right with his picture of the universe, and this upset and depressed him. Frank even came to suspect the adventures he was looking for could also be full of caveats – even if he managed to get them.

Discouraged and tired, he got drunk that evening at the hotel bar and set off toward his room with the staggering gait of a lonely salesman at the end of another fruitless day. On the way to the elevator, he encountered a flock of night faeries, dressed up like bright butterflies, with the tenacious eyes of young she-wolves. They greeted him, first in Russian, then in fairly good English, but he got confused and chickened out. Here it occurred to him that he was wasting yet another great chance – the girls were fresh and sweet, not at all resembling the poor creatures that had sunk to the very bottom. But Frank reminded himself of the diseases, robberies, and other horrors that awaited the consumers of love for hire, and he fell asleep accompanied by drunken visions, his whole soul sensing the bitter imperfection of the world.

Much was repeated the following day, but with a more mature Frank White, one who had taken off his rose-colored glasses. The holiday was over and the work week began; his throbbing head produced the soberest of thoughts. Looking around, Frank now felt strangely indifferent and impassive. Dreams faded like a magic lantern in the light; particulars became visible, revealing their inept trickery. At lunch, he drank watery Russian beer instead of vodka and sat for a long time in the empty restaurant, gazing out the window and regretting that the waitress was fat and impolite. It seemed to him the curtain was rising slowly and the keyhole was visible. The only thing left was to select the right key. Later, he again wandered the city, turning toward the boulevards instead of the center this time, wandering aimlessly down the Arbat backstreets and returning to Tverskaya by the dusty and loud Garden Ring.

This day, too, passed without meeting anyone, though progress was apparent. He was almost taken seriously and, perhaps, luck would have smiled on him if he hadn't lost faith in himself under amused looks full of artless coquetry. Frank rambled back to the hotel deep in thought, absentmindedly picked up the newspaper shoved under the door, and immediately stumbled upon the escort service advertised at the bottom of the page. His heart pounded; he fell on the bed, waved his hand, and cursed in Russian, already knowing how he was going to spend the evening.

It all turned out easier than he expected. The masculine voice on the line was courteous and velvety, he wasn't asked anything superfluous – in fact, the conversation contained not a single note of vulgarity. The administrator's manners called to mind a concert hall, elegant dresses, long-awaited vouchers to the orchestra seats. And, indeed, when he offered Frank a girl for the evening, he described her as a violinist down on her luck, a musician from a good school reserved for demanding clients.

"I can tell you're an intelligent man," the voice warbled. "You'll be satisfied: she is a Muscovite, an angel, with long, sensitive fingers…"

At this, White's heart sputtered again, and afterward he was truly not disappointed, though the violinist turned out to be a Ukrainian from Donetsk, confessing with a chuckle that she had no ear for music. They laughed together at the deceit over the phone, and then she was nice enough, especially when she disrobed without any shyness or affectation under his intense gaze. Her love seemed a bit mechanical, but the automatic nature of it didn't feel humiliating. She even said she enjoyed him, and Frank believed it, in turn shaking off his bashful constraint. Besides, the girl was called Natasha, a name ringing with sweet pain in his heart and adding content to prepaid passion.

Just before parting, as he came out of the shower, Frank saw his guest inspecting his wallet, which he had carelessly tossed on the nightstand. "I wanted to take a gander at your wife," she laughed in response to his raised eyebrows. "All Americans carry photos around with them, right? And you, I'd wager, are not even married."

She looked at him with brazen eyes, yellow like those of a taiga lynx, and grinned from ear to ear, then they kissed goodbye and only the odor of her perfume remained in the room. Frank drank some cognac from the mini-bar and counted his money, prepared for the worst, but realized he didn't remember how much cash he had, and just laughed at himself.

Overall, he had to acknowledge the evening was a success – and he admitted this and drank himself drunk again. The nocturnal faeries at the bar now looked like the guardians of a collective secret that bound them to him, as well as a good half of those sitting here in the smoky twilight. With a faint sadness, he peered into their faces, cognizant that his one life was not enough to learn all the paths through forbidden grounds. He imagined how one could live for years here, in the city of sin, in lechery and alcoholic debauchery, without once recalling a single taboo. In the morning he felt ill and wallowed in bed until midday, then went to the central park and strolled for a long while. And then everything was repeated again: the newspaper ad, the phone call, and the insinuating baritone. Shop assistants and waitresses no longer interested him. The road to truth was much shorter, and it was not worth wasting his valuable time.

On this occasion they sent him Olga, dark haired, with high cheekbones and a slightly Eastern slant to her eyes. He spent the evening with her, and then the three following nights. At first, though, it turned out embarrassing: after two hours of lovemaking and a wholehearted goodbye kiss, he, probably remembering the night before, decided to take a peek in his ill-fated wallet and discovered the pocket of his pants dangling from the chair was completely empty. This was too much, and Frank grew acutely alarmed. He remembered right away that he was in a dangerous land where crime ran rampant and no one could be trusted. With shaking hands, he dialed the number of the insidious service and shouted at the dispatcher in a falsetto, full of weakness, knowing his senses had come to him too late. The dispatcher was genuinely surprised and promised to get to the bottom of it without delay. For a quarter of an hour, Frank stomped from corner to corner, cursing his own idiocy through clenched teeth. Then, as if by some hunch, he kicked the hateful chair, forcing it toward the wall, and saw his lost wallet, which had fallen to the floor in the most harmless of ways.

Everything was there – his credit cards and his money. Frank's despair knew no bounds. The escort service, as if out of spite, gave a busy signal for a long time, and he mumbled in chagrin, his palms pressed to his temples. And once he got through, he unleashed such a barrage of emotions, mixing up his Russian out of agitation, that it fully confused the owner of the baritone, who began to justify himself without knowing what he was guilty of.

Soon all was settled. Frank White was assured with appropriate empathy that such a thing could happen to anyone, and there was no reason for worry or concern. And with regard to the girl, whom they had already asked for her side of the story, she would simply be happy with the resolution and would bear him no ill will. Frank, however, ardently insisted he wanted to apologize in person. At this, the insinuating voice advised him to do it the very next evening, in the course of receiving romantic services, which, of course, Olga would take gracefully as a combination of the pleasant with the useful. "Especially if it's for the whole night," the voice hinted cautiously, and they agreed on that, ending the conversation with considerable warmth.

The next day she came with a turquoise ribbon in her hair. She was downcast and laconic, admitting with a sigh that no one had ever before accused her of theft. Frank fussed about like an anxious newlywed, saying a lot of unnecessary words and not knowing where to place his eyes and hands. Then they quickly reconciled and headed off to dine at an Italian restaurant, and that night they hardly slept, sharing stories from their lives mingled with erotic games full of unexpected quirks. Olga brought elegant handcuffs, scaring him slightly at first, but they shone so invitingly and seemed so innocent, he was ashamed of his suspicions. However, the game they played, while remaining close to an innocuous joke, revealed something really new. Frank was bewildered; he was being offered an unaccustomed form of freedom. There was more to it than he'd realized at first sight, and he assumed Russian women were really and truly insane, perhaps ready to believe anybody who was capable of sharing their own crazy thoughts.

He was uncomfortable for a moment with her submission, which went a bit too far, but then he saw the same was expected from him as well, and Olga, his black-haired slave, was now waiting for him with an imaginary horsewhip. Then it began to seem natural and desirable; she said to him, "Trust me," and he accepted trust as the essence of the action. And, afterward, they whispered tender words, as if they had survived enough dangers together to suffice for a few years.

Olga left in the morning, and Frank White knew he was about

to lose his head. He roamed the Moscow streets, sleepy and sullen, muttering as if carrying on an endless dialogue with her. He had never told any woman so much about himself – supposing, reasonably, that none would listen; this was also new, and it imparted a strange relief. He suddenly realized he had outgrown himself – such as he was before – and he wondered with fatigued irony what else might he have to explore and how many more nights like that were needed to get used to them and not be surprised later.

After lunch he dropped into a heavy slumber, and then there was Olga again and her impetuous whisper. They didn't speak now of their former lives, but about each other and the burdens of loneliness, guardedly admitting mutual sympathy and selecting their words carefully to avoid being pathetic. Therefore, perhaps a lot was left unsaid, for which Frank subsequently suffered, squinting his eyes in the daylight.

When the next night came, Olga came too, wearing not turquoise, but a scarlet ribbon in her black locks. He lost all control and blurted out to her everything a man who had been snared by the most enticing bait could possibly say. When it came to him promising to take her away to Washington, get her a job, and, who knows, maybe unite their lives at some point, Olga squeezed his hand – from excitement or perhaps something else. Frank suddenly collected himself and started kissing her in gratitude. Later, standing under the shower, he berated his wagging tongue, recognizing he had gone too far. Returning to the room, he told her he was about to travel to another city on business. It was becoming scary to continue their nightly appointments, like wandering into foreign territory where disguised traps waited. She shed a few tears and left her phone number, which he fervently pledged to call – the minute he got back.

So, they had said and done all that was proper but, left alone, Frank sighed in relief. Something seemed out of hand; he clearly needed a reprieve. All the same, he ought to finally get to business: another city was not just a redeeming lie, and he had already gotten more from Moscow than he bargained for.

He had slept into the afternoon and was now sitting in a cafe with a view of the cobblestones of Stoleshnikov – grooming his somewhat somber spleen and reliving the last night and his words, of which he should probably be ashamed. But he felt no shame whatsoever; in fact, he liked himself for the first time in many years. Of course, he had said too much without thinking, Frank White conceded, drinking the cocktail he was brought. He had probably broken the girl's heart: she would be hoping and waiting. Perhaps she would even leave her profitable business, at least for as long as her hope endured. But one can't plan one's life around a woman's tears; that's too much trouble and the consequences are unclear. And Olga, after all, didn't have the nicest past: what if that later became a sore point for him? Frank studied with interest two young lasses languidly traipsing by, then waved to the waitress, pointing at his empty glass, and felt himself to be a freedom-loving male, full of vigor and desires.

"It's too bad for the girl," he thought again with feigned grief, leaning back in his chair and stretching out fully. "But Axel was right: there are a lot of them, and the choice is so hard!"

This false grief would have been easily forgotten, however, had he by chance known the thoughts of his recent lover, who was sitting at that very moment in a bar in the southeast of Moscow. She sipped her martini, exchanging glances with the bartender, squinting contentedly as she anticipated intense shopping ahead. A profitable client had turned up right on time; Olga praised herself for the skillful game and pitied the American simpleton who seemed such an easy mark. Her conscience even bothered her a little, which happened quite rarely, and might be considered an amusing exception. She recalled how Frank had shoved money at her that morning to get out of the situation he had put himself in, and how she lathered on some fake waterworks to strengthen the effect.

"Fucking life!" she said to the barkeep, as if he were an accomplice who should be up to date on the latest, and he nodded his consent. "I'm a Moscow bitch!" she added with pride, already slurring her speech a little, and the bartender grinned in reply. Meanwhile, Frank White, Jr., departing his café of choice, meandered in the direction of Petrovka, mentally sending Olga a fond *adieu* and preparing to forget about her forthwith and forever.

On reaching the hotel, he headed straight for the concierge and asked him to order a ticket for the most comfortable train to Sivoldaisk and also to book a hotel room, preferably a suite – thinking in passing that he had spent too much already, but in this city it was impossible not to squander money. Shortly thereafter, a cute maid brought him an envelope containing all the essentials. He checked out her legs as he signed the bill, not even noticing the pearl bracelet adorning her wrist that could have told a great deal, even if not a single two appeared in the written total. The pearl gleamed with moonlight and the girl's knees brought to mind the most immodest thoughts. But Frank White, Jr. resolutely pushed them away, ordering himself to limit this evening just to solitary drunkenness.

CHAPTER 11

The Moscow-Sivoldaisk luxury-class train was standing ready on Track One a whole hour before departure. Paveletsky Station buzzed like a beehive: it was the evening of the last Sunday in July, and the terminal was packed with people. The center of the affair was Track One itself – the most well-to-do passengers were headed there at that moment. The previous luxury liner, on route to Volgograd, had departed two hours before; the next, to Voronezh, was leaving around midnight, and the rest, for the simpler folk, were not that important. Staid porters were already approaching the cars; pickpockets and beggars filtered light-footed through the throng; guards wandered unfettered throughout the crowd, thick nightsticks slapping at their thighs – and here our protagonists were to appear, though they did not yet suspect each other's existence.

First to arrive at the station was Alexander Frolov; he was emaciated, with dark circles under his eyes, but full of determination and ready to act. Margo did not let him down: Elizaveta Andreyevna's secret plans had been partially revealed. Like a clever spy, she had detected the precise date of departure, the train number, and even the car and seat – though this was not easy: her colleague comported herself with reserve. She had to resort to a bit of cunning, which worked out smoothly since Elizaveta didn't expect any tricks from Masha. It was too early to fight for her man, so her acute female sensor remained inoperative, and she easily believed the story about some insurance policies and official forms.

"You should have come to work earlier," spiteful Masha did not fail to note, "but don't be concerned, I vouched for you. I'll go take care of everything on Friday, and if they tell me your signature's a must, I'll bring you the papers, at the house or the train station. I'll cover for you, don't worry, my friend."

Elizaveta, thanking her absentmindedly, told her the train, the date, and what seat she had in which car. Yet, when her companion, encouraged by this success, tried to draw more out of her, she snapped, "Oh, Mashka, give me a break. I don't even know myself!"

Rozhdestvenskaya chuckled silently at this obvious lie and soon called Alexander, lathering it on thick by adding that the matter was serious and could end dramatically. A man was involved, she said, who had quite a history with Bestuzheva in the past, whether it was long ago or not.

"Mash-sha, Mash-sha," Frolov intoned sadly. "Well, thank you. You are a true comrade-in-arms."

Margo giggled ambiguously enough, but he hastened to conclude the conversation; he had no further strength for words. Things were getting worse and worse. The world was not just breaking; the world was dying, decomposing into elements.

"If you cannot live, do something else," Frolov bitterly quoted a line he had seen recently. Then he wagged his head and whispered, "The same night awaits one and all..." and then, "Dying means joining the majority." Something clicked in his head; his face froze and turned into a mask. For the first time in his thirty-four years, he seriously thought of suicide.

The truths of others now seemed senseless to him. It was hard to believe that, not long before, he had been diligently entering them into his notebooks and been proud of his work. Alexander moaned and then started to laugh as he remembered yet another, "The morals of the people depend on respect for women." He stood, walked to the window, and howled thinly and terribly, "Bitch! Bitch! Whore!"

Then he sat on the floor with his back to the wall and began to think about how to do away with himself.

Frolov quickly chose a method for settling his accounts with life: the most reliable seemed to be a jump from the roof of a tall building. His apartment block on Solyanka, an eight-story Stalin-era edifice with high ceilings, suited this purpose very well. He tried to remember what part of the courtyard was devoid of obstacles in the form of flower beds or garbage heaps, and surmised the sidewalk between entrances six and seven would do nicely. After that, there was nothing left to decide and no point in hesitating anymore. The hatch to the roof was never locked; loopholes for retreat did not exist; and after suffering as much as he had, it was somewhat awkward to turn back now.

"We must believe in free will. There's simply no other choice," he said aloud. "Now, how did it go after that? 'To every folly, there is a season'? Enough of that, then! That's all!"

Smiling bitterly to himself, he considered how all his life he had feared death, at times to the point of shivering and night terrors. He had watched his health and taken care of his body, almost panicking at any sign that seemed to indicate failures in its performance. It was funny: he recalled his fears regarding apparent venereal diseases, or cheeks too bright, as if flushed with TB, or his face swelling in the morning, which could indicate kidney problems, or circles under eyes that might be caused by poor cardio function. Currently, that all sounded so silly he might laugh out loud at it, if he could find an ounce of courage to do so.

Alexander clenched his fists and prepared to rise. "Alright, enough! I'm off!" he shouted at himself. But his eyes burned; he felt something running down his cheek, recognized they were tears, and was desperately ashamed. Self-pity washed over him like a muddy stream, and Frolov started to sob, cradling his face in his hands. He wept a long time, whimpering and howling. When he eventually grew tired and calmed down, he understood his urge for suicide had flowed away with the tears, and its place was occupied now with a desire to act and take revenge. Upon whom and for what, he wasn't yet completely sure, and his plan of action was still a bit fuzzy. But it had become clear Elizaveta couldn't be permitted to throw him out of her life without even attempting to explain the reasons.

No, that would be too easy, both for her and for his lucky adversary. Something must happen from his own direct participation. He knew he was ready for many things, but killing himself was no longer among them; that would be a rather hasty decision. There were other, much more entertaining choices: why not settle the score with someone – whether it was with his former lover or else with the seducer who had trespassed upon another man's life? Or, perhaps, to do it without bloodshed – simply to destroy their impudent union, appearing at the crucial moment to their great surprise. And if even this didn't work out, at least he could bring the self-torture to its utmost, absurd degree, remaining a secret witness and obtaining undeniable proof. And then, then he would see: either the organ of his suffering would die on its own after sustaining an overload, or despair would become so dominant that no tears would prevent his last jump.

All Saturday, Frolov was almost tranquil. He ate heartily after starving through his time of torments and lay on the sofa for most of the day, leaving the house only to buy a train ticket in third class, where it would be easy to hide without attracting attention. He arrived early at the station; the train had just barely crept up to the platform. Alexander took up a position behind the shawarma stand, keeping his eyes peeled. He wanted to make certain Bestuzheva was actually traveling to Sivoldaisk: events had been developing so oddly that sudden tricks might be lurking anywhere, and he no longer wished to be made a fool of.

"We will achieve peace, even if we must go to war to do so," Frolov muttered in a low voice as he adjusted his dark glasses. To them he added a hat with a long bill and a baggy, camouflage sweatshirt. There was no way to recognize him unless you took a long, hard look.

Soon, the station area was visited by Frank White, Jr., who was excited and looked around intently. He was on guard against every trick imaginable: in particular, he was concerned about running late, getting lost, boarding the wrong train, getting robbed and beaten up, and so on. His cash was secreted in a money belt he had acquired while still in the States, and his ticket and passport were in a zippered pocket inside his jean jacket, though wearing it made him uncomfortably hot.

The journey and his entire project were entering a critical phase. Frank knew he was leaving a habitable city that, despite some reservations, could be called part of the civilized world. Now he was heading to a place the civilized world knew quite little about, and it would be up to him to find out just how much the rules of life there were suited for an untrained person. He felt a certain trepidation, but on the whole was proud of the responsibility that had been laid upon his shoulders.

Even the Russians themselves, Frank White reflected, were wary of traveling to "the interior:" his partner Nilva advised caution and the concierge in the hotel spoke of heightened vigilance and nighttime muggings. Frank prepared to be more watchful than ever, and he now scanned each passerby without letting his attention wane for a second. Soon, his eyes began to sting and his head was even spinning a little, so he decided to park himself for a bit and acclimate to the situation at the same stall behind which Alexander Frolov was hiding.

The conditions seemed completely placid, even if it was dirty and smelled burnt. A redheaded youngster with a pained face circled Frank once and disappeared. Then two teenaged girls, barelegged and cute, snatched a glance at him as they walked past. One of them even turned around and gruffly barked, "Hey, man, you got the time?" but her friend pulled her away, and they shuffled over to the commuter ticket booths, laughing loudly as they walked. No one else paid the least attention to White, Jr. He looked up and saw the large board above his head. The Sivoldaisk train was listed at the top, on the first track, and labeled with a green number. It wasn't far, which made Frank glad he came straight to the place he needed. At a leisurely pace, he walked the length of the platform and confirmed that boarding hadn't begun. So he decided to find the men's room; this turned out to be surprisingly difficult and took nearly a quarter of an hour. The bathroom itself made a very strong impression on Frank White – to the extent that he forgot his vigilance for a while. It was only upon entering the car and presenting his passport and ticket that he tensed up and focused again, looking furtively around.

This inspection revealed nothing of interest – the walkway by the business-class car was almost deserted. However, had Frank taken a look five minutes later, his eyes would have lighted upon Nikolai Kramskoy slowly making his way to the tail of the train. Nikolai was gloomy and, as usual, buried in his own thoughts. Everything was going well enough, but it was still rather ambivalent. He couldn't fathom what this meant, or what the higher planes wanted of him, pulling several threads at once.

Kramskoy had little doubt that there, in those planes, something was expected from this business trip that had come about so suddenly. All the events surrounding it, which had seemed completely ordinary at first, were occurring with an unusual force of will. As soon as he decided to go, all the recent coincidences had started to disappear. His literary friend wasn't answering the phone, and no response came from the e-mails he sent him. After spending more than an hour at a tourist agency, he was finally able to get a hotel reservation, but the only ticket available was a four-person berth – and Kramskoy didn't like to travel with roommates, especially three of them in a small compartment. Finally, on Saturday, Zhanna Chizhik called to wish him a safe and happy journey. They chatted for a while about nothing much, but something made him uneasy and gnawed at him, ruining his mood the whole following day. Later he understood: in the stories about her youth on the Volga, which he had brought up with her himself, some unpleasant notes came out, careless chatter out of place. He caught the scent of the dismal sadness of those places, of their indifference to everything in the world, and his secret thoughts of Sivoldaisk women suddenly seemed like a naïve whim. He laughed at himself and then wore an annoyed frown, as if surprised by this childishness he should have been through with long ago.

In short, the signs of fortune were becoming increasingly less discernible. Only Pugin's order remained firm, and it was possible to hold on to this foundation. Moreover, Nikolai himself became quite interested in the Pugachev story. He continued to scour the Net and search for facts – now out of his own curiosity.

Soon, it was clear that the heroic image was misleading and not authentic in the least. The Don vagrant pretending to the Imperial crown, despite his lofty aspirations, was the chieftain of the lowest class of plebes, the leader of canailles who had lost all semblance of humanity. Reports of executions and senseless atrocities terrified readers even after the passing of many years, bringing to mind another incursion, a century and a half later, not by commoners but by the Communists that time, who unleashed the same deadly energy of the simple masses in their wake. Pugachev himself, fierce and clever, occasionally cowardly, always treacherous, was more interesting than all others because he, like no other, embodied the hand of vengeance that was lifted against the nobility, who wallowed in the impotence of spirit. This was the demon of universal punishment, a symbol of *momento mori*, which they failed to appropriately heed – and then paid for that one more time at the dawn of a new age.

Nevertheless, Nikolai couldn't help but admit he thought of the chieftain with the liveliest of sympathy, which always accompanies mutiny doomed to failure and the bold determination that leads to demise. Somewhere here was also envy for the fortunate soul chosen by the higher power – for who else, if not the outlaw Yemelyan, was led by some force pushing against his back and causing him to wreak madness, putting him face to face with death and hiding him from it until the mysterious program was carried out in full. All his life, including its abrupt turn and the story of the senseless revolt, provoked admiration as a huge-scale affair designed by someone with a huge-scale imagination. Part of this admiration was due to the outlaw himself, no matter how base or foolish he actually was, or inexplicably brutal.

A plan from above could explain a lot: gallows and corpses, his panic attacks, and his inability to manage his vassals – many of whom were, incidentally, more clever and resolute than their leader. But the demon possessed him, not anyone else, forcing obedience to the sheen of his terrible eyes, before which all trembled – seeing there something not quite human. And even now, Kramskoy felt a strange shiver as he thought of the power of a will from Beyond that expressed itself in the will of Yemelyan Pugachev and made him believe in his own destiny – which was recognized by everyone.

"For behold, now I, one of the lost, have manifested myself, and walked throughout the land upon mine own two legs, and the Lord hath created me in order that I might grant you mercy."

"And whoso doth now receive this mercy, to him I grant compensation of land, fishing, timber, honey trees, beaver trapping rights, and other privileges, and also liberty and the freedoms of the Cossacks to be his forever."

"And whoso will not countenance this clemency, including boyars and landholders, those who are transgressors of the law and the common peace, let them be deprived of life: to wit, let them be put to death, and all their houses and property seized as a reward."

"And whoso doth continue in his delusion in spite of this clemency, let that man receive from me the recompense of great torment, and naught shall there be to defend him."

"Yea, though he assay to commend himself to lawful obedience, and though he endeavor to submit and render fealty, no such overture shall be received. Then he shall sigh from the depths of his heart and recall his worldly life, yet it shall not be possible for him to get it back..."

Thus did the self-proclaimed emperor dictate – since he knew not how to read or write – to his faithful secretary, who transcribed it word for word, albeit with an occasional flourish befitting the freewheeling Cossack manner. Nikolai was impressed by the style and considered the fate of this man, perhaps even supposing, like his client Pugin, he shared a connection with the brigand. Yemelyan would have also been led by signs; he probably sought them and suffered as he guessed at their clandestine meanings. Kramskoy was now experiencing the same, discounting, of course, the misleading nature of messages from the past – which is always good to bear in mind.

Reflecting on Pugachev and the whirlwind he had loosed, he caught himself at times thinking he had taken on too much over the last few years. Probably, the freedom-loving spirit of the outlaw's decrees possessed genuine tenacity and had lost very little potency over time. Kramskoy even started dreaming of an enticing future, of himself altered beyond recognition – renouncing his petty efforts, grasping a secret lever that would allow him to truly contend with the universe. Existing for the moment only in dreams, these pictures could become reality. It was only necessary to cast off the superfluous, to break away from something, to get free of the fetters, chains or – perhaps – someone's clinging fingers. Perceiving them was no easy task; everything came under suspicion. He understood he couldn't get by with a hasty resolution and just get rid of Zhanna Chizhik or Heraldic Inq, casting them down on the virtual altar as a small sacrifice. The issue was deeper and more serious; even the ruling organism had no *a priori* alibi or indulgence. The concept of higher planes might prove to be an unjustified narrowing of perspective, and the "predestination" set for him by someone would then seem a manifestation of those very same fetters and chains.

Of course, going that deep and allowing himself to doubt nearly everything, he mustn't get carried away and burn his bridges over the abyss too soon. Dreams were dreams, but the path to reach them was long. Meanwhile, here were the realities, right under his nose, and dealing with them, he must never lose his level-headedness. Kramskoy reminded himself of this every day before departure, simplifying formulas and avoiding unnecessary pathos. Still, as he approached the train, he determined with a certain solemnity to consider the short trip as his liberation from something, which he would think over at his leisure – both now and later, upon returning to Moscow.

In the compartment, to his great displeasure, Nikolai encountered a group of slightly inebriated men. He greeted them sourly, anticipating a tough night ahead; however, it was soon clear just one of them would be traveling on with him. This fellow was quite sober and the rest were seeing him off to the – as they expressed it – "decisive battle." Kramskoy was informed the man was the director of the Romashka folk band, and that the entire happy throng was, in fact, comprised of the band's singing ensemble. With that, they offered him "cognac" from a suspicious-looking bottle – though not insistently, as everyone else wanted to pour himself another.

"Open a third. Remember St. Pete's? Had to jump off while the train was moving," hooted someone in a low bass behind Nikolai as he fiercely tried to stuff his bag under the bottom bunk. Suddenly, two old women dressed as nuns appeared at the door, astonished at the surplus of cheerful laymen, and the folklorists instantly dropped down, flowed out into the hallway, and made for the exit, conversing for some reason in subdued voices.

Their time to go had already come, however – only a few moments remained before the train pushed off. The passengers on the platform, hastening to their cars, shifted into a half-run along with the porters, who had lost their stuffiness. In the meantime, Alexander Frolov had grown utterly frantic at his post as he tried to guess whether he had missed Elizaveta as she slid artfully behind other people's backs, or whether she had changed her mind about going, or even, perhaps, that thoughtless Margo had mixed something up – intentionally or by accident – which put him on a false trail. He had nearly decided to make a weak move and dial Bestuzheva's number. This was humiliating, but it could clarify the circumstances. Alexander sighed and took the cell from his pocket, but, fortunately, had not punched a single key before he noticed Liza running out of the station. He exhaled deeply, let her pass in front of him, and followed behind without closing in. Suddenly, he became perfectly calm and now had nowhere to hurry.

As for Elizaveta, she was taxed to the limit. Since morning, everything had gone wrong and was slipping from her hands. The last straw was a traffic jam caused by an accident on Tverskaya: she lost it entirely and yelled at the driver, even though it wasn't his fault and there was nothing he could do. As often happens in Moscow, the cars came to a dead halt that seemed endless, but then something shifted, the whole stream began its gradual crawl, and the driver proved resourceful as he squeezed between every crack. "A true Moscow street jockey," he said proudly of himself when it was clear they would make it, and Elizaveta shot him a kind smile. However, it didn't linger on her face for long and was replaced again by an expression of concern and frustration.

She was frustrated mainly with herself, though not for any specific reason. Her anxiety just didn't want to settle down, and no wonder: this Sunday was preceded by some very hectic days. The first warm wave of feelings that had swept over Elizaveta Andreyevna upon reading the romantic letter soon gave way to confusion that swallowed her whole. Thoughts of the happy months she had once spent with Timofey were replaced by memories of hurt – and now it seemed she was ready to explode at the first hint of that distant betrayal. Besides, it soon became clear she remembered Tsarkov quite poorly in comparison to the ill-fated nurse. The nurse had been bronze-haired, buxom, and devilish, inexcusably young in the recollections of seven years hence. So Elizaveta, looking at herself in the mirror, was puzzled as to why Timofey hadn't given word of himself for so long, lingering with indecision and allowing both her youth and his to slip away from them forever.

Tsarkov called that same day, trying to joke around and act natural, but the conversation went badly: she was desperately shy, bound and chained to words, for which she later chided herself mercilessly. He, however, took no offense and immediately dispatched her an e-mail, intending to smooth over the situation. Elizaveta, all aflame, replied with a long, sensual letter – and then wanted to die of shame five minutes after she sent it.

And that's how it continued between them, right up until Sunday. Their moods fluctuated often and were astonishingly incompatible – at least it seemed so to her, and Timofey, try as he might, could simply not predict their bizarre trajectory. She wanted to clarify something for herself in those few days, but there was too little time, and the scattered parts didn't coalesce into one. The answers seemed unclear because the questions themselves interfered with each other. And the main issue got pushed to the back, behind the rest.

Then Elizaveta made a mistake: she told everything to Zoya, her closest friend. Zoya had reconciled with her husband, winning herself and the cat a lot of personal space, and now she looked down her nose at the proceedings.

"He's not going marry you," she snickered.

Elizaveta narrowed her eyes and began saying unsavory things in return. Zoya Klimova only grinned victoriously: her position had no weak spots. Bestuzheva sensed this and took her leave, cursing Timofey and herself as well. That supposed point of support shook like a rickety bridge. All quivered underfoot, and her hands clutched emptiness.

"The world is what's inside me," she repeated to herself and looked around, realizing that no, the world was actually outside, watching her. It watched in scorn and refused to help in any way. It slipped past and gave her nothing, nor would it recognize her at all: in its gaze all interest was lacking. No attentive eye was tracking her; no man, imperceptible as a shadow, followed her anymore – Elizaveta realized she even missed the PI. A nerve stretched between them; there was a connection, an electric prickling – and now nothing was left; the center of gravity had relocated to Sivoldaisk. She thought of her aunt's *voshchanka* and laughed nervously: how does he look now, Defiort? Then she recalled the window display on Solyanka and winced in despair: enough! Here, in this city, are only boring suitors and dead eyeballs!

Finally, Elizaveta accepted the notion of revenge as the safest path from the standpoint of self-assessment. In this game, she had to remain aloof, she admonished herself. He was the one, after all, who wanted her again, and it was up to her to decide whether she would respond in kind. Traveling to see him was worth it, of course – at least to confirm in person that he was still infatuated with her.

Finding that out is always nice – besides, she could turn his head again if it happened that her former charms were not sufficiently strong.

"Having power over a man is such a sweet thing," Elizaveta repeated as a comforting mantra, though she knew at the same time that power has a form but no substance, like all pointless trinkets. One should not rely on it – as one cannot walk on thin glass – but she didn't have a good choice of motivations: the best of them also proved to be somewhat pointless. They were suitable only for thick-skinned Zoya, her cat, and the multitude of those like them. "Indeed, any thought can be completed only in solitude," she said and felt sorry for herself. "Isn't that a reason to go to even the ends of the earth?"

Meditating on revenge was comfortable; intentions came out invulnerable to scorn. But between them, at each step, were secret passages leading to quite different worlds – to thoughts as explosive as gunpowder, and to a total lack of rationality. The doors to these worlds were sealed with sincere effort, but the locks were ready to fall off – she understood this perfectly well, despite being indignant at her own foolishness. And, moreover, what if he needed help? He most probably remembered her at this very moment for a reason, she thought, noting with a certain satisfaction that Tsarkov hadn't managed to find anyone dear to him in all the years they spent apart. Then doubts overwhelmed her again. She remembered the inconstancy of men in general, and in particular recalled that same nurse, coarse and ugly, who probably didn't suspect someone was still thinking of her even now. Finally, the time for departure arrived. Having already ordered a taxi, Elizaveta nearly broke down in tears from incomprehensible fear. And then in the car, helpless in the standstill, she feared most of all missing the Sivoldaisk train.

CHAPTER 12

Frank White's companion in the double compartment turned out to be a plump but energetic middle-aged man. He quickly stowed his belongings, changed into a track suit, carefully hung up his jacket, pants, and shirt, drew the curtain over the window, and buried himself in his newspaper, occasionally scratching and sniffling. Frank, who had intended to enjoy the scenery around Moscow, was annoyed at such presumptuousness but didn't argue, being unsure of train etiquette. He sat staring into space for a bit, then decided he would bring up the issue of the curtain anyway and was just about to speak when a waitress appeared in the doorway to take their orders for dinner, and the situation resolved itself. As his bunkmate was busy with inquiring after the details of the sparse menu, Frank White took advantage of the opportunity to pull the curtain a little to the side and peer through the slit – with a very independent air.

"Well, I've decided," his companion suddenly turned to him. "I'll start with herring under a fur coat, then some goulash, I guess – and *vodotchka*, of course, a hundred and fifty grams or so. How about you? Will you join me?"

This sounded so appetizing that White Jr., who was prepared to make do with just tea because of his fear of poor-quality food, smiled in reply and also requested the herring, the goulash with gravy, and even a little vodka – so as not to miss out. Having finished his order, he caught himself thinking that he already liked the train, the waitress, and even his panting companion. Soon they formally introduced themselves and exchanged business cards, his neighbor's much more impressive than his own.

"Georgi Vladimirovich Samokhvalov, Senior Expert," it read, mysteriously enough. But he added that Frank should just call him Zhora, and launched into telling about his confusing work, which somehow involved squabbles inside the Russian Sports Commission, though Frank was unable to follow the details. But that was not important: his companion Zhora didn't need any interlocutor's support. He heartily chided the thieving officials, who were to blame for the poor performance of the Russian team at the last Olympics. This landed yet another blow against the nation's pride, which was already in dire straits.

Just then the food and vodka arrived. They gulped down a mouthful, after which Zhora cursed mildly and expressed his opinion: to hell with pride. By and large, the problem was not in pride, but rather in the loss of former greatness. It was gone and would probably never come back again. There was only an all-embracing boorishness left that would undoubtedly be there forever.

"What about you, being from far away? What do you think, at first glance?" he asked Frank White, sniffing a crust of dark bread and munching on herring. Frank followed suit and answered in complete honesty that, in fact, he really liked it there, though, of course, he was in no position yet to render any verdict on serious matters.

"You like it, huh?" his neighbor murmured. "What do you like about it then, if you don't mind me asking?"

Frank obediently started listing things and quickly came to Moscow women, which he mentioned with some embarrassment, in spite of the vodka. And here he was forced to be silent again because Georgi Vladimirovich picked up the topic right away and ran with it assertively, managing all the while to eat and drink a little at a time with great pleasure and watching White, Jr. do the same so as not to break the rhythm.

The opinion of Samokhvalov, the senior expert, coincided with White's on the whole, though, not surprisingly, he had substantially more to say on the subject. "The girls in Moscow," he declared with authority, "aren't what they used to be." And he started to explain, even getting a little worked up, "Not – absolutely *not* the same. They're a whole different breed now, as if the ones from the past just vanished or are hiding in a cave somewhere!"

Frank looked astonished and was about to object, but Zhora shook his head vigorously and wouldn't let him break in.

"Of course we know they didn't vanish," he continued a little more calmly. "They've just been locked up like Cinderellas in dungeons and luxury high-rises, in posh restaurants and swanky cocktail parties, one by one or in bunches sometimes. And you tell me, who gains from it – me, or maybe you? No, it's all frustration: the lovely faces disappear. You won't find them on Tverskaya or on Chistoprudny Boulevard anymore. Nothing but farmer daughters there, from poor villages and small, shitty towns. They hide the good ones away, or the girls hide themselves and don't show their faces on the street. They're right, of course, the streets are terrible these days, but it's still a shame. A cryin' shame for the country, I mean. Used to be, you'd go out and there was a gorgeous babe at every turn. But not now: times are changing and bringin' nothin' but grief."

"Though, you know..." and here he took a dramatic pause, raised his shot glass, and winked at White, "you know, the women in Russia are really something! Nothing's left here anymore – only greedy hucksters and thugs of all kinds. Everyone just postures and puts on airs, but the female sex is something extraordinary even still – not counting Moscow, that is. Let's leave out the capital – even though all of them, from the periphery, strive to get there one way or the other. In the rest of Russia, there's a myriad of women. Enough for our lifetime, at any rate."

"Just look how much room there is," he nodded out the window. "How much space, and it's all ours. You can't deny that, even though it's lonely as heck. Bad to be on your own – it's tough, for instance, for you and me, with vodka or without it. And it's the same for any girl – as soon as she reflects on it, she grows sad and gets depressed. But this makes her impulse all the stronger when she decides she's found a kindred spirit! A Russian woman will take any old thing for love – in the wide open spaces one doesn't get too picky – and she'll turn soft, pliable, and generous in her caresses. It may be short-lived, of course, but still…"

"Short-lived?" asked Frank White. Something in Zhora's statements bugged him. He even fidgeted and blinked, trying not to give himself away. Fortunately, his companion was not looking in his direction.

"Well, yeah, everything's just for a little while," Samokhvalov said with a wave of the hand. "Love fades, and passion evaporates into thin air. And there's no magic without passion; in the vast expanses it's nothing but swamps and swarms of mosquitoes. And the forests don't look like fairy-tale woodlands anymore, it's scrub brush and deadfalls at every step. There are no kikimoras to tickle you there, no mermaids, or any other maiden spirits – until you stumble upon some village, and there, perhaps, are just a few old crones. The rest went to the nearest city – to get drunk and screw around. So it is, and you never know in advance – but then a moment comes, and all of a sudden you have your most magical fairy tale!"

"And this is how the Russian girls are," he was nearly whispering. "It's about the only thing not to be ashamed of here. I was in Dusseldorf, lived there for half a year. Man, those German women are something. But ours are better! They're better, hands down!"

They drank to women, and Zhora got serious. "I'll tell you something else," he sighed, looking Frank in the eye. "I'm telling you: there is life here. Dusseldorf, it's all order and cleanliness, but then you come back and see: here, there is life. In the Russian woman, there is life, if you can understand that, of course. And you, I think, you are a man in the know!"

Frank White was a bit embarrassed and began to stutter his objection, but Zhora only half-listened. His vision clouded over; it was obvious his thoughts had transported him somewhere – back to Moscow or to distant Dusseldorf, or to other locales indiscernible from here.

"Me, personally," Zhora said suddenly, interrupting Frank in mid-sentence, "I used to love stout women. The kind with real hips, breasts, butts – the typical Slavic type, you know? It's strange, but that's in the past already – faded away with my youth, and it doesn't attract me anymore. These days, I'm crazy about little girls. There are such tiny little girls out there…"

"No, no, no," he hastened to add, seeing the alarm flash across White's face, "don't get the wrong idea. Not underage ones – some of them are even older than you. But they're still just like toy-breed poodles, miniature puppets. Ah, how alluring they are for me! How different everything is with them, how unusual and fun! And yet, this is a whole big drama of the heart."

He threw back his head, gulped down the final drops of vodka, and turned toward the window. Frank, after a small hesitation, did the same. Outside stretched endless fields as the sun was setting in the clouds, framing their soft edges in flame. Zhora sighed, grazed his cheek with his palm, spun the empty glass in his fingers, and put it on the table.

"A little girl," he began again. "Could be a girl over-thirty two, or even close to forty. Doesn't matter – even though age will creep up on her rapidly at some point. Her time is short, but until it's over, a tiny girl always feels very young. Young and fragile – she senses that, and she tirelessly plays it up. And she can't resist you: you can sense her weakness, her propensity to cry for no reason. She encourages you and surrenders her rights and becomes your obedient shadow… Oh, how quickly you get used to the notion that she belongs to you – even if she doesn't yet. How quickly you convince yourself she's your faithful devotee, your slave, that she thinks of you always, every day and hour. It appears it can't be otherwise: she's fragile and spontaneous, with frog feet and a child's chest. Her every gesture is out in the open – and all her essence is out in the open: it seems to you there's no way for her to put up a fight. But this is a dangerous illusion, and the little ones have a weapon – just one, but it's deadlier than what many others own. It's this: she can say 'No!'"

"Now, that's a fearful blow, a terrible hit, a deafening shot," Samokhvalov bitterly declared and pounded the table with his fist so the plates clinked and a fork fell to the floor. "She knows it, the little cunt. She knows she has no other ammunition and keeps this one in reserve for as long as she can – restraining her curiosity, anticipating her triumph. She nurtures it inside her, spends sleepless nights sensing impending victory – revenge upon the city of men, vengeance against males with their heavy breath, who want absolute power over her puny body – not giving anything in return after sucking her tiny soul dry. That's why she wears a bitchy mask – you cannot survive here without it – but this mask surprises no one, as she can outwit no one with feigned indifference or apathy. Yet she's cleverer than the arrogant or cold ones; she's passing herself off as an obedient little shadow, and then, suddenly, she can endure no more, she just wants too much to see how it turns out. A blade appears from under her corset, that same "*No*" when you least expect it. And celebration comes, a moment, ever so short, for her exultation. Later, of course, it's bad for both of you – and she cries into her pillow, sits alone, and drinks cheap whiskey or some murky concoction. She's also gotten used to you; she warmed up to you like a little doggie. It's hard for her to wean herself away and run off again into the cold. Though her eyes twinkle with a remnant of resolution, what you see there is just bewilderment and sadness. But it's too late: nothing can be changed. She wants to go back, but there's no way back – and the drama unfolds…"

The train drove on at full steam. Something squeaked in the walls, and the car shook as if from an excess of power. It was getting dark outside, and Frank White saw his reflection in the glass. He wasn't drunk but felt strange, as though he was a bystander looking in on himself, on his companion Zhora, and on the whole compartment illuminated by the deathly-pale lamp. The clack of the wheels was calming, as if to inform that nothing bad would happen – not to Frank or to anyone else. His neighbor rose, walked to the mirror and adjusted his hair, then stretched out on his bunk with a crackle, folding his hands behind his head.

"But we have something to say in response," he said firmly, staring at the ceiling. "A man, you know, he's no pitiful little cunt. Nobody can keep up with him – not a tiny girl nor any other wretched creature. Yeah?" he asked, but White was silent, and Zhora nodded complacently, "Yeah, that's it!"

"Now, a woman," he continued with a yawn, "she wants to cling to you; that's her nature. And so she does, and afterward – how's she going to take revenge? She sleeps with others as a protest, but the protest is short and limited. Meanwhile, a man seeks his ideal and may search endlessly. He may have been hurt by a refusal – this means only that the toy-breed poodle in question is not worth another word or look – but the notion of the ideal remains, and much can be devoted to it. Oh, a man can commit a lot to that, more than to any little cunt. For how many more of them are there – with similar names, with the same hair and shape of the eyes... There's such an urge to imagine they're all your obedient shadow! There's such an itch to buy every chick available – and of those there is a legion, an armada. To buy them and give all of yourself away, knowing you are yielding not to them, but to the idea – though they don't understand, as they're incapable of abstract thought. They believe you, these whores who knew hordes of men, they lose their heads in ecstasy, quiver for real, and whisper genuinely, 'You are my only angel...' Ah, what's the use in talking about it!"

He yawned again, closing his eyes, and Frank seized the moment. He grabbed a towel, muttered something, and headed to the lavatory. It grew awkward for him: he feared that, just a little more, and Zhora Samokhvalov would go too far with his revelations. Upon returning, he noted with relief that his bunkmate was sleeping. He turned out the light, undressed, slipped beneath the thin covers, and began pondering Sivoldaisk and Pugachev's hoard. Soon, his thoughts turned, as they had on the plane, to the money to come and ways of spending it. "The Frank White, Jr. Award," thought White, Jr. with a pleasant rush of excitement. But here he restrained himself, not wanting to get carried away.

This was his private dream, the whim of his mysterious American soul. Several years ago, he had firmly decided to establish a charity for the mathematicians of the country that would help him to get rich. Now it seemed that fate was going to choose Russia, and that was the most appropriate outcome. Many nuances melded into one, including the school with its special emphasis, though that emphasis left no trace and didn't incline Frank toward a love for the exact sciences. Much more could be said of the light romanticism of Russian books and the atmosphere of Muscovite life at that time. They somehow nurtured this idea in the back alleyways of his mind, connecting it to the science that was ultimately exact. For some reason, Frank was convinced that mathematics in its academic form, stripped of all pragmatism and full of severe beauty, could become the last stronghold of impracticality. Which, he felt with all his heart, had to be preserved in some form, even if the rest of humanity was utterly indifferent to the matter.

The decision to create the charity was bold – or, at least, so it seemed to him. Making it was facilitated by a newspaper interview in which Axel Timurov, wishing to show off, announced their company's intention to hire a large group of mathematicians – no less than forty. Knowing Axel, Frank knew he meant no harm by it but had merely blurted out the first thing that popped into his head. However, all the mathematicians for miles around Washington, D.C., took the notice at face value and besieged their office for several weeks to demonstrate their professional prowess.

They turned out to be hungry, unsettled and irascible, awkward in conversation, and enormously unneeded. They sent letters and faxes, inundated the company with calls and unannounced visits. Axel took cover behind White's back, who, besides other things, was in charge of hiring. It was a tough challenge, but White stood his ground and beat back the attacks, repeating with some astonishment time and again that, unfortunately, they had no vacancies left to fill. At first, the applicants didn't believe him and demanded to know the names of the lucky contenders who had gotten the jobs. Others even tried ineptly to manipulate, blushing in desperation and hiding their eyes – but eventually, they all accepted the inevitable, as they had done many times before, and agreed with Frank there had been an error, and they were not wanted there, just like everywhere else. The most active of them, a forty-year-old tensor field expert, called a couple of times more and even warmly wished Frank a happy Independence Day, but ultimately even he disappeared, admitting the futility of his efforts. And White, Jr., breathing a sigh of relief, promised himself he would deal with setting up the charity as soon as he acquired some real capital.

The clack of the wheels made it easy to think of his future wealth, and soon Frank White drifted off to sleep despite his neighbor's snoring. Life aboard the train marched to its own beat, as it had for countless years, night after night. In the doorway, a drunk, discharged soldier smoked in solitude. Not far away, an elderly accountant expressed his affection to the female conductor, who had long since wearied of words. Meanwhile, her chubby coworker, after bringing tea to the passengers and smiling at all in turn, was sweating and huffing in the arms of the pockmarked ensign she had put in her lonely berth at the Mikhailov station.

Frank dreamed of little girls with the wrinkled faces of old crones, followed by all kinds of horrors. This caused him to cry out and twitch on his narrow bunk so that he barely avoided falling to the floor. At times his hand grazed the small table, and the dishware left over from the evening hummed like a naval bell. At this, Georgi Vladimirovich Samokhvalov would croak in a hoarse voice, "Come on now, take it easy," but he wouldn't stop snoring or open his eyes.

Even worse than Frank slept Nikolai Kramskoy – as he always did on trains. On this occasion, he had also abused alcohol, staying up past midnight with the director of the folk ensemble, so he now suffered a headache and tried to subdue his incoherent thoughts. It was embarrassing to recall that while still in the Paveletsky station, he had pledged to himself not to engage in protracted road discussions or late-night drinking.

When the train had disembarked, Nikolai was sober and still

resolute in his prudence. After exchanging brief pleasantries with his
bunkmates, he went out into the hallway and stood at the window
for a full hour, his forehead pressed against the cold glass. The view
didn't cheer him; the city's outskirts made a sorry spectacle. Along
the landscape stretched the catacombs of abandoned factories from
the Soviet era – as if to underscore the futility of the endeavors once
undertaken here for naught. They gaped in ruins of crumbling walls,
the detritus of construction, rusted conveyer belts – the backdrop
to a bad movie about the horrors of the technocratic age. It seemed
the train was creeping over the terrain of an alien planet, but when
Moscow had been left behind, it became clear: no, the planet is the
same, only the country is probably different – it's unrecognizable
for some reason. The city ended, and civilization ended with it. All
that remained were traces of barbarians and Huns – their fire pits
and wrecked huts, strange tools and half-rotten pelts. Rust again
reigned over all: old machinery abandoned by some enemy, doors
falling from the hinges of box-shaped garages, and other junked iron
in the gutters and ditches. The earth was covered with wounds from
a fierce battle between man and nature, a war not for life but to the
death, where man, it seemed, had been forced to retreat.

Then everything changed in an instant – as if the train had
suddenly crossed the front lines. Fields and groves began; the colors
faded, but this cleaned up the perspective. The horizon extended to
infinity; all the reference points disappeared, and Nikolai Kramskoy,
forgetting his recent irritation, reflected then and there on the
boundless expanse of space, as a great many of his countrymen had
done before him. Like all of them, he vaguely sensed that what he
saw from the window exceeded the limits of comprehension; and
therefore, no matter how he tried to capture it, the essence of the
question eluded him, just as it eluded all.

"This is why Russians have no true rules," he thought, gloomily
furrowing his brows. "There's nothing here but inexpressibility and
sorrow. Though it would seem clear: harmony lives in nature, it's
the name by which God is called in the rustic lands. Yet out there
it's too abundant – that's why they fight against it and try to take

revenge. You have to travel abroad to understand and long for your homeland. In other countries all is meted out little by little – not enough to adjust your inner tuning fork. Only upon returning will it resonate again without false notes. Could this be what poets mean when they say, 'Here the soul is opening up?'"

"Shame on you!" Kramskoy chided himself. "You're constantly being drawn to clichés. Just like the others: everyone's reflections reveal hastiness and the impotence of formulations. Any country could be proud of its limitless vastness. Any except this one: people here don't know how to be proud of anything, and perhaps they never did. Where there's a lot of space, there's free will and farsightedness, but there's also no respite and an eternal restlessness, which results in universal sadness. The excessiveness of scale is not the easiest thing to cope with, especially for immature minds. And here all minds are as immature as everywhere else – why would they be any different?"

For some reason, Kramskoy became uncomfortable. He rubbed the scar on his cheek as a secret, somewhat embarrassing talisman, but this didn't help in the least. The city, that greedy specter, released him from the labyrinth where he was wont to wander. The thin threads ripped one by one, and the universe doffed its mask. Nikolai suddenly felt that his thoughts were thinning out, preparing to grasp a lot at once – and there was no one with whom to share them. This, it seemed to him in a flash, was the true essence of freedom. Could it be, in these expanses, no matter how great they were, no place had been readied for him? He had escaped from a kingdom of iron where he barely managed to carve a niche for himself. But could it be his salvation lay in returning as soon as possible?

"Indeed," Kramskoy shook his head, "I'm up for any kind of nonsense. The issue isn't so much about liberation, so why am I clinging to it like to a familiar fetish? 'And whoso doth now receive this mercy, to him I grant the freedoms of the Cossacks forever...' This is all just a decoy for fools who don't pay attention to what words mean. Even with Pugachev, for all his intransigent pathos, the main thing was not freedom, but a daring goal. Of course, in this bedlam outside the window no daring feat could be born – that's why he knocked about with restlessness: as a tramp day-laborer, a fishmonger, a renegade from Polish lands. If he hadn't landed in prison, and from there, almost by mistake, fallen into the hands of the Yaik rebels, maybe nothing exceptional would have happened – the authorities would just have flogged him and exiled him to Siberia. But he did end up that way – first in jail, then falling in with a gang of insurgents – and he recognized a demon inside himself and got carried away on black wings promising imminent liberty, though bound hand and foot by his own courage.

Nikolai sighed with a frown. "Daring goal," he mocked himself. "Will someone please tell me why I'm really going to Sivoldaisk?"

Behind him, a door opened. Kramskoy, as though caught unaware, hunched his shoulders and tried to assume a drowsily bored air. From the compartment exited his bunkmate in sweatpants and a T-shirt; coughing loudly, he stood nearby.

"*Russia, the magnificent vastness,*" he quoted, peering through the glass. "An evil lot and an ailing will. Or perhaps large lands made for small lives, meaninglessness on parade. Of course, it's wrong to laugh at that. You know," he turned to Nikolai, "I could never figure out what best characterizes provincial existence: is it laziness, envy, or the neglect of details? How 'bout you, now? What would you say on that score?"

"I'm mostly in Moscow," Kramskoy responded without turning his head. "It's rather hard for me to judge."

"It's tough for me too," his companion concurred, "though I get around, in Moscow and everywhere else. Actually, we're from Voronezh, but we got stuck in the capital. In the meantime, I go to Balakovo, for money. That's a long story," he waved his hand. "My name's Murzin, by the way. Savelly Savellievich Murzin. How about getting some dinner?"

Nikolai was going to flatly refuse, but, like Frank White, he somehow couldn't find the strength. The wheels knocked rhythmically, lulling his consciousness; the world seemed unreal, and any decisiveness felt inappropriate. He gave his own name in reply and soon found himself sitting in the dining car opposite Savelly Savellievich, who, without much ado, had thrown his suit coat right over his T-shirt. Between them, against all resolve, mischievously gleamed a crude decanter.

"You look like an intelligent man," his companion pronounced, downing his first shot. "You understand the concept: laziness, envy, inattention to details. I think the predominant factor is what comes last here, like in any list. From neglect of details arise all troubles, disarray, and blindness of thought. Yet it may be of different kinds, neglect. It can be forgiven, if its cause is an internal craving that devours all energy, leaving no resource for specifics, trifles. If inside is all perpetual heat and hard work – whether it's the work of the mind or, let's say, the soul…"

The train reduced speed and the brakes sang out a plaintive song of the East, like Bashkirs on bowlegged steeds or Tatars with razor-sharp sabers. "Yes, indeed," Nikolai interrupted, "no resource is left at all. That's what leads to the propensity for unworthy generalizations. Hasty deductions for no reason – they're way too naïve, but there's no remedy. When the massive scales weigh upon you, all you can do is invent nonsense, to save or else to forget yourself."

He felt a sudden urge and reached for the decanter of vodka. Savelly Savellievich joined in; they drank their second shots and began to argue about the work of the soul – as if this particular question had been occupying their thoughts in recent years. The man from Voronezh possessed a nimble mind. Persuading him was not easy, but Kramskoy too was able to find holes in seemingly flawless arguments; so the conversation became lively and even took on some uneasy undertones. Eventually, however, the interlocutors got used to each other and started to reach a consensus. Besides, the decanter gradually emptied, adding to their mutual empathy; so they quickly uncovered the heart of the matter and concluded the question was reduced to the *languishing of the psyche*, which is usually regarded as personal depth, but only suitable for justifying heavy boozing.

"The problem is that people want to comprehend the

incomprehensible," Savelly Murzin maintained, and Kramskoy could offer no objection, especially since this was compatible with the boundless spaces and limitless scales. He still asserted, for his part, that it was better to try anyway than not to think of anything at all; though he agreed with his companion that such attempts, as a rule, were useless and didn't alter the course of one's life.

"They merely distract you from your work – that's why all around is squalor and poverty," the folklorist advised. They became despondent for a moment but then undertook to convince each other that it was worth paying for freedom of spirit with a wretched lifestyle. "And if they don't understand this in some places," Savelly nodded toward the sun setting in the West, "it's just because their spirit has long been bound and free thought has died out as a phenomenon!"

The conversation unfolded in the usual fashion, without deviating from tradition. Soon, the topic turned to the national identity and its quintessence, which was facilitated by the view of rolling forests outside the window. They complained in unison that it was now commonplace to decry it, although this notion, like nothing else, had for centuries been nourishing all who were not lax in spirit – even at the expense of attention to details.

"Oh, yes," Kramskoy affirmed and cautiously expressed what had just come to mind: was there a rationale behind it, perhaps? Couldn't there be a geomagnetic anomaly in the middle of the Central Russian Plain that's responsible for the properties in question? And if so, then Russia is a sanctuary for the whole world, and everyone who comes here senses that for himself.

This thought was met with great enthusiasm, particularly since the waitress brought more vodka and the second course. Murzin eagerly agreed with Nikolai and even developed the idea by saying that detection and research about the anomaly should soon be made a worldwide project. He even mentioned UNESCO as an appropriate institution for such an effort, but with that they were slightly flummoxed and grew silent in embarrassment, somehow feeling they had gone too far.

"Our mind is weak, after all," sighed Savelly Savellievich. "We are inept when trying to interpret intricate matters. Thus, we are drawn to attribute them either to fairy tales or to completely ordinary factors. However, there still might not even be words for what is yet to be understood!"

It suddenly darkened outside. The train sped through the night, as if propelled by a mysterious force. The two men were somewhat drunk and filled with the deepest mutual trust. Patriotism started seeming uninteresting and trivial to both – the essence was not in that, but was buried deeper. Without agreeing to it beforehand, and imbued with solidarity, they began to grumble about the Fatherland. Soon they were blaming it for each and every sin, trying merely to avoid falling into overly trite banalities.

"They say, those boring, boring nations – like Germans, for instance, or Swedes – they don't even drink vodka or make a ruckus off schedule," folk artist Savelly complained, gesticulating with his shot glass. "Well, as far as vodka goes, the Swedes can also chug it like nobody's business. But, for me, a schedule and boredom is better than morose, moronic bravado. You know, Russians don't have a model of happiness – no one's figured out how to knock it into our heads. After the Soviet state collapsed, our sense of happiness disappeared. Everyone muses in solitude – and what is an average man capable of devising? Only something worthless and inconsistent to boot – no comparison with a competent ideologue or a spe-ci-a-list in general!" He nodded meaningfully, and Nikolai did exactly the same. "So it turns out that these pigs – be they Germans or Swedes – they have their little program near at hand. They can peek at it every moment and always know what to shoot for. They get brainwashed at an early age, and for the average Westerner, it's nothing but a benefit. But here everyone marches to his own drum and cacophony results, making the ears bleed!"

They glumly poured and drank another without clinking glasses. On the table, the fake flowers shook their leaves in time with the wheels. Their plastic petals gyrated in place in the hope of impregnating anything at all, yet being utterly impotent. The waitress came, gathered up the dishes, and glanced at the half-empty decanter as she put another basket of bread on the table.

"Could you grab us some pickles?" Savelly asked her, then turned to Nikolai and continued, "Yeah, I know I'm not entirely correct. There is a plus, in the same vein: the Russians have many dissimilar models, and diversity is a big deal. But as you study that positive side and get a closer look, you just want to chuck it all: the diversity boasts almost no actual differences. They're nearly invisible; it's all just idiocy, then the same idiocy and dreariness. Nobody jumps out of their skin or looks past their nose. How do you move them or stir them up? I can't tell you, and neither can anyone else. What do we do to open the floodgates? I know drugs break all the dams down, but you can't force everyone to get doped up. Vodka opens the floodgates, but vodka makes them drop like flies; they can't work and are drunk down to the last man. Love opens floodgates – yeah, it's a super-powered hallucinogen; it clarifies your thoughts and pushes you up to the sky. But love is not bestowed upon all; it's hardly granted to anyone, to be honest. Care for another shot?"

Kramskoy drank another shot and felt drunk. "I have a model for happiness," he said with slurred speech, "but it wouldn't make anyone happy, I'm afraid. I haven't been given the gift of love – I know I'm not capable of it, and I don't need it: I'm against hallucinations. I've had the chance to see those who have it. As a rule, theirs is a miserable fate."

"Come on," Savelly Savellievich frowned, "what does fate have to do with it? Love almost doesn't exist anymore – it's all lies and utter laziness. The weariness of life, that is our lot; and meanwhile, the West is invigorated and rushes ahead. Here they don't even come out for folk performances," he complained. "Though I've been told they don't go for them in Europe either. There's only one hope: literature. And there's only one big problem: life passes too quickly. What about you? Do you suffer from the weariness of life?" he asked, and Nikolai affirmed with passion that no, he didn't, as if this harbored some shameful significance.

They each chewed a pickle, and Savelly confessed he didn't suffer either, though people considered him to be a very reserved guy. At that, he leaned across the table and, lowering his voice, declared he was prepared to share a certain secret discovery with Nikolai. Kramskoy informed him in reply that he also had a secret to disclose, but the time had not yet come to share it – and this had been met by his companion with complete understanding and even enthusiasm.

"Don't," he said with conviction. "Don't until the right time. But I had no doubt you bore something like that in mind. Because," he switched to a whisper, "because you're one of *us!*" Then Savelly Savellievich made a sly face, glanced to each side, and added, "We're just a different species!"

"Yes, yes, yes," he started to assert ardently when he noted Nikolai looked mistrustful and was in no hurry to agree. "I know, it's been explained to me. A certain biologist, a spe-ci-a-list with security clearance, related the details – just like that, on the train en route from Barnaul. The whole issue, it turned out, was in the genes: they are identical, but not exactly. There's always a small difference – and at first no one wanted to take it seriously. But now they've taken a closer look, and *voila*: almost every gene has points of dissimilarity. They're called SNPs – I committed the name to memory – and it's interesting that a vast majority of people have divergences in the same spots. This explains everything, I knew at once – as soon as I heard about the majority – because for some people the divergences are distributed differently. Their SNPs are incorrect, uncommon, not the same as others have – and such an unfortunate person may suffer his whole life, tormented by the imperfection of the world, while his associates don't notice a thing. That's no surprise: it's not written on his forehead whether he has the right SNPs or not. Whether he's normal or, like you and I, in a certain sense, a freak."

"Genes... SNPs..." Nikolai thoughtfully repeated, and then he felt agitated and began to rub his temples. The words of his companion seemed filled with deep meaning, and even the vague shadow of the universal organism appeared to flash before the window. Maybe something will emerge right here – a path, a hint, an answer might appear – he thought nervously, and then, trying to keep a grip on himself, muttered out loud, "I wonder, does this have something to do with metabolism?"

"Everything has to do with metabolism," Savelly Murzin waved his hand at him. "Believe me, I'm well informed in that area. Anyway, it's quite easy to imagine how this SNP screw-up happened at one time – you don't even need any specific expertise. Look: the pithecanthropes had a tiny brain that only increased by a few milligrams in a millennium – this didn't allow them much, maybe just enough to wield a club. That's not evolution, it's mockery: a hundred thousand years – imagine it – a hundred thousand and no tangible results. But then someone, for no apparent reason, scribbles a picture with soot on a cave wall and bang: the border line is drawn. A new species is on the scene – because the old ones would never do such a thing. Don't confuse this change with the advent of *homo sapiens*. *Homo sapiens* is too general of a term, an unworthy generalization. The new mix with the old, they pair off regardless of the genes, just because of sexual attraction – really, unrestrained morals interfere terribly with genetic purity. But all the same, SNPs tell no lies: it seems the wheat has been mixed with the tares, but no, the whole truth is encoded in the sequences of nucleotides. And all who understand think to themselves: ah, what a shame! What a pity, they lament, that this truth is accessible only to a narrow circle – the ones with the test tubes and electron microscopes. But I know: it's so, yet it's not quite so. There is a discriminator..." Savelly looked around again, extended his hands, and whispered triumphantly, "*Our* people are the ones bothered by *the question*."

They drank the rest of their vodka and were now finishing the bread with pickles. The folk artist's eyes shone excitedly, and red spots stood out on his face. "The question has long been known," he murmured, looking Nikolai in the eye. "Yet for the majority it's simply white noise: not that it doesn't bother them – it doesn't even register. But the others, with their different SNPs, immediately become alert. 'For what is the mind predestined?' they ask themselves several times a day. 'What's the essence of all intentions, the arrogant attempts to get a hold on life, which merely make it worse for everyone since you can't alter the outcome?' The sense of the possibility of searching for sense: the question is fixed in a loop, and we can't break free of that loop – including those who seek answers. And those who don't are protoplasm, building material – what a pity for them, the miserable ignoramuses!"

"There's not so few of *us* as you might think," he whispered, leaning on the table. "Especially in infancy, when the page is blank and vision is unclouded. Later, their sense is confused – by mothers, grandparents, models of happiness. Of course, diversity plays into our hands: dissociation of opinions, the fragile parchment – this isn't Western-style reinforced concrete. Therefore, there should be more of *us* in Russia – this is the place to look. You know what I mean," he grinned, pointing out the window. "So long as brainiacs from abroad don't bring in their fucking models."

"Aha," Kramskoy nodded thoughtfully. Savelly crumbled the bread with his fingers and muttered in umbrage, "We'll see, in any case. All accounts will be settled in the future, mark my words: it's already moving in that direction. One big zoo – civilization mashed together with wild beasts, tribes alien to us, savage and stupid. And where the zoo is, there will the cages be. It's just not certain who's in the cages and who's outside, but that's a matter of personal perception. Either way, *our* people will unite, on one side of the bars or the other. You and I will see, though the rest might not even notice it!"

They left late, rocking from the sway of the car, and reached their compartment, content from the evening they had spent, but in the morning they avoided eye contact with each other. The night was stuffy; lightning flashed in the distance but yielded no rain. Nikolai lay awake for a long while, musing on Murzin and SNPs. It was clear: whatever he thought of his bunkmate, no message had arrived for him from a higher power as yet.

The conductor who woke them two hours prior to arrival was, for some reason, scowling and unfriendly. A long line formed for the bathroom, and though the day had hardly begun, it was shaping up to be tiresome and ungainly. The thrifty nuns fed Savelly hard-boiled eggs and gave him a piece of a pie for his tea. As for Nikolai, he declined breakfast, went into the hall, and then even relocated to the neighboring car. There, bothered by no one, he stood all the way to Sivoldaisk – feeling old, as often happens after a night of drinking.

CHAPTER 13

In dusty haze and yellow smoke, noiseless as a morning phantasm, the Moscow train approached the station. Timofey Tsarkov paced the platform with one hand behind his back, the other awkwardly squeezing a bouquet of bright red roses. He was immaculately shaven and well dressed, a little nervous and angry at himself for it. But it seemed impossible to get a grip; his heart pounded in his chest and his palms were conspicuously damp.

"Just like a teenager, wet around the ears," Timofey muttered aloud and glanced at the station clock, noting mechanically that the train was nearly on time. It occurred to him he had wandered just like this beneath many clocks, around monuments and squares, his hands folded behind his back, anxious and murmuring to himself, waiting for that same woman in a different time that had heedlessly slipped away. Young Liza Bestuzheva he remembered well and didn't doubt he would now recognize her even without the pictures provided by the private eye who had successfully implemented the Moscow-based preliminary phase. She seemed nearly the same in them – only her hairdo had changed, and her eyes had become more derisive. Years before, at twenty-one, she wore a short bob, was full of smiles, limber and slender, and her body smelled of something flowery – either jasmine or delicate rose oil.

"She's probably put on some weight now," Tsarkov thought with a sigh and recalled with displeasure that he himself had gained no less than eleven pounds since that same time. Then his thoughts became confused and succumbed again to frivolous romantic mores. He remembered how, in revenge for some trivial remark, he told her he had always preferred brunettes over blondes because they were brighter and stood out in a crowd. The following day she came to class with her hair tinted black and looked at him fixedly, staving off inappropriate jokes with her gaze, as if to insinuate, "You see what I'm prepared to do for you?" Dark hair looked awful on her; the two of them skipped the lecture and scoured all of Moscow in search of a special product to neutralize the dye. Then he assisted her in the bathroom as she nervously giggled and kept asking, "Is it turning green? Is it turning green?" because the dye was cheap and might give unexpected results. Then they laughed in the mirror and made love under the shower – to the great embarrassment of another Tsarkov, his cousin, who was visiting Moscow at the time. Cloistered in the kitchen, he had to turn the radio up full blast...

This cousin, the son of the uncle from the Urals who had gotten rich as a pawnbroker, was one of the causes, albeit unintentional, of the car accident story that eventually led to Timofey treading along the Sivoldaisk platform with flowers. On that ill-fated day he was driving back home, rejoicing at unloading a tiresome burden after seeing his guest off on the Ekaterinburg train. The cousin came to Moscow a few times a year. They didn't get along well, yet Tsarkov tolerated his presence since he had no other relatives but his uncle's family. His parents had perished shortly after he returned from the army, somewhere outside Krasnoyarsk in a mysterious railway accident that got not a word of mention in the press. On that occasion he was visited by a morose grey-headed man who flashed him a KGB badge and said some consoling words with a serious, alert look. Timofey asked questions but the man only responded with a sigh and a calming pat on the shoulder. Then, over the course of three weeks, the agency paid him a considerable compensation and its people came over a couple of more times to make him sign a lot of papers concerning nondisclosure of something that was entirely beyond his comprehension.

Tsarkov didn't mourn his parents long – they had never been close, and, once he grew up, he was alienated from them completely. His father drank a lot and sometimes got violent, being intolerant of youthful fashions, and his mother maintained a separate life, fooling around on the side, as he now understood. The family was held together only by visits from the Volga Khazars, as his father sullenly called Grandma and Grandpa, his mother's parents who lived in Elista, a city of great winds that smelled of koumiss and the dust of the steppe. His grandmother was half Kalmyk and his grandfather descended from the Don Cossacks who had once been driven from their lands and settled on the other side of the Volga. He wandered a lot and was a boisterous carouser and fighter in his youth; nowadays he still blackened his mustache with old German coloring and put a thin strip of birch bark inside his boots to produce a telltale creak. He traveled to Altai and to the Astrakhan floodplains, to the heart of Ukraine and to the Central Asian desert, to the forested Ural foothills and to the distant northern lands of which he spoke grudgingly and unkindly. In Kazan, the Tatars taught him to hunt wolves from horseback using just a whip with an iron pellet at the end; Novgorod's monks once nearly castrated him for heresy; and in arid Aralkum, he had almost perished after getting lost, riding his horse to death, and being left without a drop of water. His favorite activity was hunting with falcons, and Timofey recalled how his grandfather read to him from Dahl, "A falcon takes not his prey from the ground, but in flight he strikes, flying under a bird and forcing it aloft. Always he strikes below the left wing, thrusting his claw and slicing like a knife..."

By thirty-five, he settled down and began contemplating a successor. Taking a look around, he set his eye on beautiful Elena, the daughter of a merchant manufacturer considered to be an established man throughout the area. Once he turned his bride's head, he stole her away from her unconsenting parent and eloped a hundred miles from Elista, where distant relatives of the maiden were living. Faced with the facts, the merchant deemed it best to forgive the young couple, and they soon returned to the city to spend their entire lives there. Elena loved his grandfather with heavy-handed Russian love: she gave him no freedom and kept close tabs on him, but was devoted absolutely and would have gone without question to the ends of the earth if the former restlessness could have been awakened in him again.

An heir was not produced for a long time, despite the advice of local doctors and their own prayers, but then Elena did somehow bear a daughter when they had all but given up hope. With their arrival, a fragile peace and a certain comfort settled upon Timofey's family. The father feared Grandfather, who did not abide *horilka*, and the mother blossomed and gorged the family on every imaginable tasty treat. After Timofey's parents died, the grandparents came to see him one time, but they were not the same anymore, growing suddenly very old; and then they both expired in a single year not long before he met Liza. He grieved for them sincerely, musing more than once that he wanted the same kind of wife for himself as his grandfather's Kalmyk Elena – and so in Elizaveta, perhaps, he most appreciated her integrity and devotion. But then, after the car accident and his fleeing the capital, he had no time to think of marriage – until a threat loomed on the horizon in the form of the obsessed predator Maya.

Timofey ran his handkerchief across his forehead one last time, straightened his tie, and adjusted his grip on the bouquet whose roses were indistinguishable from the ones used to commence his hunt. "Like a bridegroom, really!" he thought with hostility. He was increasingly feeling disoriented; the thought even flashed in his mind that this was all nonsense, a waste of effort, utter foolishness, not a serious idea at all. But there was no retreat – the train slowed down, clanged, and halted. The conductress of car eight flung the door open without delay, and passengers emptied through the portal. Elizaveta was the fifth. Due to some sudden superstition, he counted those disembarking – guessing a totally different number in advance.

She was fresh and upright in her bearing and looked younger

than her years. Tsarkov cursed himself with the strongest words, imploring his consciousness to relax at last, took a step toward her, gave her a peck on the cheek with quite an impudent smile, and proffered the flowers while simultaneously attempting to take her luggage.

"Let's deal some dope for cash like a couple of hoods," he quipped clumsily as he slung her bag over his shoulder. "Well, hello!"

"Well, hello!" Elizaveta matched his tone. She smelled the roses with pleasure and kissed him thank you in return. Then she looked him in the eyes with a smile no less impudent and slightly provocative.

Compared to yesterday's stress, her condition was close to serene. The road had calmed her – with its monotonous landscapes, smooth passage of time, and the sense that all decisions had been made and nothing depended on her anymore. Her compartment mate happened to be a quiet old man who didn't ask questions or engage in conversation. He merely blinked half-blindly, then lay down, covering his face with his newspaper, and thus, under the paper, fell asleep. She kept looking out the window and thinking to herself – not of the impending meeting, but of her childhood for some reason: of summer trips to the Crimea in noisy, talkative third-class, where her father played chess with his neighbors and ran for beer to the station buffets while she watched him, frowning angrily under the fear he might get lost. Then there was university and the sports camp on the Azov – also third-class and light wine under the clack of the wheels. Then – and this was funnier – a posh Berlin train and a suave admirer with a sad face...

The expanses outside the window and the symbols of the fatherland – birch trees, endless fields, bright red clusters of rowan berries – angel blood made into water – did not excite her soul and even irritated her at first. The landscape was too dispassionate, and the fading pasturelands seemed to flaunt their innocence, like a virgin waiting to be ravished. But who knows what goes on in a virgin's mind? Elizaveta chuckled mirthlessly. It appeared that the massive heavens and earth extending into the void stretched toward each other, squeezing out the air – so you catch yourself thinking, after having a look around, that it's probably tough to breathe around here.

"They close in from both sides and sap your strength," she thought, propping her chin on her hands. "This is the vengeance space takes against those who have no love for it, while for some it is a reward and for others a panacea. Life can't break away from the surface but enters it, submerging, nearly smashed flat. The elements of nature, they arose long before man and remained the same as they always were – soulless, knowing neither pity nor warmth. A panacea for the desperate, for those alone, without faith… This place is full of poverty, and no one bothers about it: no point in trying and exerting effort when you're weighed down with the heaviest of mantles. What clouds! They may be pretty, but life beneath them is no picnic. No room for comfort here – too much flat earth and sky!"

The outside world didn't cohere into a whole as it crept to the horizon and beyond, past the limits of sight, and this was strange to her, a city-dweller used to having defined boundaries and reference points for every occasion. The capital, a symbol of verticality, had disaccustomed her to spaces yawning into the broad yonder where nothing caught your eye. But then she got used to it and even began to find in the boundlessness a certain charming despair that at times is so appealing to the female heart, like the justification of self-pity and impending tears. The provincial towns also amused her as the rapid train zipped past without slackening its pace. Stations bore simple names – Malinovka, Khokhlovka, Belotserkovets. Elizaveta hadn't heard of these places, and the words themselves were unfamiliar, as if she were trying to comprehend a new language. She got caught up in this, not even thinking of Sivoldaisk and the possible change in her life. Only when the Orthodox domes flashed by the window did she remember about Tsarkov, asking herself with a bit of irony whether he'd propose a church wedding and how she'd look in a snow-white dress before the altar.

Exiting the train and seeing him in his stylish shirt and matching tie, Elizaveta realized they hadn't quite gotten over each other. She felt attracted to Timofey, finding he had become more serious and firm without losing his former charm. She glided easily across the platform and smiled, hiding her face in the roses, while Tsarkov cracked jokes incessantly to keep from yielding ground to the remnants of his confusion that wouldn't go away.

"Want to cruise by my place to stow your stuff?" he asked, looking at her as he reached into his pocket for his key ring.

Elizaveta nodded in reply, thinking, "I wonder if he's going to come on to me right away. Better to hang back a little – everything's still a bit strange."

They went to a large Jeep Cherokee, and Tsarkov opened the front door for her.

"Your car's pretty dusty," she teased.

"Well, yeah," said Timofey with false remorse. "Careful not to smudge yourself, city slicker. This here's the sticks we're in." He got in next to her and muttered in a subdued voice, *"Our town's truly great, only the streets are filthy. Our boys are really kind, only their fists are itching..."* Then he grimaced, Elizaveta laughed, and they unhurriedly began to pull away from their parking spot into the bustling street.

Bathed in sun, yellow and decayed, eroded and astonishingly old-fashioned, Bestuzheva liked Sivoldaisk. At first glance, it was terrible; at second, it had no place for any kind of life at all. But soon, her eyes got used to the fake décor. Masonry poked through the carelessly slapped-on plywood, and the drawings covering it fell away to reveal a city frozen in its own time, as if to spite the inept owners. They sped past the former royal stables, which had become a hangout for local skinheads, past the library and semi-dilapidated church, past Emperor Nikolai University and – across from it – the Academy for the Ministry of Internal Affairs with a bunch of sweaty, ruddy-faced cadets circling around it. Timofey piloted the Jeep confidently and insolently, scaring off the rusted midget cars, and chattered nonstop like a real guide.

"Check out the facades," he said to Elizaveta, "they're intact;

they haven't collapsed, even though no one's repaired them for a hundred years. Just imagine, the nineteenth century! Nothing's changed, and moreover, here you can breathe easy, though everyone around trashes the place."

Liza obediently twirled her head and inhaled with her nose to smell the air that reeked of gasoline, just as it did in Moscow. Meanwhile, Tsarkov, without looking at the road, was already telling her, "Look, look: all the courtyards are real slums. Just walk through any gate – you'll discover a sight right out of a horror movie. Some houses are totally wrecked – the renovation money was stolen long ago, and nobody gives a flip anymore. Though, you know, every square inch of land in Sivoldaisk costs an insane amount of money," he added with a snicker, and it was unclear whether he was joking or serious. "I've lived here for seven years already, and I don't regret it one bit!"

Tsarkov wasn't certain himself whether he was twisting the truth – the city had definitely gotten on his nerves, but he could really breathe easier here, though he couldn't explain why. "Scope out the park," he pointed. "They have fairs there on Saturdays. It's pretty cool – they bring real clowns, and there are even bears on parade."

Elizaveta laughed, cocking her head, "Yeah, right. I don't believe it!"

"Come on, trust me," Timofey was indefatigable. "And besides – soon we'll be scoping out the Volga, that's the main attraction. We'll have a blast, I promise – on a good, fast boat. Or just on a beach, having a swim."

"A swim? You mean skinny-dipping?" she asked mischievously, remembering their nocturnal sorties at someone's dacha on a manmade lake.

Timofey laughed, turning through an archway into a courtyard with a rubbish heap in the middle, "Sure, if you like. We're laid back around here. *Better for us both to drown than to get shot!*"

They drove up to a cluster of expensive cars packed in helter-skelter next to a new nine-story apartment building and picked their way with difficulty to the entrance, circumventing a pile of construction debris. Then they ascended to the top floor, and he triumphantly flung open the heavy steel door in front of her: "Be my guest!"

Once inside, they were both suddenly reserved and kept their distance as they avoided looking at each other. Elizaveta threw the bag in her room, which had a separate bathroom, adjusted her hair in the mirror, sighed deeply, and walked through the apartment, all the while feeling his presence nearby. It turned out to be a nice flat, and she thought in passing there were probably few like it in this city. Furniture was in short supply, and everything smacked of an official air, but this could be attributed to the lack of a woman's touch.

"So," she summarized as she converged on Timofey in the kitchen, "it has a lot of space, which testifies to a potential lust for life. Without me around, were you just dying from longing?"

"All kinds of stuff happened," Tsarkov replied, examining the contents of the fridge. "But I'm still alive, as you can see. *A man doesn't die of despair; he just dries up.*"

"Aha, you have proverbs for every occasion!" she said as if she had unraveled some riddle, and then asked demandingly, "Well, what's the program? I have no doubt you've planned everything out in advance, right?"

"I've planned a bit," Timofey sighed with complete sincerity. "But my head's filled with you, for some reason. Whatever I planned, I forgot about straightaway. Let's go for a ride. We'll catch a bite to eat, then maybe hit the office."

"Let's go," she agreed, relaxing a little. "Give me half an hour. I'll be quick."

Tsarkov started rummaging in the refrigerator again, clanking something glass, and Elizaveta vanished into the bathroom. At their next meeting, the delight was palpable, as if they hadn't seen each other for several days; both of them blushed, and they were silent in the elevator, like shy teenagers. He drove her to the Volga, majestic and smooth. There they felt young, like before, and finally stopped being bashful. Drawing glances from the few onlookers, they ran along the waterfront, goofing off, laughing into the wind, and yelling at the boats. Then Elizaveta got hungry and the wind picked up in earnest, so they took shelter from it on the terrace of an Asian restaurant, not far from the river. Timofey told one funny local legend after another. Sivoldaisk waitresses in kimonos, including smiling Kazakh girls trying to pass as Japanese, scurried about, creating a carnival atmosphere. Elizaveta felt good; she had quite forgotten Moscow and her recent anxieties on account of the man sitting opposite her. They dined for a long time and then, sated and languorous, walked across the beachfront gardens to Tsarkov's office, which was close by. There, he became formal and strangely quiet.

His plan, sketchy as it was, was coming to life. There was no retreat – in the event of failure, he was risking a great deal. The emotions that surged unbidden should be postponed until later – after all, who knew how *later* might develop. But now, the main thing was the business at hand, and Timofey set to it without delay.

Right up until Bestuzheva's arrival, he was figuring this way and that what possible tactic might bring him to his goal. Could he rely on feelings that had lain so long dormant, on the unbearable harshness of solitude and longing? Or should he tell it like it was right away, making an appeal for solidarity? The question was tough, but finally he decided in favor of subtlety and elusiveness, believing in the power of memories and in feminine sensitivity in general, which Liza had once possessed in spades. Besides, the option of stark pragmatism could always be employed as a last resort – he could turn resolutely in that direction if his "bride" would not indulge in romantic impulse. The impulse issue was not entirely clear to him now, but there was no point in changing the logic midway through – and the same was true of the words prepared in advance. "They will come out even more naturally," Timofey resolved, calling on his long-established cynicism for assistance, which, he knew, wouldn't forsake him in a difficult moment.

Elizaveta also grew silent, sensing an imminent discussion. Tsarkov's office was full of shiny gadgets that she examined with exaggerated attention while Timofey perused the mail his secretary had piled on one corner of the desk. He had given the employees this Monday off and didn't want to think of work-related issues since the business had run smoothly up until now. Yet he couldn't help but notice with displeasure that the mail was again unsorted and left in a heap, which spoke to the carelessness of the secretary he would have to fire. Tsarkov sighed involuntarily. He had no luck with secretaries; the current one was too young and deathly afraid of him. Then he observed Elizaveta glancing with a smile at the potted geranium on a bookcase by the window. He stood up from the desk and went to her, grinning in response.

"What's up with you?" he asked, wondering whether he should hug her around the shoulders. She nodded at the pot and giggled like a little girl – the formal settings, modern office equipment, and the flat black screen of the monitor suddenly seemed to her no more than a joke. "Um, the rosanelle," he was suddenly embarrassed. "The cleaning lady brought that. Can't throw it out – so there it sits. I know, I have to get rid of it somehow."

"What did you call it?" Elizaveta asked mischievously. "Did you say rosanelle? Oh, my! That sounds like something our great-grandmothers would say. How romantic!" Then she stepped over to him, getting right up close, and said as she looked him in the eyes, "Okay, tell me, what's going on? Why are you playing games with me again?"

"I want to marry you," answered Tsarkov calmly, holding her gaze. "And as for the games, that was to create a favorable atmosphere and awaken feelings. Otherwise, you'd have just turned me down outright."

Elizaveta nodded thoughtfully. Some chord sounded, audible to her alone, taut, delicate, and responsive. At this, her invisible guards, who were accustomed to strike at the first sign of trouble, formed ranks with their spears at the ready.

"No doubt, I'd have turned you down," she laughed, swiveling and going to the window. "So do you think I still won't turn you down now?"

"I'm not sure what to think. All I do is think!" Timofey pathetically exclaimed and strode through the office, speaking quickly and fervently. From the very first words, he realized he was going astray and the situation wasn't developing according to plan. But this no longer bothered him – he suddenly believed all would work out as it should, and Liza wouldn't let him down. He should just play for a little time, without committing any obvious blunders, allowing the imperceptible to gain strength, soar in their mutual proximity again, despite the years they had spent apart. Still, he noted that the complicated scheme was justified. Something awoke, arose out of thin air, and was nearly giving off sparks – in Bestuzheva as well as him.

"You know what it's like to spend seven years here?" Tsarkov inquired with a certain strain. "Seven years, and in the beginning I didn't know a single soul. I was poor as a church mouse – who wants to deal with somebody like that? One guy brought me here and helped out, yeah, but I couldn't be one of his toadies. And to do your own thing, you've got to pay a lot – you have no idea the hoops I had to jump through!"

Liza kept standing by the window while Timofey paced and paced, fuming and gesticulating. The chronicle of recent years turned out to be more dramatic in his speech than it had really been, but he consciously poured on the emotions, missing no opportunity for exaggeration. Right there, in the heat of the action, he dreamed up part of his past full of troubles. He fantasized, mixed up facts, devising memories of what had happened to himself as well as others. For, truth be told, his road to success was smooth enough.

The first Sivoldaisk years he painted in grey, hinting at misunderstanding and poverty. Then light dawned, and Tsarkov, unruffling his feathers, tried to generate intrigue without giving things away ahead of time – arguing *via negativa* to dissociate himself from the majority, from the quick and simple ways of making money accepted here in the provinces. He solemnly swore he didn't kill or steal, didn't seize apartments by force or appropriate unclaimed lands. He didn't even take bribes – for he had no occasion to – nor did he falsify any licenses, whether it was for hunting and fishing or trading in tobacco and vodka. No, his posturing as a man from the capital didn't permit overly straightforward methods, and so he selected the refined purity of abstractions, though no one taught him to do that.

"Geometry!" he exclaimed to Elizaveta. "Elliptical orbits, trapezoids, and pyramids. No criminal overtones – just straight lines and right angles!"

He related how he began to invent clever schemes. The values of the material world changed from one form to another, switched masks, names, and owners, crossed borders, oceans, obstacles of stagnant reasoning. Everyone benefited – and if anyone did not, then they were obviously unworthy of it. He never took from the poor; only the rich were falling into his crosshairs, and even they wouldn't get involved by force. They asked for it themselves, attracted by the music of foreign words and the game of shadows that formed a picture in which so much could be inferred. The strength of abstract essences is in their depth, but the depth is also what makes them dangerous: pulling a single lever may at once destroy several buildings – speaking figuratively, and even literally sometimes. He quickly understood this and learned to employ it to his advantage at the expense of those others, whose understanding turned out to be not so quick. In a word, nothing dirty: clean hands and intricate charts on white paper – but some great prospects had opened up already, though at this point he had only managed to master the very tip of the iceberg...

"So, Sivoldaisk is the wild steppe for some; for others it's the dust grinding in their teeth. For me, however, it's a kind of breakthrough – new ideas and some achievements too," Timofey solemnly announced after a brief pause. "This may be immodest, but yes, I've done here what others couldn't even imagine. Everyone with money has something to hide – honor and profit lie not in one sack – so all of them come to me. Though there are also plenty of enemies, of course. Morals here are simple: some swim in the Volga just for the fun of it, but plenty get taken there with a load around their ankles – and so long to them. All sorts of stuff has happened, yes, but nobody ever put one over on me, try as they might – and when they attempted to, I bared my teeth at them well enough in turn. So it goes, Liza..." he sighed and lit up an English cigarette.

Elizaveta had long since turned away from the window and was watching him with a barely perceptible smile. The internal chord had slackened, becoming almost soundless. Tsarkov seemed to her like a vulnerable child, but at the same time, she sensed new strength she had never seen in him before.

"Now he'll talk about his women," she thought. "How it didn't work out with them. Who knows? Maybe it really didn't."

Timofey, meanwhile, had perched on the edge of the desk, scooted a massive ashtray over to himself, and was examining it closely – and even a bit sadly.

"But that's one thing, you know, and then there's a different matter," he said with a certain chagrin, as if he were angry at himself and at innocent Liza as well. That was partially true – he had to switch to more personal topics, and words wouldn't just come to mind. Writers have it easier, shameless hacks, he thought sullenly, recalling the immaculately written letter, and reiterated, "A different matter entirely," searching frantically for his next phrase.

"Yeah, I noticed: your place isn't that comfy," Elizaveta threw him a lifeline with just the slightest hint of a sneer. "The apartment is nice, but it lacks character – like a bachelor's dormitory or something."

"Well, you see," Tsarkov was suddenly upset, "that's exactly what my uncle said! I spent so much effort, hit all the stores, but recently he visited me and kept calling it a hostel, over and over. He's a bit of scoundrel: when I arrived in his town penniless, he turned up his nose and even tried to sell me out..." and Timofey, unexpectedly, launched into a story about his uncle that was entirely out of place.

Fortunately, the phone rang at that moment. Tsarkov grabbed the receiver, issued several short commands, and took a new cigarette from the pack. "Yeah, my uncle – but none of that's important," he said with a wave of his hand. "Never cry over spilled milk;

tomorrow's another day. I bear no grudge against him – whatever he may be, he's a relative, and I don't have much family. So you work, you slave away, and then a little thought occurs to you: where is that dear person, the one you're piling all this up for like some Egyptian pyramid? Everyone wants comfort – and some warmth, and posterity. Besides, being alone is no good in general, with money or without it."

Having finally fallen into the right groove, Timofey relaxed and even felt a sort of inspiration. His words poured out freely and his face expressed thoughtfulness and a light sorrow. He couldn't tell whether he was prevaricating and didn't wish to think about it. The empty apartment appeared in his speech again, as well as material wealth and a solitary, uncomfortable lifestyle. Then, at the center of it all, the notion of a companion was affirmed, which is where the topic remained until the end of the monologue.

At first, the part about companions resounded with a consistent minor key – Elizaveta had guessed correctly. But soon hope rang out, not yet supported by any particulars, and then, at the appropriate time, the solid fact followed: Timofey Tsarkov had come to finally realize at thirty-three years of age what kind of woman he could dwell with under one roof for the rest of his life. He understood that clearly – though he admitted he arrived at this understanding with difficulty and had committed many mistakes, arguing with fate out of pure stubbornness.

Having said all this – and flinching a little inside from a few excessive turns of phrase – Timofey crossed the room to Elizaveta, but she had turned back, facing out the window, hiding her face from him. After several seconds of silence, she finally exhaled, "Well," fixedly studying the street below.

"No, no, don't leave," she blurted out when she heard Timofey make some sort of movement. "Give me your hand. Man, it's cold. So tell me: why did you push me away back in Moscow, then hook up with that slut and cut out on me? Just don't lie, please."

Timofey sighed with a frown. His whole inspired speech now seemed to him intolerably trite. "What's to lie about?" he replied gloomily. "Don't you get it? I was ashamed and hurt, and I couldn't keep on going like a helpless nobody. Here, of course, people are just sheep mostly, but at least to them I'm someone."

"But why did I have to be kicked to the curb?" she asked without turning her head. "And then there's that nurse…"

"You saw the former me," he shrugged. "What's left to understand? I decided to change and didn't want to see that former me anymore. As for the nurse, I don't remember much about a nurse. Well, maybe I did something, yeah – to make you get mad and leave me with no explanation."

"No explanation," Elizaveta repeated. "An explanation would have probably been better."

She grew silent again, then released his hand and turned to him with a slightly artificial smile. She's still ticked off, thought Timofey, and he was right. "Well, I guess I'll consider it," she said buoyantly. "This is all rather unexpected and a bit rushed. I think we need to get to know one another again – and get used to each other, adjust."

Tsarkov realized the first part of the plan had failed. He crossed the room, pushed back the ashtray on the desk, and came back to her. She calmly looked at him, not smiling anymore and not averting her eyes. "Liza," he said firmly, "look, I need this now."

Elizaveta Andreyevna raised her eyebrows, peering at him in bewilderment. She waited for elaboration, but Timofey was silent, just grinning awkwardly. "Did you knock somebody up?" she asked finally, clearly put out by this turn of events.

"Of course not," he brushed it off with irritation. "This is much more serious."

"Really?" Liza was incredulous.

"Yes, really. Why are you assuming such nonsense – knocking somebody up?" Timofey asked with a frown. He suddenly felt very embarrassed. Quite genuinely, he was angry, at himself and Bestuzheva, and most of all at bloodsucking Maya, who was now roaming carefree under the sky of the American Midwest. I've never looked like such a fool in my life, he thought despondently, hanging his head and boring into the floor with his eyes.

"What, then?" Elizaveta narrowed her gaze. "But anyway, this is your business, not mine. That means this is nothing but cold calculation. And me, idiot that I am, I believed that there'd been some rekindling of feelings."

"Liza, it's all those things at once," he said hollowly, still not raising his eyes. "At first, yes, it was calculated. But then fresh feelings arose – spontaneously, on their own. Now I don't know myself. I swear on my life."

"You're lying!" she declared.

"I'm not!" Tsarkov shouted, scaring her a little. He rushed to the desk, snatched up his cigarettes, and went whirling around the office, forgetting all about his plans, jumbling his words and jumping from one thing to another.

For the next hour and a half, they sorted out their relationship in the best tradition of medieval romances. Peals of lightning split the air, sparks crackled, shadowy figures appeared in cloaks with hoods, daggers glinted, and swords crossed. Timofey ran around the room as if it were a gladiatorial arena, while Liza at times became a panther – though she only threatened with her claws, probably more for the sake of appearances.

Tsarkov and his inspired speech had stirred something inside her. She really wanted to believe – immediately and, to the extent it was possible, everything. She enjoyed this desire and didn't want to part with it. Believing was difficult for her, but then it clicked somehow. Sound judgment retreated in defeat – for the first time in many years. Even the spear-wielding guards dissolved like phantoms – they were, in fact, phantoms, though they had their practical uses.

She didn't want to be afraid anymore – and emptiness was scarier than deceit. Actual war didn't erupt, but something told them both: the major battles still lay ahead. For now, everything was commingled, as if in a tempestuous flood, pushing fragments of shipwrecks – their own or those of others, experienced together or apart, concocted by someone, or else anonymous, obscure. Focal points drew close and then divided again to the north and south. Liza and Timofey got mad and laughed, drew close, and then went back to their opposing corners. Her tears began flowing at some point – when the smoke had already nearly cleared. This allowed Timofey to embrace her and whisper sweet nothings in her ear – by right of the strong man he again felt he was.

Elizaveta got quiet for a few minutes, then he confessed to her, "The world is so full of shit." She nodded in agreement, and this brought them even closer. She suddenly sensed that Timofey Tsarkov had already established himself in her consciousness – in place of the vacuum that, for many years, occupied considerable space there. Liza reflected briefly that the offenses remained unavenged, and in terms of the power of her charms nothing was yet clear, but she pushed this thought away. It was too unreliable; instead, she could bank on what grew inside – or at least she could grab hold and try to keep her grip.

Here he stroked her back, running his fingers along her spine, and her body remembered something too. Elizaveta sighed fitfully, then twisted out of his arms, distanced herself by a few feet, and stopped. With her eyes shining, she loudly demanded, "Say the most important thing!"

"Lizzy, I..." Timofey stammered, looking away.

She stomped her foot. "Look me in the eye!"

"Well, alright. It's like I..." he said sullenly, turning to face her. "It's like I..."

"Don't be afraid," Elizaveta gently encouraged him.

"It's like I've fallen in love with you again," Tsarkov concluded irritably. "Is that what you wanted to hear?"

She cocked her head to the side, was quiet for a second, and admitted with a sigh, "That 'it's like' bit kind of takes the allure away."

"Well, you understand, without that I'd be lying," he declared glumly. "We haven't seen each other for long time, after all. And what use do you have for lies? Let a little time pass – all the 'it's like' bits will vanish. But time can't be rushed, and this business can't wait. What else do you want to squeeze out of me?"

Elizaveta thought a little before nodding with a grin. "You could have lied, but that's okay. 'In a multitude of words, the truth keeps silent.' Is that what you all say?"

"Who is 'you all?'" asked Tsarkov, uncomprehending.

"It's not important," she said, looked at him intently, and added with the same grin, "Alright then, I'll keep on being a fool." Then she smiled at him, walked over, and kissed him on the lips. Drawing back, she said thoughtfully, "So he's in love, and he's asking me to marry him. Well, how can I resist?" and she kissed him again, earnestly and passionately.

"I accept," she informed him. "A need is a need, if you truly are 'in love.' Like you said, 'It's better for us both to drown than to get shot,' right?" and she began twirling around the room in a playful dance.

Timofey at first looked at her in disbelief, stunned at the quick resolution, then cleared his throat and asked, "Will you take my wedding ring?"

"Why not?" she consented with barely perceptible irony. "Let's have it, since you went to the trouble to get one."

Tsarkov reached into a desk drawer, pulled out a sapphire ring in a gold setting – of very old craftsmanship – and placed it on Liza's ring finger. "Look, a perfect fit," he grinned. "My great-grandmother wore it. She left it to us."

"It's wonderful!" she cried, looking at the stone. "And heavy..." And then she added as a joke, remembering the Soul Number and the heart broken in pieces, "But my stone is diamond, right?"

"I know," Timofey said in sudden confusion. "But now this blue one here is perfect on you. So, keep it – the Wallachian gypsies told me it wards off the evil eye. And a diamond – that's for later."

Like that girl on Kuznetsky, word for word, Elizaveta thought and smiled involuntarily. Then she looked at the ring again and asked, "So, when do we get married?"

"Today," Tsarkov sighed. "But I must make a phone call first." With that, he lifted the receiver and began punching in a short local number.

CHAPTER 14

No sooner had Express Liner Twenty Nine pulled into the
Sivoldaisk station than Frank White, Jr. again became apprehensive.
The confined space of the compartment, secure and habitable, would
no longer serve as shelter when he went out into a strange city where
shelters were scarce. All sorts of dangers might lurk; he reminded
himself again of the wildness of this region. Perhaps for good reason
his bunkmate Samokhvalov, the senior expert who had seemed so
vivacious the night before, was reticent and gloomy this morning
as he gazed through the window at the gardens in the poor suburb
frosted with dust. Only once did he address Frank to ask what hotel
he planned to stay in and nodded approvingly upon hearing the
name Pallada. Frank wondered whether he had said too much, but
soon calmed down and even laughed at himself: one couldn't be
suspicious of each and every person, after all.

In the plaza adjoining the station, by the Dzerzhinsky monument
that greeted arrivals with its scrawny butt clad in bronze riding
breeches, he checked his money belt by force of habit, hailed a
taxi, and rode down Moskovskaya Street, grinning in momentary
recollection of the capital he had just left, the fascinating call girl
Olga, and those several happy days. The city struck him oddly at
first. It wasn't like Moscow, which Frank took for a miniature copy of
all Russia. It didn't resemble any place at all, but instead represented

something very strange – at least, according to his transatlantic view. He was suddenly reminded of Gogol and even said to himself, "Here it is!" acutely sensing that before him stood a true provincial hub even more caricatured than the one from the famous book. Here might have been a butcher's shop and a small grocery behind it, he figured; then, a bit farther, a post office; then a cobbler and an old inn with semi-obscured windows. The next building might have once hosted balls and banquets for the whole county, and there, in the grime near the hydrant, coachmen had probably stood nibbling sunflower seeds and spitting them out as they waited for wayfarers... He noticed the filthiness of the houses and the deplorable state of the roadbed and felt bad for this city, though it was utterly alien to him.

The car bounced up, its wheels having encountered some pothole; the driver let loose an eloquent barrage of profanity, then glanced back to mutter an apology.

"The asphalt's terrible," Frank said in a display of solidarity. "The local government probably doesn't look after it."

"The government?" said the driver in astonishment as he turned down the music – a wheezy, morose ballad. "What are you talking about? There's no government these days. You're obviously from out of town."

Frank merely shrugged his shoulders as he contemplated an unusual edifice with a portly nymph plastered on its façade. Soon, the street brought them to the waterfront, which bore no connection to Gogol, and the hotel turned out to be a quite modern structure with a bright billboard advertising a casino. At the registration desk stood a man arguing with the administrator about his room and its air conditioner, as Frank gathered from overhearing them in passing. White was attended to by a young female trainee while the administrator admonished the man who was now expressing his extreme impatience, unwilling to back down. This was Nikolai Kramskoy, irritated by a hangover and an uncomfortable ride in a stuffy automobile. He and Frank glanced at each other and turned away indifferently.

"Why don't you take a deluxe suite?" the lady administrator with a perm asked Nikolai. "Your comrade here also has a suite, quite a good one, and there's an air conditioner there."

"All right," Kramskoy sighed. "If that's what my comrade here has. Party comrades that we are... Sorry," he turned to White, "just joking."

"There's no need to be that way," the administrator said, taking umbrage on Frank's behalf. "This is a good hotel, no one complains, even folks from Moscow. Your comrade, by the way, is from Moscow as well," she added, glancing over the trainee's shoulder. "And he's fine, just checking in with no jokes."

Nikolai and Frank simultaneously cleared their throats to suppress a snicker and looked at each other now with a certain mutual understanding. Then Kramskoy was handed his key and walked to the elevator. Meanwhile, White, Jr. was detained for another quarter of an hour while the blushing trainee, a very thin girl with a long, narrow face, was getting a reprimand from her boss for errors that had nothing to do with him.

When that was finally finished, Frank went up to his room, relieved. The matter of where to spend the night had been resolved – quite effectively. He hummed a melody, took a cursory walk through his two-room accommodations, and glanced into the microscopic bathroom with its smudged mirror. Satisfied with the inspection, he stepped out onto the balcony from which, as promised, a sweeping vista of the mighty Russian river opened before him. The river truly was impressively broad, but Frank White felt no stirring in his soul. Nevertheless, he stood there several minutes as if out of courtesy, then came to his senses and said to himself, "To business, to business."

He had to act without haste, but he could also not needlessly waste time. Frank unpacked his things and laid them out carefully, after which, in a pronounced businesslike fashion, he checked his money, documents, and a photocopy of the map. Everything was where it belonged, which he interpreted as a good sign. He nodded contentedly, again donned his belt and jean jacket, carefully locked the door, and went downstairs.

It was time to get acquainted with the locale, which necessitated acquiring topographical materials. Not far from the hotel he found a newspaper kiosk, carelessly inspected the showcase, and asked, posing as a tourist, whether they sold a map of the city – preferably one with the names of all the streets. A map was available, but only in a set with a glossy guidebook – for an absolutely outrageous price. White groaned for the sake of appearances, portraying miserliness quite naturally, but the pretty salesgirl expressed no sympathy. He decided it was best not to overdo the farce and completed the transaction with an inner sense of triumph. One more obstacle was overcome. Frank seized the bag with his purchase, looked around, and hurried back to the hotel, noting with a sweet, fleeting pang that the young newspaper vendor reminded him of dark-haired Olga.

On the whole, everything was falling into place quite well: his actions were deliberate and part of a unified plan. White, Jr. went back up to his room, locked the door with a double turn of the key, spread the map on the bed, and began to search for Trinity Cathedral, which, Nilva had told him, was long abandoned by its congregants and situated on the periphery, at the edge of a ravine that most likely served as the city dump. He located the cathedral, though not without the aid of the guidebook, which came in quite handy. To Frank's amazement, however, it turned out to be not on the outskirts at all, but within the city limits and right next to the hotel, where it was hard to imagine a dump – or even a ravine.

He checked it again, twice, but there could be no mistake. Some sort of disconnect was evident, but Frank didn't want to succumb to doubts and spoil his energetic mood. Besides, the guidebook informed him clearly of a chapel adjoining the cathedral, which had been built not long before the Pugachev Rebellion. This fully coincided with the data from the precious photocopy, which was now slightly crumpled and, because of that, had taken on an even more authentic aspect. Starting at the chapel, he would need to count paces to the burial site he was seeking, so Frank took out a special marker he had set aside for that purpose and drew a fat dot on the map. "A reference point," he murmured thoughtfully, recalling his math classes, diagrams on graph paper and coordinate axes.

It remained to figure out the cardinal directions. He also took this seriously and even went out on the balcony to verify by the sun that the map wasn't lying. The sun was already high in the sky, and the river rippled with countless patches of light. Frank involuntarily admired the scenery, throwing his shoulders back, straightening his spine, and gazing eagle-eyed into the distance like a general before a decisive battle. Then he returned to his room and sighed contentedly. All estimates indicated the exact same place, approximately in the middle of the square marked in green on the map. Nilva spoke of a wasteland – this must be the wasteland. It was strange, of course, for it to be in a brisk urban area, but here in the provinces anything could happen... Frank pulled a bottle of mineral water out of the mini-bar and pensively took a few swigs. The preliminary stage complete, the main phase of fieldwork would begin.

This, White, Jr. understood, was no laughing matter. Direct contact with the place where the treasure was hidden might be quite dangerous. The space in the hotel room seemed to fill with electricity; Frank felt his whole body vibrating in a stream of particles. He reconnoitered both rooms, noting with regret that the suite had no safe, and, after weighing the possible pros and cons, decided to take all his valuables with him. Buckling the money belt, he went into the lavatory and looked into the mirror streaked with lines. Even still, it reflected something, and the image pleased White: his face was pale, slightly puffy but resolute and, he wanted to think, fearless.

Returning to the bedroom, Frank repeated the names of the nearby streets aloud in order to better orient himself, even though the cathedral was quite close by. Consulting the map one last time, he folded it and stuffed it in his pocket as a last resort: "working" at the site would have to be done from memory to avoid attracting attention. Then he checked his passport and keys, stood by the window for a couple of minutes, looking down at the bustle by the river terminal, and, pursing his lips, left the suite.

With its golden dome visible from the waterfront, Frank White found the Trinity Cathedral with ease. The church occupied considerable territory enclosed by an iron fence and, contrary to Nilva's opinion, didn't appear at all derelict or ownerless. Feeling like a spy in a hostile land and hearing the beating of his own heart pounding through his clothes, Frank circumambulated the grounds to appraise the situation. One thing was immediately not to his liking: excavations were being conducted in the churchyard – and, in addition to half a dozen men with shovels, a powerful earthmover plowed up topsoil, emitting plumes of smoke and carving tracks into the stunted lawn. Competitors, he thought with stinging dismay, and his head spun with pictures of treachery and betrayal on the part of his partner, whose honesty he was trusting less and less. Or could someone else have reached the ancient secrets at the same time? It was his own fault: he had screwed up by wasting an entire week for nothing.

Frank White resolutely turned around and went back to the main entrance. "Whatever. It remains to be seen," he muttered crossly. "They probably don't have a precise plan. That must be why they're digging on such a large scale!"

Going through the gate, he tossed a couple of coins to a begging invalid – just to get luck on his side – and immediately caught sight of the chapel doors right where the guidebook had promised. "A useful little booklet. Good thing they foisted it on me," Frank thought in passing. "Though it's a bit fishy, as if they make them especially for treasure-hunters..." But now was no time for distracting thoughts. At the heavy, iron-studded doors he stopped and turned toward the already familiar Moskovskaya Street.

The map of this part of the city, which he had memorized in his hotel suite, obediently unfolded before his eyes. "Now it makes sense," he whispered to himself. "This is southwest. Where's the excavator? Ah, there it is behind me – that puts it northeast of the chapel. So, everything is pretty clear: I need almost due west, just a few degrees south – and these guys with shovels are not competitors at all. They're just digging with no ulterior motive. And if there is a motive, then they're simpletons, and just that!"

So he'd been worried about them for nothing. Frank took a breath and, assuming a nonchalant air, twisted his head again. He needed west, almost west, almost. To be precise, that warped plank in the fence. No point in hesitating – the invalid at the main gates was already checking him out with unwanted interest. White, Jr. turned in precisely the right direction and without haste, as if going for a stroll, went toward the enclosure, counting paces the length of which he – well in advance – had calculated, averaged, and plotted to the dimensions of the Pugachev map.

Reaching the fence and selecting an indicator on the walkway beyond it, he returned to the chapel and lifted his head as if studying the sharply peaked apex. Then he lazily yawned and headed toward the exit from the grounds. The invalid watched without breaking his gaze, and this disquieted him somewhat. Moreover, when Frank drew even with him, the man said rather brashly, "Leaving already, Mr. Surveyor? For the love of Christ, give us a little something."

"What if he were to call the cops?" Frank White thought. His palms broke into a sweat, and, rummaging feverishly in his pocket, he pitched a hundred-ruble note into the greasy cap. The invalid laughed hoarsely; Frank, without lifting his eyes, scurried away. "No big deal, no big deal," he calmed himself. "He's no competitor either. It's all just in my head!"

On the sidewalk by the fence where the invisible dotted line continued, it was more of the same: filthy and empty. Frank turned his back to the bars and headed west, mechanically counting his steps. His heart fluttered beneath his diaphragm; cold sweat ran into his eyes. He could already see approaching catastrophe but didn't yet want to believe it. The dotted line led not to a secluded corner, not to an empty lot with shards of glass and scraps of old newspaper as he had recently envisioned. Directly before him towered a five-story red and white building, looking gloomy and dishearteningly official. As though on autopilot, Frank crossed the street, climbed the gently sloping stairs, and stumbled into the front doors.

Painted above them, it read: Volga Railway Administration. Twelve paces remained to the supposed burial spot. Clearly, he had to dig inside the building. It was equally clear that was impossible and the project was ruined irrevocably and forever. Frank's head began to spin. He sat down on the steps and buried his face in his hands.

The occasional passersby looked at him, perplexed, but he didn't notice anyone around. His brain was crowded with wild, nonsensical thoughts. It seemed to him he'd landed in the epicenter of an intrigue, of someone's insidious plot. Certain forces alien to a rational spirit were targeting him, Frank White, for his good fortune, and the good fortune as well of Russian mathematicians now left with nothing; though, to be honest, the mathematicians were the last thing on his mind. Then the notion of intrigue subsided, like a paranoid delusion, and all his wrath was levied against the Volga rail authorities who had obviously found the hoard before him and plonked down five floors of building with the money. He seriously considered breaking in to find the director or some other person in charge and demand his cut by showing them the photocopy as proof he had no less right than they to the treasure. But luckily, his healthy American consciousness soon reconnected with basic principles of reason. Lunacy began to recede and Frank White recovered his ability to reckon sensibly – at least enough to assume no hoard had been found there and the edifice was constructed with other funds.

He mechanically checked his belt with his passport and money. All was where it belonged – at least, the world hadn't turned utterly upside down, but had just thrown him a sharp curve ball. Frank took out the map, laid it across his knees, and again checked the angles and landmarks. He couldn't be mistaken, since the steps and the chapel were clearly visible, as was Moskovskaya Street and even the waterfront, though the waterfront had no connection to his problem. Frank's lips moved as he ran his index finger over the map: here's the cathedral and the "reference point;" here's southwest, west, south. There, further on, is the Volga, which makes it impossible to go astray... No, there's no mistake. Obviously, like many treasure-seekers, he had simply experienced horrible luck.

Folding the useless map and sitting motionless for a minute or two, Frank White resolved to take a last, deliberate step. He rose, dragging his feet as he made his way to the heavy door, opened it with difficulty, and found himself in the dim twilight of a large hall. The two uniformed guards were obviously not among his allies, and Frank, looking around, approached a window marked Office of Admissions, as it was the only place bearing signs of life.

"Excuse me," he began, and his voice trembled helplessly. White cleared his throat, heaved two deep sighs, and asked an elderly employee, "Could you tell me, please, if an old treasure was ever found beneath this building?" thinking dejectedly that she would probably think him insane.

The employee did look at him in alarm, but something in Frank White's countenance assured her she was faced not with a troublemaker but with a foreigner who was not from there and far removed from full comprehension of local life.

"You'd be better off directing your question to the museum," she said kindly, and when he inquired where the local museum was, she readily explained that it happened to be directly opposite them, right behind the ill-fated cathedral. Frank thanked her with resignation and set off toward the museum, ashen-faced and treading cautiously, as though on very thin ice.

Drops of sweat streaked down his cheeks, his chest tightened, and his fists convulsively clenched. With his last bit of strength, he tried to restrain himself from becoming hysterical and whispered with noncompliant lips, "It's okay. There's still a chance. We'll see, we'll see." Bypassing the familiar fence, he raised his eyes and saw the same indefatigable invalid, now with a young police sergeant standing next to him, arms akimbo and a nightstick in his belt. Noticing the look on Frank's face, the invalid grinned maliciously and nodded in his direction, drawing the attention of his uniformed companion.

There was no threat in this gesture, and they probably wished White no harm, but Frank assumed the worst. An abscess ruptured inside him and the protective shroud fell from his eyes; a picture of defeat took on the utmost sharpness. He understood more clearly than ever that his life had reached an impasse. This city, this cathedral, and the gates in the iron fence had become a trap into which he was lured by an unseen enemy who had once assumed the aspect of Nilva and possessed many other faces besides. And these two grinning here were none other than minions of dark forces that were unleashed upon Frank White for some unknown sin.

He convulsively gulped down air and strode toward them, no longer possessing the strength to endure the phalanx of facts that had closed in from all sides. "No, no, no," he yelled, spitting. "Don't you nod at me like that. You won't hoodwink me: I noticed right away how you're watching me and making signs to each other. I'm an American citizen! You get in touch with the consulate, and then we'll see what insinuations there are here. I know you have no evidence. I'm no criminal, and I haven't stolen a thing!"

The invalid and the sergeant were transfixed by confusion, staring at Frank as he advanced on them, still yelling incomprehensibly. But then the policeman, hearing familiar words, came to his senses, took on an air of authority, and asked rather sternly, "Haven't stolen anything? What are you shouting about then? Are you making trouble or what? If you're drunk, we can book you right away!"

"Maybe he's not right in the head," the invalid hypocritically sighed, peering from under his gray brows. "He's been wandering around here a long time, measuring something out. You reckon he's a surveyor?"

"You stay out of this!" Frank shouted at him heatedly. "I noticed you at once – you're a spy, no doubt! But without the consul present I'm not saying a thing." He turned to the authority figure. "Not a word. No, no, no!"

White raised his hand and waved his palm expressively in front of the officer's face. The cop didn't like that in the least. He grabbed Frank forcefully by the elbow, declaring with menace, "Alright. Since he's asking to be put in the *vytrezvitel*, the state will be happy to give him a bunk. We'll fix him right up."

The sergeant was young and round of face, with big ears and broad rural hands. Frank White looked him in the eye for a second, cursed in English, and venomously hissed, "Go sober up in the drunk tank yourself!" – after which he started fiercely twisting to get free, preparing to kick the officer in the shin. This was too much and could cause the affair to take a not-so-comical turn, but then, fortunately, someone's confident voice rang out, "Hey, what's going on here?" and the situation was defused, the tension gone.

Frank's savior turned out to be none other than Nikolai Kramskoy, who with a rather contented look had just exited the museum where the railway employee had sent White. Noticing the commotion at the cathedral entrance, he was about to cross to the other side of the street, but then recognized one of the participants as his fellow guest from the hotel. As soon as he heard the unmistakable American profanity, he understood all was much more complicated than it seemed. As he came up and appraised the situation, Kramskoy adopted a concerned aspect and directed himself to Frank with the traditional, "Are you okay?"

"Sure!" the other hastily replied in English. The policeman immediately released his elbow and took a barely perceptible step to the side, freeing up a modicum of personal space. Without delay, Nikolai added, "Excuse me," moved White, Jr. out of harm's way, and winked at the sergeant like one of his own, letting out a noisy sigh.

"*Normal'no,*" he gave the magic password of the Russian streets. "It's all right, finally found him. Gotta be careful with a foreigner like this one." Meanwhile, he waved a hundred-rouble bill, which was able to serve as password and countersign all in one.

"Is he with you, then?" the policeman muttered, glancing briefly at the cash and pretending he was still mad. "Look after him. He's freaking people out!" The hundred rouble note jumped into his palm in a flash, after which he turned and started looking in the direction of the Volga, taking no further interest in Kramskoy or his ward.

"Alright," Nikolai repeated as they parted company. "*Normal'no.* We're outta here," and he led Frank to the shade of large trees nearby, away from the invalid, who was suspiciously watching them depart. White didn't resist; the wind had been knocked out of him.

The moment of catastrophe was left behind; there was no return to it. Sooner or later, Frank knew, the emotions would burst forth again, but now all his limbs went numb as if under a powerful anesthetic. He obediently walked next to Nikolai, repeating the odd word *"vytrezvitel"* to himself, which he had not heard for many years.

As for Kramskoy, he was in high spirits. What he desired was nearly achieved – on the very first day, though not in the most direct manner. All the remaining time could be given to indulging in idleness – as if he had broken free from everyone and all scrutiny, examining this utterly unknown city like a new world full of its own enticing mysteries.

The museum itself – which was the main object of his trip and conveniently located a stone's throw from his hotel – made quite an impression upon him with the seriousness of its approach to business. Like the majority of local edifices, it was a dusty yellow color – in honor of the near steppe and the far wilderness. It was once home to a rich merchant famous for gluttony and a patronage of the arts. Apparently, he possessed a sense of architecture as well – one had to wonder how such a prominent structure remained undestroyed by time and the Bolsheviks, and how it was later not appropriated by the enterprising powers-that-be. Nikolai even walked around the building, inspecting the columns and strong walls. After seeing his fill, he concluded that the revolutionary attitudes in this city were fairly weak – and then purchased a ticket and went inside.

The interior turned out to be pretty decent too. The museum was amply outfitted – one could jokingly surmise it did well with people wishing to purchase certificates of their shady origins. Kramskoy smiled: Pugachev's heirs in this case came to resemble the fictitious children of Lieutenant Schmidt – history was repeating itself, and that couldn't help but be amusing. However, he lacked direct confirmation of this and soon stopped thinking about it as he finally engaged in his own affair.

At first, he strolled through the floors, stopping at the hall devoted to the Pugachev era, and pointedly nodded as he noticed the door to the director's office by the stairs. Then, zigzagging as if to cover his tracks and even laughing at his comical secrecy, he went into the room he needed and slowly walked along the walls. The document he sought hung in the very corner, indistinguishable from the other letters and appeals that formed part of the main exhibit. Nikolai paced back and forth, his hands folded behind his back, and peered at the yellowed manuscripts. Then he relaxed and began reading them one by one, paying special attention to a report by General Semanzh in which he bemoaned the lack of morale in the Imperial army.

The letter by the elder from the village of Chumovo was well preserved and looked authentic. "That's the real McCoy," Nikolai murmured derisively, studying the document from the first word to the last, assessing the uniformity of the handwriting and what difficulties there might be in altering it. They didn't appear too great: the elder had written with visible effort; lines broke, which was quite helpful, and several words were even difficult to decipher. Kramskoy shook his head and chuckled condescendingly: adding a phrase or two would be a piece of cake.

Thus the fact-finding phase of the operation concluded quite successfully. Next was the director's office, to which Nikolai set off with a confident stride. The secretary – who was around thirty-five and had a huge chest – wore the face of a woman who hated her life. She greeted him cautiously, but Kramskoy, with insolent Moscow pushiness, quickly convinced her to tear the director away from important matters for the sake of an even more substantial issue that could not afford delay.

"How shall I introduce you?" she asked pretentiously, blinking her fake eyelashes.

"Genealogical expert," Nikolai humbly presented himself. The secretary's lips moved, as if she were repeating the title to herself. Then she disappeared behind a leather-clad door and flung it open a second later announcing, "Mikhail Mikhailovich will see you!"

Kramskoy stepped inside. The director's office was large and well lit. The desk was also large, drawn out in a sort of fat letter T. The director himself sat at the head of the T like grotesque Party royalty. Behind him hung a portrait of the president and an image of someone else, smaller – Nikolai thought for a moment that this was the director himself, but on closer inspection he decided the resemblance was too slight. For a few seconds before the door slammed shut, the owner of the office looked past him – diverting his eyes toward the secretary's hips, as Kramskoy divined by the line of his gaze. Then, with some regret, the director focused on the man who had just entered and said in a velvety voice, "Milov, Mikhail Mikhailovich. Please have a seat. How, as they say, may I be of service?"

Nikolai introduced himself, sat, and looked around surreptitiously. The possessions of Milov, Mikhail Mikhailovich were arranged thoughtfully and with love. In the event a visitor should prove hard of hearing, a plate stood on the desk with the full name of its owner. Meanwhile, the walls were adorned here and there with diplomas and certificates listing sundry directorial honors. They alternated with photographs in which Milov was depicted in the company of various people against the backdrop of buildings, gullies of some kind, and other landscapes that probably had regional significance. All the photos had labels affixed in an especially large font – in the event the aforementioned visitor was visually impaired as well.

The director himself brought to mind nothing so much as a well-fed cat. Kramskoy observed the carefully trimmed moustache and well-groomed head of hair typical of a provincial heartbreaker and decided it was better to be direct. He smiled – affably but not ingratiatingly – and looked Milov right in the eye. "I have a client," he said, "who would like to buy a document from you…" naming a completely different letter he had seen in another hall, which had no relation to Pugachev. Then he took a short pause and added, lowering his voice slightly, "Very confidential, of course, no publicity. No one will know besides you and me. What do you think of my little business proposition?"

"Business proposition?" the director asked with feigned surprise. "Buy a document?" He shook his head reproachfully. "What are you talking about? We are a municipal office with a public budget. We don't do business deals here."

"I misspoke myself," Nikolai sighed, already feeling some irritation. "But the matter is not about words, after all. Call it what you like; you know better than I. For me – and for the client – what matters most is the core issue at hand."

Milov assumed a dignified air, cleared his throat, and started talking, enjoying the sound of his own voice, which actually was quite pleasant. "As for the core issue, which is always most important for me as well," he declared like a lecturer giving a speech, "it is subject to no ambiguity. On the one hand, you have business, deals, clients. And on the other, you understand, is the scientific process and, no doubt, one's reputation and academic ethics. Take me, for example, a doctor of history – what need do I have of business? You come here – not for something serious, just for a piece of paper, a trifle, not worth discussing. But we *have* a discussion, and it immediately starts wrong – even if," he inserted a meaningful pause, "even if the matter is not about words. After all, I don't know your client and he doesn't know me. And here you show up – unexpectedly, mind you, without an appointment – and practically start off with insults. No, no, I'm not rebuking you," he hastened to add, seeing Nikolai make a gesture of protest, "but neither is that the right way to do things, you understand? This is not the capital, which is full of academics and their children. For the moment we have only doctors here. But still, you know, it's not right, not right at all."

Kramskoy knew his first attempt failed, and the problem, which seemed quite simple, would not be resolved fast. The aging heartbreaker turned out to also be a demagogue with ambitions, who was used to verbosity and flowery turns of phrase. Nikolai sighed to himself and set about talking profusely to address the grievous misunderstanding that had clearly occurred through his own action. He should have started right away with the main reason he had personally made the wearisome trip. What really brought him here was the desire of his client to provide generous aid to the Sivoldaisk museum and its director personally – within his powers, of course

– for the purposes of development, improvement, and so on. As for the document in question, that was a minor issue – one of those small things that always arises when mutual aid is discussed – a secondary matter, which should not be hard to resolve at all.

Milov listened to all this without interrupting and even nodded encouragingly at several points. Then he rose, walked across the office, looking at his reflection in the glass doors of the bookcase, and noted in turn that these aid-related intentions were quite magnanimous indeed; yet not all aid could be considered beneficial, especially when you don't know who it's coming from. He, for example, had never requested any aid; and when it was imposed upon him out of the blue, he immediately wished to find out why this unknown Moscow businessman got such an unusual desire? What had actually brought him to Milov, Mikhail Mikhailovich, Doctor of History, etc.? Because everything has its own scale, and the scales must be comparable. The historical process... a scientist's dignity... municipal funding...

"For a scientist, you look way too well-off," thought Nikolai with a grin and suddenly sensed that he was tired of this conversation. "So what, then, you need some bucks or not? You finally gonna sell the paper?" he asked with intentional rudeness, standing up to look down at the director.

The expression on Milov's face displayed bewilderment, at first involuntary, then deliberately restrained. "Like I've been explaining," he said more dryly, "we don't traffic historical documents here. This is a serious institution for archives and scientific inquiry. I must tell you, your behavior is simply baffling."

"What does he want?" Nikolai asked himself vacantly, shrugging his shoulders. "What an odd duck this guy is. Well, you win some, you lose some."

"Have it your way," he blurted out in a bored voice, interrupting Milov in mid-sentence and leaving without saying goodbye. The secretary was holding a telephone receiver to her ear, justifying herself to someone plaintively and a bit shrilly. "Nice place you got here," said Kramskoy to her without slackening his pace, but she paid him no attention. "Well, now," he muttered as he reached the landing in the stairwell, "we'll need to look for other options."

The option turned up on its own – literally right there by the stairs – in the form of a short old man in huge worn-out boots and a mouse-brown suit with elbow patches. A waxen-faced girl with glasses was trying to convince him of something, repeating like a broken record, "But Mikhal Mikhalych said..." To this, the man only replied with short, caustic remarks. The girl sighed and rolled her eyes but the old man remained completely indifferent to her suffering.

"That Mikhal Mikhalych of yours doesn't know jack. You give him that message from me. Let him tell that to me, what he told you," he cut her off again, stroking his chin.

"But that's what he told me. Now what do I tell him?" the girl whined.

"Well, you say to him, 'Tell Pechorsky. Don't tell me about it!'"

"I can't tell him that."

"Oh yes, you can. You tell him that!" The old man crowded her toward the steps, clearly winning the fight.

"Oh, you're so difficult, Mark Lvovich," the girl sobbed and scurried downstairs. The old man in boots looked around victoriously, took a pipe out of his pocket, and smelled it with relish.

"Excuse me," Nikolai Kramskoy addressed him with a mysterious, conspiratorial look, "are you Mark Lvovich Pechorsky?"

"The very same!" the other answered proudly and twisted his head around again, obviously still feeling the effects of his recently achieved victory. There wasn't another soul on the landing, so his gaze fell by default upon Kramskoy as the sole witness to his triumph.

"You were recommended to me as the most knowledgeable expert," Nikolai informed him, lowering his voice to a volume of confidentiality.

"And who was it that recommended me?" the old man inquired cockily and even with a little suspicion, but it was obvious he received this information favorably.

"You know, I've forgotten," Kramskoy confessed, revealing an open, honest face. "But there's no mistake, I'm sure. You do work in this museum, don't you?"

"In this museum, young man, I've been working all my life," the old man grumbled, hiding the pipe in a bulging jacket pocket. "And I've lived in this city all my life. My great-great-great grandparents, just so you know, were settled here by Catherine II herself – you've heard of the Jewish exile, haven't you? So then, what's your question for me?"

Nikolai furrowed his brow a bit as though in doubt before saying firmly, "Come on. This, I have to show you," and went straight to the Pugachev hall. The little old man pattered beside him, his boots creaking loudly as he muttered to himself under his breath. Stepping up to the elder's letter, Kramskoy stopped, looked at the old man slyly, and said, "Here."

"Well, let's see, let's see," murmured Pechorsky. "Well, yes, a curious document. Stylistically mature, though, in point of fact, nothing special. And good preservation, yes... So what?"

Nikolai, hesitating a little for decorum, carefully grasped him by the elbow, led him to a corner of the hall, and explained the situation. He admitted he had a client, a very respected personage, who was worried that the letter, which concerned him directly, was hanging in the hall, an eyesore, right in plain view of all. The client, therefore, wished to take steps: for example, to purchase the document without publicity for an appropriate price. Meanwhile, Nikolai, as a mediator in this affair, couldn't figure out who to turn to. It was clear there was no use talking to that cat Milov. As everyone knows, it's always best to deal directly with a spe-ci-a-list – at which point he made a minuscule gesture with his palm toward Pechorsky. Because the question of authenticity is also important. And besides, it's always easier to reach an agreement with an intelligent man.

They were silent for a bit, then Mark Lvovich sighed and grumbled, "Yeah, well, it's clearly authentic – even to the unaided eye, so to speak," and Kramskoy saw he was flattered. "As far as any direct relationship, that's up to the client to decide on his own," the old man added, and asked with a certain trepidation: "So what, then? You want me to *sell* you this exhibit?"

"No sense beating around the bush," Nikolai spread his hands. "Exactly: sell it, and the deed is done. I'm sure Milov won't even notice."

"Milov..." Mark Lvovich's face twitched. "Yeah, what would he notice anyway? But you're talking about a museum piece, no less."

"Or else a personal relic," Nikolai retorted. "No one will find out, and my client will be pleased. A man, I say again, of means. Not someone full of empty promises who throws his word to the wind."

Mark Lvovich Pechorsky was quiet, then bit his lip and said delicately, "I could help you, I think. But the issue is in the details."

"If we're talking about details," Nikolai said softly but distinctly, "then just name your price."

"That's how it is, huh?" Pechorsky cringed. Thinking some more, he took out his pipe but promptly put it back in his pocket.

"Five hundred US dollars," he blurted out angrily and turned away. Then he looked up at Nikolai and repeated, "Five hundred!" and launched into a justification. "My daughter's getting married, what can I do? I know it's a lot, but you need to understand. The client's well-off, you say, and I really don't have anything for the wedding."

"Don't you worry," Nikolai soothed. "Five hundred it is. That's not too much at all."

"For you it's not much," the old man erupted, "but for me it's three months' wages! Please don't think I'm taking advantage. People just have no conscience these days."

Then he calmed down and got to business. "Tomorrow we'll do a small inventory," he mumbled as he accompanied Kramskoy to the stairs. "I'll hang up another letter from storage – no one will know the difference. In the evening, we'll meet, and I'll hand this one over. Does that work for you?"

"Nothing could work better," Nikolai assured him and then asked out of mischievousness, "but won't this Milov of yours figure it out?"

"Milov!?" snorted Mark Lvovich with contempt. "All Milov has going for him is a moustache and a secretary with a double D cup, if you catch my meaning. Figure it out? You know what he'll figure out? Nothing, that's what!"

Thus, all was falling into place just fine. They bade each other a warm farewell, agreeing to meet at the waterfront the following evening. Feeling hungry and pleased with himself, Nikolai left the museum and, a minute later, came face to face with the picturesque group consisting of the invalid, the police sergeant, and the American citizen White, Jr. – who, unlike him, had just suffered utter defeat. After rescuing Frank from the clutches of the police and retiring with him to a nearby square, Kramskoy politely inquired what that incident was about, already aware it was not so simple.

Frank declined to comment at first and just gave a muffled thanks, but then he became inflamed with a last, desperate hope, clinging to Kramskoy like a drowning man grabbing a willow branch. He feverishly spilled a bunch of incoherent facts, making up stuff on the go and jumbling his words, so that Nikolai understood nothing, but concluded that White, Jr. had encountered a serious misfortune. Convinced the issue was tangled and didn't involve a matter of immediate life or death, he suggested they go have lunch and, in the process, get to the bottom of this problem that obviously demanded thoughtful consideration. This cheered Frank up a bit, and he gladly consented. Within fifteen minutes, they were sitting in the same Asian restaurant that Elizaveta and Timofey Tsarkov had just left after thrilling the waitresses with a generous tip.

Both assured each other straight away that they wouldn't drink alcohol, but then they did order a bottle of beer each, and later yet another. Frank apologized for his temper, admitting he was confused in an unfamiliar city, and Nikolai assured him that this sort of nonsense happens with everyone. They quickly hit it off, and White, Jr. pulled the precious map from his pocket, concocting a story about the estates of his Russian great-grandfather who had left him naught but this map, which unfortunately led to a blind alley. Kramskoy instantly spotted the forgery and gave Frank a short lecture on the features of old manuscripts, even adding in jest that the crumpled photocopy smacked of some kind of treasure map, which caused his new friend substantial consternation. On the whole, though, he readily accepted the verdict, being already predisposed toward it, and dined with an enviable appetite no less than Nikolai's.

Having no reason to hurry, they sat for a long time in the restaurant. Once the meal was finished, they checked out the girls strolling along the waterfront and came to the mutual opinion that Sivoldaisk was not a bad city – and that it was even worth visiting again. Walking along the river, this idea was confirmed all the more and they decided to test it definitively by going to the main boulevard where the concentration of the female species was sure to be highest. From the waterfront they ascended toward a narrow street named after Chernyshevsky – a peevish enlightener with a sick liver – and there at the crossroads they were stopped by Elizaveta Bestuzheva, who was waiting for Timofey. He was delayed for a minute, clearing up some petty detail with an employee who was skulking about the office, despite the day off.

CHAPTER 15

An unforeseen problem compelled Elizaveta to engage the strangers in conversation. As good as Tsarkov's plan may have been, it was not ideal, just as the world itself is not perfect. It was precisely the imperfection of the world that Timofey bemoaned as he hung up the phone, as well as the fact you can never rely on others to do anything if you want it done right and on time.

On this occasion, the flaw was the two witnesses he had selected with the utmost care. The secrecy of the wedding necessitated that no people could be involved who might later become a source of rumors and gossip. Human beings in general are curious to a fault – Tsarkov had learned this well – and in this respect, the city of Sivoldaisk was no different than anywhere else. The witnesses, who were required by law to affix their signatures to the marriage certificate, would have to be sought on the sly. This he had accomplished all in good time, undertaking quite an operation to do so, and yet it had failed at the last moment.

The ones he was counting on suddenly and completely let him down, forcing him to scramble to find replacements – and that meant relying on chance. Ironically, the option he had prepared was suitable in every respect – it had paid off for Tsarkov to spend half a day in the hot sun, hanging out at the pier where tourists boarded Volga ships large and small. It was Saturday; the river terminal was working at full capacity as the crowds arrived and departed, leaving garbage and the stench of cheap beer in their wake. Timofey's back was drenched in sweat and his head ached from the unaccustomed strain but he persisted, not wishing to give up. And so, around lunchtime, he made his choice. At the most lively stall, between the air rifle shooting gallery and the karaoke booth, Tsarkov met a couple from Volgograd, Yura and Shura – whom he instantly christened in his mind as The Soldier and the Fool, recalling something he had read by a great Russian poet in his youth. The Volgograders were just what he was looking for: out-of-towners who didn't live too far away, unsophisticated and ready for adventure, but not too youthful and carefree. And, besides that, they were greedy, dim-witted, and easily swayed by the opinions of others. Such were in ample supply, but for some reason, these two struck his fancy right away – random chance, which later unpredictably worked against him.

Fidgety Shurochka's pupils darted from side to side: she was interested in every bloke that crossed her path, though it was obvious to all how tenacious her grip was on her companion, a hulking man in immense canvas trousers taking great swigs from a beer bottle and showing no less contempt for his surroundings than Byron's Childe Harold. Timofey surmised that both would be game for coarse flattery, so he told them with an ingenuous face that they appeared to be intelligent people "with dignity." Shura blushed at this, while Yura gave a self-satisfied nod. Clearly, contact had been established and the business was already halfway done. He invited them to a café, suggested magnanimously they shouldn't hesitate to pick any snack they wanted, and told them a story of romance, choosing easy words and expressing an air of agitation and gravity.

The two from Volgograd listened attentively, and when he hinted that this story could bring them some notable profit, they pricked up their ears. Timofey paused, gazed thoughtfully into the distance, and then, as if he had just made up his mind, informed them of an objecting parent who had a lot of influence in Sivoldaisk, and of the unpleasantness that awaited him and his bride if this man discovered their intentions to join their lives in wedlock against the father's will.

Here, he privately recalled his grandma and grandpa and grinned to himself. Out loud, he added there would be a wedding anyway, even if it had to be secret and quiet: for the heart cannot be tamed, much less two passionate hearts at once.

Here Shurochka gave a sigh of understanding, and even Yura expressed a semblance of empathy. Getting to details, Tsarkov informed them they had a date for the civil ceremony and a person at the registry office who wouldn't let them down. The only thing remaining was to get witnesses who weren't known in the city, and here fate had smiled upon him – none better than Yura and Shura were to be found. He recognized this at first sight and was now asking them – simply begging them – to agree; and he was prepared, of course, to cover their expenses, paying for their tickets and a hotel, and even to give them a nice sum in compensation for the effort.

Shurochka's eyes lit up. She was delighted and began to nudge her sluggish gentleman who, after showing some feigned hesitation, likewise expressed his gracious consent. Timofey breathed a sigh of relief as he crossed off another point on his complex checklist. He did everything as promised – with the tickets as well as the hotel – and Yura and Shura had actually arrived the night before, but today a vexing misstep occurred. Calling them from the office immediately after his conversation with Liza, Tsarkov heard sobs and weeping on the other end of the line, punctuated by pauses in which inconsolable Shurochka fought back tears to mumble that she and her sweetheart had an argument, as a result of which he had gotten drunk, broken her nose, and vanished into the Sivoldaisk evening. He hadn't come back to spend the night there, and where on earth he might be wandering about now, she hadn't the vaguest clue. To Timofey's justifiable protest of "How is that possible?" she merely set about weeping again, imploring him to have compassion. Her sole concern was her missing Yura, not Tsarkov's wedding, and not even her swollen nose. There was nothing to be done for it. Timofey, restraining himself from vulgarity, carefully placed the receiver on its cradle and said to Elizaveta, "There's a minor complication."

Assessing the situation quickly and efficiently, they concluded there was no cause for desperation. A replacement could be found for the weak link; Sivoldaisk was not small and didn't have a shortage of out-of-towners. And, naturally, they needed to be sought where they congregated en masse – at the entrance to the city's main hotel, for instance, which wasn't far away.

Elizaveta set off first, leaving Timofey to hammer out something with an employee who had the eyes of a frightened mouse. She took a few paces with a spring in her step, humming a tune and stealthily glancing at her ring, when she caught sight of two men before her, one of whom seemed familiar. "The train," thought Liza. "This morning... Yes, he was standing in the hallway of my car, glumly gazing out the window as I passed him, time and again. And those mannerisms aren't local. More likely Muscovite!"

The men drew even with her, simultaneously considering her with interest while at the same time averting their eyes.

"If I'm not mistaken," she addressed them, "we arrived together today."

"Oh, really?" Kramskoy reacted right away, stopping and adding some pleasantry. Frank, meanwhile, stood next to him, blushing for some reason and not knowing what to do with his hands.

"Intelligent," Elizaveta decided. "They'll do." And she smiled at Nikolai, "Yes, yes, now I remember you. You were standing by the window. And you?" she quizzically turned to Frank.

"Me too, except I was elsewhere. Different window, different car," he mumbled, tongue-tied and still befuddled. But here Nikolai came to his aid, explaining that Frank White was an American and that they had bumped into each other quite by accident not two hours before. Then, as if in passing, he paid her a nice compliment and asked innocently, "Are you here with your husband?"

"With my fiancé," Bestuzheva laughed, nodding to Timofey just as he walked up and hugging him around the waist. "These are my fellow travelers from the train," she informed him. "We just met unexpectedly."

"A fine bride you are," Tsarkov grinned widely. "I leave you alone for a minute, and here you already have company. Don't go running away from the altar!"

He immediately understood what was going on and quickly looked the fellow travelers over. They stood calmly, modestly smiling but dignified. One of them seemed rather strange, but not overly so. "They're adequate," decided Timofey and continued in his jovial tone, "About the altar: the matter's simple, yet sometimes it becomes quite tricky. All in all, we're looking for help. Would you be willing to lend a hand? And then, this very evening, let's celebrate together!"

Nikolai and Frank exchanged glances and shrugged their shoulders. Seeing their hesitancy, Tsarkov continued to put on the pressure, "Just a trivial matter; half a day, that's all. We were fixing to get married, but the alcohol demon carried our witnesses off, so now we're stuck looking for new ones. The car's just around the corner, and it's all arranged with the township registrar. And we even have a bride, standing patiently by. Our only hang-up is two reliable eyewitnesses."

"Why not?" Nikolai conceded and looked at Frank. "I could do it, in principle. What about you, Frank White?"

"In principle, so could I, yeah," he nodded enthusiastically, frightened by the prospect of again being left in solitude, alone with his grief. "A wedding! That sounds interesting, and I've never participated in one before."

"Fantastic," Timofey sighed with relief, peering at Frank with some doubt. "You're real lifesavers. I knew I shouldn't have counted on those two anyway. They were too eager for freedom, but freedom isn't in the cards for everyone!" He gestured an invitation, and the whole group set off toward his Jeep.

"That would be no big deal," Tsarkov explained, directing himself primarily to Nikolai, "but we have to do it on the down-low, you understand. Liza's dad is awfully strict: she's a Moscow girl, and they want to hook her up with a general or an oil baron. And here I am, an ordinary guy from Sivoldaisk – so, we need this to be quick and secret, and afterward I'll just say, 'It's done. We got married. Here's my wife!' No matter how strict he was, the man couldn't do anything about it then, right? And tonight, we'll all hang out at Shaman and track down some hotties to keep you two entertained – we're well stocked in that department. *Wherever the moolah is, there's no lack of pretty young things.* 'Course, since I'll be hitched at that point, I'm gonna be struttin' my stuff with my sweetie, now that I've stolen her away and made her mine. Lizzie, show 'em the ring. Let 'em see that we're on the up and up!"

Timofey was content: all was now proceeding as it should. And at the restaurant it would be good to show up accompanied by Muscovites – who had arrived, as it were, with his wife as her old friends from the capital. A blast from the past, one might say, former sins coming to light – and the public will get an opportunity to know the true state of affairs. Here she is, my secret spouse – now it's out in the open; no chance of hiding it. Soon the *patrón* would be informed – and that's alright. Let the chips fall where they may. As for that sharp-toothed Maya, she'd be enraged and fly into a royal fit of course – but what could she change when all is said and done?

The last stage remained: the aforementioned registry office in the village. Tsarkov wasn't worried about that; the director there had his own grave reasons for keeping his lips sealed. He had forged this acquaintance fortuitously, when there were still no storm clouds on the horizon. Of course, even here a gesture of fate was involved, gearing up for some trickery; and Tsarkov could only chalk it up to his credit that he recognized it in time and acted in the only correct fashion.

Incidentally, he himself had partially provoked this gesture: having just barely become affluent, he was taken with the desire to buy an SUV – bulky and black, exactly like that of the Muscovite villain who was to blame for the crisis in his life. Not that he saw any great significance in that, but he wanted to prove to himself he had acquired power over symbols, which included the ability to laugh at them as a testament to his strength. A month or so later, the universe responded by showing that it understood and appreciated the joke:

Timofey's brand new Jeep was hit by another car.

It happened on a cold, rainy evening near a nightclub in the southern quarter of the city. Tsarkov had parked along the sidewalk in a row of vehicles whose owners were already being drenched with cognac in the smoky heat. He sat waiting for a call, looking at his watch and listening to soft jazz. The phone didn't ring, and slanting rain slashed at the windows. The street was devoid of cars and pedestrians alike. Timofey imagined he was in a bathyscaphe descending into the depths of another world, where life was archaic and primitive, primordially savage and cruel to human bodies. The bathyscaphe, however, was unsinkable and reliably shielded him from everything. Tsarkov was captivated by a sense of calm only seldom experienced, but then someone's headlights were reflected in the rearview mirror and brakes squealed, followed by an impact.

The Jeep shuddered, something in it cracked plaintively, and Timofey's neck was suddenly sore. In the mirror he saw the car one spot over – a stocky old Opel – back up, pull into an open lane, and splash through puddles as it sped off. Tsarkov managed to make out some figures on the license plate and then hopped out in the rain to appraise the damage, which turned out not to be extensive – only the powerful bumper was grazed. Worse off was the car before his – which he recognized with smug satisfaction as the BMW belonging to the local soccer coach, with whom he was casually acquainted and had squabbled over some trifle. The street was empty as before – most likely no one other than Timofey knew about the incident. He got back in his Jeep and, after thinking for a moment, drove home. For some reason, he had lost the desire to have fun at the club.

Soon, he found the culprit with assistance of a police major who demanded three bottles of Scotch for his services. The Scotch, as everyone knew – including the major – was distilled right there in the area and had a strange flavor despite the Scottish label. Nevertheless, this didn't prevent Tsarkov from receiving the name and address in a couple of days as requested, after which he set off for the village of Rogozhino to see a fellow by the name of Botvinkin. In the village he found the three-story building without difficulty, with the very same Opel parked in the courtyard which, as the light revealed, was painted light blue and clearly had a smashed front end. "Here we go," thought Tsarkov, and he felt a sudden excitement, as if he were on the threshold of an adventure he had long anticipated.

Botvinkin turned out to be a balding, dark-haired man about forty-five years old. Timofey and his black Jeep scared him half to death. He began to beat his chest, confess his cowardice, and promise considerable money. Timofey took the cash – mainly not to get out of character – but he was much more interested in something else. It was as if he was reliving the Moscow story from long ago – from the opposite side of it. Botvinkin fussed and shivered; Timofey knew he could punch him – over and over, with impunity and without consequences – and he was proud that he did not, and didn't even want to.

Bidding him farewell, Timofey commented as if in passing that the main problem still lay ahead for Botvinkin. "I'm not the only one looking for you," he said gravely. "You didn't bang me up much. But the guy in front of me – him, you smashed up real good. Bad luck for you: he's a serious fellow, on a first-name basis with the governor. Soccer coach Tuvyrin – maybe you've heard of him?"

This information produced quite an impression. The owner of the Opel started shaking again and nearly shed a tear.

"Strange that he hasn't found you yet. He never lets anyone slip away. Or could it be that I was the only one who saw anything?" Timofey pronounced thoughtfully. Then he joked, "If that's true, then you're a lucky duck, especially with a last name like yours."

But it was no laughing matter to Botvinkin. The thought that danger hadn't passed and that the greatest troubles might lie ahead was obviously intolerable. He suddenly grew ashen, such that even Tsarkov felt awkward.

"Hey, don't sweat it. I'm not gonna rat you out," he clapped the man on the shoulder. "But perhaps you can give me a hand when the occasion arises."

Botvinkin, director of the Rogozhino registry office, pressed his hand to his heart as he saw him off and pledged eternal loyalty. Now this commitment came in quite handy: Timofey had no doubt he would do everything as needed – affix the necessary date and stick this business deep within the archives. And when the last difficulty that had arisen due to Yura and Shura's frivolity was finally overcome, he came to be in the best of moods: the complex operation was nearing its end.

"*Don't gallop to the altar on a swift steed*, they say, but we're brave men, aren't we? Be seated, my bride. You are our princess," he intoned, opening the door to the Jeep.

"And you, dear guests, pile in," he nodded toward the back seat. "Let's go get married. *White for marriage, black for mourning...* Never mind that our car is black, Lizzie's soul is radiant!" – and they pulled away laughing, not noticing that, one after the other, two more vehicles filed in behind them.

In one sat Alexander Frolov – still wearing the same baseball cap and dark glasses. His aspect was focused and aggressive. He chewed his lips, fidgeted in his seat, and was the very model of impatience. The car's driver was, in contrast, utterly calm. He was whistling something and held a cigarette in his mouth, unlit out of deference to the nonsmoking passenger.

Alexander had lucked out with the driver. From amidst the throng of freelancers outside the station, he had chosen him according to some inexplicable intuition, and he had guessed correctly. There had actually been no time for reflection: Tsarkov and Elizaveta were already getting into the Cherokee for which Alexander instantly sensed a blazing hatred. He asked the driver to follow the SUV, expecting bothersome questions and hesitation. But the other man, without showing undue curiosity, deftly dove into the stream of cars, daringly hit the gas, and started tailing Timofey, hanging back a little and to the side. Meanwhile, the expression on his face pleased Frolov, as it reflected a kindred spirit – fiery, sharp, and malicious. He thought they might get along, still not believing he hadn't needed to waste time negotiating. The driver, meanwhile, was clearly enjoying the game and pursued them relentlessly and skillfully, hiding behind other cars, letting the black Jeep go, then gaining on the vehicle and its carefree occupants.

En route, the freelance cabbie, whose name was Tolyan, told Frolov of his past which, among other things, included military service in the elite Special Forces. There, he was taught how to tail vehicles, as well as many other things that, unfortunately, he could now find no practical use for. As far as the military was concerned, Tolyan was most likely telling the truth. He was strongly built but moved as softly as a cat, and his face was slightly creased with suffering not befitting his fair-haired, blue-eyed countenance. What he prized most in life, his true pride and joy, was his car: a Zhiguli Nine with a nondescript paint job and a certain shabby, faded look that made it seem to blend into the asphalt, a most welcome feature in this case.

"Don't worry," he declared. "They won't get away from me. They taught us some fancy stuff, believe me. Taught us all we needed – it's a shame there's nowhere to apply it. Here, you came along, and it's my lucky day. Otherwise, it's only good for knocking someone out and snatching their wallet. But I couldn't do that. I've got principles."

Alexander assented, shooting a glance at the tattoo on his powerful forearm. This arm and the large black car ahead were the only realities to which his sight clung. The unfamiliar city held no interest for him. The yellow buildings and trees with dusty foliage, posters on columns, dim billboards, and showcases swam by, but he paid them no mind. Tolyan got silent as he braked at a traffic light, then casually nodded at the Cherokee and asked, "Your wife?"

"Well, yeah," Frolov responded dejectedly, feeling a painful pang in his chest.

"Don't be too upset," the driver said. "That's life. Mine skipped out on me, too. Because of principles. Where there are principles, money is scarce, everyone knows that – so I just keep on trolling for fares… And this hotshot," he grumbled angrily, looking at the Jeep again, "he thinks he owns the world. I'd love to put him in a basement and go to work on him with my fists!"

Pulling up behind Timofey to the new apartment building, Tolyan parked on the other side of the playground, half-hidden by swings and baby carriages. "Let's hang out here a while," he said, averting his eyes. "So, you gonna be in town with us for long?"

"'Bout two days," Frolov sighed. "You want some work for a couple of days?"

He feared Tolyan might refuse, but he agreed easily, asking for quite a small sum of money. "Two grand a day, plus gas, and we're good. I'll haul you in style." He shook his head and hastily added with exaggerated vigor, "If we get time, I'll show you around. We'll take a trip over the river – to the far shore and to Hawk Mountain. They've built a monument there now, a whole memorial, glass and stone. But at night, they say, witches still roam there naked."

"Really?" Alexander muttered as he adjusted his ball cap.

The driver gave him a sidelong glance and continued, "Besides, nearby we have an ancient town here, back to the days of the Tatars. When it flourished, that Moscow of yours was still ruled by the Mongols." Then he cleared his throat and grumbled, "Alright, don't sulk. As for the guy in the Jeep, we'll take care of that dude later. You'll have your revenge, don't worry. If you want to, of course," he added conciliatorily, noting Frolov was frowning as if he had a toothache. "Check it out: here they come. Seems a bit early. Well, let's saddle up!"

Their teamwork was proceeding smoothly. Tolyan the driver, despite his hard life, turned out to be gentle and obliging – neither the Special Forces nor his enterprising wife could spoil his easygoing nature. On Frolov he acted as a mild sedative, and the seriousness with which he regarded business suggested that this business really made sense – even adding to the hope for a positive result.

For the time being, however, the situation offered nothing positive. Bestuzheva and her companion wandered along the waterfront, goofing off and laughing. Alexander, for his part, dismally observed them from the position he had taken up in the adjacent gardens ascending the hill. He was shown this spot by the ubiquitous driver, who had returned to the car to keep the Muscovite "husband" from feeling uncomfortable. The waterfront wasn't large and could all be clearly taken in from his vantage point. Elizaveta behaved naturally and freely, not worrying about whose eyes were on her so far from her normal habitat, and Frolov's vision, devoid of professional focus, wasn't so sharp as might be expected. His emotions finally ran dry when he understood, seeing Timofey with a bouquet of roses, that the old history between them was no more, and there was another story into which his former lover had fallen long ago and for real. No place was left for him in her life; he needed to accept that as a given and to part ways with her forever. Nevertheless, he wanted to watch the film through to the end – merely as an attentive observer – not knowing what to do with it later, when the string of separate shots led to some outcome.

"They're having fun down there," Tolyan whispered, having materialized silently at his side.

Startled, Frolov jumped, glaring angrily as his partner, then he turned away and shrugged his shoulders. "They're just hanging around the same spot," he mumbled. "I'm tired of standing here. Sivoldaisk is probably not a big city at all."

"Sure, if you got cash, then it's not so big," the driver vehemently objected. "And if not, then try as you might, you'll never get past it. And there's no way in hell you'll cross the river. Catch my drift?"

Frolov nodded and was actually about to be lost in contemplation of the Volga, but then he snapped to and stared again at Tsarkov and Elizaveta, who were standing right at the parapet with their backs to him.

"Don't wear yourself out," Tolyan advised him. "Go sit down if you want. I'll keep watch here. Otherwise, if you let anger get the better of you, you'll have bad blood yourself."

"Yeah, I'm almost over it," Alexander muttered, but the driver just looked away. It wasn't easy to convince Tolyan: to his reckoning, women belonged to the enemy camp, the bearers of wickedness and the evil eye. The only exceptions were whores, some of whom were sympathetic and friendly by nature, but the rest deserved contempt, or, ideally, punishment – from whoever had the strength for it. He knew the time would come when a worthy avenger would arise to settle accounts with a wave of his magic sword. Frolov, of course, didn't strike him as an avenger, but their scheming should still lead to a day of reckoning. Otherwise, justice wouldn't triumph, and the driver had a big respect for justice that was somewhat aggressive and threatening to others.

Alexander, he supposed, also thirsted for vengeance, merely concealing it to keep from frightening his driver ahead of time. Tolyan was a bit annoyed with this and tried to hint to Frolov a couple of times that he shared his sentiments and welcomed severe action if there was a worthy reason for that.

"You can push her around a bit, I think," he said softly, as if to himself.

Alexander gave a gloomy grin. "Did you push yours around?" he asked in reply, not taking his eyes off Elizaveta.

"Well, I felt sorry for her," Tolyan unexpectedly admitted. "She was so thin and frail."

"Well, yeah, yeah," Alexander mumbled, thinking there was something here he didn't grasp. It may be in the middle of nowhere, but this city is far from simple, he concluded, and this somehow made him feel better.

While Timofey and Elizaveta dined at a riverside restaurant, the driver made a run for beef *pierogies* and drinking water. The *pierogies* turned out to be unexpectedly tasty. Frolov bit into the char-baked dough and licked the meaty juice from his fingers, noting once more – as he had before the train – his surprisingly healthy appetite. The intrigue has ended, he thought with a certain irony. It no longer stresses me out. I'll go drinking this evening – with Tolyan here. Maybe he's right – she deserves pity, and what could one expect from her anyway?

However, when the happy pair set off to Tsarkov's office, the driver shook his head and declared, "Nope, something's not right. This doesn't add up: after the train they just tossed their things in the apartment, and now, excuse my frankness, it's high time for them to go screw, but look – they went right to his workplace like busy little bees. And he never even kissed her once... I can't wrap my head around it. Maybe this isn't just hanky-panky? Maybe it's more serious than that – for instance, what if they're stealing money from you?"

"Forget about it. What's there to steal?" Frolov grinned dismissively but got tense and took a hard stare at the office doors. Tolyan's words alarmed him, and it all came back: the nervous shakes, disorientation, contradictory thoughts. Who knows, maybe he'd viewed everything in the wrong light? He'd beaten it into his head: "She's cheating! She's cheating!" But could it be that the bouquet at the station didn't mean anything? After all, a bouquet can also be just a sign of courtesy – or some other kind of sign, or maybe genuine deceit?

So what difference does it make if this guy is an old friend, he thought with a desperate hope. We know about those kinds of friends, and who can figure what's going on in his brain? There's something strange here – how had he not noticed it before? Indeed, they hadn't kissed a single time – Tolyan, he was really sharp-eyed. And the types who drive Jeeps like that would take a girl to bed quickly, without all this ceremony.

"Gimme some water," he asked hoarsely. Tolyan passed him the bottle without saying another word, feeling that Alexander's mind was busy. The sense of alarm grew. Something should have happened, but time dragged on ever so slowly, draining his soul.

She probably just didn't want to draw me into problems, protecting me from danger, thought Frolov glumly, clenching his fists. That's why she'd severed communication and broken off all contact. And he, being a real knucklehead, couldn't think of anything but his own pride. And Margo, she had masterfully messed with his head, the bitch!

When Elizaveta left the office alone, his heart skipped a beat.

And when she started talking to complete strangers, he thought she might need immediate rescue and nearly jumped out of the car. But then Timofey appeared, everyone got to conversing and laughing, and she clearly demonstrated no discomfort, so any help might seem out of place. When the whole merry band piled into Tsarkov's Jeep, Alexander realized he didn't understand anything at all.

"This wife of yours is acting pretty weird," Tolyan shook his head as he started the car.

Frolov merely shrugged his shoulders and didn't answer.

"Now what's up with these goons?" his partner whistled, noting a VW microbus, as beat up as his own Zhiguli, which turned out of its parking spot and pulled in to tail the Jeep. "Maybe another jealous husband popped out of the woodwork, eh?" he attempted to joke, but it was obvious he was getting nervous. The affair had taken an unexpectedly nasty turn.

"It seems to me..." Tolyan turned and scratched the back of his head. "Seems to me, these guys are badder dudes than the two of us!"

CHAPTER 16

The three men in the microbus indeed looked more serious than Alexander Frolov and his driver, and most resembled grotesque gangsters from a comic book. They seemed to fill nearly half of the spacious vehicle, though it still had five seats free. Behind the wheel sat the oldest of them, a raven-haired tough with the jaw of a prizefighter. Next to him fidgeted a tall man with a clean-shaven scalp who was hastily pecking the buttons of his mobile phone with thick, unbending fingers.

"It's me," he yelled into the receiver, covering the other ear with his palm. "We're following him, but he's not alone again. He's with some chick… the same one, yeah. And there's a couple of men with him, too. Average Joes, by the looks of it… Yeah, how should I know?" He was quiet for a while, then started arguing with the person on the other end, explaining himself mainly through interjections. Upon concluding the conversation, he slid the phone into his pocket and let loose a string of profanity.

"What's up?" inquired Mr. Tough without turning his head.

"It's a madhouse there," the tall man answered grudgingly. "Makar isn't around, and the boss is out too. The two of them are tied up somewhere and the others don't know shit, the gorillas."

He cursed again, not as maliciously this time, and turned away to stare out the side window. One of his ears was misshapen and turned in on itself, making his face look even more ruthless.

"Tied up, tied up... He doesn't have time for us, so what the fuck should we do?" he grumbled. "They haven't been able to get him on the phone for two hours now, and the agreement was that we do the thing today!"

"So, what's up, then? What did they say?" Mr. Tough asked angrily.

"What did they say?" the third thug with a hook nose and very hairy hands repeated like an echo behind them.

"Said to grab them all," the tall one sneered. "Then they'll get it sorted without us. Now where're we going to stick everybody?"

Mr. Tough cut him off with a frown, "Not our problem. All means all, they'll fit in here. Look, they took the road to our pier themselves! Funny, huh?"

Timofey, in the meantime, turned toward the northern exit from the city. Behind him, the Volkswagen and Zhiguli Nine stuck like glue, trying to blend into the stream of traffic. However, no one in the lead car noticed what was happening behind them. The hoods in the microbus were used to attack, not defense; moreover, they were dealing with a harmless target, and this was in a city where no one knew them. And Tsarkov had let his guard down, assuming that events were bending to his will and the difficulties were all behind him.

However, his take on events was a bit misguided. The microbus creeping after them hinted at circumstances of which Tsarkov had no idea. Even if he had heard of them from someone, he would have considered it totally absurd. Yet that didn't alter the state of affairs one iota. And this state was none too pleasant, as underscored by the ominous countenance of the pursuers in the Volkswagen. They were employed by the same *patrón* – the father of the enamored Maya – whose friendship Timofey thought was rock-solid. The *patrón*'s goal coincided completely with Tsarkov's own desire. He wanted to avoid the impending wedding – at any more-or-less reasonable cost.

Truth be told, Timofey Tsarkov had long aroused his doubts:

since the time they first met, much had changed to reveal a new side to things. Tsarkov's eyes lost their dogged sheen – that sign of hunger and restlessness. He had outgrown himself, acquired strength, and become imposing in his bearing. It even sometimes seemed he had ceased to be fearful, and the *patrón* didn't like people who weren't afraid of him. Of course, both recognized he could grind Timofey into dust with a snap of his fingers if he wished, but the readiness for humiliation had disappeared from the other's voice and face. Tsarkov became shrewd and at times expressed himself with excessive ambiguity. The *patrón* thought more than once that his smug, impudent protégé needed to be taught a lesson – not that he was growing dangerous, but he still needed to know his place. And besides, from time to time, it was beneficial for anyone to be brought back to earth from their lofty heights – just for their own good.

This situation was aggravated by Timofey being a Muscovite. The *patrón* didn't trust Muscovites, being suspicious of their insincerity and cockiness which, no matter how deeply it was hidden, would always surface eventually. "Soon, he'll begin to get uppity," he thought of Tsarkov, "if he hasn't already started." This notion bothered him. It reminded him of the utterly insulting carelessness with which he himself was treated in the capital by *apparatchik* bosses, after which he wanted to spit and grind his teeth, and had to medicate himself with expensive cognac, or maybe even vodka, in the company of young girls.

Maya's sudden whim merely accelerated the denouement: it was clear to the *patrón* that he could delay no longer. He had envisioned the groom for his only daughter as someone else – a man with prospects and a reputation, accepted in society and living in Moscow itself, not in this pitiful backwater. He had worked out a plan of action, including setting up Maya at the best university in the capital and arranging the corresponding recreation. Tsarkov was not at all suitable to occupy the place of future son-in-law: he was, by and large, nobody – and he intended, most likely, to remain nobody in the years to come. As far as money was concerned, the *patrón* had plenty of his own, and Timofey, for all his exploits, was still not nearly successful enough to merit any financial respect according to today's standards.

The discussion with Tsarkov about the upcoming engagement, intended as a test of the current status quo, was the straw that broke his patience. It was clear this man was squirming, holding back some ugly secret. This would simply not do, and for that Timofey must be punished. Weighing everything as he should, the *patrón* made the decision to finish the issue once and for all.

Being a man of old-fashioned principles, he wasn't considering extreme measures to guarantee that "once and for all" meant a permanent end to Timofey's life. The case was not so egregious: he hadn't been slighted to the extent that revenge was necessary, regardless of the means. Timofey just had to be schooled a little to put fear into him and force him to leave the city – and surrender to the *patrón* what he had created over the years. He had long been keeping tabs on Tsarkov's firm, and the business seemed promising and novel in its approach. Taking it over – through dummy corporations and the like, of course – was tempting in itself. Moreover, it imbued the scheme with needed scope, transforming it from a domestic squabble into a business matter.

On the whole, all was falling into place. The "fiancé" had to be frightened properly, so that he disappeared in the blink of an eye and never thought about further escapades – in Sivoldaisk itself or its environs. Who knew what might pop into his head when he became poor again? He could start shooting off his mouth or, even worse, decide to look up Maya and take advantage of her feelings. Anything might happen then: liaisons behind her father's back, undesirable consequences, a secret marriage – she was still just a child after all, and fully capable of losing her head.

No, Tsarkov must be driven as far as possible from the Volga, under the promise of some serious terror. He has family in the Urals, the *patrón* reasoned coldly. Let him go there where he belonged. Or let him return home to Moscow, where there were tons like him, vagrant hucksters. He wouldn't cross paths with darling Maya in the capital; no one would let him anywhere near her circles, and, besides, he would hardly look attractive there at all. She would go a little ballistic, of course – and the doting father involuntarily frowned at this, knowing full well how adept she was at pitching a tantrum, the unruly brat – but she would come to her senses. Such is youth: time heals all wounds. That mantra would never let one down. So, let him get thrown out of town – and be very happy to escape alive. And let him lose the apartment, too – no need for him to have a place to live in Sivoldaisk!

To execute the plan, he found people in Togliatti – through his old acquaintances in nefarious realms – and gave careful instructions to the most experienced of them after putting him in charge and empowering him with full authority. They were instructed to act fiercely and convincingly but not go too far and complete everything post haste – in the event of unforeseen tricks from Timofey, who might later behave foolishly from despair, which would demand yet another, possibly terminal, explanation. The *patrón* intended to wrap up all the details prior to Maya's arrival and therefore ordered the Togliatti boys to "resolve the issue" at the earliest convenience. As a result, they scheduled the operation for Monday, which, for a variety of reasons, seemed the most reasonable. The *patrón* didn't object and was quite content with this plan of action, as he confirmed by phone the night before. Of course, had he known of the innocent bystanders, the plan would have been aborted and delayed until a more accommodating moment, but his interference in the course of events was not meant to be. And the gangsters' handpicked leader, for all his experience, didn't dare change the agreed-upon date.

Meanwhile, Timofey and his companions had no idea that trouble threatened them. In the black SUV they were getting acquainted at full speed. All were talkative and lively, including Elizaveta Bestuzheva. Her doubts had vanished without a trace – at least for the present. Worlds inside shouted at the top of their lungs, even with a certain exultation, and it felt totally natural to her.

The confidentiality of the upcoming event drew the company together, transforming them into accomplices linked by a common secret. The fact that the bride and the witnesses had arrived on the same train also added mutual sympathy. All lamented that being in different cars had prevented them from getting to know each other en route – and they rejoiced at the whim of fate that had brought them together in the same city, which seemed much less probable.

"Numbers can never be understood; they must simply be believed," Nikolai declared vaguely, and the others considered him with awe, especially Frank, who was reminded of the mathematicians who could now hardly expect any financial aid.

"Sivoldaisk must be a pretty small city," Kramskoy added for some unknown reason. Some echo of condescension could be heard in this, and Timofey, who had been silent and just casting glances at Elizaveta up until then, came alive. "Well, who knows?" he smiled and explained mysteriously, *"The soul may be caged while the spirit soars,"* at which Liza rolled her eyes.

"I never knew you were so into folklore!" she said to him. "And you're a Muscovite. Aren't you stifled here?"

"I love my baby when she busts my balls," Tsarkov laughed and cracked a few more boorish jokes, clearly avoiding an answer, but the discussion drifted on its own to the capital. It turned out they had all lived a substantial part of their lives there – even at the same time and not very far from each other. As they compared street names and high schools, all were again astonished they hadn't met earlier – and Nikolai's statement about numbers appeared even more convincing. Then all focused their attention on Frank's foreignness and pressed him with inquiries, at which Timofey was especially zealous, looking at White, Jr. with a more cunning eye than at the others.

Being in the spotlight, Frank didn't clam up but, on the contrary, rose to the occasion as a true American and recounted his recent Moscow adventures rather humorously, concentrating on their alcoholic side and omitting details of a more personal nature. All laughed, and then Tsarkov asked brusquely, "So what brings you to our neck of the woods, then?"

This produced a sudden speed bump in the conversation. Frank

White abruptly lost not only his vivacity of speech but even his command of the language as he muttered something vaguely about a Russian great-grandfather and his estate. Even more out of place, he mentioned some sort of map that was supposedly genuine, though maybe it wasn't really. All the while he was looking at Nikolai as if seeking support, and Tsarkov, watching the whole scene unfold in the rearview mirror, murmured with a snicker, "Yeah, your family roots are quite elusive," and added in a low voice, "*The conquerors are kings, and the beaten are bandits,*" after which Frank shut up in embarrassment.

Kramskoy came to his assistance, feeling somehow responsible for him, and began with slightly feigned buoyancy to question the newlyweds on the story of how they met. Timofey merely grinned at this and gazed fixedly again at White, Jr., but Liza turned around and readily set to recalling their romance, which had taken place in the best traditions of idyllic youth. Then it was her turn to dissemble a little as she glossed over the last seven years; and Tsarkov, attempting to play along, didn't know right away how to answer the natural question of why he and his bride worked in different cities. As for the forthcoming wedding and its hastiness, he said nothing at all, extracting himself from the commentary by humorous banter with Elizaveta, who was admiring her new ring with exaggerated attention.

"The sapphire is a noble stone. Wear it, and you can wed Satan himself if you want," he intoned, drawing out his words. "How is it, lovely Liza, that he hasn't stolen you away yet?"

"Well, he could have – if you'd waited longer," she chuckled in response.

"*We'd been waiting, waiting, and all was for naught,*" sighed Tsarkov. "*Then we were getting married while the devils sang a song.* Such is life – some things don't go fast, and you didn't hurry me, either."

"That was out of modesty," Elizaveta dropped her eyes for effect. Then, turning to the men seated behind them, she asked Nikolai Kramskoy, "So, are you here on business or just because?"

"You could say, 'just because,'" he replied evasively. "Though there are some matters to attend to."

"Matters of the heart, I'm sure," laughed Timofey. "Lots of guys come here for our hot women."

"No, at the regional museum," Nikolai said absently, and the Jeep shook as everyone laughed. It was especially funny to Frank White for some reason, who wiped away the tears moistening his eyes. Elizaveta hid her blushing face in her hands, and even Nikolai laughed a bit so as not to be left out. Tsarkov summarized solemnly, "Pretty good group we have here," and they exchanged meaningful glances as if another common mystery had been uncovered, though everyone's secrets were completely different.

"Excuse me," Frank addressed him. "Timofey – is that your full name? Is it the best thing to call you?"

"Well, yeah. It's Timothy in your language. Although a lot of folks here just call me Tsar…"

They left the city and rolled along the highway, beside which rose a dense forest. The road was deserted, except for the microbus crawling along a hundred meters back and Tolyan's Zhiguli Nine about the same distance behind it. Alexander Frolov sat in silence, firmly gripping the armrest. His grim colleague, meanwhile, kept repeating that he was baffled about what was going on.

"Things, they are simple in this town, you know," he grumbled in frustration. "Strange stuff doesn't happen here. And if anything odd does occur, then look out! As for these guys, who the hell knows what's up?"

"You figure it could be dangerous?" asked Frolov in a strained voice without taking his eyes off the Volkswagen.

"Dangerous? Ha!" sneered Tolyan. "Anything can turn dangerous in these parts. Don't go looking for trouble, and it won't find you so easily!" He frowned and added, "People here are generally quiet, but when they get heated, they just lose control. No holds barred, that's all the rage these days. No brains, my platoon commander used to say, means no brakes either. So how's no brakes for you? Dangerous, eh? But that's the land we live in!"

They were silent a bit. "Nice weather," Alexander sighed. "Good for a picnic."

"Got that right," his comrade agreed. "Picnic's just what they have in mind. Them and the other folks. 'Cept it seems to me everybody's idea of fun is different – with their own binges and their own crowd. No chicks with 'em neither – they're not going for a romp, that's for sure. Whoa, check it out!"

The microbus had picked up speed and caught up with Tsarkov. Then, still accelerating, it slid around and clipped the Jeep, forcing him to stop. Tolyan cursed and pulled onto the shoulder as well. Frolov sighed fitfully as three people jumped out of the Volkswagen and rushed to the Jeep, wielding things that looked like pistols. They moved nimbly and quickly. One opened the driver's side door and tossed Timofey out with a single fluid motion. The other two, meanwhile, handled the passengers. Soon, all four were escorted by their attackers into the microbus, which pulled away with a lurch. Tolyan again spat out some vulgarities, pounded his fist on the wheel, and hit the gas in pursuit.

"Just like a movie," he growled through his teeth. "Thriller and comedy all in one go. And we're playing the clowns. Did you at least catch their license number?" he turned to Frolov, who was white as a sheet.

"No," the other answered guiltily and wiped his face with his palm. "I didn't have a chance. And you?"

"What are you sitting there for, then, Sherlock?" Tolyan erupted. He suddenly changed, becoming unkind and quarrelsome. "Didn't have a chance... Write this down, I did your job for you. Those plates of theirs aren't local!"

Soon the abductors' van came into view. Tolyan cut his speed and hung back at a respectable distance without coming too close.

"Aren't they going to get away?" Alexander asked with alarm.

"Better they get away than blow our heads off," the other snapped with a shrug of his shoulders. "We've already come where we weren't invited."

Frolov didn't speak, though all inside him was seething. He felt the conclusion was near and soon his afflictions would end. He had only one fear: all would transpire without him being present. The danger, as sharply as Tolyan sensed it, was not so great according to his reckoning. He didn't believe the abductors would cause Elizaveta harm, and, if worse came to worst, he supposed he could somehow manage to rescue her. The fate of everyone else – including his own, to some degree – didn't concern him in the least.

"Police checkpoint soon. They'll probably turn off before it," said Tolyan, who was now calm and even gave an encouraging nod. And, in fact, about eight hundred meters further, the Volkswagen turned right and dropped out of sight. "They're headed to the Volga," Tolyan sighed and rubbed the nape of his neck. "No doubt they've got a boat there. Whether they're local or not, they know their way around."

Reaching the spot where the microbus disappeared, they saw a barely discernible track of matted grass. It curved off in an arc, going to the side and vanishing into thickets of nettles and raspberry cane. "Well, should we risk it?" the driver asked with chagrin. "We're already neck deep in this. If we bump into them, we're goners."

Frolov, thinking he might refuse to drive further, looked at him imploringly and said hoarsely, "Let's risk it, eh?"

"Fuck!" Tolyan grumbled as he heaved another sigh, scowled, but turned off the highway, and the Zhiguli slowly picked its way deep into the woods.

They slogged through about a kilometer, diligently circumventing deep potholes and shuddering over ruts and roots, the driver swearing through his teeth the whole time, feeling sorry for the car as he cursed his own stupidity. Then he braked and peered ahead, though nothing could be made out through the trees. Proceeding forward a bit more, he decisively turned the wheel, wound between the pines, and parked right in the middle of the forest, about fifty meters off the track that could hardly be called a road.

"Why'd you do that?" Frolov asked.

"The shore's coming up soon," Tolyan growled. "What? You wanna run right into the back of them?" He cut the motor and commanded with a shrill whisper, "Let's get to that hillock on foot, double quick!"

They ran at a dogtrot to the hill just in time to see a large boat with people on the deck sailing upstream. "There's your girl," Tolyan pointed confidently. "They're hauling them to an island. You can even see the number. Remember this: A, V, four, three, three, five..."

"Which island?" Alexander turned to him, panting heavily after the climb.

"How should I know which? There's hundreds of 'em here," Tolyan spat and looked away. "A bad turn of events. Let's head back."

"How are we going to go after them now?" asked Frolov, his voice cracking. "We've got to go after them! Do you have a boat?"

"Yep, I carry one in the trunk," his companion snapped wearily. "Use your head. What good's a boat going to do you? What do we need one for – so they can sink us along with it? No, we have to return now. We only have one play: we go to the cops."

CHAPTER 17

Andrei Fyodorovich Astakhov, Kramskoy's friend in Sivoldaisk, woke up Monday in a bad mood. The window flap in the kitchen had creaked from the wind during the night and banged against the ledge. When he got up to latch it shut, all drowsiness disappeared, so Andrei tossed and turned on crumpled sheets till dawn. The alarm went off, as always, at nine. He furiously smacked it with his palm and immediately dozed off again. Then he overslept until midday, wasting the best hours of the morning.

Now he was tormented by a headache and general discontent with the state of affairs. He frowned, screwed up his face, and scratched his unshaven cheek in front of the mirror. There was reflected his angular features, high hairline, slightly hooked nose in which something Roman could be detected, and large eyes colored gray-green in the light of the halogen lamp, with a clearly distinguishable wolf-tinted yellow rim.

In contrast to Kramskoy, Andrei Fyodorovich didn't attribute drops in mood to the whims of unseen, external forces. Morning despair, as he understood it, was a quite natural phenomenon explained – along with the uneasy night – by disappointment in his own slothfulness and the assortment of failures that had haunted him for several days. The last straw was a breakdown at the regional communication center, leaving Astakhov without a home phone line and, consequently, access to the Web, which caused a host of inconveniences. That's why he hadn't responded to Nikolai's letter – and didn't know Kramskoy was now in his city, having arrived that very morning on a train from Moscow.

Exiting the bathroom, Andrei Fyodorovich cast a glance at the clock hanging above the entrance, snorted in frustration, and strode through the flat considering his daily routine, which was already hopelessly dashed by waking up late. There were only two rooms, adjoined by a kitchen and a spacious vestibule with crown molding around the ceiling. He had already become attached to his apartment and even loved it with a slightly embarrassed affection, in spite of the pink wallpaper and the naïve Empire décor. He had rented it from a youthful woman of fifty-something, though he didn't remember the landlady so much as her young daughter, who tantalized him as she walked barefoot over the floor mats as if they were the parquet tiles of a ballroom. In many respects, it was because of her feet that he came again, ostensibly to look over the place once more, and then somehow agreed to a three-year lease – although the landlady's daughter never responded to his advances.

The kitchen smelled of last night's meal. Andrei cursed and flung the ill-fated shutters wide open. Instead of fresh air and coolness, a foul, scorched odor wafted in – somewhere close by, someone was burning bitumen or a piece of rubber.

"Damned city," Astakhov shook his head. Something alarmed him: all was going awry. He even heard a slight ringing in his ears – or was his body just reacting to many days of sweltering heat, anticipating a change in the weather?

"Alright, then!" he shouted at himself and, with exaggerated vigor, headed toward the office. There he spread a thin, firm rug on the floor and began his exercises, which he had every reason to put off today. But Andrei Fyodorovich decided not to give himself a pass. He started with a Pranayama routine, then performed a few simple *asanas* and stiffened into a *Yoga Mudra* which, everyone knows, promotes harmony of spirit. Coming out of it, he grinned ironically, rolled up the rug, and threw it in the corner. Following this, he stripped down to his skin and did the Taoist Dance of the Testes – the first step on the path to the mysteries of alchemical sex – followed by a five-minute workout of the Chi muscle, directing the energy of the universe upwards along his spine. This all made him almost cheerful, but when he, prancing like Shiva, headed to the bathroom to take a contrast shower, his gaze fell upon the local newspaper whose female reporter had come by a few days previously. At this, his mood was spoiled anew.

She had done nothing wrong, as Astakhov knew quite well, which made him even angrier at himself. The girl was smiling and kind, even showing a certain piety – probably for show, but perhaps partly sincere: not so long ago Andrei Fyodorovich numbered among the "genuine" writers, which in Sivoldaisk could be counted on one hand. His biggest novel, after torturous postponements and delays, had finally been published by a rather solid firm. A review of it was even issued, though the author misquoted the title in one place. As far as the province saw it, this was a success, and it was closely followed by the local weekly, which sent the visitor who brought along a nut pie and initially touched Astakhov with her habit of blowing on her cup of hot tea, pressing her lips together like a child. Then, however, the interview went sour. Fluttering her eyelashes, she asked what all his books were about, most specifically the aforementioned novel; and Astakhov grew nervous, then became prickly and assumed a totally unnecessary tone.

He generally hated to talk about such things, and the girl, on top of that, had gotten him in a combative mood by using several clichés – albeit without any ulterior motive. Andrei, however, took this as mockery. He got irritated and turned from gracious host to an arrogant elitist, making a sweeping statement that this sort of question was not just odd, but indeed rather ridiculous. The years he had spent on this novel were not few, and he could not now be expected to relate everything in a minute or two. By the same token, if someone were interested, it wouldn't be a bad idea to pluck up the determination and spend considerable time, perhaps not years but at least a month, digesting the writing, to experience it thoughtfully and without haste. Only then could one speak with the author as an equal. "Otherwise, it's not even worth the effort," he cut her off glumly, looking at the floor.

At this, the journalist, obviously confused, retorted she might gladly spend a month on it if she could know for certain the novel had worthwhile content, and that the author was not an impostor or charlatan.

"You see," he said despondently, "you don't want to give the book a chance, but assume ahead of time that it's bad. Why should I hope for the best and assume that you're not desperately stupid?"

The girl's eyes misted over, and only then did he understand he had gone too far, attacking his interlocutor for no reason at all. They made peace and laughed a lot, and she even shot Astakhov very inviting glances, but he was still not himself and the invitation went unanswered. Even now that a week had passed, this episode still sat in his mind like a splinter, forcing him to wince and sigh.

His writing he approached painfully, not knowing how to explain its significance even to himself. Every attempt to get to the bottom of his thinking led him to pompous formulations that he feared, seeing in them a symptom of feeblemindedness, no matter how important the concept. Therefore, every time uninvited notions of beauty, harmony, or the attainability of perfection crept into his head, he became terribly angry, sneered, and jumped to the safety of pragmatics as if that defined the basis of his labors. This basis, Andrei Fyodorovich knew, was quite shaky – no money or fame awaited him – but there was nothing more to rely on. So he reluctantly convinced himself he was aspiring to recognition – at least to impart a good fate for his books. The finer motivations were not worth further reflection, for those reflections from the very beginning exuded blatant mysticism. Astakhov didn't care for mysticism; he avoided it and gave it as wide a berth as possible, replacing it, if not with something rational, then at least with what was familiar and ordinary. For example, the regret over the futility of all his efforts and over the fact that time was flying by too quickly: when his books came to be valued according to their worth, he would most likely be old, his sex appeal would have vanished, and thus he would be unable to make full use of the fruits of success.

The issue of fast-flying time provided yet another interesting perspective. Writing books, like nothing else, distracted him from thoughts of inevitable death. He had a multitude of ideas that couldn't be implemented soon, and therefore he felt his life would be long. Those who credited him with a burst of creativity probably knew what they were doing and should now take measures to keep him from slipping into oblivion until he had written all his books.

It was imperative he continue putting pressure on himself, Astakhov guessed. As soon as it eased up, all guarantees would be off – and so he was unceasingly concerned about keeping his "creative nerve" in decent shape. Doing this was easy: the nerve vibrated quite consistently on its own, not allowing itself to be ignored. Andrei even dared on occasion to reflect upon time with a sense of superiority. Indeed, he had found the strength to do something and not throw up his hands – that is, not give in to terror or despair when thoughts assaulted him regarding the finality of everything.

Hardest of all was explaining to others what he was up to and what the point of it was. Those same pragmatics he used to deceive himself didn't withstand scrutiny when spoken aloud in response to someone's innocent question. Everyone noticed their lack of a core – even if he, personally, earned only pennies and hardly made ends meet. As for those who enjoyed a comfortable living, they didn't even bother to conceal a grin and often asked with condescension why Astakhov couldn't approach the matter seriously and attune his restive muse to the realities of demand and the laws of the market. In these cases, he lost patience and could behave very rudely. Ultimately, he stopped mentioning his literary pursuits at all and introduced himself as a broker, or an exchange analyst, or a psychologist dealing with intimate areas, if he wanted to play a little prank. This shut down questions instantly; people hung a label on him and lost interest, which he was quite content with as he chuckled mildly inside.

With official literary bodies, his relations weren't very good, either – especially with publishers who didn't appreciate an author's obstinacy. Only by happenstance did his novel catch the eye of a functionary at a large Petersburg publishing house whose name reminded Andrei of a seashell or a chamber pot. The functionary condescended to grant a personal meeting and was haughty and grandiloquent. Astakhov, who had made a special trip to St. Pete's for this encounter, nearly spoiled the whole deal himself when he took umbrage with something and copped an attitude. But then he relaxed and became absorbed in another matter: the executive astonishingly matched one of the protagonists of the new book he intended to start. It was a reminder of what Andrei had heard recently: that in this city, weak and spectral gray, each person connected in some way with literature is deeply concerned about purity in the ranks – a phrase which here implied sexual orientation. Why literati cultivated in the cradle of the Revolution were so intolerant of gays, no one was able to explain, but Astakhov found the idea itself amusing. He decided to use it in one of his story arcs and now observed with interest that the owner of the office, for all his overbearing arrogance, clearly exhibited some suspicious quirks.

The publisher was fairly young, chubby, and shaven bald. His loose-fitting, untucked shirt seemed too long for him, though it did cover his full hips, even as it comically puffed out behind him. His mannerisms smacked of deliberate rigidity, as if, with all his being, he wanted to live up to his first name, a symbol of an uncompromising, irreconcilable temper – but his gaze revealed something else. The inclination of his head was a bit coquettish and his fingers had a nervous life of their own, as if tugging at a cambric handkerchief.

Andrei Fyodorovich dreamed up a story about a timid teenager, sensitive about his defect since childhood. He had then attempted to conceal it from his whole countrified family – from his grandfather, son of Nazar the blacksmith; from his father, son of Fedot the miller; and, most of all, from his exalted mother ripped from the suburbs, descended from Russified Germans. Then he grew up and broke into society, splitting for good with his country roots, but even there he had no peace: obsolete patriarchalism was replaced by the distrustfulness of his literary colleagues. Hiding from them was even harder, and despair was already kindled deep in his soul: it seemed the whole world was dogging his every step – quite sharply... This all turned out to be amusing – and the future character rose right before Astakhov's eyes. Meanwhile, the conversation flowed on and concluded quite amicably – though the publishing firm later dragged out the novel's release for more than a year.

Only Kramskoy took his writing affairs with appropriate seriousness, most likely because he himself was under the power of strange metaphysics, which Andrei never inquired after in detail. However, it was Nikolai to whom he occasionally addressed long letters in which, sparing no ink, he painted the fundamentals of playing with words. He put forth arguments and examples, extolled the power of linguistic forms, and even waxed a bit tediously while explaining why some books turn into icons, though their plot is worn and they are quite primitive in spirit. These letters he invariably tore up, but they nevertheless helped him retain his determination by reminding him, with pomposity or without it, that the pragmatism was actually nothing. The true meaning of his efforts – here it was, intact and powerful, and there was no hiding from it.

Standing with the ill-fated newspaper for a moment or two, Andrei Fyodorovich carefully folded it, smashed down the contents of the garbage pail with it, and proceeded into the bathroom. The contrast shower didn't work out – turning the hot-water nozzle produced nothing. Astakhov was about to get angry, but then ordered himself to consider this a chance to test his own endurance and washed under the cold jets, which demanded mustering all his strength. In the shower, forgetting about the journalist, he muttered homemade mantras intended to ease the tribulation, but they provided no relief and he suffered in full until jumping out and wrapping up in a towel. Rubbing himself dry and rejoicing at the long-awaited warmth, Andrei thought in passing that this week he needed to try three new yoga postures, especially *Virasana* to temper the nervous system. Then he felt very hungry, and a minute later set about the kitchen, heating the teapot and rummaging through the fridge, which had two sections like a wardrobe.

Today's breakfast was rather plentiful and included toast with red caviar, a few slices of expensive sturgeon, and a large cup of Chinese tea of a variety selected at random from five or six that were always kept in special jars. To the tea he added nuts – a mix of filbert and almonds – which, as everyone knows, promote strengthening of the Chi muscle itself, and, in consequence, the body systems related to it. When it came to food, Andrei Fyodorovich never economized – even when his financial state left much to be desired. The present couldn't be called problematic, but there was no sense losing his head either, so his expenses were meticulously controlled and overseen according to the rules he had made. There was still enough, however, for delicacies or other simple pleasures, especially in the province where life remained inexpensive compared to the pricing madness in the capital.

At one time, Astakhov and Nikolai Kramskoy had studied together at the same university and were considered friends who had much in common. Then their paths diverged briefly before crossing again during the story with the Technology T that had been sold to the gullible Dutchmen. In contrast to Kramskoy, Andrei Fyodorovich decided to toy with fate and increase his easily acquired money, for which he was swiftly punished. Fortunately, he didn't lose everything – after settling with creditors, he was left with about a third of the capital and a two-room Moscow apartment. Andrei regarded this as a final warning and promised himself to concentrate solely on writing books without getting distracted by side pursuits and temptations.

He knew it was very easy to go astray when sidetracked. The surrounding world he perceived as a freakish mixture of substances – a large cauldron where notions, guidelines, and thoughts were jumbled together. Their nature was movement and mutability. Their essence was impetuousness, which is life itself. In his youth, Astakhov tried to catch up with life, learn to run level with it, and keep pace with the others. Mastering this, it seemed he joined their ranks and went head to head with the rest. But then, through inertia, he overtook nearly everyone and was suddenly in solitude – forever. It was here he understood that only literature truly and fully grabbed him. Writing had to be done in fits; nevertheless, he soon sensed serious potential within himself and impatiently waited for the moment when he could yield to it completely. This was rather naïve – by all rights, he wouldn't be able to earn serious money – but, as sometimes happens, naïveté took the prize as it outran many in the wild race of statistics. The rules affirmed themselves through the rarest of contradictions: Astakhov received the Dutch payout and, losing a large part of it, was definitely convinced that financial success was afforded him exclusively to realize his talent.

He carefully counted up the remainder and took to planning the future, approaching it with commensurate gravity and no longer depending on intuition and blind chance. Estimating how much he would spend in a week, a month, and a year – with adjustments for *force majeure* like marriage or illness – Andrei Fyodorovich displayed the results graphically in the form of optimistic and pessimistic curves. The area between them was shaded blue – it was sufficiently large and traced out a strange figure trailing off with a long tail into the foggy distance. That was where no place remained for either optimism or pessimism, but it wasn't worth dwelling on sad matters. The bright blue living space looked impressive enough, and the countdown hadn't even commenced yet.

From this, it followed that he had to dispense his funds without luxury – the topmost of the plotted curves soon crossed a bold red line beyond which penury awaited. Weighing the obvious pros and cons, Andrei Fyodorovich shrugged and, with no remorse, left insanely over-priced Moscow, relocating to the Volga city of Sivoldaisk, where he had been born and which he remembered not at all.

This was facilitated by a divorce from his second wife, Yulia. She didn't want money – since she had left him for a man of much greater means – but their breakup had been nerve-wracking and sucked all the energy from Astakhov. Yulia was riddled with guilt; she thought, with her leaving, Andrei's life would be turned into one long torment. She wanted him to recognize this too, but he was stubborn, so she wore him down with calls and unannounced visits, being jealous and causing scenes as though she still had rights to him.

Astakhov became coarse with Yulia, but this merely encouraged her. She even began to hint she saw in him another man, one for whom she might develop new, unambiguous interest. This was too much, and Andrei, who had grown ten years younger after the divorce, cravenly fled the capital a month before the appointed term, repulsed by the very thought of the affected paroxysms of Yulia's suffocating passion.

With women, his luck was generally not good, and he took this in stride, considering it appropriate. Astakhov had long understood that no one was fully capable of sharing his abiding passion for the harmony of words and thoughts, much less endure the mechanism of its creation: him. He knew he was attractive enough, but it soon became clear to all that his response was worth little: he was too involved with himself and not ready to sacrifice anything. In this sense, Andrei Fyodorovich demonstrated even further extremes than his friend Kramskoy – but, fortunately, his interest in the opposite sex was much less strong, marked by a certain detachment that women are not wont to forgive.

Nevertheless, he was never left without some female asserting her ownership of him. The first marriage transpired in his early youth and taught him a thing or two – mainly that in choosing a bride one needed to remember the significance of one's social niche. His spouse – stout, light-haired Galya – quickly understood this and more than once bitterly recalled her grandmother's advice: Never marry a man from outside your circle. She was distinguished by a strong persistence in achieving her goals. Her principal tactic in any battle was constant pressure: she focused on the most important point and didn't allow herself a single superfluous thought. All should serve a purpose: strengthening the family's prosperity and her own small business.

At first, this attracted Astakhov. He saw in her reliability, a source of constant grounding, which he so wanted to have near as he himself tended to soar among the clouds. He also liked her crude sensuality, to which she surrendered with unparalleled thoroughness. But soon a fissure erupted between them: Galya, seeing that her newly minted husband was too extravagant in his desires and plans, cooled to him and withdrew into herself. Besides, her appearance started to change – her hands and feet thickened, while her hair, on the contrary, grew thinner, colorless, and lost its sheen. Astakhov was somewhat alarmed when he imagined what she might turn into in another ten years, and when Galya confronted him, demanding his participation in one of her projects, he engaged in open conflict leading to the split – without much regret from either side.

Soon thereafter, he met Yulia. They had a long, languid romance that ended up with a sudden trip to the Registry Office – and Andrei never understood exactly how he got roped into it. At first, though, he felt quite happy. His second wife seemed almost ideal to him. They read the same books and had friends in common. She liked his dark humor and, especially, his freedom in choosing words – which is not so far from being real or imagined kindred spirits. And Yulia wanted words – whether imagined or real. She worked as a proofreader and was very proud of her knowledge of the rules of written speech, often considering her literacy to be absolute. The further things went, the more this took root in her consciousness as the primary essence of her personality – insomuch as the other essences were dying off, one by one. In short order, she became intolerant of doubts regarding her rightness if the matter concerned spelling and grammar. And it was then that Andrei Fyodorovich first noticed in her the inclination toward hysterics, a trait that soon blossomed fully.

She had once had the habit of smiling with the sarcasm of forgiveness, such that one corner of her mouth crept up her face – and he would feel a sudden pang of tenderness toward her. But then, with increasing frequency, instead of a sarcastic smile her lips would contort into a capricious pucker, like that of a little girl about to burst into tears, and Astakhov sensed that he was rapidly losing interest. Once, he happened to point out a discrepancy in her copy editing, and Yulia took such strong umbrage at this, they didn't speak for several days. Then, about two months later, they argued over some other word. He opened Dahl's dictionary, confirming she was mistaken. Yulia, in a fury, threw a frying pan at him and locked herself in the bathroom, where she sobbed for a long time. It was clear the marriage would not survive. Astakhov got involved in several minor flings on the side, and then, one fine day, Yulia came home agitated and pale, red blotches on her cheeks. After roaming aimlessly about the rooms, she informed him in a shrill voice she had met a man who understood her like no one else. Andrei just shrugged his shoulders, which enraged her beyond words. She rampaged like a fury, accusing him of indifference and egotism, and collected her things that very evening – thus stunning both Astakhov himself and her new beau, who hadn't expected things to develop so quickly.

After this, Andrei Fyodorovich, again like Kramskoy, guarded his carefree bachelorhood quite resolutely. Romances occurred from time to time, but they were rather dull – probably because he himself didn't believe in their success. He accepted with a certain regret that other souls made a miserable combustible: they burned poorly, tended to smolder, and gave off a lot of smoke – not to mention that some of them cost a great deal. Yet within him the subconscious longing for a muse lived on. It surfaced in his incoherent literary experiments that never reached his books, where his attitude toward women was rather cynical. One on one with himself, however, he fantasized often, making up many theories about how to succeed in his personal life.

At some point, after he read about neuro-linguistic programming, he even considered whether he could saturate his next text with short, coded instructions and then sit back and wait for a result. The idea seemed productive: really, how else was he to derive personal benefit from his skills in polysemantics, the mastery of the unspoken, the rarest of abilities so scornfully rejected by mankind? To utilize their power, some subterfuge was necessary – and a command artfully concealed in a harmless description of a landscape could turn out to be an effective piece of cunning, thought Andrei Fyodorovich, and he even conducted a few tests. But with them everything came to an end: the instructions, even short ones, imperceptibly spoiled the writing by destroying the harmony of those same polysemantics, while the text itself reeked of cheap populist tripe – probably from an instinctive attempt to broaden the target audience. The result so depressed him that he stopped these endeavors entirely, telling himself with a smile that this was precisely how people sacrifice the personal for the sake of the eternal, even if it repeatedly eludes you and only tantalizes with its shadow.

Leaving Moscow, Astakhov nurtured one more illusion: about unspoiled provincial maidens, the simplicity of their desires, and the openness of their souls. That was how it turned out, in general, but far from the extent to which he anticipated. The illusion soon dissipated nearly without a trace, though as soon as he arrived in Sivoldaisk he had an ardent affair with a pretty post-graduate from the local university. Then all along the Volga brunettes became the fashion – Astakhov's very heart was smitten by her hair as black as pitch and the bronze tint around her pupils. He suddenly felt quite young, just beginning his real life, and he easily bedazzled the girl's head with the style of the capital and the elegance of his reasonings. They were also connected by a common ploy: he used her as a provincial model – making her beat the streets, shop, haggle, and brawl; he observed her with avaricious voyeurism, trying to glimpse the world through her eyes, inventing all new tricks and methods. This inspired her beyond all else for a week, maybe a week and a half. She withheld no effort and burned with the future novel nearly as much as he. But then she abruptly cooled somehow and nothing remained between them but sex, which they both continued to enjoy. Yet this was not enough; Andrei felt frustrated and disappointed. He even ditched the scarcely begun opus and never returned to it.

"In the naïve sincerity of the province, there is huge potential," he wrote to Nikolai Kramskoy, "but it's hard to bring it to the surface." And he added right away, "Short, short is the affection of the provincial girl," as if trying to reduce everything to a joke and not show he was actually wounded. Soon, however, time and the river air cured him of his melancholy. He learned not to demand much of his Sivoldaisk girlfriends and recognized that, on the whole, they were more responsive than high-minded Muscovites. He quickly appraised the essence of the local women's charm: a hybrid of cheerfulness and a provincially laidback mentality. They drew energy from the great river that was always nearby and ready to console. The propensity to console here was bestowed on everyone. It could be tiresome, or it could be funny at times, but most often it turned out to be pleasant. At the same time, it was these lands where one might clearly see the utterly hopeless dualism from which there was no escape. Astakhov sensed this with particular poignancy, walking along the quay in the warm afternoon, observing the procession of young mothers with the flawless faces of madonnas, beautiful and withdrawn, concerned only with their children, driving out all other thoughts.

These are it, though Andrei, the primary stronghold of monotony and stagnation. Inside of them is the negation of the non-ordinary, a quagmire, animal instinct. Yet at the same time they're the ones who bear love, both its cause and its source. Here is the great trap of the universe, and this is its principal joke. The rest is secondary, for nothing inspires to create as love does.

"Might I lack inspiration?" he teased himself with an unhappy grin. "Or maybe there's no such thing, and all that exists is an urge to scribble out lines. An impulse created by an internal engine of unknown properties – and this is alarming, for it doesn't last. Or am I the one who doesn't last, while the 'engine' may run forever? In any case, no one has an answer – although this is a big, big question indeed!"

CHAPTER 18

After finishing breakfast, Andrei Fyodorovich walked through the whole apartment again, constantly glancing at the clock with displeasure. Not much time was left until a meeting from which he expected nothing good. He was faced with a decisive conversation with his present lover, Anna the pediatrician. He was planning to break up, and today was the day he wanted to inform her. Like most men, Astakhov couldn't stand explanations and making scenes, and thinking of possible reactions – tears, complaints, accusations – made the muscles of his face involuntarily tense in advance.

Yet this event couldn't be avoided. He dressed with urgency, slapped his pocket to check his keys and billfold, and left the apartment, lightly fingering his Indian amulet – wooden arrows on a leather cord. At some point, he had brought it from Mexico and never parted with it since. Touching the dark wood seemed to establish contact with the shades and spirits of the ancient world, but today even this couldn't ensure good luck. Andrei Fyodorovich grinned lopsidedly and hurried downstairs, trying not to stumble over the crumbling steps.

In the stairway lingered the smell of a dungeon – somewhere below, perhaps, a large rack still creaked and implements were stored for stretching sinews. These musings were fostered further by the wire fence surrounding the prison property that adjoined the courtyard itself, fifteen paces from the back wall, and bordered a building belonging to the former KGB. Andrei imagined time and again how Stalinist detectives residing there would have looked out from their spacious apartments at prisoners exercising in the yard – the link between the victim and the executioner must not be severed for even an instant!

Nevertheless, his own windows opened on the other side, so he hadn't the slightest inkling of how the prison actually looked. Winding between the cockleshell garages, Andrei Fyodorovich came out on Moskovskaya Street and glanced around. His gloomy building of rough stonemasonry, with seven stories and three-meter ceilings, confidently dominated the space, cutting into a line of merchant houses over the brisk intersection. It looked like a fortress, and Astakhov liked it for that – probably because he perceived the whole city as a distant point of retreat or exile, a bastion on the frontier of the infidel steppe, which is precisely what it was in the times of enterprising Catherine II. Only after living here for several months did he reluctantly begin to credit Sivoldaisk with more developed features and characteristics – admiring the eccentric mixing of races and the naïve integrity of the worldview inherent in those who live in remote places.

After buying cigarettes at a booth trading in everything from bread to knock-off Armagnac, Andrei Fyodorovich turned toward downtown and treaded along the uneven sidewalk broken to pieces by a row of trees. The asphalt was dingy, and the air seemed excessively thin as sounds from the street appeared to be reverberating through the grungy mica. The sense of alarm that had troubled him since morning returned for no obvious reason; Andrei had to catch his breath, and even his heart beat faster. Slackening his pace, he peered without curiosity at the lone guard standing at the entrance to the district police department, which had once been appropriated from the "bloodthirsty *Cheka*." It was an old building and was the color of scarlet mousse. From its central wall jutted a solitary balcony, like a dais for addressing the public. On closer inspection, however, everyone could see it was subterfuge, for the balcony had no floor. The guard, recognizing Astakhov, managed a vapid nod and straightened his cap; he was hot, bored, and longing for a beer. The wind suddenly blew, and the air immediately smelled of dust. "What a horrible city," thought Andrei Fyodorovich in a fit of temper. "How did I manage to end up here?"

He wandered further, glancing from side to side in search of signs promising something positive. Like any province, Sivoldaisk was generous with signs; but today, unfortunately, nothing cheered his eye. Slowly, the cars crept along, heaving and honking, as the sun already blazed down and drops of sweat emerged on Andrei's forehead. Then he was met by a Kotlyar Gypsy with a kerchief fastened under her chin – a bad omen, portending unpleasantness and woe. Astakhov cursed under his breath and decided to cross to the other side of the street, to the shadow of a gray building with a clinic on the ground floor. It was long, like a pier, and dismal, like an abandoned casemate. On its corner, a paramedic van with a battered, rusty body was always parked and heaps of limp cardboard rustled, from beneath which protruded something that looked like used bandages. By the van, he saw a group of orderlies who had come outside for a smoke. One of them, resembling an elderly prosector with a contented face, suddenly looked at him point blank, then turned away and, continuing his interrupted story, intoned threateningly, "So I say to him, 'Well, you come to my ward...'" This conjured unpleasant images – Andrei Fyodorovich shuffled ahead, trying not to exude anxiety, but thoughts of mortality churned in his head and a cold chill slithered up his spine.

Something was amiss; space was lacking stability. To distract himself, Astakhov recalled the conversation that soon awaited him and started thinking of Anna, all the more so since she also dealt with medicine, having worked for some seven years in the best local hospital. That was where they had met when he went to reception for some trifle. Anna had encountered him by chance and told him where to go, flashing her gray eyes. She seemed utterly unapproachable in her starched lab coat with a stethoscope around her neck, like a snow queen or a beauty imprisoned in ice. This really aroused him, to such a degree that he showed his excitement and said too much – and then, without any need, promised more than he should have...

On the whole, Astakhov didn't like his part in this story. All began bright and beautiful – their fleeting encounter grew literally overnight into mutual passion. He sought Anna out at the end of the work day, hoping only to make a date for dinner, but it was she who seduced him – taking him by the hand through the hospital corridor, tall and stately with an intense gaze. She shoved him into a dimly lit closet and turned the key, hastily undressed, pressed him to her soft breast... In the broom closet, they spent a long hour, then went to his place. There, he was finally able to look her over properly, noting with pride her flawless form, not to mention her fairly quick mind. Their romance remained easy and carefree for another five or six days. Then the complexities of life began to encroach upon it and gain territory, foot by foot, gradually advancing into the foreground.

Astakhov didn't hide from himself that Anna still meant a lot to him and that his interest in her hadn't waned in the least. She continued to surprise him at times; he even made quite a few observations, waiting for a chance to bring them to life in his future books. Chief among them was the shift in perception inherent in provincial females, the majority of whom never grew out of their childish dreams. Their world was strange and multihued, though constrained to a narrow framework. Within it mingled an amusing mixture of forms capable of bewildering any onlooker. Anna was considered an educated woman, read Kafka, Borges, and Joyce, yet she was desperately superstitious and affirmed in earnest that she occasionally asked advice of the disembodied spirit of her grandmother. Her fantasies were limited to ordinary mysticism, yet distinguished by their refinement and persistence. They were populated by visitors from the past – apparitions and the dead resurrected, and house and forest sprites besides, as customary for every Russian fairytale. There were other quirks – Anna, for instance, had no e-mail address, as she took it as a mark of immorality; she believed the World Wide Web, like insatiable Moloch, was ensnaring souls into its deceitful, debauched clutches. In love, she was unfettered and shameless, but she flatly refused any means of mechanical contraception, asserting only prostitutes used those. Thus, Andrei Fyodorovich said to himself, this all proved that a Russian woman is an extraordinarily wild thing, indeed. At least he was never bored with her – and he valued that a lot.

However, apart from harmless eccentricities, she had a very real husband, causing a multitude of problems. Their childless marriage had long since grown odious to both. About a year ago, Anna had finally decided on a divorce, but then the bothersome spouse became a cripple as a result of a drunken brawl, and she couldn't dare to leave him without a push from the outside. Cheating on him, though, seemed perfectly natural to her. She did it with relish, making up nonexistent shifts at work. He had a hunch something was up, made scandals, tried to humiliate her, and even roughed her up at times, like any average Russian man whose life was wretched. Anna didn't conceal from Astakhov that this was all becoming unbearable – the new was aggravating the old, tightening the situation into a hard knot. Here she hinted ever more transparently that the time had come to buck up and break the knot in one blow, by which she meant their life together. Leaving her husband and living alone was something she no longer thought possible. This, to her understanding, was a cowardly retreat – in contrast to changing her status on account of true love. Of course, her inconsolable spouse would fly into a rage and not leave them in peace, but Andrei, as a man, should be able to cope with such difficulties.

"You'll have to give him money, threaten, and scare him," she said melodiously. "We'll have a very happy life, won't we?" Stretching, twisting like a cat, she folded her hands behind her head, exposing her armpits. Then, snuggling up to him, she confessed with feigned shyness, "I've dreamt for so long of having a real family, of children…"

So the situation was worsening by the minute, and, in Astakhov's opinion, the point had come to really "buck up" and make a manly decision. It wouldn't be the one Anna wanted, but there was nothing to be done for it: their living environments were incompatible, like the sea and dry land.

"That, of course, would be the cleanest case," Andrei Fyodorovich noted, grinning glumly. "To live out the ends of my days in the province, amid family squabbles, runny noses, diapers. To throw away literature, drink myself into obscurity and give up, complaining bitterly of my fate. Realization of the national idea, grassroots nihilism *au naturel*. No thank you, don't hold your breath. And besides, the inner engine won't allow it."

He barely missed colliding with the lone drunk stumbling over the whole sidewalk, then stopped and looked back in the direction of the recently seen orderlies. They had already gone back through the doors, obviously hurrying to get to their wards with enemas, syringes, and probes. "A woman needs her husband like a fish needs a bicycle," he muttered, repeating this saying that Anna so loved, like any married Russian. The whole story irritated him immensely – he knew forgetting his lover wouldn't be easy. Thinking of her thrilled him; he wasn't even sure he wouldn't reconsider at the last moment and, instead of a decisive explanation, take her home with him – though she hadn't gotten enough sleep after the night shift.

Andrei Fyodorovich regarded Anna's unlucky spouse with overt hostility. He represented a typical specimen from the local tribe of men – one who was good for nothing but was hot for gimmicks and certain, for some reason, that he should be taken seriously. There were plenty of those around – half-drunk, ignorant, and not knowing how to do anything well.

"'You won't lead me on. I'll smoke you out,' he probably threatened his unfaithful wife. But what does she care – having gotten used to his impotence long ago?" thought Astakhov glumly, squinting at the sun, then asked himself for the thousandth time, "Why does everyone here think he's so clever? They're all the same: wily cowards, full of the deceit of the downtrodden, a national virtue in a class by itself. They love to crowd together in the herd, but each is asocial – that's why we're considered savages in other countries. Could it be an experiment performed by nature itself? If so, it's grand enough – with a sixth of the world involved, no less. It could create a massive force of will – as a challenge to worldwide entropy. But there's no strength here – all are weak to a man. That's understandable: nature cannot afford to be overly generous.

Andrei pondered a logical line upon which a conflict could be constructed. "This will need to be jotted down later," he frowned. "Experiment, proving ground, special role. In opposing columns: cunning – gigantic call; weakness of spirit – the indifference of the stars. And add the feminine principle: heartlessness – and sudden tenderness; deceit – and sacrifice, readiness to surrender all…"

He picked up his pace a little and grinned upon recalling how he'd tried to persuade his graduate student girlfriend of the congenital nobility of Russian girls. She didn't believe him, and she was right: here in particular, in the boondocks, Astakhov despaired of his theories, recognizing that noble genes had long since disappeared from the Fatherland's chromosomes. He was especially disappointed by thick ankles and large palms – the heritage of the Volga peasants who hadn't a whisper of aristocracy among them.

"The grad student, incidentally, had pretty decent wrists," Andrei Fyodorovich noted. "But she did articulate well: a typical quality here – in mimicry or adaptation, nothing more. Social perturbation, change in regime, a sharp bend in the track… Men, inclined toward contemplation, lagged behind the train in its abrupt turning; meanwhile, the females, well, they're tougher and try to cling to the handrail. And cling they do, to their praise."

He drew even with the Kirov monument, thinking in passing, "Here is another occasion for irony. Funny things should be written from life here. Why are my texts so overly serious? Take this, for example: on a street named for one hero stands another, untimely in his arrival, whose features on top of that look every bit like a typical Sivoldaisk mobster. The union of the old, the new, and the very latest… But why does everything seem so despicable today?"

He was met by two old women bundled in shawls despite the heat. They walked, holding on to one another like hook-nosed witches. Andrei Fyodorovich turned hastily away and stumbled, nearly falling. Shaking his head, he hurried along further, watching his footfalls attentively, thinking, "You cannot let down your guard in this city for an instant. Its provincial calm is insidious, like the surface of a mysterious undertow – even here, right downtown, where no place remains for any mystique."

Astakhov imagined Anna going to their meeting spot, also probably worrying for no reason. Their story was harder for her, of course; he was still incomprehensible to her – a visiting prince living a strange life. But she had a resource: she was accustomed since birth to the large river. She could go to the shore, stand for an hour or two, convince herself agonizing was useless and that time flowed the same as always – she had evidence of eternity at her fingertips. He, however, was an outlander. The Volga couldn't teach him the indifference that was in the blood of those who grew up on its shores. Though, of course, it was in its power to change anyone – he had, in fact, already started writing differently: not as tightly or as densely as before. In the past, his phrases used to come out in clumps, intractable to the touch; he tried to force more meaning into even the shortest paragraphs. The river had opened his eyes to the futility of endeavoring to fit huge things into small spaces. Immense content required large forms: you couldn't encode or compact it with a clever algorithm. Narration should be fluid – no point in fretting over the number of pages. As for phrases, they could be long or short – it changed nothing either way.

Andrei Fyodorovich started thinking about his current book and frowned. Here, too, was a deadlock. The skein was winding tighter and tighter – he wondered, did Anna feel this as she was still a quarter hour's walk away? The universe pulsed, playing like a cat with a mouse – grabbing here, loosening its grasp there. Now its muscles were clearly tensed – and that meant something. It was perhaps an indicator, an attempt to get his attention, give him a signal. Breathing became harder with each block. Something was sure to occur – could it be to him? Just, please, not with Anna, she didn't deserve it!

He stepped on the cobblestone at the entrance to a fashionable café and froze in place, petrified like all who happened to be in the vicinity. The wail of a horn and the desperate squeal of brakes sliced the air with a chord that stung nerves, immediately after which a dull blow resounded – and then shouts, the tinkling of glass. Astakhov knew in an instant – it had happened. Then he rejoiced, for it hadn't happened to him. Only later, with a millisecond delay, did he recognize the picture imprinted on his retina: a cargo van, speeding along Komdiv Chapayev Street; the other car, a Mercedes with tinted windows, cutting off the van at the intersection; and in an instant, both of them fused into one heap of metal, smoke, splattering, and glass raining down.

"The truck probably ran a yellow," observed Andrei mechanically. "Rushed upon the oppressor of the proletariat in the finest traditions of the Red Army. Might not be a *tachanka*, but there's plenty of class antagonism anyway." Then he snapped out of it, sighed fitfully, mumbled out loud, "Ambulance, an ambulance!" and started to look around for a pay phone, forgetting entirely about the cell in his pants pocket.

An ambulance truly was needed – for the Mercedes driver, who was still alive. The blow from the van impacted the rear door, where the sole passenger sat. He had been killed instantly, as had the driver of the van, who really was trying to make a yellow light that had already turned red. But if the driver's death didn't affect our heroes at all, then the demise of the important passenger had the most direct relationship to them. In the back seat of the S-class sedan was traveling none other than Timofey Tsarkov's *patrón*.

Just like Astakhov, he hadn't liked this morning either. However, being a practical man, he didn't look for any complicated reasons behind that. He woke up with a pounding in his head that had begun to torment him again over the last weeks and he lay long in bed, wondering whether this was the result of an approaching cyclone or else the harbinger of a more serious issue that might be worth discussing with a doctor. Then his mistress, a beauty-salon owner, called him and complained for half an hour about problems that weren't worth a dime. But mainly, today was the day that the action on Tsarkov was set, and the *patrón* was tortured by doubts as to whether all had been planned properly or if there might be some unforeseen snag.

So he got in the car, glum and dejected, unhappily wiped the back of his neck, and chewed out the driver over some triviality imbuing him with significant fear. The first thing he wanted to do at the office was to close the doors and discuss the details again with the head gangster from Tolyatti, but he didn't live long enough to manage that. An anonymous emissary of fate, who had already "restored his health" that morning with some vodka and beer, confounded all the plans of the *patrón* – and many others – by crashing into the new Benz and providing two hours of work for the rescuers extracting the bodies from the crumpled automobiles.

Andrei Fyodorovich had never beheld anything like it. He wandered toward the honking traffic jam, agitated and pale, noticing nothing around. There was no more to see; the incident had already happened. The tension in the air subsided, as if a taut string had snapped. The universe's live round hadn't hit him, but had whistled by pretty closely. He would still have to consider the meaning of that.

Two blocks from the ill-fated intersection, life was already moving along in turn. It was crowded; young Tatar women spread out along the sidewalk glibly traded their wares. A cheeky girl from the clothing shop tried to catch Astakhov by the sleeve. "Come to our place for jeans. We have new Turkish shirts too," she chirped in falsetto but shut up and took a step back when she saw his face.

The square came into view – with the market that looked like a stylized train station and the Sermyazhny Brothers' Circus with its mirrored façade, behind which a vanishing act was apparently being prepared. There, Andrei regained his senses a little. His hands weren't shaking anymore, the metallic taste in his mouth disappeared, and his thoughts again acquired a semblance of symmetry.

"*Déjà vu*," he muttered. "Well, no, not really. What am I on about? Not *déjà vu*, but rather a premonition of an unknown nature. Still, an overabundance of the unexplainable always carries some creative impulse."

It occurred to him that the complexity of space-time, which humanity hadn't as yet even approached understanding, was truly valuable in an everyday sense. At least it gave no one the right to reduce phenomena to something primitive – despite the fact that all around, wherever you looked, the primitive flowered in full bloom.

"Copulate, reproduce," grinned Astakhov, addressing no one in particular. "What else are you capable of? I'm not mad at you; we're all equally naïve. Herein is hope – could it be that all is designed more complexly that we think, and the spirit does not end its life at death?"

Soon he saw Anna – she was sitting on a bench by the fountain, having moved for some reason from her usual place by the statue of the seal with a ball on its nose. When he approached, they were separated by a train taking children for a ride, and for half a minute they studied each other through the ornamental windows of the cars painted in cheerful colors. Something in her look seemed odd to Astakhov, some detachment or a shade of acceptance – he even considered whether there might be a cause here for new presentiments, and sighed wearily.

"Sorry I'm late," he said, kissing her on the cheek. "There's a terrible accident at the intersection with Moskovskaya. I'm afraid there are injuries, if not worse."

"Yes, that's horrible," responded Anna, intently looking him in the eye. "Worse for them, of course, than it is for me. But it's so bad for me now that I can't even feel sorry for them."

"What's wrong?" Andrei Fyodorovich was astonished. "Something with your husband? Let's go to a café and I'll buy you lunch."

"You know," Anna pronounced the words slowly, "it seems to me that you've decided to dump me. Is that right?"

An invisible wall rose between them at once. Astakhov lifted his hand, wiped his temple, and said, not averting his gaze, "Yes, that's right."

"Well, dump me, then," Anna shrugged. "What's the point of eating too?"

And she turned and ran off before he had a chance to say another word.

CHAPTER 19

Meanwhile, news of the accident that had abruptly ushered Tsarkov's *patrón* into the next world had yet to reach the kidnappers or their captives that Monday afternoon. Once launched, the action continued, though it had lost all meaning. The plan developed by the thugs and confirmed by the *patrón* – who had no intention of dying so soon – would be fulfilled point by point, despite the drastic change in the cast of characters.

The world-weary boat, sailing away from the deserted dock concealed by bushes, was crossing the Volga. The river here spread out broad and free, and the opposite shore was lost in uneven haze. A small wave rippled in the sun; the current flowed smoothly, as serene as a slumbering beast. All around breathed tranquility; the wide expanse was bewitchingly peaceful, but the captives had no interest in the beauties of nature. They crowded in the middle of the deck under the guard of two ruffians lounging in seats along the side. At the helm stood the owner of the vessel: an ordinary-looking man, constantly spitting overboard. Timofey pressed a handkerchief to his cheek; the rest were unharmed and merely exchanged glances without uttering a word.

They still couldn't wrap their heads around the situation. On the one hand, what was happening seemed ridiculous – the transition from everyday life to the plot of a bad thriller had been too abrupt.

Conversely, there was no doubt about the depressing reality of events: the black pistols bore no resemblance to toys, and the demeanor of their captors indicated they were not to be trifled with. The abductees were thoroughly searched and their mobile phones confiscated. When Tsarkov started to protest, he received a pistol butt to the cheek in response. Before they boarded the motorboat, the shaven-headed thug looked over the whole company, and this inspection left an unsettled sensation in the pits of their stomachs.

"We're going for a ride on the river now," he pronounced quietly. "So I want you to make like you're on a little cruise – cool and collected. If anyone decides to act up – to go for a swim or raise their voice – they get a bullet. Got it?"

All understood that's really how it would be. Silence ruled the craft, contradicted only by the even rattle of the motor. In twenty minutes, they had traversed the river and began to wind through narrow passages amid countless islets. At one of these, the boat plunged into the rushes, frightening a large heron, and was soon moored to a rickety wooden gangplank. Perhaps once there had been a health resort there or a recreational retreat owned by one of the neighboring factories that had fallen into disrepair and ruin after the fall of the Union. Through the pines could be seen the remnants of cottages – houses of cards made of plywood full of holes. Among them wandered two dogs, and right by the water stood the guard booth – a small shack from old Soviet times, dug into the earth and leaning to one side. Next to it, one could envision a decrepit drunkard with an ancient rifle, but there was actually a tall, broad-shouldered guy with a telltale bulge under his shirt. Grinning, he looked at the arrivals. "You're here," he declared. "Seems to be a lot of you."

"A lot is not a little," responded the man with the shaved head glumly. "Not our business, anyway. Careful with them – that one in the tie might want to play the hero." Then he yelled at the captives, "Hurry up, this is no vacation. Unload; the trip is over."

All climbed onto the shore, balancing with difficulty on the rotted boards. The detainees wore a somewhat dumbfounded look, but on the whole, they'd already begun to come to their senses.

Timofey contemplated his feet and tensely thought about something. Nikolai and Elizaveta apparently still couldn't believe this was really happening. Only Frank retained his full composure, seeming to say that what had occurred completely met his expectations.

"Listen!" Elizaveta began, but no one even looked at her. Only Tsarkov finally lifted his eyes and said quietly, "Hold on, Lizzie. I don't think these guys have got a clue," at which the senior thug, who had been silent up until then, sarcastically chuckled and shook his head.

"Well, move it," commanded someone, and the entire group began marching toward the interior of the island, winding along a narrow trail through tall pines and thickets of blackberries over which bees buzzed. Pine needles crunched under their feet; it smelled of fir and river water. The crowns of the trees closed in above their heads and the light falling upon the trail dimmed, like in a fairytale forest. "Don't lag behind, sweetie," the broad-shouldered guy addressed Elizaveta and looked at her with interest, almost clicking his tongue. "You're from the capital, for sure," he added. Bestuzheva, without meeting his gaze, drew even with Timofey and walked next to him. The track soon brought them to a wide glade where a large new lodge stood. Upon it was emblazoned the inscription *Administration*. Another dog was sniffing about but ran off quickly once he saw the people. "Velcome hoam," the broad-shouldered guy continued to joke. "I'm going to unlock this now, and we'll pack you in like sardines."

"Don't mess around, Yurets. Hop to it," the hood with the shaved head chided. The other shrugged, flung open the door after only slightly fiddling with the lock, and made a broad gesture with his arm: "Be my guests!"

Along a stairway that began right at the entrance door, the abductees were led down into a large semi-basement. Narrow windows beneath the ceiling were protected with grillwork. In the center, a massive billiard table dominated, surrounded by sofas stretching along the walls. At one of the corners, by a bar, was another door, standing open, behind which a washstand could be seen.

One of the guards dragged a large package of drinking water into the room. "Have a drink, relax," the skinhead grinned crookedly. "The latrine's there, by the bar. There's no grub, but that's no big deal, you'll manage. Sit quietly, don't make a fuss – the door is strong, and outside there's no one but us. If anyone starts a ruckus, we'll calm 'em down straight away!"

The gangster stopped talking, looked over the captives as if expecting objections, and winked at Elizaveta, giving her the same crooked smirk. "Don't worry. They're not gonna hurt you. It's all about this one, the hotshot," he nodded at Timofey and turned to leave.

"Hey, listen, where's your boss?" Tsarkov directed at his back in a pretty firm voice. "Who is there to talk to, anyway?"

The hoodlum turned back around and sized him up with a glance. "The boss is coming," he said through his teeth. "You'll talk your head off with him, whether you want to or not. In the meantime, sit your ass down and don't pull any crap." With that, he slammed the door behind him and bolted the lock.

For some time, all were silent. Timofey was withdrawn and immersed within himself; the rest, looking in his direction, didn't know what to say. Elizaveta Bestuzheva went to the wall with the windows at the top and attentively studied the glass; Nikolai picked at the leather upholstery of the sofa; and Frank, opening a bottle of water, sat staring at a single point and taking short gulps from time to time.

"*By mistake, like a finger in molasses,*" Tsarkov finally said. "Looks to me like we're really screwed. Here's the mousetrap, snapped shut – but I don't get it: where was the bait? Where's the fucking cheese? I don't remember biting at somebody else's pieces."

"Smart trick, huh?" Nikolai glared at him sullenly. "Did you drag us along with you on purpose? Like insurance, or some such thing? Why the hell did you do it if you knew you were being hunted?"

Elizaveta shuddered and turned around, but Timofey desperately shook his head. "I didn't get so much as a whiff of it!" he said firmly. "Not a whiff. There's no hunt for me, everybody here gets on famously with me. I don't even owe anyone money. And almost nobody owes me either, come to think of it."

"Yeah, sure," Kramskoy waved his hand. "It makes no difference now. They know who you are, that's obvious. They couldn't care less about us though."

He leapt from the couch and started walking back and forth, hands folded behind his back. "Just like a stork," thought Elizaveta as she turned and laughed out loud with a short, nervous giggle. Tsarkov looked at her with surprise and sighed.

"Yeah, they know me, but I don't know them, that's the trouble," he said. "If I live through this, I'll get to the bottom of it, of course. *You beat a bear and he learns his lesson,* so they say...There's no point in you chewing me out," he added, addressing Nikolai. "I don't set people up, that's not my way. You guys, I don't even know you – but Liza's my girl, and here she is, just like the rest of us. Or do you also think I used you as cover?" he suddenly asked Elizaveta.

"That's ridiculous," she said softly and went up to him. "Don't be silly, I'm with you. We came together, we leave together – just like in a movie."

"Do you believe *me* that we suspected nothing?" she turned to Nikolai and Frank. "We were just on our way to get married, and these guys showed up like a thunderbolt out of the blue."

"A bolt out of the blue? More like a shit storm," grumbled Nikolai. "And how do you come by such horrors in the provinces? What do you think, Frank? Is it like Hollywood?"

"Well, I believe him too, not just his bride," Frank White said softly. "Though it was just today that I swore off trusting Russians. You're right, Liza, we'll leave together. And Timothy, in my opinion, isn't lying."

"Well, okay then, he isn't," Nikolai shrugged. "Let's agree he's clean and didn't suspect a thing. No problem – it's just a shame that the wedding will be postponed."

He sat back down on the couch, folded his hands behind his

head, and assumed a deliberately indifferent air. "The wedding won't get away from us," Elizaveta grinned. "And besides, let's stop arguing, that's enough. Instead, why don't you take a look: the glass is broken."

Indeed, one of the windowpanes was broken at the edge and outside sounds were coming through the hole. Everyone approached and stared at the window, though it was clear this brought them no closer to freedom.

"You need to speak more quietly," Nikolai muttered, "or else they'll overhear us, you know."

"They don't give a damn," Tsarkov waved his hand. "We're sitting here helpless as rabbits. Why listen to us – especially these flunkies?"

He withdrew and stared again at the floor, meditating upon something intensely. Nikolai looked at him and grinned. "Here, you see," he said, "they may call you Tsar around these parts, but you're still not God. Don't be offended, I'm just making a pun. You know, like the one about Captain Cook."

"Yeah? What about Cook?" Timofey glumly inquired.

"It is instructive," Kramskoy grinned again. "When the aborigines saw Cook, they took him for a god – that's why it didn't occur to them to devour him. But he made a mistake – he learned too many native words or got overly close with one of the tribal girls. Then it became clear: he was no god – and they ate him on the spot. Obviously, sailing the seas was not for him."

Elizaveta shot Nikolai a lingering glance. "Who are you really, Nikolai Kramskoy?" she asked seriously.

"He's a lunatic," grumbled Timofey. "But no matter, I'm not offended. I hope he's not upset at me, either. After all, everyone's in shit up to their ears because of me."

"Quiet!" Frank White, Jr. hissed and pointed at the broken glass. Voices could be heard from outside – obviously, the gangsters had left the building. It soon became clear that two of the men from the Volkswagen were taking their leave of the broad-shouldered bloke named Yurets. The goodbyes lingered; one of them recalled a dirty joke, and the whole trio laughed heartily for several minutes. Finally, someone, probably the bold guy, said hoarsely, "Alright, then. You're in charge here," and the voices subsided. A quarter of an hour later, the familiar clattering of the boat motor sounded off in the distance. The captives exchanged glances full of meaning: clearly, only one man had been left to guard them.

"What now?" whispered Tsarkov. "Is this our chance? Huddle up, let's talk."

They crowded into a corner of the room, as far as possible from the entrance – and the broken glass, as well. Nikolai, after a moment's consideration, threw open the bathroom door and started the water running in the wash basin.

"White noise," he explained. "Now no one can eavesdrop on us."

"Lunatic, really," said Tsarkov to this. "But at least that makes our secrecy top notch. There it is, then..." and they began to discuss a desperate plan, without which there was little hope for a favorable outcome.

Timofey stated as much in plain terms, and nobody opposed him. The thought arose of its own accord that nothing good awaited them since the captors hadn't concealed their faces. What they'd done to trouble the mysterious boss, wherein lay their guilt, and whether this was all some tragic mistake was beyond their understanding, and they decided to leave their theorizing until later. Only Kramskoy occasionally looked pensively at Timofey, but even he was forced to admit he had no reason to suspect him of duplicity. They had to focus on particularly practical questions, especially the main one of "What to do?" without wasting time on the Russian favorite "Whose fault is it?"

They whispered exhaustively, though the options were few. Violence must be answered with violence, selecting the right moment and a vulnerable spot. Only one scheme materialized: attack the guard while he was watching over them in solitude, commandeer his weapon, and escape from the billiard room. Then they could seek a further path to freedom. "At least in the open air we can shoot and yell," Timofey summed it up, and all agreed with him.

Much more of an argument was caused by the central part of the plan: physical contact with the broad-shouldered thug who, though he seemed more good-natured than the rest, was still extremely dangerous.

"Any of you ever serve in the Special Forces?" Tsarkov asked Nikolai and Frank, and when both of them shook their heads, he sighed, "Well, the chances are small then."

"The main thing is to make him open the door," murmured Nikolai, nervously rubbing his palms. "There's still more of us than him. He can't watch us all."

"Well, yeah, but where the door is, that's where the bullet is too. Whether there's a lot of us or a few, everyone wants to live," Timofey retorted peevishly, but he admitted there was no other solution and they started to determine a sequence of actions to reduce the risk of fatality to a minimum.

Eventually, the operation was devised, and it turned out to be quite simple. Somebody would pretend to have a seizure – a nervous breakdown or an asthma attack. And the guard would take the bait: the untimely demise of a hostage hardly fit into the "boss's" plans. The candidate to play the one stricken ill was debated hotly – this person would be the first to engage the guard in a struggle in order to immobilize him for a brief instant while the others rushed him from behind. Each one was itching to be the hero, including Elizaveta, who insisted, not without reason, that one would expect a trick least of all from her. The three men, however, told her a resounding "no" and subsequently brushed aside Timofey's candidacy, since he obviously represented the most important figure to the bandits. This left Nikolai and Frank, and the choice, quite logically, fell on the latter – as a foreigner, his general health could betray him as it confronted the harsh Russian realities.

Tsarkov cavalierly asked White, Jr. if he would chicken out at the last minute, at which Frank reacted vehemently, taking umbrage at such a lack of faith. But here Elizaveta stroked his shoulder, and Nikolai and Timofey acted as though they trusted him like their own selves, so he calmed down and even turned a little pale from pride. The roles of the rest were quickly assigned, and with that the discussion concluded – on a productive, albeit alarming note.

"Time to fish or cut bait," Tsarkov said gloomily. "Let's try hard, otherwise they might kill us," and all grew silent: the threat was close and real.

They decided to implement the plot an hour later. "Hey, guard!" yelled Timofey; and when there was no response, he shouted at the top of his lungs, "Yurets!" pounding with his fists on the door. "Checking communication lines," he whispered to the rest with a wink when footsteps resounded on the other side and an unhappy voice said, "What's with the racket?"

"When do we talk to the boss, Yurets?" asked Tsarkov insolently. "How long you gonna hold people, anyway? They got nothin' to do with this."

"To some folks I'm Yurets, and others call me Yuri Petrovich," the guard droned from behind the door. "Don't be rude or I'll put you back in line right away. You'll talk to the boss whenever he feels like it. Sit tight for now, stay healthy!" and footsteps retreated up the stairs.

"We have contact," Timofey said contentedly and sat down next to Elizaveta on the sofa.

"Does it hurt?" she asked, pointing at his lacerated cheek.

"No big deal, just a scratch," he brushed it off. "There's no clarity – that's the problem! Abducting people – there's no such thing around here, yet these toughs, they aren't just toying around. They'll shoot your head off for real."

"You know," said Kramskoy to him from the neighboring couch, "I'm certainly a lunatic as far as you're concerned, but I must say none of this is strange to me. I was expecting something like it – though not in such a form, of course. I don't know your life, but in mine right now everything's suddenly warped and strained – and it's not clear where it's taking me, pushing me, pulling me..."

"No, no, don't get the wrong idea," he added calmly when Timofey assumed an open grin of sarcasm. "I'm fully sane, maybe even more rational than you. But some higher power has taunted me for a long time – and in that, there is no insanity. I knew something was to happen on this trip, and perhaps the veil would open a tiny bit at last – that's probably what's occurring, something preposterous, with a meaning of its own. Or could it be that some force is toying with you, not with us, while you're trying to figure it out according to your own weak means?"

"Sure, a force, the Hyperborean Cock," grumbled Tsarkov, hugging Liza around the shoulders. "Don't feed me any mysticism; you're no priest. If we get out of this, I'll get in touch with all my contacts – let them search. I don't like getting hit in the face with the butt of a gun..." He shook his head as though in thought, and added, "But I find it hard to believe in your thesis. It seems to me higher powers hardly see us; they're way out of our league. Lions don't smother mice, you know."

"So what then, Nikolai? Is it because of you that we're suffering here?" Elizaveta asked defiantly. "It was wrong of you to bring this on us."

"No sense confusing consequences with cause," answered Kramskoy coldly. "Or attendant contingencies, to be logically coherent. If not for you and your wedding, perhaps I would have had a much less dangerous adventure. And our American friend all the more."

"Contingencies, you say," Tsarkov sneered. "Sure. You can really get smacked around by a contingency in this country – or without a contingency, just the same. As for the cause, I'm the one for Lizzie, as she is for me – and what the consequences are, we haven't figured out yet. We'll get married – then okay, the consequences will become clear. And when I find the guy who ordered us here, I'll arrange some fucking consequences for him, all right!"

"As for me," Frank White chimed in, "I think Nikolai's right about forces. I have a clear example. I didn't see it at first, but now – yeah, I do, very much so!"

"How interesting. What was it that happened, then?" Elizaveta encouraged him. She snuggled up to Tsarkov and seemed as peacefully tranquil as on an outing in the park. Kramskoy's words helped her as well – she understood she also wasn't a bit surprised. All had been turned upside down – so what? In the last few days, this wasn't the first time. She was changing into someone else, and unusual things were supposed to happen to her. The person she was before would scarcely have come to be here with Timofey. But now she possessed an antique ring and a totally unknown future. And as for her previous life, no, she didn't miss it at all.

"I..." Frank began, and his hand shook as he painfully selected his words. Like the rest, he realized in a second that what was happening to him – beginning with when he had met Nilva – represented one unbroken chain of events leading to a predetermined finale. Here on the island, all would be resolved – this was the last ordeal, the decisive shakedown. He began to convulsively pick out facts and faces, and a name flashed suddenly in his head: Olga! This was not in vain – her or her handcuffs. White, Jr. felt that he feared nothing, he was prepared to fight the guard one on one, and he blurted out, quite unexpectedly even to himself, "My thing is, I want to marry a Russian woman!"

"Not bad," Timofey appraised and geared up to crack a joke, but Elizaveta squeezed his arm. "A Russian woman," she repeated, looking Frank attentively in the eye. "Any Russian woman, or one you already know? After all, there are different types. Marrying a Russian – that could end up being quite a reckless feat."

"No, no," Frank White blustered. "Somebody I'm already acquainted with. I know her well. For a week now," he added, feeling awkward for some reason.

"And who is she?" Bestuzheva continued interrogating him. "What's her name? Where does she work? How old is she?"

Frank gazed at her helplessly and woefully raised his eyebrows.

He was so comical, everyone immediately cheered up. Even the danger was apparently forgotten – the question of White, Jr.'s bride pushed it to the background.

"Um, her name, uh, it's Olga," he announced with difficulty. "She's still at university, quite young. She's going to be an architect," he declared with some doubt, but he now looked at Elizaveta with much more courage, as if accepting the call and preparing to stand firm to the end.

"An architect?" Bestuzheva queried again. "Yes, that's really nice. But tell me, have you been involved with other girls here? Have you had affairs with them? That's not good – just meeting someone and having a wedding right away."

She spoke with a crafty smile, behind which something inquisitive was hidden. "Yet, of course, such love does occur," she added softly. "Life in general is like that sometimes."

"Once," admitted Frank White, "I had a Russian girlfriend. I attended grade school here – quite a long time ago."

"I bet her name was Tanya. Or Natasha," Tsarkov brusquely interrupted.

"Yes," Frank agreed, and blushed. "Natasha, but she was different. And now Olga's different, too. We met on the plane," he said for some reason and bit his lip.

"Ah, do tell," Liza demanded. "Now's the perfect time for a romantic story." Frank White started to refuse, but she was unshakeable. "No, you have to, you have to," she assured him, as if joking, knowing he lacked the strength to argue with her. And, of course, Frank yielded.

"We sat there together, by the emergency exit…" he began, then faltered, was silent a bit, and said, "No, there was something else. I have to start with higher powers. The thing is, I came to Russia to look for treasure."

Everyone turned their eyes to stare at him, and Nikolai exclaimed, "Well, yeah, I should have guessed! How could I be fooled with the estate story?"

"What then? Find anything?" Tsarkov asked with interest.

"No," Frank admitted. "And, probably, there was no chance. But better to lay it all out in order."

He began to speak confidently, almost without mixing up his Russian, beginning back in his days in school in Moscow. His subsequent life, full of disappointments, he described quite briefly, hastening to move on to essentials – Axel Timurov and the programmers from Russia, and then to Nilva from St. Pete's, who destiny had apparently chosen as its wily emissary. When he heard about the manuscripts from the time of Pugachev, Nikolai couldn't suppress an exclamation of astonishment; and when Frank got to the part about the treasure map, he grabbed his head and laughed out loud.

"No, no, don't think I'm laughing at you," he said through his chuckles. "Just how it all coincided – Pugachev and now this present absurdity. And how we ran into each other, and I didn't understand it..." He was unable to calm down for a bit, whispering something under his breath. In the meantime, with a rather confused look on his face, White, Jr. described the morning's fiasco, not forgetting to mention the cripple and the cop, from whom Kramskoy had saved him, fortuitously appearing nearby. Upon finishing, he leaned his head to the side and said uncertainly, "So, there it is."

The story made a strong impression – especially on Tsarkov, who twirled his hand in the air for a while, trying to express some sort of emotion. Then he said with derision, "Well, Frankie, how can I put it delicately? You're rather gullible, eh?"

White grinned sourly and agreed, in the sense that, yes, it was probably excessive, clearly expecting further jeers. But here Elizaveta came to his aid.

"This is very interesting," she said. "And it's all so logical. I wouldn't even blame you if I were your wife or girlfriend. But you left out the main thing – your fiancée the architect and the plane, the plane!"

"And Pugachev too," interjected Nikolai. "Please explain: what do you know about him? This is quite a tremendous coincidence."

"No, Frank, you'll excuse me, but hereabouts they'd say you're a sucker," Tsarkov blurted out, grinning ear to ear.

"Hey, now," Liza raised her palm. "It seems to me we're getting off topic." She looked around at those present, fixing her gaze on Frank, and firmly said, one at a time, "I. Want. To. Know. What. Happened. On the plane."

"Well," said Frank and blinked hesitantly, "alright then. We sat next to each other, where the emergency exit is. At first, I was shy and couldn't speak at all..."

His thoughts arranged themselves, meanwhile, into a very coherent picture. The nights spent with the dark-haired courtesan, awkward promises, and tender words – all this fused together with the fantasy being born in his head. The plane artfully put the pieces into place – and Frank, who wasn't good at lying, now easily fabricated on the fly, passing off as truth what should have occurred between them if this world were designed just a little better.

This story had actually happened to him once, though it involved not Olga but an entirely different girl – a tall Italian with whom he flew from Washington to Seattle. Frank had noticed her at the entranceway to the cabin and, when he ended up next to her, he really did lose the power of speech and couldn't even say "Hi." The girl had no time for him, however. She sat with her body turned away and her eyes downcast, then she started rummaging in her purse, looking around tensely, as though she had lost something. A moment later, she calmed down and stared blankly into the distance. He thought she might be sick in the head, but that wasn't true – she was just afraid of flying.

When they lifted off, her lips began to tremble; Frank White noticed this because he kept glancing toward her side. She was beautiful and she smelled pleasant, but her strangeness looked disturbing. And she really frightened him when they gained altitude.

The Italian sat by the window but was afraid to look out of it. Then suddenly she turned toward the emergency door and started to grope with her hands like blind people do – over the whole surface and around the handle. Frank, of course, became concerned. He didn't know how the safety catch was constructed, and, though he surmised the door couldn't be opened easily, he didn't want to test that theory. And so he struck up a conversation with her.

The ice between them broke instantly. The girl admitted straightaway she was scared and wanted to leave; and when he gently but persistently explained to her this was impossible, she asked with whitened lips if she could sit closer to him, away from the window. Thus they sat until the end of the flight – at first just discussing all sorts of things, then holding hands like a couple in love. He recounted his whole life to her – and she listened without interrupting, devouring every word and not tearing her gaze from his face. Frank knew this was only because she was frightened beyond measure, but he was flattered all the same. And when fear momentarily triumphed and his neighbor began to peer at the ill-fated door, he caressed her knee without any timidity and whispered tender things until she calmed herself and reclined into her seat.

At times, her fright seemed to recede completely. She stopped shaking and even tried to take care of him – placing a pillow under his head and persuading him to close his eyes. This was also a novelty; he had never had women tend to him. He yielded to the strange sensation, but a minute later heard, "Why aren't you talking? We're falling, aren't we? Would it be better for me to get out?"

Certainly, he could have gone to the flight attendants and explained they had a psycho sitting by the emergency exit hatch. There were probably regulations outlining such a case, but Frank couldn't fathom betraying his terrified neighbor to the cruel world waiting outside – just beyond their fragile cocoon. This would have been horrible treachery – he could already hear shrill voices, see a multitude of strong hands, a syringe, and a straightjacket... Their closeness seemed to be absolute – as if they had fallen into a deadly trap and only a miracle could save them. In five hours of flight, he left his seat only once – to visit the lavatory in feverish haste after spending some considerable time convincing his companion there was no need to touch the door while she was alone. Upon returning, he saw she was sitting still, spine erect, a big bundle of raw nerves, and his heart fluttered at the notion that someone needed him that much. During the landing, she became even more scared, and he cradled her like a child. When the plane's tires rattled against the tarmac, she burst out crying, burying her face in his shoulder.

Her tears, however, soon dried: she applied lipstick for several minutes, looking into a small mirror – then abruptly became distant, a casual seatmate and a foreigner with her own life. He then thought ruefully that the magic of their intimacy was lost forever – and he wasn't surprised, being ready for this – but now, imagining himself and Olga in the neighboring seats on the plane, he saw with utter clarity it wouldn't be that way with her. Everything would have just begun – and she would have turned to him with a smile, showing she forgot nothing. There was no doubt of the new reality now – he seemed to recall it frame by frame: they retrieved their baggage and went out together into the hot Moscow morning, into a city of greedy brutes, of those confident in their own rightness. "Will you call me?" Olga asked and he nodded, and the magic was right here, affirming itself with inexplicable strength. And he called her – that very evening, unable to wait any longer. They met and soon went to his hotel; and she came to their next date with a turquoise ribbon in her hair...

"That's how it happened," Frank White concluded, somewhat confused. "That's how we met, then we spent a week in Moscow. I understood: they brought me here as a test," he muttered, becoming tongue-tied again. "That is, there were other matters, but now I know – they were only to conceal the main purpose."

"Oh, Frank, turns out you're a romantic," Elizaveta drew out the word slyly. "It was a delight to listen to, honestly. And what about her? Does she know yet?"

"No," Frank confessed. "But I'll tell her soon. If all ends well."

The reminder was timely – everyone, including Bestuzheva, sobered up and got serious. The environs of the improvised dungeon – bars on the windows, a pack of bottled water – left no doubt the danger was real, and a chill ran up their spines. With that, Frank's bride and the Pugachev hoard were forgotten in an instant.

"Well, now," Timofey said in a barely audible whisper, "is it time to start the comedy? You ready, Frankie?"

"Yes," he replied in English, and flashed a thumbs-up. "But I need to hit the washroom."

There, standing at the sink, Frank looked at himself in the filthy mirror and again, as in the hotel room that morning, nodded approvingly. He was collected and feared nothing – feeling like a knight defending the honor of his lady love. The path to further exploits was open. Frank White, Jr. exited the bathroom, stamped his feet by the front door, and lay on his back – right on the cracked, dusty floor.

CHAPTER 20

Tolyan's Zhiguli Nine, shaking and bumping over the potholes, quickly reached the city center. Alexander Frolov was silent the whole way, leaning against the window with his eyes closed. His face softened and not a drop of strength remained in it – the recent pressure gave way to indifference and apathy. He had suddenly realized nothing more depended on him: Elizaveta was in the hands of others, and there was nothing he could do to help her. Whatever happened would occur without his involvement, and the injustice of this turn of events bothered him more than the abduction itself. He felt a cruel trick had been played upon him, and the entire voyage to Sivoldaisk now looked like an utterly hopeless effort.

The driver, on the contrary, was energetic and focused. The situation seemed to awaken instincts in him that were hidden from outside eyes. *"Two fools are fighting with a third watching,"* he muttered through clenched teeth. "This is just like with us. Interesting movie, this thriller here – someone in that group is a big wheel..." and he swerved the car right and left, like in an off-road rally.

"They had guns – did you notice?" he addressed Frolov, unperturbed by his silence. "That's no joking matter – guns can fire without breaking a sweat. From their ugly mugs, I'd say they were our boys, not Cauckies. Hard to tell from a distance, though."

"You know anybody on the force?" Alexander responded when

they parked at the district police building. "Otherwise, I'm sure they won't listen to us."

Tolyan became silent, then cursed and said, "I do know someone. Don't worry. And now you'll get to know... all my secrets. They'll hear us out right away, just like real VIPs," and he angrily slammed the door shut.

Before them was the very same mansion colored in ripe raspberry that Andrei Astakhov had glumly walked past that morning. Rows of narrow, identical windows imbued it with mercantile austerity – it could have been a multi-dwelling residence or a mediocre brothel where they knew how to count money and offered nothing for free. For the police it seemed excessively playful; there was something freaky about it, not urban at all. But the guardians of order were obviously immune to the dictates of style, and here the crimson edifice was not considered too odd.

None of this affected Frolov, who was obediently walking behind Tolyan. He noted only external decay and a balcony with no bottom, expecting to see something like dried-up wood or dusty carpet inside, and even shuddered in surprise when he entered a hall trimmed entirely with glass and real marble.

"Remodeling," his escort nodded at the walls. "The pride of the city. The cops really tried hard. There wasn't enough money for the second floor though." He confidently squeezed through a small but noisy group of Armenians desperately arguing with a sweaty lieutenant and brought Frolov to the window of the duty officer, who was shifting something around in the desk drawers.

"Hey, listen, we need an investigator," Tolyan said, sounding somewhat vague, clearly falling back on habit before the living symbol of power. "We have business, and it can't be delayed."

The officer, a sergeant with a thin, short moustache, inspected him with undisguised contempt. It was clear the visitor was of no interest to him personally, nor to the district police department as a whole. "Well, what sort of business do you have?" he asked idly, with the look of a man who had seen everything there was in life. "Maybe you'd rather wait in line like everybody else?"

"You call Nikitina for me, Valentina Pavlovna," said Tolyan crossly. "And if you don't, you'll have only yourself to blame; then there'll be hell to pay for your negligence."

The duty officer again gave him a derisively haughty look, but he reached out to the switchboard, punched some buttons, and drawled lazily, "Valentina Pallna? There's a gentleman here for you."

"Rusakov," Tolyan added loudly, so that it was audible in the switchboard microphone, "regarding an urgent incident." Then, grabbing Alexander by the elbow, he took him aside. "She's coming down now," he whispered. "Don't be afraid of her. She's a good girl, you'll see."

"What do I have to be afraid of?" Frolov shrugged. "Who is she? A real investigator? I've never seen…" He stopped short: from the stairway a very beautiful woman with a tired face crossed over to them quickly.

The inspector, Valentina Pavlovna Nikitina of the Criminal Investigation Unit, had attended secondary school with Tolyan. On top of that, she was his first love – an unhappy affair, as it should be in one's youth – and she remained the most important reason why he hadn't totally given up on women yet. Deep in his heart, Tolyan still believed that somewhere there existed others like his Valentina, and he hoped to meet at least one of them in the future, no matter how distant that future was. His hope was weak: he realized how rare such turns of luck were. Nevertheless, his high-school sweetheart represented the ideal that reconciled him to humanity, a fact he thoroughly hid.

At thirty, Valentina still looked attractive: tall, fair-haired, with a full chest and huge eyes in which men drowned as in space, blissfully giving in to zero gravity. In her youth, she had been slim and graceful; she smelled of violet like a woodland fairy, and Tolyan had been enamored with all the ardor of his not-quite-seventeen years. He often fought over her with older guys, and tried to court her clumsily, with shy letters and confused words. By the end of their last year she noticed his persistence and picked him out from the others, and right before graduation she even yielded to his passion

– smiling with an inscrutable, slightly perverse smile. He, however, was too insecure and timorous about his strong hands and she was totally inexperienced, despite her affected depravity. Nothing worked out for them, and later, utterly disconcerted, he never got up the resolve to approach her again. She quickly tired of his sighs from a distance and soon acquired new admirers. Yet she maintained a certain warmth toward Tolyan, having learned early to appreciate selfless, patient devotion.

Valentina ended up with the police by accident, coming along with a longtime friend, but, in a rather unexpected development, she displayed remarkable character and persistence. She advanced quickly in her career, to the envy of many men, and was promoted to the unit that handled the most important cases. Now no one was misled by the bottomlessness of her blue eyes and her soft voice, in which the growling of a predator could undoubtedly be heard.

She turned out to be a strong woman, but even all her strength couldn't withstand the intrinsic negativity of the job, which soon changed her, making her nervous and hard-assed. She learned not to let anyone offend her, to elbow her way forward and bite off what was hers. She never felt sorry for herself and wasn't open with anybody, ever. At work Valentina spent way too many hours. She ruined her stomach on bad take-out food, and her personal life was reduced to wretched episodes occurring at the very same workplace. At some point she understood she'd had her fill of that lifestyle and, mostly as a protest, decided to marry a man considerably weaker than herself. Her spouse was petty and irascible. He sensed he fell short of her in every respect and, because of that, was impetuously jealous – not just of other men, but also of any emotions she experienced in his absence. At times, this seemed unbearable, but she showed patience, seeing in marriage a support, albeit a shaky one – in spite of the storms and tempests that raged ceaselessly at her job.

Seeing Tolyan in the company of an unknown man, Nikitina decided her friend had gotten tangled up in some trivial mess. Walking right up close, she greeted them efficiently to convey that every minute counted and threw Alexander a professional glance, surmising he was just an ordinary type and didn't pose any threat. "What is it, Tolik? Got yourself in a bind?" she asked with a sigh. "Did you wreck your car or get in a fight? Just hurry it up, it's a zoo around here."

"Valentina, Valentina," Tolyan shook his head. "I can see you have no faith in me. And here is such a case that you'll no doubt get a promotion for it. Kidnapping – ever heard of that? Or seen it in a film somewhere? Take us upstairs – I'll tell you the whole story."

"You have a whole story, huh?" Nikitina hesitated, but something told her they weren't joking. She inspected Frolov again, this time quite closely, and nodded toward the stairs: "All right, if that's how it is, let's go." And she yelled at the duty officer, "Pankratov, I want you to make visitor passes for these two in a bit," without even giving him a casual glance.

"Passes," the officer shook his head. "I can't make passes without identification," but he didn't argue and just made an unhappy face instead. Valentina Pavlovna frustrated him terribly, but she was a tough nut and well she knew it. "Skank," he muttered through his teeth, remembering how she had brusquely rejected his advances a few years before, and snapped hatefully, "Whaddaya want?" at the innocent old woman waiting obediently at the window.

In the meantime, events at the abandoned tourist site were taking a decisive turn. The captives, not expecting help from the outside, implemented their plan. All exchanged glances involuntarily – with a serious and slightly bewildered aspect – and looked at Frank White lying at the door on his back. He gave the okay sign and inhaled hysterically a few times with a rasp.

"Great," Timofey whispered. "Do that. You," he turned to Nikolai, "remember: grab his hands. I'm on his feet – and Lizka, you snatch the gun, if we don't snag it ourselves."

Elizaveta silently nodded, her eyes aflame. Tsarkov thought in passing that he had never seen her so beautiful and raised his fist: "Let's do it!"

"There's no air, oh, oh," groaned Frank, wheezing like a true asthmatic. "I can't breathe... my condition... I can't..." Then he turned toward the threshold and said with a strain, *"Help!* I'm choking!"

"Look, he's almost not breathing," Timofey yelled a little louder than necessary. "Yo, guard, we got a guy in bad shape here," and he pounded his fists on the door. In the meantime, Nikolai knocked against the window bars with an empty plastic bottle and Bestuzheva, as a skilled nurse, fawned over Frank, folding back his shirt collar.

"Help!" Frank shouted occasionally, "I need some air! Let me breathe! I have asthma!"

"Hey, Yurets, what's your deal? You deaf?" Tsarkov raged. "Now the American's gonna kick the bucket, and then you country bumpkins will be in a world of hurt. You just try waving your guns around when the CIA shows up! Come on, open up. Let him get out and take a breather."

The whole performance was intentionally very loud. Sitting on the porch, the guard heard the commotion at once and tried for a minute to appraise the situation, which certainly sounded urgent. He was already a little alarmed anyway – his mobile phone couldn't catch a signal and still no boss came to the island, though, according to the plan, something should occur by the evening of that very day. Intuition told him the operation wasn't proceeding smoothly and lots of trouble still lay ahead. Now he'd have to handle one of them on his own.

Sighing and swearing, he walked around the perimeter of the building and, kneeling, peered through the dark windows of the billiard room. "Hey, you mooks! What's going on in there?" he shouted and knocked on the glass. "Turn on the light so I can see you."

"The lights are out," responded Nikolai. "They don't work. We got a guy suffocating, a foreigner. From the United States of America – ever hear of that country?"

"Help!" groaned Frank. "Give me some fucking air! No air for breath, no air at all..."

He had suddenly developed a distinct accent; there was no doubt of his foreign origins. "What assholes!" the ruffian growled, by which he could have meant the captives or his tardy colleagues. In a single movement, he jumped to his feet and shuffled to the main entrance, muttering sullenly. "Hey, you!" he barked as he descended the stairs. "All of you come up to the windows and keep your mouths shut, or else I'll shoot!"

Through the keyhole he also managed to make out a little. Three silhouettes loomed against the opposite wall, someone unseen wheezed by the door, barely squeezing out non-Russian words. The guard tramped around some more, trying to find a spot where the ailing man fell into his field of vision, but he still couldn't see much.

"What are you waiting for, Yurets?" Timofey yelled impatiently. "Come on, open up, drag him outside. He's going to die and you'll have to answer for it."

"I don't think he'll croak," the thug snickered. "He's too young to kick off yet. I'm not letting him outside. No way."

"What do you mean 'no way?'" Elizaveta interjected. "You don't get it. He's dying – here, look, he's not breathing at all!"

Frank, as if to confirm this, gave an especially plaintive moan and let out something similar to a child's whimper.

"Yeah, I don't get it, and who does? Do you?" the guard snapped. "Who do you think you are, sweetie? Doctor Aybolit? If he's still alive, then he's probably breathing some!" He was quiet for a second, then declared, having obviously made a decision, "Enough! If he wants to live, he'll start to breathe little by little. All right, everyone sit quietly. Don't make any ruckus."

"Wait, hold on!" Understanding Yurets was about to leave, Timofey stepped from the wall to the door, looking fixedly at the opening in the lock. "Why are you being such an animal? Show some humanity, man!"

The crook shifted from one foot to the other, quickly considering something. "Well, what can I do to help?" he asked almost jovially. "You know what kind of doctor I am? A bone crusher. If somebody needs to have an arm or a leg broken... I'm even squeamish around blood," he added and laughed.

"Well," muttered Kramskoy, "that's a sign of a refined personality." He took steps behind Timofey toward the door and asked loudly, "Listen, Yurets, do you believe in God?"

"What do you care?" The guard became angry. "Don't bug me about God. What I believe in is no concern of yours. You think about yourself!" He began to climb the stairs, whistling something catchy. Frank breathed even harder, but it was already clear their captor didn't buy the illness trick.

"Hey, hey, listen," Tsarkov hastened. "When will somebody finally come to talk?"

"When he needs to, that's when he's coming," the thug said, turning around halfway up. And he added irritably, "Who the fuck knows who gets here and when? *They'll come when the devil dies – and he's not even sick yet!*"

"Ah," Nikolai droned, "so you're afraid, yourself. They dumped you here with us and everybody bailed on you. I can tell something's fishy."

"Who do I have to be afraid of? You, pipsqueak?" the guard asked menacingly. "Shut up or you'll be sorry!" He struck the railing twice with his palm and walked away, spitting on the steps.

"Yurets!" yelled Kramskoy, making a sign to the rest. "You're small potatoes, a Rambo wannabe. You're afraid – just admit it!"

"If he comes in, you get his leg," he whispered to Timofey, and the other, nodding in agreement, slid over to the door jamb.

The thug halted. The captives froze, hanging on every sound, but all appeared to be in vain. "Amateurs," he said. "Who are you trying to play like a fool? If it's me, then I'm not going to be played. As for you, bud, we'll have words later, in private."

"Sure, we'll have a chat," Nikolai promised him. "You and I are practically family now."

"Screw family," the guard gave a brief chuckle and, without further delay, ascended the stairs.

In the billiard room a ponderous silence hung. Frank White rose from the floor, extended his hands in a gesture of helplessness, and took a seat on the sofa. The rest settled in as well and avoided looking at each other. Only Liza reached out to Tsarkov and nestled against him, taking his hand again.

"Yes, Lizka, you can throw the fish a worm, but you can't make him bite," he tried to joke. "Our monkeyshines weren't successful, but we'll see. Apparently their business isn't coming together, either. And you, Frankie – you deserve an Oscar for that performance," he nodded to White, Jr., grinning with noticeable effort.

"A performance of a traveling circus," grumbled Nikolai Kramskoy. "What a shame this circus works for free. Somewhere in Argentina, we could have made some coin as street actors."

"Why Argentina?" Elizaveta asked without particular interest. Nikolai didn't answer but merely shrugged his shoulders. Everyone's mood was ruined. The prospects in view were dismal. Their plan, however naïve it was, gave the hope of a happy outcome, and now it was difficult to find a reason for optimism.

"And Frank did pretty well learning the native words," Bestuzheva said suddenly. "Like Captain Cook, only better. He's probably tender with the native girls too. What do you think, Nikolai?"

She wanted to cheer him up, but Kramskoy remained silent. He felt beaten down, unresponsive. The ruling organism had obviously planned a dirty trick or simply forgotten about him, having cast him off as an unnecessary detail.

"Are they testing me?" he thought vapidly. "Checking my strength or flexibility, so to speak? If only they could have given me a signal, the jokers."

"I'd have been good with the girls as well," he muttered. "It's a pity we're occupied with other things now. What do you say, Mr. White? How do you like the newest Russian reality?"

"It's all right," responded Frank after a brief pause. "I even think they're not going to kill us."

Everyone laughed involuntarily. "A clairvoyant," sighed

Kramskoy. "I love American humor."

"All the same," added Frank hesitantly, "we can still try when they come for Timothy. They have to open the door, after all..."

"Forget it," Tsarkov interrupted. "It won't be just one of them; there'll be a lot. A lot of big, bad dudes. They'll cripple you or shoot right away," he said sternly, tugging at his cheek. "Still, let's not give up hope. We'll sit here, nice and cozy, and wait for events to unfold. We'll tell some jokes, a bunch of stories – nothing to sulk about, like in a churchyard."

"*Even churchyards have guests*," Nikolai grumbled. "And I'm glad it's not us yet. Let's have a story, then – who wants to tell one? Frank here did his part already."

"Kramskoy," Elizaveta said, "you tell one. You're the most unexplained riddle here. And that scar on your cheek is somewhat odd."

"Just your average scar," answered Nikolai glumly. "And as for riddles, mine won't win any prizes. My enigmas are hardly enough to shake a stick at. Though... There is one unusual thing: look how interesting it turned out for me to get hooked up with Frank White!

"We met by accident," he explained. "We didn't know anything about each other. Of course, Sivoldaisk is a very small city, but still. He was brought here by a mythic treasure trove, and I came for a document that also doesn't exist in reality. But the basis for both our hunts is the same and quite real – Pugachev. And one can now contemplate further: did we meet so we could be captured? Or is captivity an independent issue, and *they* are looking for something else from us?" He shook his head.

"You are indeed a lunatic!" Tsarkov sighed. "Don't worry, captivity is a separate thing; it's me who stepped on some bastard's toes. And our American friend just got scammed for a thousand bucks – not by a higher power, but by an ordinary con man, what's his name, Silva? Actually, if not for you, the cops at the precinct would have beaten the crap out of his kidneys, too."

"Wait, hold on," Elizaveta patted him on the hand, then turned to

Nikolai and asked with a glint in her eyes, "That document of yours, is it a secret?"

"Of course not," Kramskoy replied. "What could there be secret in it if it doesn't even exist? Everyday stuff with a bit of romantic flavor, if you want details."

"So tell us all about it," Liza wouldn't relent. "There's nothing more interesting than romantic details. Especially everyday ones."

"What's there to tell? And besides, I'm no storyteller." Nikolai stood to stretch his legs and went to the window. Halfway there, however, he couldn't hold back and turned to Elizaveta. She didn't break her eyes away from his gaze, but narrowed her eyelids and bit her lip slightly. "Is she bewitching me or something?" he thought suddenly, and was surprised at himself: What nonsense! Though anybody's nerves could give out here.

He sported a terse grin as he said, "Better somebody else. Or maybe we should give the dice a throw?" Elizaveta smiled at him in response and tilted her head to the side, still without averting her eyes. "Like a cat," flashed in Kramskoy's head. "A forest cat or water nymph – with bright green eyes. She's probably a lot of fun. That fiancé of hers is lucky. Maybe I really should tell – about Pugachev, and the document too."

"The lady's asking," Timofey supported her. "Why do we have dice if there's free will?" He lounged on the sofa, but his palms were restless, rubbing one another.

"That's what I'm lacking," Nikolai noted to himself, turning away from Liza and the rest. "Fine. You win," he grumbled. "I'll tell it for the sake of free will. Once upon a time, there lived an outlaw by the name of Yemelyan..."

It darkened in the billiard room. Evening fell. In the corners behind the couches, shadows thickened. "Actually, he was no criminal, but rather a simple Cossack," Kramskoy said, peering at the barred windows. "But that was at first, and later destiny played a very strange role. He was turned into a figurehead in local turmoil – just to defend apiaries and fishing trade – but ended up becoming the self-appointed tsar, inflicting terror upon half the empire. However many impostors there were in Russia, it was in him, Emperor Pugach, that people believed in with abandon: everyone who crossed his path, who ran to him from the steppe lands through bog and smoke, in blizzards and impassable mires. He never studied the art of war but possessed intuition and courage – and seized fortresses one after another as he won over whole garrisons for himself. He was the chief of a rabble, the leader of a most vulgar horde, a real master of treachery and atrocity. And he knew no doubt – as if he felt someone's hand was guiding him toward an unattainable goal. This knowledge was conveyed to the rest: all who looked into his eyes, kissed his hand in an oath of fealty, or only heard about him from others who had turned already to the new faith and were set to devour anyone alive who didn't gape in awe at this messiah's advent. And he was, for them, a messiah – a fair tsar and a most fearsome devil, demigod, and defender of the oppressed. His campaign was full of triumphs; he seemed omnipotent and invincible. Immortality itself apparently touched him. Was it not for this reason that he feared neither cannon shot nor bullets? And indeed, no bullet or cannon ball took him, and he was ferocious – ferocious and ruthless, advancing tirelessly up the Volga, only rarely affording himself a respite – to give rest to body and soul."

"And so," Nikolai made a strange gesture, "so he was an inveterate beast and didn't need a warm den. But he chanced upon the village of Chumovo – a local place, not far from Sivoldaisk – and there a snowstorm flared up, dumping on everything in the vicinity. Yemelyan ordered a halt, to wait out the inclement weather and get a semblance of rest for a brief day or two. In the evening, as was customary, they held a feast. Pugachev and his confidants glutted themselves on grilled meat and homemade wine. And serving them was the farmer's daughter, fair-haired and gray-eyed, with slightly high cheekbones from a trace of Tatar blood, tall and stately from her Cossack roots. Her braids were plaited in a headpiece, and her cheeks reddened – from the heat of the oven and the virile talk around her…"

"Yes, the farmer's daughter. History didn't record her name,"

Nikolai continued, shooting a glimpse at Elizaveta. "Perhaps she was called Eudokia or Maria, and she was simple-hearted – just like her mother. Or maybe she bore a classier name – Darya, Natalia or Katerina – and she lived in her own little world, loved to look into the oven coals or wander the woods in search of enchanting herbs. She believed in legends and omens, feared the forest sprite, whom she called the Old Man of the Woods, as everyone did. For her part, echoing him, she loved to sing without words, as if enticing the fairy spirit, which might transform into an owl or a wolf, or even a man with a knapsack, and then howl and whistle, luring her into the wilderness. There she felt at home, better than in the village – where the young men admired her but nobody caught her affections, and the boisterous roundelays didn't interest her in the least. Thus she lived in anticipation of something – or someone, as the case may be – and in the months since June she was troubled by sinful thoughts, beginning with the sultry nights when the mountain ash bloomed and the sky blazed with summer lightning. They tormented her all autumn, and in sleep she found no rest. It seemed that someone scraped at the window, knocked and tramped through the attic under the roof and even caressed her with a shaggy hand as she slept – for her good, for her maidenly joy. A few days before the appearance of Pugachev and his horde, the fire in their hearth suddenly went out. 'For an unintended guest,' said her mother pensively, and her heart pounded. And as soon as she saw the fearful man with the dense black beard, she knew: here was the guest, and he had come for her."

Nikolai again looked briefly at Bestuzheva and gave a barely perceptible grin, but the room had already darkened, and faces were indistinguishable. "The farmer's daughter," he continued. "How many such girls chanced upon the ataman's way? There were others, more smiling and saucier, but this one he studied all evening – thoughtfully, almost with grief – and at the meal he became silent, not responding as his brothers-in-arms egged him on. Later, in the entrance hall, he caught her by the elbow, burning right through her with the fiery coals of his eyes, and said briefly, "Come to me tonight. I won't harm you. I'll be loving you.'

"She looked at him, petrified with fear, but when night fell, the fear vanished. And she went to him in a white linen gown – tall, stately, quiet – and didn't leave for nigh on three days, to the horror of both her parents, who wouldn't dare disturb their terrible guest. Then Yemelyan was again set ablaze inside, and the farmer's daughter, in an instant, became a burden. He went out to the porch and told his men to ready the horses – the snowstorm had passed and it was time to move on. But leaving his Eudokia-Katerina-Darya was not so easy, and from that day on he never expelled her from his heart. He thought to bring her with him – and she pleaded, nearly begging on her knees, 'Take me with you. I'll be your slave.' But he did not – dark and terrible, he only looked into her face, his brow furrowed like a gloomy demon, and said, 'Don't be foolish, girl. It's death for you with me. Live your life instead.' He left money and a squirrel-fur coat that had been worn not long before by some landowner's wife, then patted her on the cheek and left, with no promise to return. And she, in her term, gave birth to twins – swarthy, with large heads. And though one of them soon died, the second remained – and survived to grow to manhood. Only they gave him a different surname, out of diffidence and superstition. That is the whole story, and the document... The document is a fiction, the fantasy of a master. That master is me," he bowed preposterously, "and my customer is a rich man, a distant descendant of Pugachev in a way."

"What a shame they split up," Elizaveta shook her head. "And you, Kramskoy, you're quite a tale spinner!"

"Why shouldn't they split?" Timofey Tsarkov grinned. "It's plain as day: Ataman Pugach and a simple girl – they had a romp and sayonara, baby. There was nothing to hold them together – neither poverty nor a common goal. What kind of goal could they have, anyway? Nothing but hoodoo."

"Common goal," Liza repeated softly. "And what about just love?"

She sensed some sort of new uneasiness. It became clear to her that seven years had not passed in vain and Timofey, as he was now, might not resemble the man she once knew at all.

"Common goal," she said again to herself. "Well, I never thought of that. Or of many other things. Might it be that he's figured out everything for the two of us?"

"What's eating you, Liza?" Tsarkov asked, feeling her estrangement. "You jealous of Eudokia, the farmer's daughter? She was gray-eyed with braids too. Our narrator is observant, I see."

"For me, she's not Eudokia, but Masha," said Elizaveta, trying to sound nonchalant. "And the story really is good. Who are you, Nikolai Kramskoy?" she asked, just as she had a few hours before.

Nikolai paced back and forth, than looked at Liza again. "Who are you? Who are you?" he echoed her question. "No matter who you are, your name is that of a nobody. So any joke about that issue turns out not to be funny... I probably would like to have been an artist," he admitted suddenly and, having embarrassed himself, fell silent.

"Kramskoy the Artist already lived a hundred years ago," Timofey remarked brusquely. "They, artists, are a dime a dozen. There's not enough money in the world to keep them all employed. Though, of course, all of us here are ready to applaud noble ambition. Your ambitions, probably, aren't modest – and you, I bet, possess a large-scale plan for the ages."

"Whether it's for the ages or not, who knows? But there is a plan, yes," Nikolai said seriously. "That is, there was at one time. Then I ditched it, and it's my own fault. That's why I'm not offended by you, even though you ridicule out of turn."

"Yeah, whatever," Tsarkov waved him off. "What ridicule is there? *A wolf also bares his teeth, but he's not laughing.* And I'd become an artist along with you – to draw Liza's portrait."

"You're a master at baring teeth, but you're no wolf. As for the portrait, strange as it is, you nailed it," Kramskoy sneered and again began pacing the room. "A portrait... That's the best thing that can be done, and done in so many ways! It occurred to me once: you can compose it from the tiniest letters. From the letters there will be words, and from the words the history of a prototype: the contents of the portrait will increase many times! Only I don't know whether anyone will appreciate it – that's the problem with excessive contents. They don't even read books now if too much is written in them."

"All the books will be burned soon," Timofey butted in with a joke, but nobody laughed.

"A portrait in letters – that's good," Frank muttered. "Although I've heard of that somewhere before."

"Well, yes," exclaimed Nikolai, disappointed. "I'm certainly not the first to conceive of it. All ideas have already been repeated many times. As have thoughts, quotes – all available in hundreds of copies, such that you almost can't distinguish it. The universe takes care that what is important doesn't pass away. It duplicates, protects its assets, but, still, the essence is in implementation, nothing else. You have to execute ideas – only in that is there depth. Sometimes, you get into such a tangled mess… Though I can only assume that. To be honest, I've never attempted to paint. That's a shame – I should have plucked up courage and tried, but I was waiting for something, looking for clues. And what if there are none?"

His palms broke into a sweat and his voice trembled treasonously. He shut up without finishing to keep from betraying himself.

"As for the contents, I agree with you," said Tsarkov from the darkness, not joking anymore. "It's a touchy issue these days. You look around, it's one freak after another. Digressing, back to the apes, it's evolution in full circle – and there you are yourself, right in the midst of them, with nowhere to go. Such terrible sadness grips you then…" He yawned nervously. "Downright deathly, like the grave."

The words hung in the air and didn't want to fall. Someone sighed convulsively. "We shouldn't be talking about death," Elizaveta said, climbing on the sofa and clasping her knees as she folded her legs. It was clear she was afraid, and she didn't want to conceal it.

"Hey, Yurets!" Tsarkov shouted, jumped up, ran to the door, and knocked on it with his heel. Then, after waiting a little, he shouted again, but the guard didn't respond.

"The devil only knows where they are and what's up," he said in a fit. "This is what the riddle is – and it's much weirder than Pugachev, the People's Tsar. What's a village girl to him? He wanted to govern from no less than a throne – yet he ended up not on a throne, but in an iron cage. And now we're in a cage instead of in a restaurant with starched tablecloths." He burst out with a forced laugh, cleared his throat, and asked White, Jr., "So, what do you think, Frankie? How did the lot of tsar fall to Pugach?"

"It's hard for me to judge," the other shrugged. "That's probably what happens when you're born under a certain star."

"Ho, ho!" Timofey grinned. "Something's a bit too murky. I would say the same about myself, yet in my life there's no die to be cast. Admit it – you were probably born under a special sign, too, and now you're secretly waiting to get your due, right?"

Frank recalled the treasure he had failed to find and felt regret prick like a needle, but this receded immediately into a far corner – to the refuse heaps of the insignificant, to things that didn't involve him. "I've been told," he said with complete seriousness, "that my star is quite common. There was a Chinese girl – she was well-versed in that stuff. She drew out these charts – I forget what they're called."

"Well," Timofey noted absentmindedly, "I suppose she has a better grasp of it than us." He took a noisy gulp from his water bottle, put it on the billiard table, and again shouted at the top of his lungs, "Yurets!"

"He's not answering, the bastard," he complained to no one in particular. "Maybe he's sailed away already, who knows? There's nothing worse than when things don't make sense."

"*An eagle flies, fire is in its mouth, and at the end of its tail is the death of man,*" Elizaveta cooed quietly, hiding on the corner of the sofa. "*A bird flies high, its feathers red and yellow, and at its end is the death of man.* Here's a real riddle for you. Who wants to guess it? My grandmother sang this to me, the one on my father's side." Her voice cracked like she was going to cry.

"It's all right. It's okay, Lizka," Timofey went over and sat next to her. "We'll get out of this, don't you fret. Somebody'll show up, give his name, make demands. They're looking for cash, no doubt. And I'll cough it up, buy our way out... Hey, friends," he addressed

Nikolai and Frank, "why don't you share something else, distract the lady from her thoughts."

"You share," retorted Kramskoy glumly. "It's your turn, not ours. And the lady's yours, too."

He was haunted by bad premonitions and irritated at everything and everybody. Having spoken his piece, he was ashamed of his frankness, and of the thoughts he concealed even from people he knew.

"How foolish it all is," he mused in impotent rage. "Higher power, predestination, signs – it's all bullshit in practice. Pugachev was also led by signs – merely so his ruin could be more magnificent. Could the very same thing be happening with me? Could this be our astral connection? What a joke!" He grinned mirthlessly and shook his head.

"Why me?" Tsarkov grumbled. "I'm not a lunatic, and I don't know stories like that. Well here, for example…" and he was quiet for a moment. "For example, Sivoldaisk stands upon an air bubble. Someday it'll pop, and that's it: the city's screwed. And we'll be adrift at sea. Or here's another: once, long ago, a Persian khan remained nearby to winter with his retinue. Thus, the city starved all that season in order to feed him!"

Nobody expressed interest; only Frank shifted weakly in the dark. "N-yes," Timofey scratched the nape of his neck. "Well, a fire broke out in our opera theater, but that happens in theaters everywhere. Or how about this: once a whole pond disappeared. A great big pond, almost a lake, right in the middle of the workers' quarters. So the grunts, accustomed to everything, could no longer live or even breathe there. They abandoned their homes and scattered to stay with their relatives – so much rubbish of all kinds was found at the bottom. The chemicals were terrible, even flies died. Now only the ravens are there; it doesn't bother them at all."

"Suddenly revealed secrets always come at inopportune times," murmured Kramskoy. "Even for the grunts."

Outside the window, some bird cried loudly and a dog howled straightaway – with melancholy and despair.

"*When above the church a raven calls, then in the town a dead man falls,*" Liza purred. "*When raven wheels above the eaves, a dead man drops in the hut beneath...* All well and good for you to chatter away," she said suddenly, "but when they caught you, you didn't make a peep. There were three of them, and you are three men. Plus me, a puny woman."

"But they have guns," Frank answered guiltily. Nikolai only snorted and said nothing. "What are you on about, Lizka?" grumbled Tsarkov. "You saw how it went down."

"The local wood sprite has beguiled me, just like the farmer's daughter." Elizaveta sighed fitfully. "He's beguiled us all in some sense and then ensnared us in a thicket. What do they call him? The Old Man of the Woods? But what does he need me for? He won't get any berries from me, or mushrooms. And nobody's stroking me with a shaggy hand – that, they say, is for wealth. And I didn't catch sight of my intended in snow water – he appeared by himself and muddled my head."

She squirmed in the dark, arranged herself more comfortably, then smiled: "And I know some more things." And she began to speak expressively, as if reading a book aloud:

"*The straw upon which the dead man lies is burned beyond the gates.*"

"*Be the coffin unseemly large – then another death in the house you'll wake.*"

"*Shavings from the coffin are not burned, but in the water they are dropped.*"

"*And if the deceased looks with one eye open, that means...*" she sobbed, "*that means he's looking at the one who's next!*"

And suddenly she burst out crying bitterly, childishly, burying her face in Timofey's chest.

CHAPTER 21

The self-appointed detectives, Tolyan and Alexander Frolov, wandered after Inspector Valentina along the corridor at the district police department. There, on the second floor, was neither marble nor shining glass. The walls gleamed a dirty lime-gray, and the loose parquet creaked intolerably. Valentina Nikitina strode lightly, without noticing the surrounding squalor. The hallway reeked of carbolic acid and stale tobacco smoke, but behind it, like a guiding thread, stretched a nearly imperceptible trail of French perfume, which Alexander unconsciously sniffed, almost flexing his nostrils.

The investigative unit's office was confined and smoky. It was stuffy, despite the open, screened-in windows. The screen, rickety and full of holes, was to protect against insects, but it did a poor job: several gray flies had found their way inside and now beat against the frames. In the office, besides Valentina, sat a small man with a crooked spine, whom Tolyan flippantly addressed with, "Hey there, Laurenty." Meanwhile, from a doorway leading to the adjacent room, a portly superior entered, bearing the epaulets of major on her uniform. She paid them not the slightest attention; her target was a youngish field detective perched on the corner of a chair. She towered over him like a cliff, and when he hastily jumped off, she patted his shoulder and said glumly, "Take off, Igorek. Report there that I sent you back." The detective started to respond, "Please, Maria

Ivanovna, maybe I…" But she threw him an even more despondent glare and he leapt from the room, slightly grazing Frolov's shoulder.

This episode amused Alexander. It even occurred to him that crimes in Sivoldaisk were investigated exclusively by women, but this, of course, would be too brazen a generalization. *"What they now refer to as feminine used to be called suspicious,"* he remembered from his ledger and felt an instant longing for his Moscow apartment and the thousand pages scribbled in his miniscule handwriting. In the meantime, Nikitina, offering a pair of uncomfortable chairs, sat down at a desk opposite them, leaned on her arm, and prepared to listen – with something maternal in the look she was giving Tolyan.

In the process of his account, however, her eyes grew inflamed with avid interest. Even her appearance changed: it became clear she had a strong grasp and sharp, albeit graceful, claws. Without interrupting the driver, she rummaged in a drawer, pulled out an empty folder, and stated matter-of-factly, "All right; let's open a case." Then she lit up a cigarette, squinting from the smoke, and began to quickly fill out some kind of form. Laurenty, who really looked like a KGB monster with his bald pate and round spectacles, approached and expressed interest in an indifferent tone, "Has something happened, Val?" But Nikitina shot him a look clearly saying to get away from her territory, and he returned to his desk without another word.

Soon, the stout major materialized again in the same doorway, tossed some papers on Laurenty's desk, and asked casually, "Whaddaya got, Valentina?"

"Multiple kidnapping," she quietly responded. "This afternoon at Priton. We're just starting the file – I was about to come see you."

The major stopped, studied Frolov and his driver, and nodded to Nikitina, "Well, okay. Come in, then."

Valentina was gone for about a quarter of an hour, during which time Alexander was nervous and fidgeted in his chair, fearing they didn't believe them and would kick them out. Tolyan was silent and sullenly gnawed his fingernails. Laurenty shouted at someone over the phone, "It's me, Vitalik. What are you doing there, anyway?" and he let loose a barrage of profanity. Nikitina came out, wearing a very contented look, and was about to address some question to Frolov when her mobile rang, and for another ten minutes she calmed her husband, who had some angry words of frustration with her about something or other.

"No, well, I called an hour ago… Where? You were just at Zavodskaya Street yesterday – what kind of crap are you doing on Zavodskaya?" could be heard in the room. Tolyan grew even darker and picked at something in his palm, while Inspector Valentina purred silkily and evenly into the receiver, so her husband finally abated and hung up after one last irritated tirade. "Well, now," she sighed after disconnecting, "what do we have here? Okay, give me the plate numbers."

Tolyan pulled out the crumpled piece of paper and dictated the tags of the boat and microbus; this set the police machine in motion under full throttle at last. Vitalik-Laurenty shouted again at someone on the phone while Nikitina, blushing and becoming even prettier, worked the switchbox and kept running into the chief's office with a stern, purposeful look. At some point the detectives remembered Frolov and his driver. As she ran past, Valentina threw them a glance and declared brusquely, "All right, you guys get going. There's nothing more for you to do here!"

Tolyan was about to get up but Alexander looked at him so pitifully that he cleared his throat and awkwardly asked, "Do you mind if we, um, sit here quietly for a bit? The man's really busted up, as you can see. And besides, what if you need some more testimony from us?"

Frolov also cleared his throat as if he were about to add something but thought better of it and merely nodded. Valentina pursed her lips, but then just waved her hand, "Fine, sit." And with that she dashed off, leaving in her wake the same, almost imperceptible, French aroma.

They ascertained the owner of the Volkswagen quickly, but the microbus, as one would expect, turned out to be stolen. With the boat, discrepancies were revealed in the records, and Vitalik, without shouting now but quietly and suavely, like an inquisitor, promised the registration holder serious trouble if he didn't deal with this business that very second.

"Do you realize they're going to string you up by the balls? No, think about it. They're going to hang you by the balls for this!" he muttered in an oily tone, then phoned somewhere else, whining, begging, insisting, and on his bald dome large drops of sweat shone. Major Maria Ivanovna got involved in the case as well, and from her half-open door resounded a couple of outbursts of boisterous vulgarity, such that it even startled Tolyan a few times, and he looked in her direction with admiration. Then everything calmed down at once, and Valentina and Vitalik-Laurenty began readying themselves to leave.

"We found the owner," Vitalik winked with a grin. "The senior mechanic at a battery plant. He's got a rap sheet starting when he was a kid. We're going to go have a chat."

"This is the one!" whispered Tolyan to Frolov and, plucking up his courage, asked Valentina, "Listen, Val, can we tag along with you guys?"

"Are you out of your mind?" she asked in amazement. "Who are you, the SWAT team? No way – and make sure I don't see you there at the address." Then she looked at miserable Alexander and sighed, "All right, Tolik, here's my new cell number. Call me in an hour or so."

Pankratov, the duty officer, gave them an ill-favored look but spoke with surprising reserve. "Enter your details here, precisely as they are in your passport, and sign here legibly, in the box," he murmured with even a bit of complaisance, which really surprised Tolyan.

"See, we're practically heroes already," he quietly told Frolov as they walked away from the window. "They can't keep a secret, cops: they gossip like ninnies."

"Yep," the other agreed listlessly once they were outside, rubbing his shoulders from the chill. Despite the warm evening, he felt a feverish shudder.

"Well, you're a nervous wreck," Tolyan eyed him critically. "You could do with a cold one right now, and it's high time for it. Now, let's think…"

He looked around and pointed a finger, "Ah, there's a store right there!" And in fact, on the other side of the street, in the middle of the square with gaunt trees, stood a small structure, almost entirely of glass, adorned with a gaudy sign that read Taste of Dreams. Beneath it was painted the frightening visage of a pie, but this didn't stop Tolyan, as he nearly dragged his buddy by the hand directly across the road, amid honking cars.

"We need a brewski, ma'am," he blurted out from the doorway as he vigorously stepped toward the counter. "Our dreams today have the taste of cold beer."

The shop assistant, a brittle, elderly woman, looked at him, perplexed. "We only have pastries," she said sheepishly. "For beer you want the café, over there to the right. They have a summer veranda, too." She pronounced it *ve-rahn-dah*, in a somewhat Oriental manner, despite her round Russian face and fair hair pulled together in a bun.

"The *ca-fay* with the *ve-rahn-dah*," the driver mocked her, offended for some reason. "I *underSTAHND*. They probably sell it there at a mark-up, eh? But we're no tourists – you could sell some to us as local boys."

"Yeah, well, I don't have any beer," the saleswoman bristled and looked suspiciously at the silent Frolov. "And you two, I don't know you either. Go to the café and drink there."

She picked up a rag that looked none too clean and began to wipe the counter pointedly. The stench of bleach wafted from it right away. Alexander frowned and turned toward the door.

"You don't look very nice, mama, despite all your pies," Tolyan told the shopkeeper and added to Frolov as they walked away, "To lose such great customers, what an idiot!"

It was empty in the cafe right around the corner, but the beer was surprisingly good. "Just as I thought: it's marked up," the driver continued to grumble, inspecting the empty tables. But Alexander, without paying attention to him, killed off a half-liter bottle in a few gulps and reached for another.

"You're a piece of work," Tolyan shook his head in respect. "Well, no matter. Everything's under control now. They won't get away – Valentina will have them under her thumb!" He lit a cigarette and sprawled in his chair with the look of a man who had just finished some difficult business.

"Many start to take revenge before they've managed to be offended," Frolov muttered after a moment's silence. "But this is clearly not the case with us."

"Not bad," his partner extolled. "Did you come up with that yourself?"

"Not at all," Alexander responded absentmindedly. "I read it somewhere and made a note of it."

"Ah," Tolyan nodded. "The capital, it shows: the ideas, the thoughts. You all probably read books there every day."

"It's a matter of personal taste," replied Frolov, still with the same vacancy. "Hey, isn't it time to call?"

"Don't rush me," the driver said sternly. "We agreed: in an hour – so, in an hour it will be. Otherwise, they'll just tell us to screw off, you got it?" He rose, went up to the bar, and returned with another two bottles, whistling on the way at a gaggle of babes with long, bare legs. "Will you say something else like that?" he asked Alexander. "Something, you know, clever, astute. It's not often you get to talk to an intelligent person around here."

Frolov started to refuse, but his friend wouldn't relent. "All right, then," he conceded. "You know how they say, *No military plan survives an encounter with the enemy*? It's interesting to note," he added with a grin, "that I had no plan whatsoever. And here's another: *War is mainly a catalog of blunders.*"

"Now, that one you definitely made up yourself," Tolyan

declared. "A serious person wouldn't say such a thing. I've also met my fair share of military types, by the way."

"No," Alexander shook his head. "That's not mine. It's from Winston Churchill. A rather serious man, you might say."

"Fine, Churchill it is," agreed the driver, but it was obvious he didn't believe him. "Everyone has a bad moment – and can blurt out any kind of foolishness in frustration. And those Brits – they're strange anyway, no matter how you look at it."

He lit a new cigarette and continued, "Fact is, we expect too much from abroad. It's because of that Moscow of yours – no offense – which has got both eyes firmly fixed on the United States. As for us here, it's all the same: the wind blows but brings you who-knows-what. Except chicks, the stupid creatures, they just want to marry and get away – 'Ooh, gimme a foreigner!' In my opinion, that's more trouble than it's worth."

Frolov grunted something and furtively looked at his watch.

"Don't worry, I'm keeping an eye on the time," Tolyan grumbled, insulted. "You think two bottles would make me drunk? It's early still, don't fuss. It's a pity, though, that you don't smoke."

"True," Alexander unexpectedly concurred, "but I can't. It makes me cough."

"All of you there are sissies," Tolyan nodded. "That's because your Moscow is the center of the world. The center, it's always poisoned in a way. And as far as life abroad, we have everything here too; it's no worse than the USA. Everybody says, 'Bermuda, Bermuda,' but right outside Sivoldaisk our Camel Gorge will give Bermuda a run for its money. People vanish there, all right, and whole expeditions, down to a man. It should be made into a movie, I guess."

"Yeah?" Frolov asked without particular interest. He twirled a bottle cap in his fingers without taking his eyes off it.

"Absolutely! I'm here to tell you," Tolyan declared, stressing the I. "My brother-in-law told me, back when I was still living with my ex. They just don't write about it in the papers – they're not allowed. Before, it was so there wouldn't be any panic, and now, it's just out of habit."

From the café bar, a pockmarked barmaid traipsed over, collected empty bottles in her arms, and shot a crazy green eye toward Alexander. "You men going to want any more beer?" she inquired playfully.

"Later," Tolyan responded firmly. "You can leave for now. Don't push it."

"Ha." She wandered back to the bar. Frolov noted mechanically that she also smelled of French perfume.

"Out of habit," his friend repeated, addressing him again. "And once, my brother-in-law told me, a group from his Institute disappeared, and neither hide nor hair was heard from them again. Searchers went out, and one of them also vanished into thin air... And another was bitten by a snake," he added thoughtfully.

Frolov nodded, continuing to fiddle with the bottle cap. The driver leaned closer and said with meaning, "It's a mistake for you not to believe. You're all Doubting Thomases there, but here things are real, not a bunch of poppycock!"

"Remember how I was telling you that here in ancient times stood a large city," he continued. "Wealthier than Moscow, all in Tatar gold. It stood for the longest time, then *poof!* Can you imagine? Gone underground, all in one day. There are ruins left, but no one visits them; ruins are nothing special. Too many ravines here, anyway – we're just slipping into the Volga, slowly but surely."

"Come on, call already," Alexander pleaded. "I can't wait any longer."

Tolyan muttered discontentedly, "Why am I playing host here?" But he obediently took out his phone and dialed the number. "She's going to tell us to fuck off," he whispered with desperate melancholy in his voice, and then spoke into the receiver, "Val, Val, hi. It's us."

Contrary to his expectations, Inspector Nikitina was favorably disposed. This was due to the positive unfolding of the investigation, which had every chance of becoming a big success. The owner of the boat happened to be at home, as was his entire family, which consisted of his middle-aged girlfriend and half a dozen cats that could be smelled from the street. The situation was muddled slightly by that fact the mechanic wasn't suitable for interrogation as he lolled about the bed in a deep narcotic sleep. However, judging by indirect signs, he should regain consciousness in seven to eight hours – and then he would sing like a canary.

His partner, on the other hand, a kind woman somewhat fearful of life, was rather talkative and obviously delighted at the opportunity to converse with somebody besides the cats. She informed Valentina and Vitalik that her man had piddled with his boat all day, sailed away somewhere, and blown off work. Her persistent – albeit reasonable – questions he refused to answer, and he even flared up a little, as attested by the fresh abrasion on her face. However, she wasn't too upset: her initial version, in which the mechanic was out carousing with floosies, dissipated on its own – since he had come home sober, in a buoyant mood, and with money. From now on, there would be piles of money, he declared, and he bragged about buying a motorcycle and an imported suit, after which he celebrated excessively and got stoned, mixing in home-brewed vodka for good measure – which he did quite often, though not every day. She even thought at first that he would die from his indulgences, but now she saw that no, he wouldn't. He'd sober up by morning, though he wouldn't be so fresh. But that was okay, she'd gotten used to it a long time ago.

Overall, the picture appeared clear, fitting the case perfectly. They left two policemen with the mechanic so as not to miss his return to the world of reality, and the inspectors went back to the department to deal with the daily grind. Valentina bade a warm goodbye to Tolyan and instructed him to phone the next day, promising to keep him informed.

"Well here," he summarized, relating what he had heard to Frolov, "you and I have now done what we can. We'll wait till morning and hope for the best – nothing else depends on us."

By all indications, he was pleased with himself and his contribution to the police action, but Alexander wasn't at all content with what had been achieved. "What do you mean 'wait till morning?'" he twitched. "This asshole's going to spill the beans tonight!"

"Come on," grinned Tolyan. "Tonight... Policemen sleep at night. Regardless of that, it's dark. Where are you going to take a boat?"

Alexander froze, looking rather stunned, but Tolyan was not to be assuaged. "Around here, even if a body's reported, the police don't go at once," he explained, slowly firing up a smoke. "They wait a couple of hours, until evening comes. The day is over, they say. Work only happens in the daylight. And as for us, we don't even have a corpse!"

Frolov exhaled through clenched teeth and wiped his face with his hand. All his tension dissipated and was replaced by indifference and apathy. "Hey, don't get steamed," the driver sympathized. "Look, everything's off to a good start. We'll chill till morning – the deed is done. It's in God's hands now. I suggest you crash at my place – what do you say? We'll buy some grub, a bit of vodka, then order us up some girls..."

"No, you'll have to excuse me," Alexander shook his head. "I don't do women for hire. I've got a conviction about that, sorry."

"A conviction?" the driver asked with sincere amazement. "First time I've heard of such a thing. I see, you're from the capital, and you're an odd character anyway; but 'round these parts everyone knows: all of Russia is nothin' but hooch and whoring. Really, what else is there to do in these lands? Look, the Volga's a kilometer away, and beyond that's nothing but the steppe. And so it goes for thousands of miles – get to thinking about it and you'll drive yourself mad. Better, you know, to be distracted and not think, and agree that the only wisdom is babes and vodka... Well, so what then? Another beer, maybe?"

He made a sign to the barmaid and showed her two fingers. She nimbly stepped from behind the bar and placed two uncapped bottles before them. "Would you like a little something to eat?" she asked languidly, again glancing at Frolov.

"Go on, Manya, leave us alone," Tolyan brushed her off. "We'd like to eat somewhere else, some place cleaner."

"My name's not Manya. It's Ve-ron-ica," the girl drawled, offended, and went back behind the bar, shuffling her feet.

"You hear that? *Ve-ron-ica*," grumbled the driver, gazing after her. "Has some spunk, too. The way she was checking you out – you caught her eye, Mr. Visitor. But she won't do for us, no sir."

Tolyan took a sip from his bottle and thoughtfully looked around. Then he scratched the nape of his neck, frowned, and said, "Actually, we don't buy women, we rent love. And love comes in many varieties: you may get lucky or not, no way to tell in advance. It's simple there in the capital: pay for something, and it's yours! Here, though, everything's more complicated."

"Yes, really," he added in response to Frolov's puzzled look. "Here, it turns out when you pay, you get the whole package – with all her troubles included. Well, and love too, of course, if she fancies you, because where else are the chicks here going to release all that? Guys hereabouts are so-so, rubbish – and there's no place to meet any others, except in a hotel working as a whore. And so it goes that you purchase the full package, and later you don't know what it was or how to escape from it. And sometimes you don't know what else to wish for, either – I mean, you're just asking yourself if there's anything else to wish for. And besides, if not with money, how would you get all this from them? They're simpletons, every one. Their heads are filled with whatever their moms and grandmas stuffed in there. Marriage, family, kids – but they don't appreciate the most important things inside themselves!"

"Very amusing," Alexander murmured and finished off his beer in one gulp.

"I haven't convinced you, huh?" Tolyan asked and nodded knowingly, "I can see that I haven't. You aren't a philosopher when it comes to women; you're more into war. Yet we were tracking a girl, not a tank... Fine, don't be put out. If you don't want to, then you don't. We'll meet some decent girls in light of that. If you, as they say, see the difference."

"Could we just skip it entirely?" Frolov asked, tossing a few bills on the table. "I hardly slept on the train, and this turned out to be a hell of a day."

"Forget that, man," Tolyan chided sternly. "That just wouldn't be proper. We worked hard, now we have to relax. Anybody'll tell you that!" He drained the rest of his beer and continued, "Come on. You gave the orders this afternoon, now surrender the initiative. I'll entertain you, provide the refreshments and the cultural program."

They got in the old reliable Zhiguli Nine and slowly drove down Moskovskaya Street. "Well, it's up to you," Alexander broke the silence. "Though, if we're hitting a club, I don't even have anything to wear."

"Why go to a club?" Tolyan said in surprise. "At a club, the decent ones are hard to find. They're all looking for sugar daddies, to put it the Moscow way. We'll head to the Prospect: there are all kinds there – we can hook up with some college girls. The main drag is not that long, but it's a real hang-out," and the driver careened to the right, onto Chapayev Street, where the traces of the morning's accident had already been cleaned up. He honked at a yawning cyclist, braked at the curb, and said enthusiastically, "Here we are, then. Hop on out."

On the Prospect, which had been turned into a pedestrian promenade, the evening life was in full swing. Well-dressed crowds sauntered from one end to the other, mingling, fanning out into the alleys, and rejoining the main flow. Those strolling were mostly women – of all ages and to suit any taste. Frolov came back to life and looked around with unanticipated interest.

His apathy had almost passed, and Alexander recalled how in his youth he and his best friend would go out on the hunt for romance, carrying a string bag with a waxy codfish. They called it "catching them by the fish's tail," and it was quite an amusing affair. "Hi, we're from the constellation Pisces, and we urgently need two more stars," his perky friend usually said. The phrase worked flawlessly, though the actual words weren't so important – youth and a carefree look meant much more.

"The fish's tail," murmured Alexander with a smile, straightening his shoulders.

"What's that?" Tolyan asked him.

"Oh, I just remembered something." Frolov again let out a short snicker. "You know, we used to have a lot of fun when I was younger," and he laid out the trick with the fish in brief, though it didn't incite much enthusiasm from his driver.

"No, that won't fly here," Tolyan said with doubt. "They'd be weirded out, think we're on dope or something. Better to do it without the fish. Especially since we have no fish, and where would we get one, anyway?"

"Yeah, I was just joking," Alexander tried to backpeddle. "Just something I was reminded of."

"Well," Tolyan nodded, "it's all fine and good to be reminded of stuff. Maybe it's best if you keep quiet – the main thing for us is the result, after all. Or here, even better: you go sit on that bench. I'll go chat up some babes. Otherwise, we'll be wandering all night."

Frolov shrugged his shoulders and took a seat on a vacant bench as his partner dissolved into the crowd. He didn't have to wait long for the "result": in a quarter of an hour, Tolyan returned with two girls. They were young, comported themselves modestly, and examined Alexander with frank curiosity. One of them, tall and portly, with the body of a cow and a sad half-smile on her lips, introduced herself as Sveta. The second was her polar opposite: small, fragile, and playful. "Lik-ka," she squeaked her name, as if stumbling over the *k* in the middle. Frolov thought Lika resembled a monkey from some kind of Russian jungle. It occurred to him that both were probably dull and obtuse, but it was soon clear he'd guessed wrong.

The girls actually did turn out to be students – very quick of tongue, in fact. They chirped on about nonsense while the whole company went to the top of the avenue where Tolyan's faithful Zhiguli waited. Frolov continued to catch them shooting glances at him, and then the driver whispered in his ear, "Don't be surprised – I fed them a line that you're a movie director from Moscow. That's why they're ogling you so much."

Alexander merely grunted; it was all the same to him. Moscow seemed far away, like another planet. There, in that life, he could be anybody at all; right now it had no meaning. He felt this evening would make it easy to forget himself, which was precisely what he needed now, and he didn't care about the rest.

Upon reaching the car, the girls demanded to know the plan for the night. "What plan?" Tolyan asked, glancing slyly at Sveta. "It's our Moscow friend's birthday today. We want to celebrate, and it's boring with just the two of us. That's the whole plan, nothing else."

"A birthday!" Lika turned to Frolov, her eyes wide. "Oh, we wish you the best from the bottom of our hearts. Only we didn't bring any gift…" She exchanged glances with her friend, and both of them started giggling.

"A gift? What for? You're the best gift!" Tolyan said melodramatically.

"What a crock," thought Alexander, flinching inside. "It's pure soap opera." But the girls took the statement quite favorably. Apparently, their meeting was going well, with the ritual performed in the right way.

"What were you planning for the celebration though?" Lika inquired, getting down to business. "Going to a bar or partying at home?"

"Yeah, what do we need a bar for? They're all smoky, with people spewing profanity," Tolyan grinned from ear to ear. "Better to do it at home: we'll drive over, get some vodka, a few shish kebabs, tomatoes, fruit…"

"I don't drink vodka," Sveta interrupted. "Get me white wine!"

"And I don't eat shish kebabs," her friend chimed in. "We'll take crop milk!" And she burst out laughing upon seeing Tolyan's contorted face. "No, we're just kidding. It's a joke. She'll drink both of you under the table."

With that, the discussion concluded. The group piled into the cramped Zhiguli and valiantly sped headlong over the broken asphalt of the Sivoldaisk streets, plotting an easterly heading to the packed bedroom community where Tolyan resided in a one-room apartment. On the way they stopped at a recently built supermarket to acquire the essentials. The girls took the shopping seriously. Vodka, at cheerful Sveta's insistence, was purchased in large quantities, to which was added some cheap sparkling wine. As for the shish kebabs for sale by the impertinent Georgians under the neighboring tent, they decided not to buy much. "So we don't overeat like pigs," Lika insisted with the voice of a schoolmarm, and Frolov unexpectedly burst out laughing, much to everyone's surprise. Then it was time for sweets, and right at the end, for vegetables and fruit. At this, Lika seized a banana and began to peel it with dexterous movements.

"She's a monkey, for sure," Alexander thought with a certain affection. Then he remembered Elizaveta and the abduction, was ashamed for an instant, but forgot all about it right away.

In the stairwell of the cement-block building, he very much wanted to hold his nose with his fingers, but was prevented by the bags of food he carried in both hands. Fortunately, they reached the second floor quickly. The apartment, despite its strange layout, appeared quite cozy, and the process of cooking together turned all four into friends. Frolov noted his driver was very affable toward his casual girlfriends and didn't seem at all like the misogynist he had appeared to be that afternoon. However, he did not reflect on this fact, considering it to be yet another testimony to the peculiarities of provincial life.

Then, for nearly half the night, they ate, drank, and sang songs. It so happened that Sveta and Lika were soloists with the university choir, which they declared with somewhat naive pride after the first several shots. Frolov asked them to sing – being sure they would decline. But the girls accepted the request with enthusiasm, and there was no need for persuasion.

"Everybody sings around here," Tolyan waved his arm around, already thoroughly inebriated. "The whole female sex – how else should they express themselves?"

"So what are you saying? We have nothing more?" Sveta laughed vulgarly, and looked at her frail girlfriend. Lika cocked her head slightly, and began:

> *The steppe lies all around,*
> *and the road ahead is long…*

Their voices really were surprisingly good. Alexander quickly softened – both from the vodka and from the sad songs. Tolyan blustered at first, posturing as a tough guy, and looked at the singers with condescension. However, he was soon moved and began wiping his eyes and conducting with a fork. And when the girls went out on the balcony to smoke, he drew near to Frolov and whispered with feeling, "These chicks here are fucking great singers! And as for us, what do we want? Just to bang them, huh? Although they're real beauties, without any sin in their souls!"

They ate again, drank even more, and sang one song after another – now as a foursome. Neither Alexander nor Tolyan could hold back, though their drunken vocals left much to be desired. The girls, however, didn't object; they sat with their hair down, like maenads in the pagan wood. Their eyes burned like coals, and their faces, it seemed, became older and more severe, as if a part of their life went into the song or into space a thousand miles hence.

> *I was drowning once in sorrow*
> *a serpent born of mischief*

they intoned, gazing through the dark window, and Tolyan picked up the tune, nearly sobbing from an abundance of emotion:

> *burn away, my smold'ring ember…*

And even Frolov, recalling the long-forgotten words, joined in with a hoarse falsetto, though before that he had never sung anywhere.

He was seeing the Bacchanalian priestesses in double; they blurred, became multi-sided. In them, he concurrently recognized youth, maidenhood, and the future, womanhood, and even something of old age – with the purity of long-lived sorrow. They were not here, but far afield; they were not together, but separated by distances common to these places. The song connected them as one: it seemed no one could remain disengaged – and yet, each one *was* disengaged, on their own, alone. Even dying was not scary – it was the same as departing into the beyond, setting off. To leave, to close one's eyes and remember the very same: the wide expanse, infinity.

Alexander's head was confused and jumbled, he forgot where he was and why. He didn't even notice how the vodka bottles on the table were replaced with a big teapot, and the plates with leftover hunks of meat disappeared. All were drunk and filled with love toward each other. Tolyan sat, his cheek propped on a hand. The girls huddled against one another, half embracing, their heads close together.

"Do you know the one about the coachman?" Alexander asked with a tottering tongue, and the driver, as though regaining consciousness, supported him, "Yeah, do you know that song, Svetka?" The girl nodded, patted her friend on the back, and began in a deep, strong voice:

How sad, how foggy all around,

Lika turned to her and backed her up with anguish:

despondent is my path, and desolate…

And then Tolyan and Frolov, with a serious, even sullen look, started to accompany them, a bit off tune. Thus, all together, they finished up the main song of the forlorn Russian byways – and then it was silent. The evening had wound down to an end.

"All right, then," Tolyan rose awkwardly and looked at Alexander. "Sheets are there in the closet. You, as the guest, get the master's bed, while I and Svetlana, the *Svet* of my Eyes, will get the kitchen sofa; it's small but cozy. Come, my queen," he said to Sveta. And she, without arguing, accompanied him, as proud as a peacock.

Little Lika gazed at Frolov openly and invitingly. "You don't have to," he told her, confused by something despite the vodka. "If you want, we can even sleep with our clothes on."

"Do you like me?" she asked with slight tension in her voice.

"Of course," he replied, completely sincere.

"Then turn out the light." Lika stood up from the table, went to the window, and spread the curtains. "Look, there are some fires on the mountain. So beautiful... And I don't sleep in my clothes. That gets them all rumpled."

They sat in the twilight, and, as he stroked her head, Frolov felt happy for the first time in the last several weeks. The light cast by the streetlamps allowed him to see only the outlines of objects and a strange smile on her face – reminiscent of an ancient painting. Then she pulled him into bed herself – declaring it was time to relax. Frolov was drunk and didn't remember much: only that same smile of hers in the unsteady patches of street light and the shamelessness of a small, lonely creature looking for tenderness. And he recalled also how she, at some brief moment, with her face contorted, rested the tiny soles of her feet against his chest and looked every bit like a Japanese Nihonzaru monkey that had mysteriously ended up on the dusty Russian plains.

CHAPTER 22

Frolov was awakened by sunlight, as sometimes happens in one's serene childhood. For a time, he frowned and smacked his lips, then composed himself and opened his eyes. The pillow beside him was empty, like the room and, it seemed, the whole world as well. Lika had vanished, as had all the rest. In the air hung the spirit of an operating theater or a sterile chamber – a glass case with implements of torture, a sickbed to which he was strapped with wide canvas belts...

Alexander sighed deeply, collected his strength, and sat up. Yesterday's events made themselves known: there was a ringing in his ears and his head was weighed down with a great heaviness. Frolov patiently waited out the first, most unpleasant minutes, then carefully stretched and looked around the room. He had indeed been left alone, but the surroundings were ordinary and peaceful. From the feast there remained not a trace – some unknown gnomes or fairies had probably taken care of that. Alexander's nose twitched as he sniffed at smells that again, like yesterday, reminded him of something French.

He cleared his throat and said aloud, "Yeah, not bad." His gaze fell upon his own clothes, scattered in disarray by the bed. He recalled his tiny lover and her shamelessness, thinking with some regret that they would likely not meet again. And right there he groaned as he was pierced with the thought of Elizaveta being in the hands of bandits and by his own inaction and drunken beastliness.

"Swine!" he cursed himself and dressed hastily, no longer paying heed to the headache or the ringing in his ears. After pulling on his jeans and a shirt, he covered the intricately crumpled bed with a blanket, heaved another grievous sigh, and headed to the kitchen.

His partner was lying on one side with the palm of his hand under his cheek, sonorously snoring with abandon. Frolov took a look at his powerful shoulder adorned with a tattoo reading KITTY, and said hoarsely, "Listen, Tolyan. Come on, wake up." The other appeared hopelessly deaf to his words, so it was necessary to shake him a couple of times before the snore was replaced by dissatisfied grumbling, and then by a languid, albeit astute, query, "What time is it, brother?"

"Half past eight already," answered Alexander. "Come on, get up. Time to make a phone call."

Tolyan rolled over on his back, rubbed his fists in his eyes, and said into space, "My head's killing me. Man, we really tied one on last night."

Frolov uneasily paced the kitchen, then seized a teapot and began to fill it with water from the tap. "You got me up too early," Tolyan complained to his back. "Not a damn thing has happened yet, mark my words. First the girls woke me up – they have class at the crack of dawn – then you. By the way, I gave them each five hundred rubles, for coffee and a taxi."

Alexander silently rummaged in his pocket, then went to the room, found his bag, and handed the driver money. "Here, this is for the girls and for you, for yesterday. Now, would you call the detective, please?" he said dryly and started to ignite an unresponsive burner. Tolyan grumbled a little more before shuffling off to the bathroom. When he returned, he picked up the phone at last.

The conversation turned out to be difficult. Inspector Nikitina's mobile was unexpectedly attended by her husband, who was impolite and brash, and who inquired venomously who was calling, on whose behalf, and regarding what. After that, he finally gave the phone to Valentina, who began the dialogue by berating Tolyan for the call being too early. Then she tempered her wrath with mercy and reported that the owner of the boat had come to his senses, confessed everything, and was ready to cooperate fully. So, all was proceeding as needed, reinforcements from SWAT would arrive soon, and a car was coming to pick her up; though the whole business would probably be directed by someone else – and at this point the obvious injury could be heard in Nikitina's voice.

"Could we possibly tag along?" Tolyan cautiously inquired. "We're already up to speed anyway."

Valentina replied with the habitual, "Are you out of your mind?" but added, "Fine, tell your Moscow guy we'll take the hostages, if they're still alive, to the Volga precinct right away. That's at the main pier, by the River Station. Head that way," and she broke off the conversation without even properly saying goodbye.

"Well, that's a stand-up guy for her, the Othello of pricks," Tolyan muttered, throwing the receiver down on the table in a fit.

"What's up?" Alexander asked impatiently, shifting from one foot to the other.

"A whole fucking movie," the driver shook his head. "SWAT and a bunch of top brass. Looks like they're going to take away Val's piece of the pie. In any event, they're soon setting sail after your beloved."

He quickly and sensibly recounted the whole conversation to Frolov and categorically shook his head at the other's hasty pronouncement of, "Let's go!"

"We're not going anywhere. It's too early yet," he declared, unperturbed. "Even Val's at home, with her hubby the prick. And, look, it's started to rain – what kind of fools are we to get soaked standing on the pier?"

Indeed, the morning sun had disappeared behind the clouds; the sky became gray and drops began beating against the window pane. In the kitchen it grew dark, and Alexander's soul was dreary and despondent. Yesterday's pursuit and the hoodlums with guns, the drunken night and singing, Lika – whom he now only vaguely remembered – and her greedy caresses: everything was jumbled into a phantasmagoric spectacle, as if he had imagined it all during a long, drunken spree. He was thinking of Elizaveta with pity mixed with hurt, and he hated himself, feeling like an impotent scriptwriter who had failed hopelessly with the plot of his story. "If only it could all be over," he thought with irritation and began to pour out the tea into cups.

They breakfasted without appetite and, in an hour, were getting in the long-suffering Zhiguli Nine. Frolov held powerful field glasses in his hands, which Tolyan had uncovered in the far recesses of his wardrobe. The rain by this time had totally let loose; the asphalt was covered with puddles and the windshield misted over right away.

"Quite clearly," the driver grumbled, "it's fixing to be a rotten day. The night was certainly better, don't you think?"

Alexander looked at him gloomily and said not a word.

The previous night, though, did not seem good to all. For the captives sequestered on the island in the Volga marshes, it turned out to be distressing and very long.

After Elizaveta's tears, no one was inclined to speak. Everyone lay down in his own corner, and then came the silence broken only by sounds of the forest and the ever-vigilant river. The hostages' dreams were uneasy, but nobody tossed and turned or groaned, as if they didn't wish to give away their presence in the protective darkness.

Frank White, Jr. dreamt of Li Chung, the Chinese girl who had once told him about the triviality of his star. They had met in astronomy class and then gone to a student party. Soon, she became his girlfriend, showing him favor unlike White American girls. They were drawn together by their attraction to the starry sky, and it was this they spoke of when they were alone. Under Li's influence, he became interested in the works of the ancient Chinese, who, not knowing of the telescope, nevertheless devised cohesive schemes of the universe – particularly in the teachings of the *I Ching*, the classical *Book of Changes*. Frank even recalled the twelve Chinese hexagrams of the solar cycle, admiring their titles, which concealed challenging riddles. He quite understood the hexagram named *The Difficult Beginning*, but struggled with the differences between *Ji-ji* and *Wei-ji*, which were translated in the books as "Already the End" and "Not Yet the End" – though the former preceded the latter. It was at this point his astronomy lessons ended and his interest in Chinese astrology died away – along with his interest in moonfaced Li Chung, in whose fellowship he somehow sensed an excess of spirituality.

In his dream, she ordered him about imperiously and severely, forcing him to do ridiculous things – and he couldn't resist, for she sported a huge, curved dagger tucked in her belt. It sharply contrasted with her mourning attire – snow white in color, as was befitting in China. She looked stunning, and, captivated, he couldn't take his eyes off her. Much of the dream's cast was familiar: somewhere in the background flashed Nilva, and the spiteful invalid at the Trinity Cathedral gate, and even Axel Timurov, who had gone gray and fat, wearing a horned helmet on his head for some reason. But all of them were of little consequence and generally incorporeal – the main character was still Li Chung with her blade.

"Death, that is good," she said, planting a graceful leg in a white boot on his chest. "If they kill you, you'll put in a word for me before Yuhuan, Master of the Sky!" White's tongue didn't engage in an argument, though his mind worked lucidly and he recalled everything that had happened in reality: the misfortune with the treasure, his sudden abduction, and – most importantly – that in Moscow dark-haired Olga awaited him.

Frank felt guilty – before Olga and before the blood-thirsty Chinese girl, but most of all before the army of destitute Russian mathematicians, though they weren't part of his dream. Many times he desired to wake up, but the tenacious vision wouldn't release him. He even tried to cry, but no tears gathered beneath his eyelids.

Meanwhile, the dagger-wielding tormentor wore a sly grin, as if to say, "Wei-ji, Not Yet the End," probably deceiving him all the while – just like every woman he ever knew.

In contrast to Frank, Nikolai Kramskoy spent the greater part of the night with his eyes open. He stared at the ceiling and bounced between thoughts of the oddities of coincidence, capricious luck, and the immense indifference of the higher powers. At the same time, his musings, departing from abstraction, continually turned to things so concrete, they were almost pedestrian. He longingly remembered his Moscow apartment, a couple of favorite restaurants and their best dishes – pork filet, for example, or roasted duck. Danger aggravated all his feelings, especially the lust for life and the taste for it he had managed to cultivate in recent years. The capital was desired and immeasurably distant – yet, thinking of it, Nikolai chided himself that he had grown lazy and long since journeyed to other countries, wallowing instead in the cares of the small businessman.

How great it would be to fly far away, chuck everything, go to Patagonia or to Fiji, or, perhaps, to the Chilean Cordilleras. What was keeping him in his hometown, except a handful of habits? The world was much more than a few polluted streets – didn't he know that? Business wasn't bringing in much and it surely didn't feed his soul, while journeys promised a great deal: new experiences, desires, women... Or another option: why not take Zhanna with him, who had never even been to Europe? How many delights and new emotions there would be – for her, and for him as well. He could tell and show her a lot – and he'd grow enormously in her eyes. There certainly was something to that, so how had it not occurred to him earlier? – And Kramskoy began to enthusiastically imagine the benefits of traveling together, momentarily even forgetting about the danger and his fears.

Then he recalled arrogant Pugin, who probably thought the order he had placed was the center of his – Nikolai's – every hope and thought. This now seemed so ridiculous that Kramskoy nearly chortled out loud – and he certainly would have, even letting loose some profanity, if he had been alone. It became even more obvious to him that he had exceeded his brief long ago, trying to prove something to himself that was unprovable and didn't mean much, anyway. All the same, the universal order might finally take offense: he had been given money, and, as a result, independence and freedom; he must never pretend he didn't understand that. The only ones who had the right to assume a servile posture were those with no other choice. But he had a choice – so he needed to choose rightly and follow what he had chosen for good. Otherwise, the money could be taken away – a more terrible punishment was impossible to imagine. His guilt was still not too great, but the higher powers were always ready to shoot their cannons – sometimes at the smallest stirring in the bushes.

Nikolai counted to one hundred to distract himself. He fell into a slumber without dreaming; he was merely shrouded by a viscous curtain, like fog over a bog, hovering above the moss. The sky, which was not visible, pressed against his breast. Causes and effects, arising in blind whirlwinds, sucked him into the vortex, like the center of a funnel cloud, a path leading to the abyss. The forest and the steppes, the river and the boundless lands – all of them concealed the energy of indifference. To comprehend it meant taking a very dangerous step. Kramskoy woke up in a sweat; his heart pounded and beat in his temples, and alarm rose right away – an insistent fear for his fate. He lay there, without moving, listening to the rustling outside the window, and then forced himself to reflect again – on anything at all, simply to kill time. About Pugachev or Zhanna Chizhik, or the strange couple, Elizaveta and Timofey, who didn't resemble a bride and groom at all.

The odd pair, meanwhile, occupying the largest of the sofas, symbolized a paragon of harmony. Elizaveta, after having her fill of crying, slept deeply, her head resting on Tsarkov's lap. She dreamt of nothing good – her imagination produced only menace and wild chases. The location was unfamiliar, and none of the villains who had captured them figured among the images, but Timofey was not there either, and that disturbed her greatly. Lacking the strength to wake, she shuffled uneasily and clung to his clothes as if trying to convince herself of his presence. He tightened his embrace and Elizaveta fell back to sleep, but in her new dreams no place was found for him again. She was left alone and had to overcome her misfortunes on her own.

Fear, however, no longer tormented her: it had evaporated along with her tears. She remembered her recent weakness without shame, as if understanding that now she had become stronger and wouldn't be her former self anymore. Timofey was not in her dreams, but she knew, waking or sleeping, that the two of them were close, battling side by side. He had simply left for a while – perhaps he was seeking her in other lands or maybe he was caught and held in confinement somewhere else. She wished to do everything together with him: to escape, to sacrifice, to win. That was her recently discovered sense, and she clung to it just as she clung to Tsarkov's clothes. No, he wouldn't leave her, wouldn't forsake her as Eudokia-Masha had. He was no black demon, nor was she a farmer's daughter. Why on earth had that Kramskoy with the scar told his fairytales? She had nothing to do with Pugachev nor with Kramskoy himself – regardless of whether he was an artist or who-knows-what. She was here because they were inseparable, she and Timofey. This fully justified what had happened: even the danger, although real, was kind of ephemeral for a time, but Timofey – here he was, beside her, with no evidence of ephemerality.

As for Tsarkov, he, like Nikolai, nearly didn't close his eyes. His brain worked feverishly without pause; he, better than anybody, understood the full gravity of the threat hanging over them. His own fate concerned him most of all, but the destiny of the others, who were involved in this story through some fault of his, was also a significant matter. Occasionally, he cast his eyes upon Elizaveta and softly, grievously sighed. The rest of the time he was consumed by just one question: "Who?"

Over and over, he scrolled through the combinations and schemes in his head, remembering customers and his meetings with them down to the smallest details. Closing his eyelids, he could picture all his demanding clientele, a whole string of self-satisfied faces resembling, mostly, pig snouts or the muzzles of weasels. Once, he recalled, he was surprised that such people were now counted among the vanguard, having turned into the new rulers of life. In the days of his Moscow youth it was difficult to imagine them openly walking the streets. Then the streets became filled with them, and afterward, they again vanished from the sidewalks as they relocated to spacious offices and flashy cars. Tsarkov learned to have dealings with them, but he was always on the lookout, sensing his strangeness. And now he was remembering the particulars of each transaction in a vain search for a hint at today's incident, which was completely mysterious to him.

Besides clients, his memory touched upon countless other people whose interests could be affected or not taken into consideration. Link by link, he traced chains of intermediaries, trying to guess who among them might decide on a sudden act of betrayal and resort to this subterfuge. This was a grueling process; his thoughts tumbled one over the other, from local land barons to brewers from Samara, from insolent officials who had gone mad from licentiousness to fly-by-night Ukrainian firms, or the Baltic bankers whose hands were still dirty despite their European passports. At times, he even thought of his employees, whom he had selected carefully, pulling them out of the morass of a semi-destitute life, cleaning and feeding them, keeping them warm. Each of them was no more than small change, but Timofey knew how many surprises were occasionally concealed by triviality. He had to be wary of them as well; someone who seemed reliable could fall in with dangerous men and reveal nasty, unforeseen traits.

Thus, there was much to think about. Personal affairs – the hasty wedding and even the whole episode with star-struck Maya that had occupied him entirely over the last weeks – had completely flown from his mind. The new danger was more direct and real, and it was necessary to attend to it in short order. However, these painful reckonings didn't lead to anything: Tsarkov felt he was running in circles. There was too little basic data, and no deduction could help. Only one thing was clear: something very important had gotten out of control. Therefore, Timofey repeated to himself, if he managed to get out of there alive, his first step would be to go have a talk with his *patrón*.

The *patrón*, meanwhile, lay in a crowded morgue attached to the medical wing of the state university, but of course Tsarkov knew nothing about this. Moreover, this event immediately took on a strategic nature: information about it was only shared with a select few, with every effort being made to keep it from getting out. One of these few was Colonel Nesterov, chief of the district police department, who tensely reflected what this unpleasant occurrence meant in terms of re-arranging forces: who would win or lose, and, in general, what would happen now? With whom should he work, and on whom could he depend?

The near future appeared bleak to him. Connections laid down by many years were threatened with serious devaluation; some minor sins could come to light, and, consequently, the head of the district police remained in a nervous, acrimonious state. Even the episode with the abduction, which smacked a little of the fantastic, didn't seem so dire against this background. On Monday evening, he heard out Valentina and her chief with an impenetrable look and right away agreed to strengthen their group with six troopers from the local SWAT division. With that he considered the matter settled – as long as events didn't become clearer and the press didn't interfere. However, the following Tuesday morning, it was reported to him that the hostages' Jeep, belonging to Timofey Tsarkov, had been found on the highway outside the city. Nesterov knew enough to connect the man with the *patrón* who had abruptly been ushered into the hereafter. The situation was taking on new facets – two linked, high-profile cases had occurred at the same time, which, of course, couldn't help but be cause for concern.

The colonel's gut told him the car crash was no more than an accident, but he still arranged to place a guard at the hospital room where the driver of the Mercedes was coming to his senses, and strictly forbade access by anyone from the outside, including close relatives. Then, thinking for a minute, he summoned his deputy, a ruddy, hulking fellow named Alenichkin and asked gloomily, "Listen, Mikhail, you're in tight with this Tsarkov, the guy who launders the cash, right? That Petrovich that got plastered by the truck – isn't he his *capo*?"

"I wouldn't say I'm tight with him, but we've talked a few times," the deputy responded cautiously, well aware of both the accident and the abduction and having already managed to connect the dots. "You got something on him, huh?"

"Not at all," the colonel frowned. "Looks like he got nabbed though – by unidentified persons of the underprivileged classes. Yesterday, as it turns out, just when they were sticking Petrovich in the morgue. You're probably up on it, yeah?"

"Well, yes," Alenichkin muttered. Then he rubbed the bridge of his nose and added, "But I didn't breathe a word to anyone, no way."

The chief became angry. "Fuck that 'yes' noise! If you're up to date, then start thinking with your head. Gimme a fucking clue, got it? Is there something to this, or is it just a ruse? Get down to the bottom of it – I'm putting you in charge. And search the Jeep immediately. Look for substances and stuff – you know what I mean…" and with a wave of his hand the colonel dismissed his subordinate so that, left alone again, he could get back to difficult thoughts about changing loyalties and duties.

Despite Tolyan's fears, the portly major placed the operation to free the captives under the direction of Inspector Nikitina, who was slightly nervous but gave no sign of it. Besides the SWAT members sitting in an unmarked van, her team included Vitalik-Laurenty and the same two sergeants who held vigil like nurses by the bed of the boat owner, waiting for him to regain his senses.

Spending the night in uncomfortable chairs in a stuffy room that stank of cats clearly didn't improve their mood. So when the mechanic came to, he felt the full brunt of their uncompromising state of mind. This yielded a result: he told them everything right away, admitting that at first he just lost his head, and then the armed thugs intimidated him so much, he couldn't refuse to continue participating in their deeds. The gangsters, according to him, had tried all evening to contact someone and then said they'd come by again early in the morning to go back to the abandoned campsite, but for some reason, they hadn't yet materialized. This troubled the sergeants a little, since the arrival of the main team was still a disturbing hour and a half away.

Valentina, when she got there, saw the police cruiser sitting by the house, which her subordinates hadn't even thought to park elsewhere. Whether this was through carelessness or cowardly intention was anyone's guess. She burst into the house like a Fury, such that the owner with the busted-up face shriveled and shrank back at the sight of her, and she gave the operatives a frightful dressing-down for their lack of concealment. This angered them even more, and, based on the looks they shot the mechanic, it was clear he'd have a tough time if they had a chance to get their hands on him again. But no such opportunity presented itself and they were left on a stake-out with two SWAT members to wait for the tardy crooks. The rest, meanwhile, set off under the command of Nikitina to rescue the victims on the island.

The stake-out proved minimally useful. As Valentina surmised, the gangsters had been frightened off by the police car. They already knew the man who ordered the action was dead, so they resolved to disappear as soon as they could grab their remaining accomplice. Approaching the mechanic's house before first light and discovering the police were already there, they observed the situation for about half an hour. Then, not able to make sense of anything, they headed for the North Pier to rent some kind of boat.

By the time they managed this, it was already quite light outside. On the creaking and rusty – albeit high-speed – vessel, the bandits scoured the channels for a long time, crying out all around, "Yurets! Where are you, you big brute!" until their friend finally responded and ran to the shore, waving his arms. The loud shouts startled just the river gulls and the few fishermen who had been out in the shoals since early morning. But neither the gulls nor the fishermen paid them any mind, just like everything else that happens moment to moment on a big river. Only the captives, not sleeping by this hour, were immediately on guard when they heard the noise and bustled about, throwing each other meaningless signs.

"They're yelling something," Timofey whispered. "They get lost or what? Morons!"

Nobody backed him up; only Frank chuckled softly and crept on tiptoes up to the battered glass.

"Here I am," they heard the guard call out, then the chirping of the boat motor and a few obscure commands. The engine cut off and the thugs spoke excitedly about something, but the words couldn't be made out.

"They've arrived," declared Tsarkov. "Bright and early in the morning. Maybe it's better that way." He nervously paced back and forth and, lowering his voice, said, "When they come in, don't move a muscle. They're not going to stand on ceremony. And don't strike up any chit-chat. I'll do the talking."

The talking, however, never took place. A few minutes later, three thugs ran up to the house and began to clamber around up top. "Leave that here," somebody commanded hoarsely. "Let's take the jackets and get to the boat. Yurets, don't stand around like a bump on a log. Get a rag and wipe down the doorknobs."

"Doorknobs, doorknobs..." came the disgruntled mumbling. "What if I touched something inside? The bottles have fingerprints on 'em too."

"If you touched anything, that's your loss, fool!" the hoarse voice growled mercilessly. "Well, let's hope they don't find you anyway. Too late to do the inside with those assholes in there. Come on, wrap it up. Get a move on!"

"Hey!" hollered Tsarkov. "What about us? Open up, you bastards!"

"Shut up, fucker," the hoarse one replied angrily. "Don't you dare call me a bastard! Yurets, step lively, let's head out!"

Something rattled, a door creaked, and hurried steps moved away from the house. Then the outboard motor fired again and soon faded into the distance. Investigator Nikitina's team was still converging on the mechanic's house as the gangsters were making a getaway – from the island, from the hostages, and from the whole venture, which had clearly been doomed from the beginning.

"They left," said Tsarkov, perplexed. "All of them, as if we weren't even here. Have you guys ever seen such a thing – in a movie or anywhere else?"

Nikolai laughed, walked to the sink, and started to splash water on his face. Frank White looked on uncomprehendingly, as if he still understood nothing. Only Elizaveta was serious, fresh and full of energy.

Her head was spinning with, "We're saved! I knew it, knew it!"

She smiled and looked tenderly at Tsarkov. "You're my hero!" she wanted to yell, but she checked herself and only said briskly, "Come on, we have to get the door open. Why are we wasting time? What if they come back?"

"They're not coming back," Timofey waved her off. "Someone spooked them, isn't that obvious? What a stupid country – nobody does anything right. It's all half-assed, all the time – nothing but a bunch of retards!"

For the next two hours, the prisoners tried to break down the door or bend the bars in the window. They achieved little, due to the complete lack of hand tools.

"What do we do then? Do we starve to death here?" Tsarkov finally exploded, throwing to the ground the useless faucet arm that he had so painstakingly unscrewed in the bathroom. "First they nab us, lock us in a basement, and then just leave us like dogs!"

"Simmer down," Nikolai glumly told him. "It's because of you that we're stuck here, so you've got no place to complain. Do you think we can break open the piping?"

"Why? So you can flood everything, genius?" Timofey started to retort, but here White, Jr. rushed to the window, froze, and lifted a finger. "An engine," he whispered when all were silent and looking in his direction. "A motorized boat. There's someone coming again, either to us or close by."

"You've got great hearing, Frankie," Elizaveta said. "For some reason I don't hear any..."

"He's right!" Tsarkov cut her off. "A launch. If I'm not mistaken, the same one that brought us here. Are they returning after all? Well, one way or the other, all will be decided now."

All was actually resolved rather quickly. Upon reaching the island, Valentina's team divided into two parts. The four SWAT troopers rushed to reconnoiter the territory, and the investigators, with unholstered weapons, walked the trail through the woods that the mechanic showed them as he bent over backward to oblige. Soon, forgetting caution, all descended on the house from which excited shouts emanated.

Especially zealous was Timofey Tsarkov. "Well now, you cops take the cake," he drawled with caustic admonition, coming up next to the barred window. "It's been two hours already since the thugs split – somebody spooked them. It's a little late to be poking your nose around. How're you going to catch them now, virtuosos?"

"Quiet, you!" Elizaveta tugged at his arm. "That's enough. Let them open the door." But he didn't relent, pacing the room, going to the window again, and cursing through his clenched teeth.

"They've screwed me, don't you understand?" he lashed out rather sharply when she tried to approach him again. "How am I going to find their boss now?"

Liza only understood that she didn't understand anything. Timofey stopped looking like a hero, though she conceded heroes came in various shapes. He had become quite another person, not resembling his former self or even the man he was yesterday, to whom she was beginning to grow accustomed. She became uncomfortable but mastered her emotions, smiled, and said as easily as she could, "Come off it, forget about this boss. Let's just leave here. Tomorrow, even – let's just leave and be done with all of it!"

"Don't be ridiculous," Timofey brushed her off. "Where would I go? My business is here!" Then he glanced at Nikolai, who was carefully studying the two of them, went up to Elizaveta and awkwardly patted her on the shoulder. "Hold on, let's get off of this island – afterward, we can talk at home."

They messed around with the door a while – to more sarcastic commentary by Tsarkov, who, tired of walking back and forth, sat down right on the floor and leaned against the doorframe. No one paid him any further attention, including Liza, who was discussing something quietly with Frank White. Finally, the lock yielded and the prisoners were free, looking slightly bedraggled and shivering in the drizzling rain.

"Inspector Nikitina," Valentina introduced herself officially as she stood by the door with a frown. "Are there injuries? Is any medical attention needed?"

"Where's your supervisor at this crime scene, Inspector Nikitina?" Timofey inquired brazenly. "My name's Tsarkov, Timofey Timofeyevich. What district are you with anyway?"

"I'm in charge. Save your questions for later," Valentina snapped, shooting him an intense look. "Are you all okay, I asked? If so, let's go."

Somewhere not far off was a squeal and the barking of a dog, then a loud curse resounded as the senior SWAT member reprimanded one of the troopers. The entire company stretched out in a chain along the familiar path back to the dock. Elizaveta's feet were instantly soaked as she stepped into grass wet from the rain, and she wrapped her arms around her shoulders against the chill.

Once on the launch, as the fidgety owner pulled out an awning to protect against bad weather, Vitalik-Laurenty gave the recent hostages their mobile phones back. "There are no prints on them. I checked," he said to Valentina in response to her questioning look. "Let them call their relatives. They must be really worried."

None of the four, however, was in a hurry to get in touch with anyone. Only Tsarkov skimmed through his missed calls and raised his brows in concern.

"Listen, Detective," he turned to Nikitina, "where are we headed now? They pulled me out my SUV, so it'd be good to go pick it up. Could you maybe send one of your men with me to check it out? And we need to drop off my fiancée at home – it's basically on the way."

"I already told you: questions later," Valentina responded indifferently. "Right now we're going to headquarters, where we'll work with you a bit. Then we'll decide about the SUV, the fiancée, and the rest."

"Who decides? *You?*" Timofey was offended. "I've never even seen you before." And he added, angrily turning away, "Bi-itch."

The SWAT team commander, a short, powerful Tatar with bowed legs, looked point-blank at Timofey and suddenly asked, "Who do you think you are, runt? Do I need to teach you some manners?"

"Uh-oh," Tsarkov turned toward him. "And who do we have here? You must be surprised, huh, to be all squinty-eyed like that?"

"Well then, let the lesson begin," grumbled the Tatar as he took a step toward Timofey.

"Don't touch him!" Elizaveta shouted, grabbing Tsarkov by the elbow and standing next to him. "Or beat us both up, if you want."

"Semyonov," said Valentina in a tired, displeased voice, "cool it. You, at least, calm down. Some fighting elite you are, both of you." Timothy pulled at his arm, trying to free himself as the trooper looked at him scornfully, stepped away, and spat overboard.

"It's like I was telling you," whispered Kramskoy to Frank, "everything comes to naught around here." He was quiet for a minute, then added, "Though maybe I told it to someone else, or never even said it out loud."

No one uttered another word all the way back to the River Station pier. The captives and their liberators wouldn't even look at each other, especially Tsarkov, frowning and withdrawing into himself.

CHAPTER 23

Sorting out his relationship with Anna and the terrible car accident left a weighty impression upon Astakhov. All day, he languished about the apartment, taking short forays to his desk, but he was simply unable to work. Evening likewise failed to bring relief. As a result, after meandering for an hour or two along the central streets, Andrei Fyodorovich convinced himself that today he needed to get properly drunk. And this was exactly what he achieved in an open-air cafe on Samarskaya Street, in proud but burdensome loneliness, talking to himself in a low voice.

On Tuesday, as always after drinking to excess, he woke early and couldn't fall back to sleep. His thoughts rushed about incoherently, his mouth was dry, and his eyelids stung as if filled with sand. Turning and sighing, Andrei Fyodorovich tossed about in bed all morning until the sun disappeared behind the clouds and rain began to pelt the window. "That's all I need," he groaned discontentedly, then suddenly calmed down and, after lying for a moment longer, jumped up and seized a pen. But the rush was brief: in a quarter of an hour, Andrei put aside his pen and paper, rose, kicked the totally innocent chair, and went to the bathroom.

He had no strength today for yoga *asanas*, or even simple respiratory exercises. After a shower, feeling refreshed and cheered up a bit, he took a seat at the table again and slowly read through what he'd written. As usual, it seemed to him that it was penned by someone else.

The metamorphosis of rain is long morning sex. Damp, indistinguishable from a dream. During an anti-cyclone one does not wish to wake up at all, he read, his head propped on his hand.

The clacking of heels against cobblestones are the steps of women that nobody loves. That is not news. But there is no remedy for it.

Astakhov frowned and shifted his gaze to the window. It was clear he couldn't use this in his new book. And the part about women, that was not accidental, no.

"What a foolish broad!" he swore, meaning Anna, and buried himself again in his hasty lines.

I am an ingenious doctor, knowing it is better to remain silent. The gray veil of water will pervert all utterances anyway. I went through this hundreds of times – and came up, gulping for air. As my eye meets more of the same – a wearisome morning rain.

From me they flee on worn-out heels – they who are too fainthearted. It's funny and makes me laugh; then I slumber again – in the hope of a wet dream. How boring is reality in the mud-gray light! How foolish are sudden urges – as are words, all words!

Here the text broke off. "Not much," Andrei Fyodorovich noted aloud, then rubbed his temple, took a half-scribbled page and stuffed it into a thick file that advertised *Other*. "That's the truth: something other," he muttered with displeasure and ordered himself, "Kitchen, to kitchen," as if forcefully changing the rhythm of a poorly begun day.

After a breakfast that was unusually meager, Astakhov, despite the rain, decided to take a walk. Something drove him from the house; he didn't even want to look at his work desk. He sauntered along Moskovskaya Street, his usual route, after opening his umbrella with the ivory handle that had been left to him by his grandfather.

The street was wet, slippery, and unkempt. Nothing pleased the eye – it seemed despondency reigned all around, the abandonment of a city nobody needed. The rain drizzled, without picking up, but also without abating; under his feet it squeaked, and cars sent muddy splashes flying.

"As soon as the weather gets rainy, you see the filth accumulated here for centuries," thought Andrei Fyodorovich, turning aside from a cyclist in a wet black cape who resembled an Angel of Death dispatched from on high. "As did the habit to not argue with destiny – one recalls it immediately when a sad occasion arises."

There was no lack of sad occasions in the city, yet it stood firm, not wishing to die – though new buildings here and there slipped into ravines as if the earth didn't accept them. Century-old houses collapsed from decay and sank into the polluted soil, but their fate had long ago ceased to bother anyone. It contained more of the same: drunken poverty, childhoods spent in dirty corners, the stench of dumpsters in the open air. And everywhere were masks instead of faces, if you took a proper look. That wasn't surprising: their everyday life was nothing but a struggle against the humiliation common to all. And there were no means to combat the thought that death would come soon and forever.

On the lower section of the street, Astakhov slackened his stride – he liked this place most of all. Old merchant buildings had been constructed here in a close row, cars were few, the hustle and bustle was left behind in the faceless downtown. Looking around, he waited for something in his soul to respond but, perhaps because of the rain, only irritation and disappointment built up inside him. Andrei again felt, with surprising acuity, that the province was capable of exhausting anyone after several weeks, not to mention the years he intended to spend there.

In this city, there's no place for great passions, he thought bitterly, again recalling his breakup with Anna. The amplitude of emotions is insignificant – they ripple in a small wave, visible only when sparkling in the sun. You want to keep looking into them, like polished bronze, but there's only your own reflection, and it grows dull faster than you can imagine. Meanwhile, everything all around continues as before – your efforts are like tears in the rain. Your aspirations, your talents – there is none to admire them.

"I must recognize," he murmured gloomily, "what I took as an experimental error was, perhaps, the true essence of the phenomenon. Which means the phenomenon actually isn't there – it's just a trifle not worth examining. The theory is to blame, for it is blind. Theorists have it much easier, and women love them more. They have clean hands and an inspired countenance. I should try to change my methods – maybe for good."

He understood suddenly, as he had a few times before, that he must leave there right away. He must return to the capital, to struggle and to suffer like the rest. Here was a peat bog, albeit in the dry steppes – a gray, foggy expanse where words dissolved into the void, the end of all hopes, a cemetery for courageous plans... Andrei thought with horror that he would never write anything there, pressed down by the leaden sky, sucking air in gulps, but then he got hold of himself. He knew panic attacks didn't last long, and this one, too, would pass, nearly without a trace. As for the sudden determination, it was fleeting. It wasn't so easy to escape from this swamp, this stuffy provincial life, pejorative and plain, predictable and cozy, that had buried many before him. And he also had to remember: money, money!

Astakhov reached River Station and stood for a little while at the main city pier, telling himself, here is the widest of all open spaces, admire it, that's what you came here for. The vision blurs, and the soul is scattered, thinning to the point of helplessness. That's okay: souls are finite, almost all of them. And besides, is depth in demand nowadays? Here the majority has no soul at all – only in some does a maelstrom roil or a black morass appears.

The Volga flowed, powerful and steady. The mackerel sky reflected and painted it in dim lead, but any weight was of no consequence to it – whether of hanging clouds, or barges loaded with coal and timber, or small, nimble motorboats. On this weekday morning, there were few passenger vessels: just one ship was preparing to embark on a northerly heading – toward Nizhny, or Kazan, or even Moscow. It gave a booming blast on the horn and picked up steam – and right there the brass band on the shore burst into the march "The Farewell of Slavyanka," according to the old tradition that was never broken.

"A hungover steamer accompanied by hungover brass, sailing on a drunken river," Andrei chuckled. "How could I make a note of that? What a shame I have nothing to write on. The wreath of multicolored flags on it is the most naïve of forgeries. The promise of a fiesta which, everybody knew, would never happen. But oh, how you wish to believe in it and, along with that – how you want to be deceived by someone's naivety!"

Andrei Fyodorovich descended to the embankment and walked to and fro along the water. He ended up at the distant end of the mooring, contemplating the fishermen who were watching floats barely distinguishable from the small rubbish, then he saw two men with large binoculars and marveled to himself at how out of place their tense posture was. That very instant, one of them exclaimed excitedly, "There they go!" and added, looking over his shoulder, "See, the brass came, too," such that Astakhov, intrigued, decided to observe a little.

Nearby, in front of the local police building shared by land-based cops and the river rats, stood a small group of people in uniform. One of them, bearing the epaulets of a major, appeared to be in charge, just as wide-eyed Tolyan indicated. This was Major Alenichkin from the Kirov Police Department, who had arrived in person to take command, as his chief had insisted. Beside him stood two lower-ranking officers glancing indifferently at the river and at the overcast heavens spattering down rain.

Soon the launch pulled up – with Valentina, the SWAT team, and the former hostages. The musicians who had seen the steamboat off had already dispersed, and the rescuees, as well as the police, were met by only a few casual gawkers. Among them was Astakhov, who noted with surprise that the two with the field glasses, who, supposedly, were more interested in the event than he, moved back and even hid behind a garbage bin – obviously wishing to remain unnoticed. He was about to consider that but forgot about it immediately: the boat was moored to the shore and, among the rest on the wobbly gangplank, descended none other than his Moscow friend Nikolai.

"Hey!" Astakhov cried and rushed toward him, causing a small alarm in the ranks – for the participants as well as the spectators. However, all calmed down once they were convinced the unexpected acquaintance harbored no threat. The friends were permitted to clap each other on the back and enjoy an emotional exchange: "Why didn't you call? I kept calling and calling… Well, my phone was… I had no idea…" after which they firmly led Andrei away, explaining that now wasn't really the appropriate time.

"Like I was telling you, Sivoldaisk is a very small city," murmured Nikolai and promised to get in touch that very afternoon, after which the whole group entered the police building and Astakhov slowly wandered back home – confused, but for some reason upbeat. The rain had ceased, though underfoot it was still wet and dirty. Passing by the trash containers, he twisted his head but those two had disappeared, as if vanishing into thin air.

"To hell with them," decided Andrei Fyodorovich. "I have to go home, maybe I'll write something," and he resolutely turned toward the Pallada Hotel, where free taxis were always waiting. On the way he muttered in a low voice, "A hungover steamer sailing upstream on a drunken river…"

In the meantime, at the Volga police precinct, small dramas were developing. Major Mikhail Alenichkin immediately began to cross the t's and dot the i's. First of all, he took Inspector Nikitina aside and told her sternly, "So, Valentina, I'm taking over the case. You go to the office and make me up a report and I'll work with them, without you." She glared at him, frowning, and was about to object, but the major grunted and groaned, and she dropped it at once. Then he continued by asking venomously, "How are you with the suspects, by the way?"

"There's one," Nikitina nodded at the mechanic surrounded by tall SWAT troopers, who, noticing this, squinted ingratiatingly in reply. "The others are being searched," she added with exaggerated vigor, but the major caught her uncertainty with his trained ear, scowled, and shook his head.

"You didn't screw something up, did you?" he pressed callously. "You were the one in charge, right?"

At that moment, Valentina's phone rang. Her eyes scanned the number on the display; she rejected the incoming call and was about to say something, gesturing with her free hand, but the major had already lost interest and was looking away, over her shoulder. The phone rang again. He turned his head in annoyance, snapped at her, "Come on, Nikitina, go," and spun around to leave.

"Mikhail Ivanovich," she pleaded to his back, but Alenichkin didn't even turn. Meanwhile, the phone kept ringing and ringing. Valentina shot the major a scathing look and made her way to the exit, shrilly screeching into the receiver, "I'm busy! Busy! Where? Where am I? At work! Where else would I be?"

Having established his leading role and issued a few brief orders, the major came into the room set aside for the victims and threw them all a sharp glance before approaching Tsarkov, who had jumped up to meet him, and shook his hand. "Listen," Timofey began animatedly, "it's great you're here. My Jeep was left right on the highway. It's got my keys and all our stuff in it!"

"I know, I know," Alenichkin interrupted with a broad smile. "The police are ever vigilant. Our boys are already dealing with your Jeep – we'll go there with you soon. We're going to get statements from each of you now. I'll take yours myself, and my man will handle your colleagues. Or are these friends rather than colleagues?" He again looked searchingly about the room and let his gaze fall on

Bestuzheva, which caused her to blush and stare at the floor.

"Yeah, they're friends. Hang on," Tsarkov said hastily. "I just need to make one call really quick. For some reason, Semyonych isn't picking up," he complained to Alenichkin, who earnestly rolled his eyes.

"Which Semyonych? You don't mean the Old Man, do you?" the major asked with forced surprise. In reply to Timofey's nod he drew his response out dramatically, "Well, you're really not up to date! It's what everybody's talking about: the Old Man got crushed in his cool Mercedes – just yesterday afternoon. The car's a total wreck, and Petrovich was at the Pearly Gates in a jiffy. *The wolf did not spare the flock, and now the wolf is not spared.*"

In the room silence hung and all stiffened as if in freeze-frame. "Are you jo-joking?" asked Tsarkov at last.

"No way," the major responded contently, enjoying the effect. "Who jokes about such things? I'm a man of authority, after all! Hold on, I'll see if that office is available over there," and he went into the hallway, closing the door tightly behind him.

All were silent, trying not to look at Timofey, who sat in an inconvenient pose, his eyes fixed on the wall. Then Frank White cleared his throat and asked quietly, "What was it, Timothy, a relative?"

"No," the other replied reluctantly. "Worse than a relative. Much worse..." But he wouldn't elaborate and just hunched over and wrinkled up his face.

Elizaveta walked over to him and gently stroked his hair. "Yeah, Lizka," Tsarkov smiled crookedly, "strange business. We'll have to work it out now. I just don't know how."

He recoiled from her hand, rose from his chair, and began to walk back and forth, nervously rubbing his fingers. Bestuzheva sat down in his spot; it was clear everything had changed suddenly, and not for the better. "Are we going to retrieve the car together?" she directed her question into space, trying to make her voice sound normal.

"The car?" Timofey stopped in place, as though he had just

regained consciousness. "Well, there's no point. You'd better go home. I'll have a one-on-one with the major, maybe get something useful from him. There's so much going on now..." Tsarkov contorted his lips and averted his eyes.

"You go ahead, rest up. Get some sleep," he continued. "You sleep and later, in the evening, I'll come. Let me give you the keys. It's a good thing I had a second set made for you." He began rummaging in his pockets, saying in a low voice, "I don't get it. Did I lose them?"

"Here they are," he sighed with relief, and this sigh didn't please Elizaveta either.

"What's up, fiancé? You want to run away?" she asked, as if joking. "We don't have a common goal anymore?"

Timofey stared at her in confusion and she smiled back as tenderly as she could, but all jesting flopped – the tension in the air grew. The emptiness between them, it seemed, had become impenetrable to signals; she understood she no longer possessed a sense of him: he had become incomprehensible and alien. The smile slipped from her face; she bit her lip and looked down, but then, just at the right moment, ruddy Alenichkin ran into the room and tapped Tsarkov on the shoulder, "Let's go!"

"See ya, Lizka," he said with exaggerated nonchalance. Then he nodded to Nikolai and Frank, "Stick around. We're bound to bump into each other," and left, following the major.

"*He wooed his bride, so tender, sweet. But now the groom has got cold feet,*" intoned Kramskoy, then lifted his hands as if to shield himself from Liza's withering glare, "I'm kidding, just kidding. That's just a saying we have, Lizaveta. That's all."

She merely nodded and went to the window, which was reinforced with iron rods. "More bars," she said morosely. "When will all this be over?"

They didn't have to wait long. A sharp young captain quickly wrote down everyone's statements, asked a few questions, and, flashing a gold tooth, told them, "All right, you're free to go. If anything comes up, we'll find you. Cheer up, beautiful," he winked at Liza, opening the entrance door for them. She was about to make an arrogant face but then got lost deep in thought again about something that clearly had no connection to the Volga regional police.

Outside, it was drizzling once more. The recent prisoners, having found freedom at last, stamped their feet awkwardly and began to say goodbye.

"No, stop," Nikolai suddenly called out. "That's not right. What are we, strangers to each other?"

His eyes shone feverishly; he was utterly agitated. Something exulted inside him, and he felt like talking loudly, sharing his pleasure, laughing. "A test," whirled in his head. "I just passed the test!"

He studied his companions who, obviously, couldn't share his feelings fully, and in reply to Elizaveta's amazed look, he added, "No! That's no way to be! We've just been through so much together, and now we split like nothing happened? I suggest we all go out to a restaurant this evening – we have to celebrate, to drink to our success."

Frank supported the idea and Liza, hesitating slightly, also promised to be there if nothing unforeseen arose. With that, they parted after exchanging phone numbers. The men ambled to the hotel, which stood nearby, while Elizaveta walked to a taxi stop where several shabby cars idled in the rain.

All this time, Frolov and Tolyan sat in their Zhiguli Nine, looking fixedly at the police building. The binoculars weren't necessary; events were clearly visible. When Timofey left with the major, the driver was about to start the engine, but then he stayed put with Alexander's silent approval.

"See, they've separated," he declared thoughtfully. "He's up to something, and she's got her own business. I imagine those two are off to fetch the Cherokee, and your girl's not with them. There has to be a reason."

"There is, there is," grumbled Frolov. "When she wants

something, she gets it, one way or another. That means she doesn't want it – meaning it's no simple matter."

He was tormented by guilt and nagging impatience. Elizaveta was here, nearby, and he loved her more than before, but everything connected with her remained inexplicable. The owner of the black SUV ceased to worry him; the affair was much more complicated and intricate. He rehearsed versions in his head, each one more outlandish than the last, but he understood all were worthless and the solution was still far away. His companion was silent and didn't engage in conversation. The rain tapped on the roof in tune to his uneasy thoughts and it seemed the waiting would never end, nor would the bad weather that made the world a joyless gray.

"There they are!" Tolyan exclaimed and Frolov snapped to, forgetting at once what he had been reflecting upon. The time had come for decisive actions – this he felt with his whole body. "So, they have no car," the driver declared. "They'll catch a ride or else go to the hotel together. No, not in that sense," he calmed fretting Alexander. "To sit for a bit, get something hot to eat... Look, she went off alone to grab a taxi. Now we'll tail her very carefully!"

Without any problem, they escorted the sluggish taxi to the entrance of the courtyard to the building they already knew, where Elizaveta got out and headed for the edifice. "Look, she came back to his place," Tolyan said with significance. "What does that add up to? That means... Hey, where are you going?" but Frolov wasn't listening anymore. Something in him shifted, some fuse burst in a short flash, and he, unexpectedly even to himself, understood he could withstand no more. Flinging open the door, he ran after his lover, shouting desperately, "Liza, Liza!" without even figuring out what he would say to her and how he would explain his presence.

Elizaveta didn't at once gather she was the one being yelled at. Frolov managed to run almost right up to her before she turned and stared at him with eyes wide.

"Hi," exhaled Alexander, out of breath and looking up at her like an obedient dog. "Listen, Liza..."

"You!" she interrupted, and he shut up in confusion. "Where did you come from? Wait, hang on a moment," she wagged her finger sternly when she saw Frolov intended to say something. "Such coincidences are impossible. Of course, I've been feeling like an utter fool these last days, but I'm not *that* dense. Does this mean you've been following me this whole time?"

"Well I... you know... to understand," Alexander murmured, feeling immense shame for some reason. "I didn't know what was happening: not a phone call, not even a how-do-you-do. You disappeared, and that was it. End of story."

"Let me get this straight," Elizaveta quickly summed up something in her head without listening to him. "That means, in Moscow, this was all your doing too? And what about the other one, my fiancé? Are you in on this together? Answer me!"

"In on *what* with *whom*?" Frolov was startled. "And what, you have a fiancé? Who? That guy in the Jeep?"

"Yeah, the one in the Jeep, or maybe he doesn't have a Jeep anymore," she averted her eyes. "And maybe he's not my fiancé anymore, either. Whatever. The two of you can't be operating together; you're totally different. Two unrelated, inept snoops. Some people have higher powers following them, but I only get types like you."

Probably because of fatigue, melancholy and the self-pity heaped upon her. Elizaveta felt how fed up she was with other people's desires and their steadfast attempts at getting into her life. "So, what is it you need?" she asked Alexander coldly.

"I just wanted to help," he retorted. "I thought you were in danger. I have a friend here; we saw everything – how you were attacked by those three men. We were the ones who called the police, by the way."

He became silent, but she was also quiet and simply looked at him with a blank expression. Then she blinked and asked firmly, "So you came from Moscow after me? Made a special trip, just to call the cops?"

"Of course not; that was all incidental – and funny, actually," Alexander screwed up his face and tried to grin. "I came from Moscow, in a third-class car, to get to the bottom of everything. I know it looks like some melodrama, but..." he hesitated, then waved his hand, "Aah, you know..." and looked right at her. No strength remained in him to play it cautious and be coy. Better just to slash away with the scalpel to get rid of any superfluous parts, toss them away like ballast and... what? To become less, grow thin, fly away without ballast?

"Naturally, I couldn't understand a thing," he said even a bit combatively, "but here's what I know for sure: I want to be with you – forever. Decide now; I can't wait anymore. I'm all out of sorts, I do the stupidest stuff – the drama is too absurd already."

Elizaveta was reminded of Tsarkov and became even angrier. "Here we go again," she mused. "I've become quite popular. And everyone thinks something's funny – why don't I get the joke?" She shook her head and asked coldly, "So, what will you do with me if I agree? You won't tame me; I'm much stronger than you."

"I'll adapt," Frolov grinned again. "Being without you is worst of all anyway." He calmed down and even relaxed a little – now with a much more confident countenance.

"How romantic," thought Elizaveta. "Everyone's trying to get me not into bed, but to the altar. And not just anywhere, but out here in the boondocks. Maybe there was a reason why this town seemed like another planet to me. A patriarchal backwater, the very heart of severe mores."

"Well, for me, being without you is not worse, worst, or whatever," she shrugged. "For me it's just *nothing*!" Then she clasped her arms about herself and looked around in alarm. The irrational was offered in excess – so that her realistic, practical mind nearly refused to work. It was hard to force herself to concentrate on the conversation and take what she heard seriously. Frolov didn't fit into the events that had happened over the last days; it was still difficult to believe he was actually here in front of her.

"Listen, are you sure I'm not dreaming you?" she asked. "Really, for the last several days I've felt like I'm in a dream."

"Sleeping Beauty," murmured Alexander. "You want me to kiss you, so you can wake up?"

He reached out toward her, but she recoiled as if frightened. Such an absolute rejection was reflected in her face that he at once grew cold inside. They stood facing one another, looking deep into each other's eyes. No further explanations were necessary.

"The quickest way to end a battle is to lose it," Alexander attempted to joke. "Or here's another, *Someday they'll declare war, and no one will come."*

"What? What's that?" asked Liza with surprising anxiety. "I don't understand what you're rambling about."

"They're quotes," Frolov sighed, wondering painfully whether he had any moves left. "Other people's thoughts. You wouldn't be interested."

"Damn! Don't you have words of your own?" Elizaveta was angry again. "War, battles – a bunch of bullshit, really."

"What's the difference?" he responded absently. "It's just more interesting that way. Whether they're my words or someone else's, you're not hearing me anyway."

They stood in silence for a few seconds, clearly not knowing what to do next. "Well," Alexander finally asked, "is that all? Forever?"

"Well, yeah," responded Liza as though it were self-evident. "Don't you see it yourself? Listen, just go. I'm so tired, and I have nothing – NOTHING – to say to you."

Frolov turned and stumbled to the car while she, ascending in the elevator, felt she truly had no energy left. "Well, here you go: at least someone loved me, and now even he will begin not to," flashed in her mind. "Not to love me as much as he's able – and soon he *will* be able. It's easy; it would be for anyone."

All her inner worlds became as cold as space. This was a rare feeling – as if the cosmos itself had reached out a hand to her. The small universe inside couldn't compete with it, mighty and immense,

utterly beyond, drawing out all her strength and life. She was sorry
to the point of tears for her freedom, which she had in abundance
until recently for her desires, plans, and naive thoughts.

"Better for me to just dream of a prince, and may that prince
never arrive. I don't want to adjust to everything around," thought
Elizaveta as she leaned against the elevator door. "I don't need this
– riddles, higher powers. I don't even have anyone to lose my head
over – could the issue be with me? Do I have an overly simple soul?"

"And why am I always waiting for something?" she muttered
heatedly as she got out of the elevator. "Even Frolov has help – other
people's thoughts written down in notebooks. But as for me – nobody
would give me a hint!"

She fiddled with the three locks for a long time, then finally
slammed the door and went to wander the rooms – the same as she
had done yesterday morning when Timofey was beside her and her
heart anticipated surprises. She suddenly wanted to see him right that
instant. She hesitated, then picked up the cell phone and resolutely
dialed the number, but the other end was silent, responding only
with long beeps. "Where, oh where are you, my fiancé?" Bestuzheva
sang sadly, coming into the living room and curling up in a large,
soft easy chair.

"No problem," she whispered to herself. "It'll still work out for
us. I am Venus; my stone is diamond."

Her eyes misted over. She blinked and covered her eyelids.
"Timofey, Timofey – and there is no meaning in anything else," she
declared sadly. "If only I could latch on to this. I'll fall for him again,
he's not so bad."

She wanted to doze off, but slumber evaded her. Her head hurt,
and colored spots floated before her eyes.

"Timofey, Timofey," Liza murmured again, but her thoughts
soared everywhere at once, jumping from one thing to another
and finding nothing to catch hold of. Words flew from her lips,
but they weren't born within. There, inside, it was as if someone
were stubbornly whispering, "Nothing will come of it. You cast

away others pitilessly – and so they will do to you. An eye for an eye, ferocity for ferocity," and she shuddered and opened her eyes. "Timofey!" she said loudly, and the same inner voice whispered in reply, "Everyone for themself."

And she knew this was the truth and became quiet, as if she had wearied of fighting. Her glance slid around the room, not lingering on anything except the mobile phone that lay right there on the coffee table.

CHAPTER 24

At six o'clock in the evening, after eating his fill and making himself presentable, Nikolai went out to the embankment to a Gagarin monument where Mark Lvovich Pechorsky was to wait for him. After what he had endured in the past twenty-four hours, his surroundings seemed artificial, yet familiar and dear at the same time. The jagged asphalt of the sidewalk, the tall lindens in the adjacent square, unembellished flower beds, and the dusty grass – everything welcomed him as if he had returned from a long journey. Only the Volga herself flowed by without noticing, indifferent to him and everyone else.

Pechorsky approached the statue almost in step with Nikolai. He was clothed in his usual mouse-brown jacket with elbow patches, like an old-fashioned clerk. Under his arm, he carried a shabby briefcase and wore an extremely focused expression.

Evening was already drawing near. Music resounded from the open cafes, and there was an increase in the number of those out for a stroll. Everything was ordinary and peaceful, only Mark Lvovich looked around anxiously, in sharp contrast with the rest of the public. Coming up to Nikolai, he twisted his head again, extended his small, dry palm for a handshake, and whispered, "Let's step aside. Over to the trash heap. I don't think anybody's there."

"It reeks," Kramskoy said, astonished, but, seeing the old man was nervous, he only shrugged his shoulders, and they walked to the nearby garbage pile, half-hidden by sprawling bushes. There Pechorsky noisily exhaled, muttered, "What then, shall we get to it?" – and with a very dexterous movement unlocked the ancient case. "Here, look," he removed a transparent folder from its plastic binding. "Here it is, the original on top, and I made some copies too, just in case. And I brought you a newspaper so you can hide it. Put it in the paper and carry it like this, so it won't fall."

"All right, all right," Nikolai murmured absently, then briefly scanned the contents, nodded, and held out five hundred-dollar bills, "Here, take this, like we agreed." The other slid them into his pants pocket with a rapid motion, then thought a moment, removed one, and looked it over on both sides.

"Say, are you sure they aren't fake?" he asked, looking distrustful. "I admit I can't tell the difference. I've only seen these notes once or twice, but I've been told they're often counterfeit."

This struck Nikolai as funny, and he struggled to conceal a smile. "Do I really look like the kind of guy who would try to cheat on such a petty sum?" he asked with genuine curiosity.

Mark Lvovich blushed and started to mumble an apology, but Kramskoy just waved him off and took the file from the newspaper. "Forget it," he said. "Don't apologize. Especially since, actually, people *do* cheat on all kinds of things. Come on, how about we step away from the garbage?"

Pechorsky, sensing the business so alien to him was concluded, cheered up at once. "Of course, of course," he stated a bit fussily. "Let's go that way, toward the river. In fact, if you don't mind, why don't we take a little walk? After all, this is your first time in Sivoldaisk, and the weather's so nice now."

Nikolai consented – he had at least an hour before his meeting with Astakhov. They returned to the monument with the rocket and a wistful Gagarin in a flight helmet and, without haste, they passed on. Mark Lvovich was suddenly enlivened – it was obvious the tension had left him. He talked incessantly, waving his arms, and seemed to wonder at his own loquacity.

"Please forgive me for being so talkative," he turned to Nikolai. "It's just that you and your dollars really provoked me. Not that I'm blaming you, but understand: it's the first time in my life I've done something like that. It's theft, which I find unforgivable. But for some reason I'm not ashamed – I just really feel like wagging my tongue."

Kramskoy said something calming in reply. Nothing irritated him today after his release from captivity.

"Yes, yes, theft," the old man nodded. "But enough about me. The city and these people around are much more interesting subjects. I think a lot about everything here, even though I have no one to speak to. And the city just goes on with its life, though it's old beyond measuring…"

"Yeah, it's drowning in muck," Pechorsky continued hotly, "sinking into the earth, and the Volga erodes its shores, but here, look, the sun sets and music echoes, as if a play is performed every evening. Ships sail, decked out like Christmas trees, and the women adorn the street with themselves – wearing bright clothes, proudly holding their heads high, as if serving some cult. Every festivity in the world takes place only because of them, and, look, they're never tired!"

Stepping aside for a noisy band of teenagers, they descended the stairs right to the water and stood there for a bit, peering into the distance. The river here was unclean; a small wave pushed debris and iridescent spots toward the parapet, but Nikolai still breathed in chests full of the evening river's freshness. On the opposite shore, occasional fires burned. He mused that somewhere out there, amid the reeds and bogs, lay the lost island where they had spent long hours of captivity, but nothing tugged inside him and his thoughts were light and peaceful.

They walked on and soon reached the Rotunda – a round Greek pavilion with columns, near which a spontaneous bath had been organized. The bathers, mainly elderly, numbered not a few, despite the filthy water. The waterfront curved to form a semi-circle and further on all was wild – the remains of a wharf and rusted rods upon which seagulls perched.

"Sometimes, when it gets dark, amazing things go on here," Pechorsky perked up again, turning around, his eyes flashing at Nikolai. "The lighting is the reason – though perhaps not the only one. A steamer sails past, there's music and dancing, everything is transformed: glowing beams of color, twinkling lights, another life. And you look at this small pool, and you see a full-chested mermaid with a fish's tail swimming there, though you soon realize it's just a large woman in the water *électrique*. I mean, in a rainbow of spilled gasoline. And then, though the steamship is full of life and fun, you don't think of the noise, but of the quiet and intimate. And the mermaid notion is not just some longing for another life, but a longing for love!"

Nikolai nodded and interjected a few words; meanwhile, Mark Lvovich kept chattering away. It was clear he had missed having a listener and enjoyed the moment, which, he knew, was brief.

"Before, we, the Russians, used to make claims," he grew excited. "We spoke of being chosen by God, of a special path. That's all nonsense: the issue is merely in distances and sizes. This is the starting point, which leads further – to the wide shoulders; tall, mighty girls; great vocals. And true passions – maybe because almost every beauty here has a drop of southern blood in her. Now, though, things are getting worse – everything passionate relocates to your neighborhood, to the center. The capital city pulls all to itself, like a funnel cloud. It whirls, draws in, and doesn't let go, but it knows: distant lands cannot be fully owned, and so you just need to plunder them down to the last cent while you still can. And then barricade against them all with a high wall. I wouldn't want to end up there, behind the wall."

Pechorsky halted and turned around, outlining the horizon with his free hand. His eyes burned; he stroked his chin comically, pressing the old briefcase to his chest. His elbow patches and worn shoes and his grotesque, bureaucratic appearance didn't match his passionate speech, which was worthy of the most ardent dreamer.

"You see how much sky there is here?" he said fervently. "It's everywhere – and every local woman is linked to that great resource. And in that capital of yours, what will she have? There she'll immediately be orphaned. She'll end up behind the wall – her humble soul will be mixed with chunks of asphalt and poisoned with exhaust gas. And they'll tell her: 'Here it is, the city, love it to death.' And she'll search for the human among the dog-headed symbols, but, of course, she won't find much. How could she, with her impulsive mind and her soul, naive to the limit? She'll just learn not to notice the dog heads around. She'll adjust bit by bit to the foreign routine, becoming like the rest and ceasing to be a burden to her men who once expected so much from her. They desired warmth and simple things – she possessed them but couldn't share, and they soon realized they would receive nothing. That's the law of your capital: don't give anything away for free. Even better: don't give anything away at all. Isn't that why they drop like flies in your big city, even before reaching fifty? They die early here too, of course, though mainly from vodka."

"Well, you know, uh…" Kramskoy gestured with his palm in the air. He was offended for Moscow, particularly since the old man was laying it on so thick. Everything was more complex but not quite so bleak – and even if it were, it wasn't for an outsider to judge. For some reason, the inhabitants of the capital have never been eager to return to their rural roots. Take Zhanna Chizhik, for instance… Here Nikolai remembered her and winced from some troubling feeling.

"No, you're exaggerating," he grumbled, glancing askance at Pechorsky, who immediately shut up and prepared to listen. "Forgive me, but that's a typical provincial viewpoint. You have a lot of sky here, but a counterbalance is needed: if there were no Moscow, it would have to be invented. And people *would* happily invent it, plastering its legend on the map, with everyone itching to go there. And it would thrive and give hope that at least somewhere there was life, since here there's none!"

His interlocutor was silent, looking subdued and not even attempting to argue. "I came on too strong for him," thought

Kramskoy and felt ashamed. "All right, don't be upset," he grinned as congenially as possible. "This is an age-old dispute – urban sprawl versus the countryside. Take ancient Rome, for instance, or these days, New York."

But Mark Lvovich was in no way hurt. "I'm not upset at all. Why would I be?" he responded with the same enthusiasm. "I'm quiet merely because I'm trying to articulate an answer without saying unpleasant things to you. After all, you're quite right of course, but, at the same time, you're completely wrong. And the issue here isn't about capitals. The matter mostly concerns the current times – those in which bad taste predominates. With a big city one can argue, but with bad taste? No, no way. Poor taste is all-powerful – it crushes and smashes, knows no mercy. And there among you all, bad taste is now the norm. It turns all of the real – forgive me for saying so – into shit. Though maybe you can't see it from the inside."

Nikolai had no answer. Meanwhile, Pechorsky heaved a deep sigh and waved his hands, almost dropping his case in the process. "No one," he cried, "no one can challenge the dullness of the average masses; the whole world is comprised by it. Only large capitals stand out – this is their essence, if indeed they have one. They select the best of the best and give them all a chance – like Moscow not so long ago. I remember that: I lived there as a graduate student and later went there a lot. And a chance was offered to me, but I didn't take it – purely through my own fault. Now I no longer visit Moscow, I hate it. Because, look, what does your city choose? And whom does it choose, whom, I ask you? The same as those who rule there!"

"But not all..." Nikolai began; however, Mark Lvovich cut him off. "Yeah, yeah, yeah," he said in a rush, "I know, I know. Don't think I'm angry at everyone indiscriminately. I just don't like it when they rob the innocent, and that's why I'm not ashamed of these dollars today – not one bit! Let this be my exploit, though nearly no one will see it. And, speaking of humble souls: your city robs them too. But where does it manage to put all this stuff? Where does it hide it like Molière's *The Miser*? I don't know, I don't reside there – but I feel it because you can't forbid me to feel. It could give much in return, your city, but this country has never had such customs. For this reason, it's clouded over and again by darkness... Ah, what an aroma," he suddenly declared, looking at a kebab skewer on a grill that smelled of charred fat. "What a pity I can't have any. Are you up for a beer? I believe I'll indulge in a bottle today. Or, perhaps not... No, I won't."

Pechorsky made a gesture of denial and looked questioningly at Nikolai, but the other was in no mood for beer. Something again stirred up murky images from his subconscious – someone else's words found a response there.

"Darkness," he repeated thoughtfully. "You know, that's very true. Such symbols are alien to me, of course; they're primitive and worn out. Good and evil, that's for simpletons, but darkness... It clouds over, just like that. You're right – and everything very much rises into place."

"I don't understand what you mean," Pechorsky sighed, "but it must make sense to you. I'm certainly not suited to be a prophet."

"Me either," muttered Nikolai, who was still tensely reflecting on something. "Too long to explain, anyway. It's a whole philosophy: higher powers, the metabolism of the Universe... But it seems I came up with a version. And Pugachev fits perfectly – this was a warning, I must have seen it. Pugachev and darkness – it's so easy to detect the link. Of course, Sivoldaisk isn't the most obvious of places, but it's necessary to begin somewhere!"

"Well," Pechorsky shrugged his shoulders, "if you're talking about revolt, then no Pugachev is to be found now. There are no tsars anymore, even self-appointed ones. There are just tycoons; they don't lead wild hordes. Furthermore, nowadays no wild hordes remain in these miserable, emasculated steppes. In other countries, yes, there are – and they look attentively at these expanses too. As for me, some Russian Pugachev would be better –otherwise it's just too unfair. A foreign tsar, self-appointed or not – it's just too much, we don't deserve it. But then, perhaps, I'll never know; I'll probably not live that long."

They had already reached River Station, where a big white steamship was moored. *Prince Dolgoruky* was emblazoned on the hull.

Mark Lvovich nodded approvingly, "Prince, that's nice. Sometimes, they just give them silly names… Well then, time for me to be off. Take care of yourself and have a safe trip back!"

He again grew fidgety and felt ill at ease. Nikolai said a warm goodbye, and Pechorsky scurried off toward the bus stop, shuffling ridiculously in his huge boots.

"What a funny character," thought Kramskoy, glanced at his watch, and started wandering toward the hotel. The crowd on the streets steadily increased. "As if it were a holiday," he noted with a smile. "The old man was right. And it's only Tuesday, but still…"

The conversation with Pechorsky, the specter of Pugachev, and the impending darkness somehow flew from his mind. Nikolai walked along, inhaling the river air and snatching glances at pretty faces. His heart was cheerful; he even whistled like a schoolboy mounting the steps to the hotel, from which a band of local businessmen noisily erupted in expensive suits that hung crooked and disheveled on their mighty shoulders.

At that very moment, far from the waterfront and the carefree crowd, Elizaveta Bestuzheva was standing in front of a mirror, closely studying her face. She was headed to the same place as Kramskoy, though in a considerably different mood. The cause for this was a discussion with Timofey, who had called a couple of hours prior to confirm her worst fears.

The call found Elizaveta in the kitchen where she, attacked by pangs of hunger, was greedily consuming sandwiches – with ham, cheese, and strawberry jam – and washing them down with coffee and milk. The phone rang as she was buttering her next slice of French baguette. Elizaveta shuddered, dropped the knife, and grew nervous, having suddenly lost her appetite.

"Listen, Lizka, all is not well," Timofey began in an utterly gloomy voice, and it was clear to her right away there would be no wedding. "I need to disappear now. Don't judge me too harshly."

He spoke unwillingly, as if the whole discussion irritated him in advance, and Elizaveta felt offended. "What do mean disappear? What about me?" she asked, sounding a little more plaintive than she intended.

Tsarkov became annoyed and somewhat rough. "Can't you see," he said sternly, "I can't think of you right now. Problems have arisen that are over my head. Wait, at least until the main issues get resolved."

Liza understood he wasn't joking – something really serious had happened to him. How she should behave she didn't know, but she was hurt to the point of tears – she felt she was being discarded like an unneeded toy. She was desperate not to be dumped just now, so she tried to compose herself and told him as calmly as she could, "Hold on. Can't we work it out together?"

Tsarkov became even more nervous. "What do you mean, 'together?'" he mocked. "You just don't get it, I can't even explain this!" And he continued with genuine bitterness, "My *patrón* – the godfather I've told you about – kicked the bucket yesterday while we were stuck on the island. Got into a car accident with some schmuck – and without him I'm nobody, nothing! Now everyone is after me, and the police most of all: they want to pin a rap on me so I'll pay them to buy my way out of it. They tossed drugs in the Jeep to set me up. So just what is it you want to do *together*? You want to do hard time with me, or what?"

"Wait, what is this they pinned on you? What rap, what are you talking about?" Elizaveta couldn't grasp what was happening. All she had heard seemed like nonsense or a bad dream, even less real than yesterday's abduction. "But you have a friend there, that major who met us on the shore. Couldn't he take care of it somehow?"

"Yeah, a friend," grumbled Tsarkov. "It's him who's fishing for cash, that friend. Friends like that are a dime a dozen. Better for a pack of jackals to have your back than them."

There was a pause, and Timofey could be heard wheezing into the receiver.

"So where are you now?" asked Liza, just to keep the conversation going.

"In a safe place," he laughed somewhat helplessly. "At the *dacha*, under house arrest, as they call it now. The police will back off – Alenych promised, that major you called friend. But, still, I'll have to pay and hole up for about a week. That's what I'm trying to figure out now: where to hide and what to pay with. And after that, I don't even know."

"Well, I can wait it out for a week or so," Bestuzheva said quietly. "If the issue is just waiting a week." Then she faltered and asked in a quavering voice, "Do you want to be with me or not?"

A heavy sigh could be heard on the other end.

"I understa-a-and," she drawled. "Sure. You don't need a wedding now. And I'm a fool... Well, why aren't you saying anything?"

Tsarkov sighed again and said, "So, um, if you leave, give the keys to the neighbor across the hall. Her name is Sonya, Sofia Pavlovna. But, of course, stay as long as you want. That's just in case you have stuff to do."

"Ah, there it is..." Elizaveta said slowly. So then, the thought flashed in her mind, here it has all ended and you're being thrown away. Just like a little dog tossed out into the cold. What else did you expect?

She bit her lip and said in an icy tone, "I'll leave, don't worry. Tomorrow, bright and early. I just have no strength for it today – neither for the station nor the train. You should have started with that – there was no need to make all that up: investigation, drugs..."

"I didn't make it up!" Tsarkov yelled. "I told you the truth; what else do you want? I just don't have time for you now, you got it? You know nothing – how I'm stewing here and who I'm engaged in this game with, whether they're just trying to frighten you or really gobble you up, guts and all. How can you judge – you're just pulling down a steady wage in that capital of yours! They may just leave me dog-poor, naked; I'll have to start over from zero. What kind of wedding can I have now – and what of you, and all the rest?"

"Oh, yes," Elizaveta repeated after him, "that 'all the rest' is the very point. Life has thrown the heroes on different sides of the barricade. It's clear, at least, that you don't love me – and probably never did. And here I was – ready to nurture a rush of feelings for you in myself."

"See there," Timofey noted, "you haven't started to nurture it yet, the rush – that's good. If, let's say, you already had the feelings, then you wouldn't need to nurture anything. And so, all in all, we're even. We don't owe each other anything."

"If you were here right now," Bestuzheva said wearily, "I'd claw your face with my nails. But you're not, so nothing'll happen to you, except for charges from the planted drugs – unless your 'friends' come up with something else. All right, you go work things out, *fiancé*." And she hung up without waiting for him to answer.

She sat for a while, staring at a fixed point, and again squinted involuntarily at the phone. She wanted Tsarkov to call back, for him to justify himself, feel guilty, but the cell was hopelessly silent. Then Elizaveta began to cry – with spiteful, helpless tears, wishing upon him all sorts of troubles. If Timofey were to fall into her hands now, he'd have hell to pay. She felt like a tigress whose den had been ruined, an Amazon insidiously robbed, the mistress of palaces turned to dust by someone's malicious slander.

"What a bastard!" was resounding in her head. "What a rotten, hypocritical liar! May all his problems come true. If only he couldn't get out of them – then he'd land in the slammer for sure. They'll really make his life sweet there!"

She felt sorry for herself, sorry for the cancelled wedding, for the universe inside and all its scarcely glimmering lives, which, taken separately or together, began to seem dreadfully deserted. "No one, no one cares," Liza whispered, hurt. "Everyone strives to prove his spitefulness – and this one too, the hero in the Cherokee. As for the Cherokee, they'll take it from him – or how does it work here? Let them take it away and leave him destitute – so that women despise him and not a one would want him, ever!"

After crying, she dried her eyes with a napkin and looked around. Her appetite had completely vanished; food caused disgust – as did the well-tended aspect of the brand-new kitchen where, like in the whole apartment, a spirit of abandonment reigned. A luxurious cage, thought Elizaveta. A provincial urban dream. He imagined I'd be charmed by this comfort of his? That sort of thing might impress some local – well, let him impress, if he still can. But girls like me won't be seen in this kitchen anymore – there'll never even be the slightest trace of us here!

She yanked the spoon from the jar of jam and looked at it thoughtfully. Drops slowly ran down – angel blood turned to sweet poison, scarlet candied roses. Inside, offense pricked her acutely, and Liza, surprising even herself, scooped out a bright red glob and splashed it full force on the wall.

The result was striking: against the sky-blue surface spread a bloody blot. "Cool," Elizaveta praised herself, "here's the trace for you." She gathered another spoonful and put one more glob near the first. For several minutes, she appraised her work, then rose and flung open the doors to the refrigerator and the kitchen cabinets – in search of additional art resources.

"You wanted to get married? You wanted me to be a housewife? Well, let me do the housewife act then," she muttered, studying the shelves. "All right, what do we have here?"

Her survey didn't reveal much, but she nevertheless succeeded in getting hold of something. In addition to the strawberry jam, she also found cherry. "Now we'll give you the sweet life, even without the slammer," Liza said and deftly unsealed the half-liter jar. "Now I'll give you a picture for dessert!"

She began to wield the spoon, carefully aiming, like an abstract artist. Together, both substances produced an interesting combination of colors, and the cherries also looked beautiful on the light floor – tragic and defenseless. "You wanted to be a painter, Nikolai

Kramskoy?" Elizaveta inquired loudly. "Well, you're too late. Here, in Sivoldaisk, the painter is me! I never knew I had talent."

In the refrigerator she found some eggs that were also put to use. Soon the walls were decorated to her satisfaction, and Liza admitted the result wasn't bad. "The picture of my life," she murmured, glancing around. "Just like Jackson Pollock. Though he did it differently, of course."

She turned a bag of milk over in her hands but decided that milk spots wouldn't match the color scheme. On the other hand, the jar of honey came in handy: she generously used strands of it to decorate the surface of the ceramic rangetop. With that she had to stop – her fantasy drew to an end.

"You complained about living alone, huh?" Elizaveta glumly pronounced. "Well, that means you're used to cleaning. What did you expect? You had a guest. You invited me yourself; I didn't ask to come. So, let your whores work a little; they aren't princesses like me, they should be accustomed to it." She again gave the kitchen a critical look and, proudly arching her back, proceeded to the living room, trying not to step in anything sticky.

There her fervor subsided. Elizaveta walked doubtfully along the sideboard and book shelves, but it didn't occur to her to break dishes or rend the books. She always took pity on innocent things, and, besides, these were refined and graceful. Absentmindedly admiring the glasses of crystal and tea cups of Chinese porcelain, Liza seated herself in the familiar chair and attempted to sum things up.

After the tears and the ruined kitchen, her thoughts didn't clear up at all. Her head spun and her soul was increasingly filled with sadness. There, the offense and discontent with the world settled, and behind them appeared something else – a trace of a strange despair, alarm made as hard and strong as a cold, tenacious lump. The room was alien, and the city beyond the window was hated and even more foreign. In the entire expanse, wherever her imagination reached, there was neither sympathy nor warmth.

"What am I doing here?" Liza wondered and shrugged her

shoulders, perplexed. "That damned letter is to blame for all this!"

She tried to envision Tsarkov but realized she couldn't recall his features. It wasn't clear whether this made it easier for her or not. Elizaveta sat for a while, as if listening to something, then said with a sigh, "Oh, well. I'll have to forget him," but the words rang hollow. In them was no conviction, and she herself lacked strength – as in a fever or a bad dream. It even seemed the issue wasn't Tsarkov after all, nor was it the affront or the ruined wedding.

This frightened her. She began persuading herself, whispering something almost incoherent. "Who is he to me? No one, and to hell with him," she muttered, rubbing her shoulders. "I imagined way too much and came here like such a star from the capital, such a refined bimbo. He was probably afraid of me. He should be pitied, and nothing more. Actually, our lives are radically different. Though in some way, of course, he's better than others."

For a fleeting moment, Elizaveta recalled Moscow and a series of men, uninteresting and unnecessary, and then considered how all last week she had been fooled, swayed by romantic bliss. She sniffed with irritation and threw up her hands. "No, but what a jerk!" she exclaimed, and complained to herself, "We women are gullible. We believe everything they hurl at us – flowers, candy hearts, the Soul Number..."

Time crept by. Bestuzheva sat without moving, looking directly ahead. Then something jingled on the balcony – she snapped to and looked up wildly, but through the window was nothing but low clouds.

Probably a cat, thought Liza and turned her head, scoping out the room again. How bare his place is. There aren't even any knickknacks. That's enough remembering; he's not worth it anyway. He's clever, and so am I; he dodged me, and I shall flee.

The lump inside shifted and her whole body responded with an involuntary shudder. "Whom *should* I remember, then?" she asked aloud and helplessly spread her hands. As late as yesterday, everything was so fun – Tsarkov was there, there were plans, and much could be seen ahead. Now emptiness arose from every corner, and the feeling of hopelessness oppressed her. The room seemed like a prison cell but there, past the walls, awaited hostile air, a space devoid of meaning, which could not be measured or taken in with the eye. The city was also lost in it, dissolving into the river, fields, woods, and yellow steppe. It was as if she felt their presence, felt their breath and scent. In them was indifference that killed hope – and now she knew how rare it was for any kind of hope to exist.

Elizaveta thought the hearts of all who lived in this city must have thick armor. The elements here defied reason – or any sympathy toward each other. "Such is life," she declared plaintively and was dumbfounded by the truth of these words. She remembered Kramskoy and felt suddenly that his higher powers were not as ephemeral as they seemed – and they were probably cruel and unkind.

Men have it good, she thought with rage. They look for signs and symbols, believing in every kind of nonsense. But I've got nothing to believe in, and I don't understand hints at all. A simpleton, in a word. The only thing I know how to do is seduce, and even then, not everyone.

Liza twisted up her face, frowned, listened to herself. It wasn't getting better, only more painful. Her palms were as cold as ice. Her eyes, unseeing, looked at the opposite wall. "I need to do something!" she exclaimed in despair and remembered right there about the restaurant, seizing on the thought.

"I'll go have fun and drink!" Elizaveta told herself. "And I'll have a fling, maybe even with Kramskoy himself." She raised a hand to fix her hair and noticed the ring on her finger.

Wow, he forgot his grandmother's relic, she thought. I bet they really did put the screws to him. Should I leave it here on the table? No, I'd best take it with me. If he wants it, he'll come retrieve it himself. Serves him right; let him be mad.

Elizaveta burst out with a nervous snicker. It was clear her consciousness was persistently looking for a chance to provoke Timofey into making contact one more time. "Stupid!" she chided herself, noting meanwhile that the ring, a visible and material object, compensated to some extent for the estrangement of the world. In any case, it was unbearable to sit there anymore, indulging in self-pity. Gathering all her strength, Liza climbed out of the chair and went to the bathroom, unbuttoning her blouse on the way.

Under the hot shower she warmed up at last and the anxiety crawled away, somewhere into the depths. After she dried off with a towel, Bestuzheva approached the mirror and nodded glumly at her reflection. Her mood was improving bit by bit.

"Whom should we play today?" she asked aloud, shaking her head. "An infantile mademoiselle or a European lioness? A sexpot who has just spent a stormy night, or a nymph with rosy cheeks?" She splashed water on her face and studied it in search of swelling and traces of recent tears. The result satisfied her. Besides, the wrinkles were few and her skin seemed quite young.

It'll endure a lot more yet, thought Elizaveta, and this greatly increased her cheerfulness. Piling on foundation, she felt the creator was waking in her again – it was pleasant to make herself anew, observing how from this girl who had been so upset an hour ago, another person was being born. With precise movements she put shadow on her eyelids and painted her lashes. And she noted from the mirror that a very beautiful woman was already looking back at her.

That's because, another pleasant thought flashed, she was like that from the very beginning. She didn't even need to put on much makeup, just to shade slightly here and there. Yes, nature hadn't deprived her eyes of depth; they were a little damp now and this gave them a special charm.

"Here's my revenge," Elizaveta said and applied blush – and her cheekbones turned a translucent pink, as if bristled by a man's whiskers. Her aspect became a little excited, promising much to those who wanted to get burned. Finally, the time came for the lips. She paid them special mind and, as a worthy addition to the blush, she made them bright with a slightly blurry kissing contour.

"Well," she appraised the results, "good, quite good!" And she finished the process with a transparent sheen, damp like a genuine kiss. The mirror confirmed she was irresistible, and Liza didn't doubt this was really so. Right then she remembered Timofey and his Cherokee and how, on the way to the Rogozhino registry, she had wanted to ditch the old cover, totally transforming herself into someone else.

"Here it is, the lizard skin," murmured Elizaveta, knowing with certainty she couldn't change, ever. The heavy lump returned again for an instant. She felt immensely lonely, but with a desperate effort she drove the feeling away. It promised new tears, which couldn't be permitted because of the carefully applied makeup.

CHAPTER 25

The Volga Shaman Restaurant was held in particular esteem in the city. Folks went there to have fun in the old manner, which meant a lot of things – from food and drink to a drunken brawl. At dinner there it was possible to live a whole life and long remember it – stories about binges at the Shaman were handed down by word of mouth. Besides, the kitchen was run by a famous Serbian cook who had garnered skill in preparing Russian dishes, and the prices approached Moscow rates, which added points for those who could afford to spend an evening there.

Elizaveta Bestuzheva appeared in the main hall after the men had already assembled. She entered energetically, looking directly ahead with a faint, victorious smile – so nobody would suspect that in her affairs of the heart all was not well. Their table was located right at the center, not far from the dance floor. Kramskoy and Astakhov sat next to each other and briskly conversed about something. Meanwhile, Frank White was silent and gloomy, fingering a napkin and looking off to the side.

Elizaveta's appearance made an impression – just as planned. Nikolai paid her a compliment and was ready to develop his theme further, but she stopped him with a gaze, thanking him all the while with deliberate modesty. It wasn't worth belaboring the obvious and, besides, looking at Kramskoy, she realized with disappointment that he wasn't even interesting enough for her to flirt with, much less have a quick romance. The only one suited to be the lover-protagonist was Astakhov, who was diligently averting his eyes; Liza decided he was quite an attractive man. In him could also be divined the luster of the capital; she was about to guess the nature of his occupation but surmised that, in this regard, she had no idea. "What's the difference, dear?" she admonished herself. "He probably trades in land or houses," and she shot a dazzling smile at Frank, who was looking at her with a certain shyness.

"Well, here we are," Kramskoy said contentedly. "Nearly all assembled. I don't know about you, but I'm just now beginning to comprehend what an improbable adventure happened to us. A small city," he waved his hand over the restaurant dining hall, "can also be quick to unleash occurrences. And where is the last participant – if not to say, the man to blame? Where's the groom called Tsar?'"

"The groom skipped out on us," Elizaveta responded nonchalantly. "His adventure proved to be too improbable. We decided our feelings were still immature; it'll be the four of us celebrating. I hope nobody minds."

Fearing sympathy and questions, she passed a challenging look to each of the men, but, despite their surprise, all treated the news as they should. Nikolai muttered something incoherent and began to look for the waiter while Frank White, blinking, burst into a tirade about unfulfilled plans, citing himself and the mystical treasure as an example. Andrei Fyodorovich, who had been silent till then, became vividly interested in this story, and Frank laid it out for him, beginning way back with the shifty Nilva.

"Not bad, not bad," muttered Astakhov. "Actually, Nilva is a very funny last name!"

At this, Frank was suddenly embarrassed, and Elizaveta came to his rescue. "Nothing funny about it," she interjected. "He's just a petty loser, from rags to rags. Whether here or there in the States, he's nothing. And you, Frank," she turned to the American, "are a true knight. Taking fire into your bosom. What a pity your stars didn't help you. It's that Chinese girl who's to blame, the bitch. You really should marry a Russian."

"He's a knight at heart, but his deeds are insane," said Kramskoy, fidgeting in his chair. He, like Astakhov, was jealous that White, Jr. was getting all the attention. "As far as plans go, mine never work out, either. And stars don't help – they don't know much, the stars, especially in this country."

"As for me, I now have no plans at all," Andrei engaged in the conversation, trying to maintain a playful tone. All looked at him, and he added clumsily, "Work just isn't coming together, that's for sure," and he signaled the server, "Hey, waiter!"

"The service here, you know…" he grinned guiltily, turning back to Liza, and grew silent without finishing the phrase. She clasped herself about the shoulders in her habitual gesture and rubbed them with her palms as if she had a chill. Her recent despair had abated for a time, but she was restless: agitation hung in the air, saturated with invisible electricity. At the tables surrounding them sat men almost exclusively – broad-shouldered mobsters with identical buzz cuts, jetsetters who were former thieves, their crafty lawyers and accountants, officials looking haughty who only fawned over their bosses, ubiquitous Chechens who fawned over no one… Nearly all were still sober; they darted heavy glances at the company of strangers who had intruded upon their territory. Most eye-catching, of course, was Liza, the tempting prize who, according to inexplicable but sure signs, didn't belong to anyone sitting with her.

A waiter in black-and-white livery, with a thin wave in his hair slicked down to one side, finally approached them and inquired with servile swagger, "What would we like, gentlemen?"

"Vod-ka!" Bestuzheva piped up loudly and distinctly. From the next table men turned their heads toward her. "Vodka, cucumbers, salmon," she continued without heeding anyone's attention, "and a lot more. Let me read from the menu."

The vodka and appetizers were brought quickly. Elizaveta, after drinking with everyone to their release from the island, again engaged Frank White – as if she had found safe harbor and took cover there from everyone, whether they advanced upon her openly or secretly. "Red fish, white fish, pickles…" she pointed at each delicacy in turn. "And here, too, look – beet salad. And some herring and rye bread."

Frank ate voraciously, not forgetting about the vodka either, which soon affected all. The first to become inebriated was Liza – not too much, but noticeably to the inquisitive eye. White, at last, was left on his own; Elizaveta leaned her cheek on a hand with her elbow bent and looked at Astakhov point-blank – as if they were sitting alone.

"What do you do, anyway?" she asked huskily. "We're past formalities, aren't we? Or am I mistaken?"

Andrei Fyodorovich frowned, sighed, and related briefly and somewhat boringly that he wrote books, serious ones – making it sound very banal. He anticipated her reaction, however, with bated breath, and didn't conceal this from Kramskoy's jealous gaze.

"Oh," Liza made a surprised grimace, "you must be famous, then. Maybe even rich. Tell us."

Nikolai sneered, and Astakhov only gave a guilty smile and shook his head. "Nobody knows me," he said, making a helpless gesture. "And they don't pay any money for books in Russia – so you won't get rich that way. I was once engaged in other things," he added, exchanging glances with Kramskoy. Elizaveta murmured, inspecting both of them, "Ah, so that's how it is…" and she covered her shot glass with her palm as the waiter came over to fill it.

"That's enough for the moment," she told him. "We're having an intelligent conversation here." She turned back to Astakhov with a charming smile. "Why do you write them if they don't bring money?" she asked innocently. "And what, does no one want to publish them? Or maybe they're just not good enough?"

"She is sharp," thought Andrei. "Passes herself off as an airhead, but her eyes betray her."

"At least I'm trying hard," he replied, matching her tone. "Sometimes the text is even decent. Though now everything is in a quagmire, that's true. And the reason I write is simply because I cannot *not* write."

"I know *exactly* what you mean," Bestuzheva nodded seriously. "Though, you understand, I really can *not* write... Look, what's going on over there? Has the dancing started?"

The dancing was still a long way off; the musicians were only checking their equipment. The restaurant, meanwhile, already seemed almost full. In the uniform rumble of voices, shouts and laughter continually rang out. The tobacco smoke grew thicker, and burly men wandered about the hall, searching for acquaintances. Looking around, Liza again felt ill at ease.

"A bad theater," she thought. "And such a heavy design: red velvet on the walls, yellow brushstrokes. It always begins with theater and ends in beastliness. And the beastliness is inevitable; there's no escaping it."

"No dancing yet, but there definitely will be," said Kramskoy, who'd also looked around. "And all the other things, as well."

"Yes, yes," Elizaveta nodded absently. "Such are our years; all still lies ahead." She picked with her fork at the almost-empty plate and addressed Astakhov rather sternly, "Actually, that was an evasive, cowardly answer! What does 'cannot *not* write' mean? Too many negatives. You're a strong, self-assured man – say what you really mean! What's the main reason – vanity or something? Or maybe even more – immortality, as you writers would call it?"

"Not bad..." Nikolai Kramskoy was surprised, but Liza didn't look at him.

"I'd be happy to answer," Andrei said with a smile, holding her gaze, "but this doesn't yield itself to verbal expression." Then he added slyly, "Immortality is also evasive, is it not?" and poured himself some vodka. "And vanity – how does one do without it? Can one really admit his own pettiness?"

"Gentlemen and their ladies!" resounded from the platform. "Please give me your attention and put down your glasses. We will now have a competition for the funniest joke. As my brother Gosha from Odessa used to say, a day without a joke is like a night without a babe, ha ha ha."

At the tables nearby they began to guffaw loudly, and a woman's squeal sounded from somewhere. Obviously, mirth was picking up its pace.

"The first to try his luck will be Vovchik from the proletarian suburb," the master of ceremonies announced. "But before he starts, let me show you a magic trick. Look at this red scarf: I'm shoving it down my trousers..."

A new burst of laughter erupted. "An illusionist," sighed Kramskoy. "Same as Andrei, except he does it with words. That's all the present is good for: producing illusions. And the past, only for examining snapshots, cravenly convincing yourself that life is long."

"Vod-ka!" said Elizaveta, pushing an empty shot glass to Astakhov. "Illusions are a necessary thing, don't you think, mister writer?"

"I guess, when they end..." Andrei began seriously, but here the microphone wheezed under the attack of the proletarian Vovchik. "When they end, there will be nothing to live for," he concluded his thought, paused briefly, and looked questioningly at Liza.

"A New Russian takes a look at his Mercedes and says, 'Hey, why is there a rifle sight on the hood of my car?'" "Ha, ha, ha," chortled the neighboring tables. "Yeah," shouted Liza to Astakhov, "that's precisely what I'm talking about. You're all looking for a remedy for fear. Frank, you're our resident romantic – are you afraid of death too? What's your idea of immortality? Or yours, Nikolai Kramskoy?"

A new bottle was brought along with a large portion of sturgeon. All set upon the food; only Bestuzheva, who had put her fork aside, looked at the platform in astonishment. There, the parody of a striptease began – two tall girls coiled entwined around the M.C. as he tried to pull off their clothes. The laughter in the hall started to abate – as if the quota for comedy had ended for the day.

"If I'm so disgusted by them and they're enjoying themselves so much, does this say something about me or them?" she inquired pensively. "Could there be something wrong with me? No matter what, I won't give up – I don't want to admit my own pettiness. Especially now, when I'm a free woman again." She glanced briefly at Astakhov, then continued loudly, "All right. Who has a word to say about immortality or anything else lofty?"

"The most likely possibility is cosmic cataclysm," began Kramskoy confidently. "Collision with a large heavenly body – if a suitable body encounters us. In that lies all hope."

"So what?" Frank White failed to comprehend.

"What, then?" Elizaveta blinked and leaned toward the platter of fish. "Gimme some before it's all eaten. Otherwise, I'll get drunk."

"So here!" Nikolai raised a finger. "The fact is everything will scatter into detritus, into the smallest bits of space dust. And those who are lucky – who are chosen by destiny or happenstance – will be preserved in this dust by their molecules, their unique chromosomes interspersed within the silicate capsules. In the silicate, their genes will travel billions of years; beyond that, one can only imagine what becomes of them. Theoretically, it wouldn't be difficult for some distant aliens to recreate copies of us and even improve them slightly. Only memory won't remain – the capsules are primitive devices, they don't even have batteries."

"It's not interesting without memory," Elizaveta sighed. "But sometimes one must be content with just a small part – and not complain. I, for instance, ruined my fiancé's kitchen: the total worth of our story is the price of a kitchen repaint. And the music is just about to start," she noted, looking over her shoulder. "Where, oh, where is my lamb chop?"

The humorist conjurer had disappeared from the stage, and the band was preparing to get down to business. The hall hooted and whooped; drunken exclamations could be heard from all corners. Somewhere a quarrel broke out, and at the other end a shrill female voice was hysterically going on about something.

"Dark energy," Astakhov thought, looking around like Liza and catching himself copying her gestures. "Aggressive tribes, the lords of local life. The time of simple reflexes – one must give them the road. Otherwise, they'll lay it out themselves – directly through you!"

The waiter, looking like a faded starling, finally brought Bestuzheva her piece of meat, and she bit into it with sharp teeth – greedily, as if she had eaten nothing all day.

"What a woman!" thought Andrei Fyodorovich, observing her stealthily.

"Immortality must exist!" Frank White was admonishing Kramskoy in the meantime. "The first life is nothing more than torture by senselessness, a preliminary selection..." but Nikolai almost wasn't listening to him. He grew dark, reflecting on something, looked askance at Astakhov, then at Liza, twitched, and reached for the bottle.

"I need to drink more," he declared angrily. "I'm almost sober. Here's a toast..." but at that instant the music burst forth in all its multi-watt might and no one could hear a word.

"*This girl, Zoika, wrote to me a letter...*" the soloist hoarsely crooned, imitating the famous aging bard. An approving whistle rang through the hall.

"They press us, oppress us – and we are just silent," murmured Elizaveta, gestured dismissively, and again attended to her meat. "Every individual is a small, specialized mechanism..." Frank White muttered. The others drank, ate, and were also saying something inaudible because the orchestra played tirelessly, and over the table one could catch only occasional scraps of words.

"This afternoon I saw a strange man, but I can't describe him properly," stormed Nikolai Kramskoy. "He was bound hand and foot, and yet he was happier than I am. I suddenly understood: the most annoying thing is when you want to get free, but then realize nothing is really holding you back!"

"What's that?" Liza leaned over to White, Jr. He screwed up his face, suffering and trying to prove his point, gesticulating desperately, "Yes, they allow us to show ourselves in all our glory! They allow that, and then whisk us off to where there are no disturbing questions. And the others are tormented, counting their lives: is it the first or not the first, the only one, or will there be another?"

"Yes!" Elizaveta exclaimed, comprehending almost nothing. Then she looked directly at Astakhov again and asked derisively, "So, writer, what's your most disturbing question?" and he yelled in reply, laughing, "What's that?" the same way she had a few minutes before.

Finally, the music ceased for a brief while. "Well, answer," Bestuzheva pestered Andrei. "Answer quickly before we go deaf."

"It's funny to imagine," he smiled, "that many years from now, my best reader will think that his life is great while he buys artificial flowers for his plastic women."

"Bravo!" clapped Elizaveta. New chords were already heard from the stage; even the shot glasses shook, resonating to the bass strings. *"In a cold cell in Kresty, my heart pines with longing..."* the suffering singer warbled. The dining hall endured along with him; everywhere, they poured drinks, imbibed, and lit up, softened and swollen-cheeked in tearful prison romanticism. The walls, remembering the Party hotshots, glared indifferently at the new owners, having long ago tired of being surprised. "Vod-ka!" Liza commanded loudly, and everyone at the table rushed to pour her some, but she drank it a little at a time, keeping an eye on Frank as well, to make sure he didn't get carried away. Someone tall, with shirt untucked, approached from the side and invited her to dance; but she looked cold and quiet in reply, silently shook her head, and the man wandered away.

Astakhov looked after him for a moment and turned to Nikolai, who was still arguing without hearing anyone: "...the higher power, could its role merely consist of thinking it up for oneself?"

"But what if there's nothing higher at all?" Andrei winked with a smile, wishing to reduce everything to a joke. "Though, look, our meeting wasn't coincidence." He grinned cunningly at Liza. "Somehow, I don't believe in simple happenstance."

"And in fact," Elizaveta supported him, addressing Kramskoy across the table, "maybe you were necessary here just to acquaint me with him."

He, as though not hearing her, continued his own topic, "Battling meaninglessness… Predestination… Yielding is not an option…" But Astakhov heard Liza very well and, inspired, flashed an even broader smile. "What a woman!" he thought again and backed Nikolai up, "Yes, battling with all our might. In battles there are victories – the most pleasant of them!"

The dancing had begun long ago. In a free spot on the floor stomped several young girls and a group of men with thick stomachs. Three more from the same crowd squeezed onto the platform, rapaciously glancing at the flushed Elizaveta. She, in the meantime, having finished her lamb chop, sat moving her shoulders in time to the music. And, it seemed, she had ceased to be interested in the conversation.

"*Remember, girl, how we strolled in the garden…*" the singer began.

"Ah," Liza sighed, "I love this song so much!" She turned and began to study the dancers with greedy eyes. All around was noisy, smoky, and drunken; jailbird anguish was replaced by a thirst for delirious fun. Then the song drew to a close. The soloist announced a break, and in the impending silence Kramskoy's voice resounded with unexpected volume.

"He wasn't given the treasure," he pointed to Frank. "That is his great misfortune. I sincerely empathize, and I'm sorry. For I was once given money – and it wasn't for nothing. Someone wanted me to develop an outside viewpoint. So I developed it, and then – Pugachev! Then kidnapping, like gangsters in a movie! My eyes were opened, believe me. Perhaps I should warn everyone, but I just don't know how."

Elizaveta turned to him with a perplexed look. She wasn't drunk, but rather alert and annoyed, as with a sudden obstacle. "Really, you're a lunatic," she said angrily. "Tsarkov, my damn fiancé, was right. Doesn't it occur to you, by the way, that the ones from whom something is expected know that precisely and don't need to rush about all over the place? And besides, do you think nobody here has eyes to see? Are you the only one smart enough to observe all?"

Her irises sparkled, her cheeks burned; she was very beautiful. "She's great!" Andrei Fyodorovich noted again, and he felt suddenly that here it was, an illustration for something about which he had long sought the words. Such are the women of your dreams, sounded in his head. A hackneyed stereotype, but still accurate!

"Interesting," he said into the distance, as if not addressing anyone. "Has any of you ever noticed: sometimes a conversation, quite innocent in nature, resembles a sexual escapade more than many sexual escapades?"

Kramskoy sat, torpid and withdrawn into himself, while Liza looked attentively at Astakhov as if she had just seen him for the first time. "Here it is," she surmised. "Now, this one is hitting on me right in the open. So quick and so boring, and all just like usual. It's amazing that in a single day one can become tired of all men at once."

She remembered Timofey and the heavy lump inside that wouldn't leave. Her intent to have a fling suddenly seemed ridiculous to her. No, there would be none; that would not save her from anything. The best of all would be to ditch the writer right away – at least some small revenge would come of it.

Everything that had crumbled continued to crumble. What she wanted to free herself from now grew ever stronger, welling in her chest. The shells, new and old, seemed to have been thinned to a micron, and under them lurked an emptiness that would need to be dealt with very soon.

"My ex-fiancé finds it easy to breathe here, but I'm choking," said Elizaveta, frowning, and Astakhov glanced at her with surprise as he recalled his morning walk.

"How do they live in this town – any one of them?!" she exclaimed in a rage.

Her thoughts flashed and then grew ponderous; she forgot for an instant about Astakhov, as well as everyone else around. Before her eyes passed a multicolor whirlwind of the events of this impossible week, which would suffice for years in an ordinary, quiet life. The PI, shifty as a shadow; the old actor in the Mephistophelian raincoat; the barefaced liar Timofey and his ring; gangsters, guns and captivity; scarlet spots on the kitchen walls. There was room for nothing more – not for a lover, or dangers, or worries.

"When I tell Masha, she won't believe it," Liza thought glumly, remembering her office mate. "Or more likely, she'll die of envy. I can't fathom it: all this dragged on and on – and for what?"

She needed to compose herself. "Don't get offended at me," she turned to Nikolai, as if not even noticing Andrei Fyodorovich and his expectant look. "I'm the same as you – enshrouded in doubt – but it's like I know about everyone beforehand. You and I are almost twins, but we just don't have a common goal."

"Common goal?" Andrei asked with interest, butting into the discussion.

"Well, yeah," Liza waved him off. "That's another thing from the fiancé textbook. Romance from the sticks. Are you familiar with it?" She turned her head, asked imploringly, "When, oh when, will the music return?" and pushed her glass toward Kramskoy, "Vod-ka!"

He obediently poured some for her and for all the rest. Elizaveta took a gulp and felt better. "That's it. Enough complicated stuff," she declared. "As long as there aren't any songs, let's recite poetry. You, mister writer, how about some of your own, the best you've got?"

"I don't write verse," Astakhov threw up his hands. "I have some drafts that are like poems, but they're still basically prose."

"Ah, pretty please, don't wimp out on us," Liza insisted, and again looked right at him, propping her chin on her palms.

"All right," Andrei said dubiously and shrugged his shoulders. "Here's one, for instance." And he began to recite unhurriedly in a hushed voice:

I threw a handful of pearls on the dirty floor.
Then I reconsidered and called the maids.
On their knees they crawled, gathering the gems into a tin basin.

Knowing that I would count them all to the last.
I repeat mistakes no longer, I affirmed to myself.
And I looked at their hips and thick calves.
I was free to take right here everything I want.
Here, in the shed full of ugly sounds.
With one of them I could even be gentle.
But you can't recognize her from behind.

"Well, you're talented," said Liza seriously when he finished. "Talented and, no doubt, you have a terrible ego. But you've got a long way yet to match mine."

She looked everyone over and awarded them the haughtiest of smiles. Something still remained within her power. She knew it wouldn't last long – she had to enjoy the moment summoned from the cruel world.

"A handful of pearls on the dirty floor…" rang in her head. "What was that you were saying about predestination?" she asked loudly and declared, "That's a terribly depressing thing! You, for instance, will fulfill your predestined task, you'll transfer a message from one higher power to another, and then become no longer needed. And I'll always be wanted: I am Venus, my stone is diamond. And I am simply made, I don't even have batteries inside. So, all everyone wants is my body. And, in revenge, I remember no one – no one at all. Wow, here they are!"

On the stage the musicians appeared, to whose ranks were now added two girls in short skirts. The hall began to clap and howl, shouts were heard, "Come on, Marusya, fire it up!"

"Ah," Bestuzheva folded her hands behind her head. "What's the reason for all your complications? I don't know what I want; I'm nearly drunk, and I like it. Let's have a dance now – what else is needed for happiness?"

"You escorted me from the shady garden, a nervous shudder suddenly took you…" the band singer burst from the platform.

"Woo hoo!" shouted someone nearby.

People from all directions tumbled toward the dance floor. Elizaveta sat a minute with a pensive, absent expression, then sighed, "Well, this is simply nostalgic ecstasy," and she slipped out from behind the table, catching greedy eyes watching her. "Each of them also believes he's the local Tsar," she thought along the way, glancing around for a moment. For some reason, she wanted to cry again, but she knew she couldn't allow that.

At the platform, in the crowd of waving, loose bodies, her sharp eye picked out a fragile girl with a bare midriff. Elizaveta appeared next to her in a shot and nudged her shoulder slightly, "Scoot over, angel." The girl was ready to retaliate but, upon encountering Liza's tender look, she smiled hesitantly and turned to face her. "*You and I walked along, and I laughed, how I laughed; then you gave me a copper brooch...*" Elizaveta accompanied the strong-voiced soloists, and she focused her dark pupils on the dark pupils opposite, gradually accelerating her movements, pulling her partner into her own rhythmic cocoon.

The girl turned out to be a gifted student. Soon a space formed around them, into which nobody tried to intrude. All merely looked on – with open lust. Elizaveta and the girl, coiled like thin snakes, clung to each other and stepped back without breaking their gaze. They slithered over the threadbare parquet like patches of light on a frozen lake. It seemed their bodies were linked by elastic threads through which pulses of energy surged. The whole dance was raw sensuality, and the crowd's tension grew stronger – blood poured into the eyes of the males, saliva dripped from their canines. It was hard to say what drew them in more – the maturity of desires and knowledge of their power, or the youthful rush, impetuous and ardent, the readiness to submit without fearing the costs.

The orchestra finished the song and immediately began a new one. "*My little ring, cast in gold...*" the singers intoned. "*My girlish heart, claimed by no one...*" Liza echoed, her eyes sparkling. "Ooh, ooh," some drunken idiot shouted. Women glared enviously, not daring to step closer. Meanwhile, two men of Eastern aspect, swarthy and dark-haired, appeared next to them, dancing side by side and encouraging each other with guttural yells. As if on command, short-haired guys with round Slavic faces also crowded in. The air clearly smelled of danger. Right then the music ended, and with it, the dance.

The musicians took a breather and exchanged words among themselves. Liza's youthful partner looked at her devotedly, biting her lower lip. Clapping was heard from the hall: Frank White and Astakhov applauded as if in orchestra seats. Kramskoy, though, sat dark and gloomy – it now seemed to him he had killed the meaning of something important by saying it out loud. The higher powers are unreasonable and blind; no enlightening event awaited him anymore – not here at the restaurant, nor anywhere else. On top of that, the girl with the exposed midriff reminded him of Zhanna Chizhik, and the thought of her pierced him like a needle.

"Some Salome, fuck it," he murmured angrily and reached for the vodka. Elizaveta stroked the girl on the cheek and headed back to her table, but here one of the Easterners gruffly seized her by the elbow.

"Want some champagne, beautiful?" he asked, showing very white teeth.

"Get lost!" she retorted contemptuously and tugged at her arm, trying to get free, but she was held fast, with no chance of release.

"Why are you so rude?" The dark-haired guy was hurt. "Stuck up, huh?"

The round-faced locals moved in on them but ran into the second Southerner; some kind of commotion started, and here two more men broke into the group. One of them pushed Elizaveta's offender in the chest and shouted, "Hey, let her go, you cocksucker!" The guy, surprised, released Liza's elbow, stumbled, and nearly fell, but swiftly appeared next to her again on strong, springy feet. "Oh, Lord," Elizaveta moaned, recognizing her intercessor. "You? Why on earth are *you* here?"

It was Alexander Frolov, who had shown up just in time. After the showdown at the entrance to Timofey's house, he was about to head right to the train station, but Tolyan the driver persuaded him "to watch the film till the end," at least through this evening. Frolov consented; it was all the same to him. They had sat in silence until Liza got into a taxi, and then they settled in at an open bar right by the front doors to the Volga Shaman and began to methodically suck down beer.

In an hour or so Alexander came alive. "We got drunk yesterday, but we'll get even more wasted today," he muttered, looking into his mug. "That'll dispense with any impediments and barriers. We can behave as if we are tsars and tyrants, and we can have concubines, grog, and anything else – as much as we want!"

"What's that? More Churchill?" the driver asked respectfully.

"No, I came up with that myself!" Alexander pounded his fist on the table and burst out laughing at the top of his lungs. In him spoke none other than the freedom-loving spirit of his grandfather. Tolyan merely nodded assent and wasn't at all surprised when, once he'd gotten thoroughly plastered, Frolov said with a shrug of the shoulders, "What are we sitting around here for? Let's have some fun – I've had my fill of this shadowing. Let's go inside – at least we can grab a decent bite." With that, they went to the restaurant, just in time for the very beginning of the conflict.

Seeing Liza being held by a swarthy Eastern guy, Alexander rushed to help. He wasn't afraid; his instinct for self-preservation had disappeared. A fight broke out at once; everything started spinning like a cyclone. It was hard to determine who was beating whom, or who was getting beat up. From all sides rang shouts and growls, groans and female squeals. Fists and contorted faces flashed; Hong Kong shirts, German tees, and Italian jackets were ripped and torn. Frolov and Tolyan were also ardently involved in the fray, as were Nikolai Kramskoy, the writer Andrei Astakhov, and even Frank White, Jr., who was the first to notice their Liza was at the eye of the storm. Elizaveta herself was trying to tear away from the hands of a painted-up chick who had latched on to her clothes. Meanwhile, the dancer with the bare midriff pulled the girl's hair and screeched, "Let her go-o-o!"

Right then the security guards appeared, frantically waving night sticks, plus a police squad that had been on duty around the corner. The orchestra banged out some Gypsy number, and the world seemed artificial, like a phantasmagorical dream. Still, everything was undoubtedly real: there were wounds and knocked-out teeth; one of the Easterners was plowed to the floor and kicked ruthlessly; and a short-haired guy, perched on his haunches, whined and clamped his palm to his thick thigh, from which blood gushed...

It took a full half hour to calm all the brawlers down. The orchestra, by this time, had long grown silent, and some of the victims were brought into the foyer, where a brigade of paramedics waited. The police detained seven, among whom were Tolyan and Frolov. The driver had sustained almost no injuries. As for Alexander, he had a split lip, one arm in a sling, and he looked very pale.

Elizaveta approached the detainees, and all of them, including the cops, stared at her. Only Frolov fixedly examined the ground underfoot.

"Are you in charge?" she asked the lieutenant, a tall Ukrainian with the restless eyes of a cocaine addict. When he nodded with a snort, she smiled radiantly and pointed at Alexander, "He's a friend of mine. Can you release him into my custody? He was just defending me; he didn't assault anyone."

"Sure, we'll release him, why not?" the lieutenant boomed, winking at the sergeants from the unit. "We'll figure stuff out at the precinct and let him go. If he didn't assault anyone... What a hottie! Want to come with us? We've got a spot warmed up for you in the car."

He reeked of onions and man sweat, and he looked at Elizaveta with the arrogant confidence of one who could do whatever he wanted. She suddenly felt fed up – with Sivoldaisk and with all the events of the last days. There was no strength left: not to prove herself, not to take revenge on anyone, not even to simply communicate with this world.

Something, however, seethed within her and threatened to boil to the surface. "Have you seen yourself in the mirror, jerk?" she asked with cold hatred. "Go, wash up. You stink from a mile away."

The lieutenant was dumbfounded, but he quickly recovered and growled, "You bitch! Who do you think you're talking to?" He took a step in her direction, but right then, fortunately, Kramskoy and Astakhov intervened. The two of them took a long time to calm the unit warden, who was in no joking mood. However, he eventually bent to their supplications and, with a regal gesture, refused several hundred-ruble bills held out to him by Nikolai.

"Go on then, Moscow scum," he said contemptuously. "And look after your broad to see she doesn't lose her tongue. And you meatheads," he turned back to the detainees, "get a move on outside!"

They led Elizaveta to the table. They poured her vodka, cold and crystal clear, but she just looked at the glass and shoved it away. All her vitality evaporated; even her shoulders fell slightly, and a crease marked her forehead.

"Here it is, my cosmic cataclysm – in small provincial scale," she said and asked Astakhov, "Do you know what a Soul Number is?"

"Um," he drawled, twisted his fork in his hand, and said with a sigh, "in a way. If, by simple arithmetic, you reduce the day and month of your birth to a single figure, then you come up with a number concocted by the Hindus. It is considered significant throughout all one's life, but it especially shows its strength during the first thirty-five years."

"Then a person wises up," he continued after a silent pause. "The person's soul matures and he doesn't aspire anymore to the unnecessary, concentrating his thoughts on what has been given to him to fulfill. That's when the next hint snaps into action, the so-called Number of Fate that's calculated in a slightly different way. That's what points out the road to happiness." He chuckled and looked briefly at Liza, but she didn't appreciate the joke.

"You know everything, don't you?" she said. "Aren't you bored with all that? What I know is that numbers lie. The same as signs."

Elizaveta turned to Frank White, Jr. and patted him on the

shoulder. She was fearful: the elements exulted, and the world was falling to pieces.

"Good bye, Frankie," she said, somewhat confused. "Farewell, everyone; I'm off to the station. Maybe we'll see each other again in Moscow," and she stood and walked to the exit. All froze; only Nikolai made a move as if to stop her. He even yelled something, but she didn't look back and he fell silent, as if tired of arguing.

Silence hung over the table. "I am a true warrior, fighting repression," Kramskoy grinned. "First, I rescue Frank White here from some angry cops, and just now Liza." He took a cigarette from a crumpled pack, raised his eyes to Andrei, and asked gloomily, "See? I fulfilled my destiny, introduced you to her, and – what was it she said? Then I was no longer needed. And you, I observe, are no longer necessary either."

"That's what you told me on the boat," Frank interjected. "Remember? All here comes to naught."

"Not on the boat, but on the lousy launch," Nikolai corrected him with displeasure. "Don't take it seriously – I was just stating the obvious. Everyone wants this not to be true, but what? Where is there at least one counterexample, tell me?"

"Yeah," Andrei Fyodorovich murmured without listening to him, "that's how they toss us away. Anya dumped me, by the way – I wrote you about her. And this one, Elizaveta, she was great! Where are her men – and what's the deal with that fiancé?"

Frank White frowned and looked away. "They were a cute couple,"

Nikolai shrugged, filling his shot glass. "Someone died and everything went to pot, a million problems all of a sudden. The two of them should both move someplace else."

"In other lands the women are different too," Frank grumbled rather darkly.

Kramskoy nodded in agreement, "Different women, different pleasures."

"Different boredom," Astakhov added. "Though, of course, I'd like to believe they wouldn't bore each other. Who does that fiancé remind you of? Some kind of crook?"

"No," Nikolai shook his head. "He's like a broker or a trader. Some important type, by local standards. Not a real wolf, more like a wolf cub, but not a vicious one. All the same..." he smiled, suddenly remembering Murzin the folklorist. "All the same, both of them are from those bothered by *the question*. The one which is closed into a circle. The sense of our ability of looking for a sense."

Astakhov reflected, scratching his cheek. "The question's not bad," he admitted. "But there's no grasping hold of it – like a dog chasing its tail. Something doesn't add up – either on purpose, or, more likely, by accident."

CHAPTER 26

Andrei Fyodorovich was mistaken, which happened to him quite often. Intentions and accidents had already converged, assembled in a chain one after the other, but he looked for harmony in other spheres and drank vodka, lost in thought. Also reflecting on their own matters were Kramskoy and Frank White, Jr.; only Elizaveta wasn't thinking anymore about anything at all. She rode in a taxi under dim streetlights down the Moskovskaya Street, heading back to Moscow, far away from everything that had happened to her in the city that she no longer even possessed the strength to hate.

In fact, there was no hatred as such left in her now. Feelings retracted into the depths, and their acuteness was dulled. She even felt a sort of kinship with the city. Like her, it was a victim, not a guilty party. It consisted completely of the yellow dust, invisible in the dark, that wafted on the air and squeaked against your teeth, covering the pavements made of paper and the buildings made of thin cardboard. The world was hostile and she knew the enemy by sight, but she didn't feel fear before him. She was troubled by something else, and this alarm had no name in any tongue she knew. Some bitter protest grew in her, and she didn't want to drive it away, even recognizing its impotence.

Gathering her belongings only took a short time. After handing over the keys and smiling crookedly at the slovenly neighbor, Liza returned to the waiting car and ordered impatiently, "To the station. I'm in a hurry."

"The Orenburg Express?" the driver asked knowingly, steering the taxi through an archway.

"Yeah, yeah," Elizaveta nodded, having no knowledge of the train schedules. "Please step on it!"

Outside the station she tossed the cabbie some money. He looked at it thoughtfully and said, "Hang on, miss, let me walk you in. It's night, after all."

Liza refused, but he, not listening, picked up her bag and walked to the illuminated entrance. Inside the building full of people, the driver looked around, said with satisfaction, "Well now, we made it," and put the bag on the floor. "Have a nice trip, miss." He turned back to Liza and saw she stood transfixed and pale, her eyes open wide. Slightly to the left, leaning his shoulder against a column, grinned Timofey Tsarkov.

"He with you?" the driver asked, tracking the direction of her gaze. "Or is he trying to frighten you?"

"Y-yes, he's with me," Liza answered, forcing herself with difficulty to snap to. Then she turned to him, "Thank you. Take care," and she froze again, lowering her hands. The recent protest dissolved in a flash. In place of the cardboard scenery there was again stone, glass, and the dirty floor underfoot. She was surrounded by a human racket and the thick smell of the crowd. Realities encroached from every side, concentrating there in the station hall.

The driver shrugged his shoulders, looked at Timofey again, and wandered away. Tsarkov, meanwhile, having removed himself from the pillar, slowly came up to Elizaveta and nudged her modest travel bag closer with his foot. "They'll steal it," he explained. "This is a train station, after all, not a five-star hotel. Who was that schmuck seeing you off?"

"Cab driver," she said softly, then somehow shed her stupor, looked Timofey in the eyes, and sternly inquired, "Did you come for the ring?"

"Nope," he responded. "For you. That is, first for the tickets – and then to go with you, the two of us. I'm off to Moscow, to the capital; it seems we're heading the same way. My plan has changed – and the new one is even better. Now I think we can start to nurture that rush of feelings between us. Something tells me that won't be too hard."

"Have you lost your mind?" asked Bestuzheva, crying inaudibly to herself, "Don't believe it, don't believe it!" She knew already that she desired precisely this and nothing else, but she was deathly afraid of being deceived again. Even more terrible was the thought he would suddenly disappear, leaving her alone; but she knew every thought could be restrained somehow. With a desperate effort of will, she called on her remaining common sense, repeating like a cruel mantra to herself, "He's lying!" She bit her lip and started to reach for her bag, but Tsarkov grabbed it first and turned around, shouting over his shoulder, "Come on, follow me. We're already running late!" Only then did Elizaveta notice the oddly shaped rucksack filled with something heavy hanging from his shoulder, and she realized all was in earnest and he wasn't joking.

"Wait, hang on," she started to protest, "what if I don't want to? What if I despise you now – what are you presuming, anyway?" But Timofey was taking broad strides, urging her on with impatient gestures, so she had no choice but to fall in behind. "No, I can't do this," she yelled at his back. "You didn't even ask me. I already parted ways with you forever, don't you get it? Hey, stop already!" She stomped her foot and froze in place. Only then did Tsarkov halt and turn toward her.

For a second or two, he looked searchingly into her face, then smiled again and said slyly, "It's pointless for you to go on like this: there are no more tickets anyway. Nina the manager gave me the last ones, and even those are third class. You won't leave without me, and the next train is at seven in the morning. Accept your fate and don't lag behind. We're on track eight; that's up over the bridge."

Liza wanted to say something, but he again strode forward, leading the way in the dense crowd. "What a crackpot!" she exclaimed and hurried after him. They reached the first platform and, along with the other passengers, began to climb the steep iron stairs. Elizaveta was soon winded – both from the ascent and from the sudden surge of emotions. "Hey now, you wait. I'm about to cry," she muttered after Tsarkov, knowing he didn't hear her. "You already dumped me – and what? Now you're messing with my head again? How on earth did you turn up here?"

The metal trembled from the multitude of feet. Below, locomotives droned, inspectors called out, cars clanked as they coupled. "I had you figured; I'm a man of action," shouted Timofey, nearly breaking into a run. "I knew you wouldn't wait till tomorrow. I rang Sonya, she said you left the keys with her and were gone. Well, obviously, I think to myself, she's off to the Orenburg train – so I played ahead of the curve, as they say. Careful, we need to go down this way. The steps are warped. Don't trip."

"Well, no, what?" Liza wrung her hands, hesitated a moment, and began to descend after Tsarkov. "You're still a creep – I want to slap you hard, really hard! Here, let me carry the bag. Your shoulder must be about to fall off."

Timofey, paying no attention to her, deftly ran down the stairs, went to the platform, and looked around. "Our car is there – number twelve." He waved his arm. "The train is about to pull in."

They walked quickly in the direction he indicated, but then a melodious trill resounded from the speakers, after which a female voice announced with a certain coquetry, "The Orenburg-Moscow, due to late arrival, is now arriving on track one. Attention, the train is arriving on track one. Due to the delay, boarding time has been reduced. Attention... Boarding time is reduced."

Tsarkov stopped short, mopped the sweat from his brow, and laughed, "No way. You've got to be kidding me!"

"What? Are we too late?" Liza asked in alarm. "I can't believe we won't make it. What if we run?" Her heart sank. Something collapsed again, without even managing to adopt a concrete form.

"We'll make it. No worries," Timofey grabbed her bag with his other hand and again took to the stairs, barking, "Follow me!"

Elizaveta felt an astounding influx of force. The chaos was all-encompassing, but in it something steady began to dawn, something not unfamiliar. Perhaps not a point of support, maybe just a willow branch, but it was possible to hold on to it, and in this, there was a chance. "To track one, the first track," she repeated to herself and tripped up the steps next to the panting Tsarkov, trying to help him with the load he flatly refused to share.

"What if you run away, my bride?" he laughed. "Better if I carry it myself!"

"You were the one who wanted to run away," she yelled, her eyes flashing. "You rejected me, *again*!"

"Well, not really," objected Timofey. "Who in their right mind would reject you?"

"Once more you have a slick plan and all are against us!" she turned to him.

"My plans are generally very cunning. But I'm not going to be cunning with you anymore," he murmured, stomping along the ironwork. "Here, to the left – run ahead!"

With them on the creaking stairs climbed others who had been deceived by the schedule, the late train, and the coquettish announcer on the loudspeaker. From all directions echoed complaints and curses, bulky trunks flashed, and contorted mouths cried out. "The exodus of the nations," thought Bestuzheva for a moment. "The line to board Noah's Ark. Are we really not going to make it?"

"And I also understood," Tsarkov said to her, gasping, "I understood I'm not afraid of you anymore. Before, I feared you – I did. But now – no, I'm sorry. I realized that and decided, we'll go to Moscow together!"

"So this is why you dragged me to this city?!" Liza laughed. "And where do you intend to live now? With me?"

"Why with you?" he boomed, offended. "I know places – to wait and sit it out. But I'll come visit you, with flowers even."

"With roses?" Elizaveta smiled, but he couldn't hear her because of the surrounding noise. "See, he isn't afraid," she murmured to herself and began to descend behind him to the first track, where a dark blue mass waited.

"That way! Go that way!" Timofey yelled. "If it starts moving, jump into any door."

"Okay!" she shouted in reply, looking around anxiously and trying to determine the numbers on the cars. Everywhere, frantic people scurried about. Someone painfully banged a suitcase into her knee, but she didn't pay attention to anything as she attempted not to lose sight of Timofey's back and not stumble on the rough asphalt along which, it seemed, they had already been running for a lifetime.

Then everything suddenly calmed down, as if the sounds had all at once disappeared. They sat on the bottom bunk in the third-class berth, silently contemplating the platform sailing by. It had become nearly deserted, only security guards in black shirts stood there, and a man in his fifties with a baby face and mad eyes wandered after the train, waving his hand at someone.

"Yesterday evening I felt all of a sudden, something was coming, something terrible," Tsarkov muttered, looking out the window. "A catastrophe, I thought at first, a flood, maybe, or the city falling into the earth. And then I understood – all at once. Thoughts came together and I resolved: I'll not lose you again! And I'll still show the local jackals what's what."

Liza said nothing and just squeezed his hand, painfully sticking his palm with her nails. The whole car slept, breathing uneasily, except for the man sitting across from them on a carefully made bed. "Would you young folks care for a cognac?" he asked without turning away from the window. "Yes," they replied simultaneously, then toggled on the night lamp and saw he had a scar on his cheek resembling that of Nikolai Kramskoy.

The three of them drank cognac with dark chocolate. The night lamp was switched off again, and only a faint profile could be seen of the man opposite. He still didn't look at Timofey and Liza, though nothing was to be made out beyond the window. Only the occasional lights flashed by, and the glow of distant Sivoldaisk gradually dissolved into the horizon. Darkness fell, night reigned, and dreams came into being, though not everybody saw them.

Frank White, Jr. wasn't sleeping; he stood on the balcony, shivering from the wind, and looked – afar toward the river and the steppe, and upward, at the stars that wouldn't aid him with their counsel. "It seemed so logical: bait, trial, reward," he whispered in English. "Well, there was indeed bait. And trial too, I believe."

Somewhat earlier, having just gotten back to his room, he called Olga's personal number she had given him on their last date, warning him it should be used only in an emergency. Olga answered after the fifth ring. She was slightly drunk and didn't recognize him right away. Once she did, she was surprised but lost interest in the conversation straightaway.

"So, what's up? How are you?" she asked with a yawn. "Come on, speak up fast. I'm a little busy here." In the background some smooth jazz was playing, and men's voices could be heard. Frank felt his heart would rip out of his chest and fly into the abyss.

"Olga," he uttered, "please, will you marry me?"

She was silent a long time, then mumbled, "Hang on," and yelled in frustration at someone close by, "Bug off, will you! This doesn't concern you!" Then she sighed and said tenderly and warmly, "Frankie, you're still such a child. Go home. It's better for you there – much, much better, trust me."

"I see," he replied. "Well, bye." He depressed the hook and stood a long while with the receiver in his hands. When he came to his senses, he opened the balcony door and went out to the Volga, majestic and tranquil, to the quay still full of the people, to voices and music, and the scent of kebob grills with their coals extinguished, where the vendors now only hawked beer. In his soul it was lightless and bitter; he felt he had endured the biggest loss in his life. The city below exulted frantically, as though it were for the last time, and Frank White knew he was seeing this place for the last time, and for some reason, this also weighed heavily on his chest.

Then the music stopped as if on command and the coast became empty at once. Only the occasional drunks wandered, wobbling, also unneeded by anyone this night. And then the streetlamps began to go out one after the other – both on the embankment and in the city itself as far as the eye could see. Soon everything around was plunged into darkness; only the water gave off an oily sheen in the moonlight. At that moment, Frank understood something about this country; inconceivable grief engulfed him – a reflection of the great despondency of the open expanses. Thus it was here over the centuries, and thus would it always be – and what a terrible thing that is, an unlit city!

"*It's hopeless,*" said Frank White loudly into the summer night. The bleakness of big open spaces, for which even the horizon was no more than a detail, revealed itself to him with flawless clarity. Its scale was beyond measure, but its power still wasn't absolute. Frank knew that even there madmen sufficed – those who dared to challenge its supremacy. It succumbed deceptively, until it swallowed them once and for all. But others would appear in their wake and fight with all their might...

He wanted desperately to seize the tantalizing essence: why? The rustle and smell of the essence were somewhere here, but he knew it would not yield itself up – it was as elusive as the Firebird Olga. "Already the End, Not Yet the End," he murmured. You couldn't grasp the flame with your hand, but could your palm at least catch its reflection? Strange hexagrams, not resembling anything, appeared to him in patches of river light. "Land of Love," "Land of No Love," he named them. "And the second follows the first."

It occurred to him right then how easy it was to just drop dead, in a hotel room, without having learned whether another life – better, simpler, more sensible – lay ahead. Easy to vanish, and nobody would notice the loss – how would they notice, when it's so dark all around? The stars twinkled, divulging no secrets. He knew only that somewhere overhead the sky hung: it was real – it, and the great river. And, clinging to this knowledge, Frank White, Jr. soared between the river and the sky, having suddenly forgotten all names and faces, cherishing like an eternal treasure the boundlessness of his sadness – a proof he was still alive.

Nikolai Kramskoy wasn't sleeping either. He had come to the hotel with White and said goodbye to him casually, but then ambled through the corridor, moving his feet with difficulty, as if spent by an effort exerted in vain. The nature of the effort was unclear, but Kramskoy had no time to contemplate. Once he got into his room, he, like Frank, rushed to the telephone, but at Zhanna's house no one answered. He listened a great while to the long tones, then drank water right from the tap and wandered in circles, whispering something through clenched teeth, feeling pitiful and confused. Did he really need this woman, who was almost still a girl? And if so, then why? Freedom, lack of freedom – where are they, what are they? How does one achieve freedom that is not death? And who was he, anyway – a bystander or not? A mere observer or someone else?

Then he called reception, requesting a headache pill and a book to read for the night. The attendant, a plump, elderly lady, brought several worn-out paperbacks. He opened the first to the middle and was dumbstruck by the suddenness of recognition – of his dreams, and fears, and his thoughts.

She gave him an amethyst – so that he would put it in his glass at supper. Color must be compared against something, she said, and undiluted wine is only for barbarians wearing animal skins. And then, to spite her, he began to play the animal in her presence. He snatched her up, lodged her with himself, and forbade her to go outside. He forbade her to depilate her body, to use the phone, or to speak distinct words. And she took the game seriously; they switched to guttural sounds. He would come in the evenings and take possession of her – always with the light on, not allowing her to disappear under the sheets. He would bring her to the point of screaming with his caresses and then bury himself in her soft flesh. In the dark stains of her armpits, in her lion's mane, in damp smells and tangy flavor. Then she left him, like an obsolete city, and took the stone with her. He roamed the world, looking in every corner, in all the brothels and haunts of vice. He asked, already without any hope, after the bacchante with lion's hair. And he drank wine without adding water, knowing the taste and the color were not important anymore. Because his instincts were dead forever and nothing could be brought back – neither this woman, nor their passion, nor the stone.

"Neither the woman, nor their passion, nor the stone," Nikolai repeated aloud and winced as though from a toothache. The thought, circling in his head, was unbearably painful and his cheek burned – as if the old scar was reminding him of itself. Fantasies dissipated; there were almost none of them left. He knew they would appear again – and betray him again. And only Zhanna, not answering the phone, would remain – as would these lines.

Kramskoy tossed the book into a corner of the room and flung himself on the bed – obliquely, on his back, hands outstretched. His lips stretched into a grin; he tried to laugh, but drunken tears flowed down his face.

"So this is what I waited for? Is that all you want to tell me?" he whispered, glaring at the ceiling. "Is the world really devised in such a crappy way?"

He again let forth a snicker similar to a whimper and shook his fist upward: "Damn you! Damn you and all your riddles! All the same, you can promise nothing but silicate capsules. It's not enough. No, not enough!"

Nor did Astakhov sleep – coming home, he hastened at once to his desk. Something from this night must be seized and kept – an imperceptible stroke, added to the picture, at last established the weighted balance for all.

"Liza, Liza, a simple soul," he muttered with a smile, reflected for a minute, and reached for the folder holding the manuscript of his recently begun book. Opening it, he absentmindedly perused some pages, then jumped up and stood, afraid to move.

Very carefully, almost on tiptoe, Andrei Fyodorovich walked to the shelf and retrieved a stack of white paper. Then he returned just as slowly, pulled out the chair, and sat down. It suddenly became clear to him what the plan of the future novel might be, and he wasn't sorry for anything – not for Anna, nor for the time and the lines spent for naught.

"There will be another book – and this will be a great book," he declared. "There everything will be different, and precisely as it should be!"

He looked at the written pages and frowned: no, this won't do. He would have to start over – and it was okay; he was well acquainted with that necessity. Even the name couldn't be left unchanged. This would be a new illusion come to replace the old; it had to be called something new. For that, it was even worth inventing a word that didn't exist – to hell with being afraid they won't understand you! He crossed out the title at the beginning of the manuscript, crumpled up the paper, took out a clean sheet, and penned at the very top: SEMMANT.

Meanwhile, the Orenburg Express flew through the steppe – steadily, tirelessly, like an eternal wanderer. Liza and Timofey sat, their heads inclined, whispering something barely audible to each other. Their neighbor with the scar had long since gone for a smoke; the rest around them snored and sniffled, tossed and turned, cried out in their slumber.

"That whole embankment of yours is covered in bottle glass," said Elizaveta. "How does that feel, to walk on broken glass every day?"

"You caught me, but I'm not a victim," she said. "Though those who seek you-know-what often end up being victims."

"You orchestrated so much around me," she said to him. "I became the center of something, and there I reigned. You'll get no such thing from the higher powers. I am Venus, I sense that now!"

"The soul may be caged while the spirit soars," murmured Tsarkov in reply. "Don't be angry at me. I knew it wouldn't turn out smoothly, but I had to go for it."

"Now nobody will call me Tsar," he grinned. "Will you be able to handle that?"

"I'll have to manage," Liza had matched his tone. Then she added, "You'll laugh, but I only pretend to be strong."

"Me too," Timofey concurred, and she shook her head, not believing him.

They didn't dream of other lands for the moment, nor of unknown seas. The journey had just begun, and the signs were full of meaning – on their own, regardless of the place. And any hexagram, even one devised by the prophets, broke up into the symbols of a well-known code. Affirming that complications are powerless. Foretelling the impotency of all prophets.

"I always wanted a ring with a sapphire," Liza confessed and touched the cold stone.

"Do you know what the Number of Fate is?" she asked, biting her lip.

The car rattled like a fragile ark, groaned on the rails, cutting through space as usual. The train rushed from station to station, across the most indifferent of the plains. But its indifference was concealed by the night, by merciful darkness in which nothing could be seen. And the plain appeared different as the cosmos opened above it. The shadow of meaning passed by unheard – promising, then sweeping away.

Night held sway, and a dream was born – the dream of an angel from the remains of myth, the thought of which so painfully wounds the heart. And one wishes to gather the remains together and confirm the myth isn't miserly but huge – huge and magnificent, by all measures. The part of it that could be grasped was merely a clue to the mystery of this vastness. The apathy that appeared outside the window was just a reason to believe in the warmest response of all. It's evasive, the response of the most soulless of lands, but there is an illusion – and its soul is simple. And, for that, everyone is prepared to battle, unperturbed by the distances and dimensions. In cities that crumble to the ground or stand for the ages. In the emptiness and beyond – where emptiness does not rule. On both sides of the railroad tracks and the great river. And even on both sides of heaven – which, alas, hangs so, so low.

Also by Vadim Babenko:

SEMMANT
THE BLACK PELICAN

SEMMANT

An excerpt from the novel published in 2013

CHAPTER I

I'm writing this in dark-blue ink, sitting by the wall where my shadow moves. It crawls like the hand on a numberless sundial, keeping track of time that only I can follow. My days are scheduled right down to the hour, to the very minute, and yet I'm not in a hurry. The shadow changes ever so slowly, gradually blurring and fading toward the fringes.

The treatments have just been completed, and Sara has left my room. That's not her real name; she borrowed it from some porn star. All our nurses have such names by choice, taken from forgotten DVDs left behind in patients' chambers. This is their favorite game; there's also Esther, Laura, Veronica. None of them has had sex with me yet.

Sara is usually cheerful and giggly. Just today I told her a joke about a parrot, and she laughed so hard she almost cried. She has olive skin, full lips, and a pink tongue. And she has breast implants that she's really proud of. They are large and hard – at least that's how they seem. Her body probably promises more than it can give.

Nevertheless, I like Sara, though not as much as Veronica. Veronica was born in Rio; her narrow hips remind me of samba; her gaze pierces deep inside. She has knees that emanate immodesty. And she has long, thin, strong fingers... I imagine them to be very skillful. I like to fix my eyes on her with a squint, but her look is omniscient – it is impossible to confuse Veronica. I think she is overly cold toward me.

She doesn't use perfume, and sometimes I can detect her natural scent. It is very faint, almost imperceptible, but it penetrates as deeply as her gaze. Then it seems all the objects in the room smell of her – and the sheets, and even my clothing. And I regret I'm no longer that young – I could spend hours in dreamy masturbation, scanning the air with my sensitive nostrils. But to do that now would be somewhat awkward.

THE BLACK PELICAN

An excerpt from the novel published in Russia in 2006
The first English edition coming in 2013

CHAPTER I

To this day I remember the long road to the City of M. It dragged on and on, while the thoughts plaguing me mingled with the scenes along the way. It seemed as if everything around me was already at one with the place, even though I still had a few hours to go. I passed indistinct farms in empty fields, small villages, and lonely estates surrounded by cultivated greenery and forest hills. Man-made ponds and natural lakes skirted the road and reeked of wetlands, which later, right before M., turned into peat bogs and marshes, with no sign of life for miles to come. The countryside was dotted with humble towns sprouting out of the earth, the highway briefly becoming their main street: squares and clusters of stores glimmered in the sun, banks and churches rose up closer to the center, a belfry whizzed by, silent as usual. Then the glint of the shops and gas stations at the outskirts said farewell without a word, and just like that, it was over. The town was gone, without having time to agitate or provoke interest. Again, the road wound its way through the fields, its monotony wearing me down. I saw the peculiar people who swarm over the countryside – for a fleeting moment they appeared amusing, but then I stopped noticing them, understanding how unexceptional they are, measured against their surroundings. At times, locals waved to me from the curb or just followed me with their eyes, though more often than not, no one was distracted by my fleeting presence. Left behind, they merged with the streets as they withdrew to the side.

At last, the fields disappeared and real swamps engulfed the road – a damp, unhealthy moor. Clouds of insects smashed into the windshield; the air became heavy. Nature seemed to bear down on me, barely letting me breathe, but that didn't last long. Soon I drove up a hill. The swamps still sat a bit to the east, retreating to the invisible ocean in a smooth line overgrown with wild shrubs. Now the trees grew dense, casting the illegible calligraphy of their shadows over the road, until, several miles ahead, the road became wider, and a sign said I had crossed the city limits of M.

Find out more about The Black Pelican at
www.blackpelicanbook.com

ABOUT THE AUTHOR

V adim Babenko left two "dream" jobs – cutting-edge scientist and high-flying entrepreneur – in order to pursue his lifelong goal to write full-time. Born in the Soviet Union, he earned master's and doctoral degrees from the Moscow Institute of Physics & Technology, Russia's equivalent to MIT. As a scientist at the Soviet Academy of Sciences he became a recognized leader in the area of artificial intelligence. Then he moved to the U.S. and co-founded a high-tech company just outside of Washington, D.C. The business soon skyrocketed, and the next ambitious goal, an IPO on the stock exchange, was realized. But at this peak of success, Vadim dropped everything to set out on the path of a writer and has never looked back. He moved to Europe and, during the next eight years, published five books, including two novels, *The Black Pelican* and *A Simple Soul*, which were nominated for Russia's most prestigious literary awards. His third novel, *Semmant*, initially written in Russian and then translated with the author's active participation, is published exclusively in English.

Find out more at www.vadimbabenko.com

www.ingramcontent.com/pod-product-compliance
Lightning Source LLC
Chambersburg PA
CBHW031031030726
47497CB00004B/1097